Praise for A. Bello and the Emily Knight series

'Emily Knight is back in all her brilliant, brave glory! She's a fabulously inspirational heroine of colour, a girl who's not afraid to take ⁓n even the most perilous of missions. An action-packed race ag⸱⸱⸱ soon kicks-off, with lively, engaging dialogue pepperi⸱⸱⸱ ⸱nd some heart-warming moments of love and f⸱⸱ ⸱e the drama.'
LoveReading4Schools

'This is a great fantasy st⸱⸱ anyone else that loves young ⸱y is progressing and I can't wait t⸱⸱
JBronder Book Reviews

'Another enjoyable thing about th⸱⸱ ⸱⸱s diversity. There is such a gap in diverse representation in pu⸱⸱ ⸱ning and while it's improving, it has a way to go. Not only is Emily a diverse character but so are her friends.'
The Contented Reader

'A thrilling adventure, sizzling with magic.'
Sophie Anderson, author of The House with Chicken Legs

'I was like, where is book 3? Please don't leave me hanging like this! Emily Knight I am. . . Awakened is the kind of novel that I really wanted growing up.'
Just Read It Reviews

'If you haven't checked out this series for you or your children then WHAT ARE YOU WAITING FOR!? Go check it out now and see why I love this series!'
Popthebutterfly Reviews

'A. Bello represents the long-awaited evolution of diversity in the literature world. Creating a character like Emily Knight who provides YA readers of colour their own heroine to look up to! Really excited about this series!'
The British Blacklist

Also by A. Bello

Emily Knight I am. . .

Emily Knight I am. . . Awakened

For the latest news, competitions and exclusive material
from A. Bello visit:
www.a-bello.com

EMILY KNIGHT

I am...Becoming

A. BELLO

Thank you Sophie
for all your support!
Do you know when Gemma asked
to be my agent, what sealed the
deal was that she repped you!

ABello
x

Hashtag PRESS

Published in Great Britain by Hashtag Press 2020

Text copyright © Abiola Bello 2020
Copyright Cover illustration © Alexandra Artigas 2020

The moral right of the author has been asserted

All rights reserved. No part of this publication may be reproduced,
stored in retrieval system, or transmitted, in any form or by any means
without the prior written permission of the publisher, nor be otherwise
circulated in any form of binding or cover other than that in which
it is published and without a similar condition being imposed on the
subsequent purchaser.

All characters in this publication are fictions and any resemblance to
real persons, living or dead, is purely coincidental.

A CIP catalogue for this book is available from the British Library.

ISBN 978-1-9161617-8-8

Typeset in Garamond Classic 11.75/14.5 by Blaze Typesetting
Printed in Great Britain by Clays Ltd, Elcograf S.p.A.

Hashtag PRESS

HASHTAG PRESS BOOKS
Hashtag Press Ltd
Kent, England, United Kingdom
Email: info@hashtagpress.co.uk
Website: www.hashtagpress.co.uk
Twitter: @hashtag_press

Acknowledgements

Thank you to God for all the opportunities that have come my way since the release of my first book. It's so challenging writing a book for a series. Emily Knight I am. . . Awakened did so well that I put pressure on myself to make this book even better. When I finally calmed down, the words flowed easily.

Thank you to my editor Tiffany. This was the first book of mine where she said, "Don't worry, it's really good!" I screamed! I'm so used to her editing notes that I was dreading it!

Thank you to Ale for always bringing Emily to life in drawings. Only you can do that. And this cover is fire! Literally!

Thank you to Kate for making the inside and outside of my book so beautiful.

A special thank you to Helen for always being my support system and loving Emily just as much as I do.

To all the bloggers and readers—thank you! I'll let you in on a little secret. This was actually meant to be the last book but as you can see it's pretty big! So we have one more book to go xx

To Helen
Thank you for being on this ride with me! x

CHAPTER ONE

Homecoming

A bell chimed in the distance. The leaves rustled; a bird hidden high in the tree tops held a flawless note. The wind blew in her face, whipping her long hair back. Emily Knight stood in the middle of the garden with her eyes closed and her body poised. Waiting.

She felt Julian Kena's power. Strong. Almost to the point of suffocating her, like she was being pushed from all different angles. It was impossible to pinpoint where he was, until his power suddenly disappeared. They had been training together all summer and Julian's power kept getting stronger and stronger.

Emily tilted her head to the side and listened. His power appeared, for a split second. Emily opened her eyes and glanced to her left. She couldn't see him, but she could feel his power. It kept appearing, in bursts, each time stronger than the next. Emily took a chance and swung her leg, kicking Julian hard in his midriff. He buckled over with a loud, "Oof," and dropped to the floor on his knees.

Emily crouched down and rubbed his back. "You cool?"

"Yeah," Julian said, shooting her a sharp look. "You didn't have to kick so hard."

"Sorry," Emily said, suppressing a smile.

Julian straightened up and rubbed his stomach. He grinned. "That was good. What did I do wrong?"

"You hid your power well but when it came back, I kept sensing it in the same direction. You're so powerful that when you weren't hiding it, it was overwhelming."

"I like overwhelming," he said, looking pleased with himself and Emily playfully nudged him. "Okay, so I have to keep my power hidden until the last second. Next time, you won't have a clue."

"Is that right?" Emily laughed and wiped her sweaty brow. She closed her eyes. "Do you sense that? It's like a weird feeling in the air. I can't explain it."

Julian sat on the floor. "It's called hope."

Emily opened her eyes and stared out into the distance, still amazed by the sight in front of her, even though it had been weeks. She couldn't get over the transformation of their home.

Julian had moved into his grandfather's house in the elite Legends Village over a year ago but Emily had lived in the Village her entire life.

Emily had never seen images of her father and brother floating outside her doorstep but the Village was covered with huge, colourful banners reading 'Welcome Home Thomas & Lox.' There were nine-foot high flags with their smiling faces surrounding the mansions. Balloons and streamers were hanging from every tree.

People were finally believing that Neci could be defeated—for good this time.

The decorations were nothing compared to the ones in Central London. They had even made statues of Thomas and Lox so the public could take pictures with them. The Prime Minister gave a speech, thanking the Knights for their bravery in these dark times. Only some months ago, the newspapers had run with the slogan 'Where is our Knight?' and Emily had dealt with the brunt of everyone's frustrations. Now it was like Lox running away to fight for Neci and Thomas going to find him had never happened.

Thomas Knight was the leader of the legendary Five Warriors. He fought for years alongside Cecil Archinia, Niles Thompson (who were both murdered by Neci and now their ghosts reside at The Osaki Training School), Hubert Jenkins, and the only female, Roberta Taniana.

Thomas wasn't only a strong warrior, he was a public figure and everyone adored him, but it all changed a few years ago when Neci returned in her trademark black cloak and white mask.

Neci was one of the strongest warriors and her battle against Thomas Knight—to this day—was the most famous battle. Even though Thomas won, he let Neci go. She disappeared for years and Thomas became an even bigger celebrity. But when she came back, she brainwashed Lox, then a teenager, into believing Thomas was holding him back from his full potential and she was the one that could make him a great warrior. Lox and Thomas already had a shaky relationship and Neci played on that. Lox believed Neci and ran away with her.

Their mother, Leah, died from breast cancer and her last wish was for Thomas to find Lox and bring him back home. Thomas had spent years searching the world for his son, while leaving his youngest child, Emily, in the care of her godparents.

Lox returned as a young adult and, at first, it was to recruit Emily to join Neci but Emily had refused. Then Neci declared war against the Five Warriors and anyone who supported them. Emily begged Lox to stop running and reunite with Thomas; without him they didn't stand a chance of winning. She didn't think Lox would actually listen, so no one was more surprised than her when Lox and Thomas ambushed Neci and her warriors on live TV. Everything changed after that.

The media now chanted, 'Our Knights have come.' The hostility Emily had received during the absence of her father immediately stopped and she was receiving more support that she was used to. Thomas's face, which appeared only for a second on the television screen, had been on the cover of every newspaper and magazine worldwide. It was the most 'liked' picture in history on social media.

Thomas's reappearance seemed to have shaken up Neci because since the ambush no one had seen or heard from her. Emily knew better than to think Neci had given up—this is exactly what Neci wanted. She'd been craving for a re-match against Thomas for years, the only warrior to ever defeat her, but for some reason the attacks Neci had orchestrated throughout the year were on pause.

Emily felt like she could finally breathe, even though she knew it was just for a short while.

Since Thomas's return, everyone felt safe, having full

confidence that he would once again be their hero. It seemed like every day was a celebration, like the war was already won. They had already forgotten Neci. Emily wished she could forget, but Neci always haunted her dreams.

It didn't seem to bother anyone else that Thomas or Lox hadn't been seen for weeks since they had ambushed Neci but it was all Emily thought about.

Except for that image on the screen, Emily hadn't seen her father since she was seven years old, when he left to find Lox. Emily had craved attention from her father and had even gone as far as to steal, hoping to garner front page coverage and show her father that she needed him. But that didn't work. What brought Thomas back was the reason he had left in the first place. Lox.

Emily sighed. She was turning fifteen tomorrow and it would be the best present to have them both home. She couldn't remember the last time she had celebrated her birthday with her family.

"Do you think they'll like all of this?" Julian asked, pointing at the decorations.

Emily went to answer, but then stopped. She knew her dad would be more used to a celebration, seeing as everywhere he went people wanted to praise him, but Lox was a difficult one.

"Hopefully," Emily said returning to reality after getting lost in her memories. Without thinking, she pushed back Julian's black hair that had stuck to his forehead. Julian stared at her and Emily blushed. "Sorry I—"

He gently held Emily's hand and interlocked their fingers. His creamy skin with Emily's brown skin. Emily stared at their hands feeling a range of emotions. Whenever she was with Julian, it felt like the most natural thing in the world. They seemed to fit. Both were related to legendary warriors and they were on the elite team, where they were trained by the best warriors to fight against Neci. Julian understood the pressure without her having to explain it to him. Last term at school, he had her back when no one else did and he helped her battle one of Neci's warriors, Blade, the ice man.

But when she's with Wesley Parker, one of her best friends, and he looked at her with his large, hazel eyes, it's like she would forget to breath. He could understand her better than anyone. Sometimes even better than herself.

When she was at school and around the both of them, she felt uncomfortable. Wesley didn't like Julian and Emily always felt stuck in the middle, that was until Wesley got into a relationship with Harmony Loving-Dale.

Julian was single, and had made it clear to Emily that he liked her. She even went on a date with him last week where they had lunch at his house before watching a movie in his cinema suite. And she had dressed up wanting to impress him, letting her foster sister, Cathy Lee, do her makeup.

She had even held Julian's hand throughout the movie, and at one point she thought he was going to kiss her. He did, but only on the cheek, and she'd felt disappointed, wishing he would kiss her like he had in the ice room. At first, he had kissed her because they had fallen beneath the ice and Emily, in her panic, wouldn't breathe under water (even though all warriors could do it). Emily was losing oxygen so Julian had helped her. Emily had begun to breathe but they had continued kissing.

The idea of committing to Julian was hard for her knowing that her and Wesley had something special. If only she had been brave enough to share how she felt, he wouldn't have started dating Harmony Loving-Dale.

"What are you thinking?" Julian's brown eyes searched hers.

"Just when I'll get to see him," Emily said, confusing herself if she meant her dad or Wesley.

"Are you nervous about seeing Thomas?"

Emily nodded. "It's been so long, I just want him to. . . like me."

"Emily," Julian said, pulling her close so she could hear his racing heartbeat. "He's going to think you're amazing, just like everyone does."

"Alice doesn't like me, neither does Tanya or Mr Watern—"

"Okay, most people," Julian cut in.

"Am I interrupting?" a deep voice called.

Emily jumped away from Julian. Her godfather, Michael Meran was staring at them quizzically over his glasses.

"No, no." Emily blushed.

"I have some good news. Your dad just rang."

"What?" Emily said. "Why didn't you call me? What did he say?"

"I'm sorry it was a very quick call." Michael smiled from ear to ear. "Your dad and Lox will be back in time for dinner."

Emily felt sick to her stomach with nerves. She had waited for so long, but what if it wasn't a great reunion? Emily knew that Lox had a love/hate relationship with their father, so it was confusing that they were even hanging out together. The knot in her stomach felt tight, making her clutch her belly.

What if Lox took off again? Would Dad leave me?

Emily turned on the tap in the bathroom sink. She splashed water on to her face and inhaled deeply.

"Relax," she muttered to herself. "Get it together."

"First sign of madness is talking to yourself," James Evernham, her foster brother said, leaning against the bathroom door.

Over the summer, James had had a mini growth spurt. He was wearing one of Michael's t-shirts, which used to come down below his knees, but now it was hanging just above it. His brown hair was finally cut short, so it was no longer in his eyes.

"Shall we add mad to the rest of the list?" Emily asked, wiping her face with a clean towel.

"It can be our secret." James grinned. "How cool is it that Thomas and Lox are coming back?"

Emily nodded, not trusting herself to speak.

James frowned at her. "Aren't you excited?"

"I just want it to go well."

"Why wouldn't it? I'll finally have a brother." James big green eyes glistened and Emily couldn't help but genuinely smile. James's happiness was infectious. She hadn't even thought about the impact this would have on the rest of the family.

"You know Lox was the youngest Warrior Champion? When he comes you should ask him to show you his skills. He can start training you up."

"I have to be a warrior first." James looked down at the marble floor.

"You are a warrior," Emily said confidently.

"How do you know?" James asked with his eyes wide.

"I can just tell. The warrior gene kicks in when you turn thirteen and that's when your powers come, so you only have two years left."

"I would love to be able to fly and create fireballs. Do you think I'll be really strong like you?"

"No way!" James hung his head and, Emily grinned. "You'll be even stronger!"

"Thanks, Emily." He hugged her before he left the bathroom. Emily wished she could be easily convinced like James.

By the time Emily was ready (five wardrobe changes and three different hairstyles later) she went downstairs to see the house busier than it had been in years. There was a chef and caterers in the kitchen and dining room. A full cleaning service had been hired and they were busy hoovering the carpet and polishing the tables, while her godparents, Sally and Michael Meran, were having a full-blown argument in the corridor.

"Are we just meant to pack up and go?" Sally shouted, with her hands on her skinny hips. "This has been our house for years. Do we give up our bedroom for him?"

"Thomas won't kick us out, you know that," Michael said. "We don't even know what his plans are. . . he might not even stay."

"Why wouldn't he stay?" Emily asked and they stopped arguing immediately. "He's not staying?"

Sally shot Michael a dark look.

Michael took off his glasses and rubbed his eyes. "Of course he will stay, Emily. I just meant. . . he just didn't go into much detail."

"He never does," Sally muttered.

"You're not leaving me are you?" Emily asked alarmed.

"No, honey," Sally said, holding out her arms and Emily ran into them. "We're family, aren't we? Hey, why don't you go check on Cathy? Make sure she's wearing something appropriate for dinner."

Emily nodded, heading towards the stairs. She stopped and turned around to see Sally looking furiously at Michael.

"And there's nothing else wrong?"

Sally instantly replaced her frown with a smile. "No, everything is fabulous. It has to be because I'm not cooking." Sally forced a laugh.

Emily nodded again and headed for her foster sister's room. Sally and Michael had fostered Cathy when she was a young girl and some years later they fostered James, Rosy Lang-Sheen and Yvonne Saunders. Emily was the closest to Cathy as they were only a year apart.

Cathy's bedroom was down the hall from Emily's. Emily opened her door to see Cathy rummaging through her wardrobe. Her double bed was hidden under a huge pile of clothes. Her blonde curls tumbled down her back and she was singing softly to herself. Cathy turned around when Emily came in and smiled mischievously.

"What do you think?" Cathy asked, showing off her red halter neck dress, for once at a reasonable length.

"I like it," Emily said, pushing some of the clothes to the side of the bed, so she could perch herself on to it.

"Do you think Lox will like it?" Cathy asked, raising her eyebrows.

"Don't," Emily said, blocking her ears with her hands. "Don't start."

Cathy laughed, but Emily knew she wasn't joking. Cathy's lust for Lox seemed to be the only thing she could speak about all summer and it was driving Emily crazy.

"What time exactly are they coming?" Cathy asked, as she gathered the clothes on her bed.

Emily removed her hands from her ears and shrugged. "Michael said dinnertime, so about an hour."

"And they're back in time for your birthday," Cathy said, dumping her clothes at the bottom of her wardrobe. "What?" she said, when she noticed Emily staring at her. "The maid will do it."

"We don't have a maid! We haven't had one in years."

"Well, we're bound to get them again when Thomas comes back." Cathy shrugged. She flopped next to Emily on the bed. "I can't wait! Chefs and clean rooms again! Can you smell the food? When was the last time food smelt that good in this house?"

"Hmmm," Emily said, half listening. "Do you know what's up with Sally and Michael? Sally seems to think they're going to be kicked out."

For the first time in the conversation, Cathy looked serious. "What? Would we have to go?"

"No, of course not," Emily said. "You're family and without you guys, I would have been where exactly?"

"Right," Cathy said, looking at her pink nail polish. "Besides there's zillions of rooms, loads of space for everyone."

"Exactly," Emily agreed. "It's just weird that Sally doesn't seem happy."

"Maybe because she was closer to your mum than Thomas. Remember, her and Leah were best friends."

"I guess." Emily said.

"Hey, you don't seem happy that they're coming. This is what you've always wanted."

"I know." Emily sighed. "I just have this feeling that it's all going to go wrong."

"How much more wrong can it go? We're going to war remember?"

Emily laughed because Cathy was right. How much worse could it possibly get?

"It will be cool for Dad and Lox to meet Michella, Wesley and Jason tomorrow. . ."

For Emily's fifteenth birthday, they were having a barbecue in the garden and she had invited her best friends from school to celebrate with her. She was nervous about seeing Wesley. They hadn't spoken properly since school ended a few weeks ago. She had only seen Michella once in the summer, which is how she knew that things with Wesley and Harmony seemed to be going well, and that really bugged her. She was hoping Wesley was dating Harmony just to get at her for not revealing her true feelings for him, but according to Michella, they were going strong and Wesley seemed happy. Emily knew, as his friend, she should be happy for him. She was trying to be, but it was hard.

"Michella and Jason aren't still together are they?" Cathy stood up and held the red dress against herself in the mirror.

"Yeah they are," Emily said.

"It's just ridiculous that the hottest guy I've ever met in real life is all loved up!"

"Wow. Over Lox already?" Emily said, throwing a pillow at her. Cathy ducked and the pillow bounced off the mirror before falling on the floor.

"It's good to have options," Cathy said defensively.

The dining hall was covered with vases of fresh flowers and the best china that they owned was laid out on the table. The room was lit by candle light. Emily's heart clenched when she smelt the familiar smell of cinnamon, which reminded her of her mother.

Emily picked up a glass, studying the pretty floral pattern. As soon as she put it down a young, bashful man came out in his white uniform and polished it off before putting it back on the table and returning to the kitchen.

Emily smoothed out her blue dress self-consciously. It clung to her body and Emily finally noticed the defined muscles in her back and arms. She never paid attention to her body because she was always in her training kit. She almost replaced the dress, as she felt she looked too muscular, but then Sally walked in and commented on how beautiful she looked.

Her six and seven year old foster sisters, Yvonne and Rosy came into the dining room looking around in awe. They looked very sweet in their matching pink dresses. Yvonne's hair was beautifully braided and Rosy's hair was tied up into a perfect ballerina bun. James thundered down the stairs behind them and skidded to a halt.

"Woah," he said, looking around the dining hall.

James was wearing a green shirt that matched his eyes and black suit trousers. His hair had been brushed back, so Emily could see his handsome face. He went to pick up a fork and Emily slapped his hand away.

"They've just been polished. You look very smart."

James rubbed his hand and looked at Emily's worn shoes resentfully. "These new shoes are giving me blisters."

"Okay, okay, is everyone here?"

Sally entered the room and the kids gasped. Sally, who lived in leggings and Michael's oversized jumpers, looked nothing less than stunning. Her hair was freshly washed and had been straightened so you could appreciate how thick and long it was. Her face had been professionally made up, so her small grey eyes looked large and her cheekbones were sharp and defined. She was wearing a figure-hugging black dress on her slim frame and black stilettos.

"Wow," Emily said.

"Mummy, you look like a pop star," Yvonne said.

"Thank you, sweetheart." Sally blushed. "Everyone take a seat. Cathy! Michael!"

Michael arrived in the living room in his black suit. He pushed up his black framed glasses and looked at his family proudly.

"Don't we clean up nice?" he said, as Cathy appeared next to him.

One of the waiters poured fruit juice into their glasses. Sally and Michael were offered the option of wine, which they both declined.

"I think I need a clear head tonight," Sally muttered. Soft

music drifted around the room and Sally smiled. "So, this is pretty."

"What time are they coming?" Cathy asked.

"Shouldn't be too long," Michael said.

They fell into silence. James tapped his foot impatiently on the floor. Fifteen minutes later and nobody had rang the doorbell. Cathy drummed her fingers on the white table cloth and absentmindedly played with a strand of her hair.

"I'd like to make a toast," Sally suddenly said. Emily and Cathy glanced at each other. "I just want to say to you, Emily, how proud we all are. You've come so far and I know your birthday isn't till tomorrow, but this is probably the last time we're together as just us, so happy birthday."

"Thank you," Emily said.

"What do you mean last time? Are we leaving?" James frowned.

"Of course not," Emily whispered, squeezing his arm.

"I hope that Leah is proud of the way we have raised you. So I want us to raise our glasses." Sally held up her glass and everyone else followed suit. "Let's toast to Leah for creating such an amazing daughter, who we have had the privilege to raise—to Leah."

"To Leah," everyone echoed.

"Mum, I'm starving!" James moaned.

"I know, baby. Michael, I think we should—"

The doorbell rang. Everyone looked at Emily and she froze. She wasn't ready to see them. Emily placed down her glass and Cathy grabbed her hand.

"They're here!" Cathy sang.

Michael, who could see the anxiety on Emily's face, stood up. "Shall we go together?"

Emily nodded and slowly got up from the table. Sally squeezed her hand as she walked past and Michael guided her towards the door, holding on to her shoulders.

"What if he doesn't like me?" Emily asked, spinning around.

Michael kissed Emily on the forehead. "What's not to like? Come on."

They walked to the door. The bell rang again. Emily took a deep breath. Her hands were sweating badly as she opened the door. . .

CHAPTER TWO

Family

Lox Knight was tall and muscular built, with battle scars along his tattooed arms. His gaunt face looked fuller, like he was finally eating, and there was a sparkle in his light brown eyes that Emily had never seen. His long, Afro, black hair was tied up into a low bun. He had on clean, black bottoms and a leather jacket that looked new under his bulging rucksack. It was the first time Emily had lain eyes on Lox and he didn't look anxious or paranoid.

"Lox," Emily said, running into his open arms.

He lifted her up and held her tight. "Hey Emily."

"Thank you for coming back."

Lox chuckled. "You threatened to kill me if I didn't remember?"

"Lucky escape," Emily whispered in his ear.

He put her down and embraced Michael into a hug.

"Long time, Lox," Michael said.

"You look well," Lox said, patting Michael on the back.

Thomas Knight was walking towards the door. The

resemblance between Thomas and Lox was unquestionable. He was the same height and build as Lox with the same dark skin, although his eyes were dark brown. His hair was cut short and when he smiled at Emily, he showed off dimpled cheeks and dazzling teeth. His worn blue Dojo kit clung to his statuesque body.

"Hello, darling," Thomas said, which brought tears to her eyes.

He dropped his heavy bag on the floor and wrapped his arms around Emily, kissing her cheeks. He smelt of grass and a familiar smell that Emily couldn't put her finger on. Thomas held her at arm's length and studied her.

"Look how beautiful you are. Just like your mother." He placed both his hands on either side of Emily's face. Their faces were so close, she could count every eyelash if she wanted to. "I will never, ever leave you again. I'm so sorry."

Emily didn't want to let go in case he disappeared. She wanted to hold on to him forever.

"Shall we say hello to everyone?" Thomas eventually said. He kept his arm around her shoulders. "So good to see you again, Michael."

"We have missed you," Michael replied, as they gave each other a one armed hug. "Come on, let's go and eat." He picked up Thomas's bag and led them into the dining hall.

Emily watched Thomas and Lox look around the house, which hadn't changed much except next to the Knight family pictures were group pictures of Emily, the Merans and their children.

When they entered the dining room, Cathy, James, Rosy and Yvonne stood to their feet and clapped excitedly.

Although, the kids weren't warriors everyone in the world knew Thomas and Lox Knight.

"Sally!" Thomas said, embracing her. "You look stunning."

"Thank you," Sally said, eyeing him. "You look good, Thomas. Hello, Lox."

Lox hugged her but Emily could see Sally tense up. She hadn't forgiven Lox for kidnapping Emily a few years ago.

"That can't be Cathy!" Thomas gasped. Cathy blushed and walked around the table to greet him. "Oh my! I haven't seen you since you were a little girl. Lox, do you remember Cathy?"

"A bit differently," Lox said, looking at Cathy up and down appreciatively.

Emily scowled. The last thing she wanted was her brother flirting with her foster sister.

"This is our son, James, and our daughters, Rosy and Yvonne," Michael said gesturing them to come over. "James desperately wants to be a warrior."

"You do?" Thomas asked. He bent down on one knee, so he was level with James, who nodded enthusiastically.

"Emily said I would be stronger than her, and that Lox will train me," James gushed.

Lox smiled at him. "Oh definitely. You'll be the strongest one in the house."

James green eyes widened and he looked at Emily as if to ask if it was true. Emily nodded and James grinned.

"Well, there's no question about it then," Thomas declared. He winked at James and James's smile grew even wider. "And how adorable are you two?" Thomas hugged Rosy and Yvonne who giggled. "Sally and Michael your family is beautiful. I am so happy for you both."

"Thank you. You boys must be starving. Shall we eat?" Sally suggested.

"Yes please," Thomas said.

Dinner was perfect. Everyone was talking and laughing but Emily barely ate. She was so excited. Lox finished each course the fastest. He scoffed it down as if someone was going to take it away from him.

"How are you finding Osaki?" Thomas asked Emily before, eating the chocolate flake in his vanilla ice cream.

"Good, I'm learning loads. I'm on the Ogragon Dojo team and I'm a Fighter not a Distracter."

"You are?" Thomas grinned. "What position do you play?"

"I'm the fifth fighter. We won the cup last year. Lenny Kinkle—my best mate Michella's brother—is, I mean was, our captain. He just graduated."

"Kinkle?" Lox frowned. "Is he related to the Dojo player Janette Kinkle?"

"Yeah, that's his sister. I've met her. She always gives me some really good battle tips and Lenny just got signed to the London FlyAways."

"Talented family," Thomas commented. "So what about your friend? Michelle? Is she on the Dojo team?"

"Michella," Emily corrected. "No, her brothers are on the team and I guess training with them wouldn't be fun, but you'll meet her tomorrow."

"Tomorrow?" Lox said.

An awkward silence fell on the table.

"It's Emily's birthday," Sally said in a frosty voice.

"Chill, Sally, I was teasing." Lox said, scooping up his ice cream. "Fifteen right?"

Emily nodded, happy that he remembered. Sally gave Lox a cold look.

"So, how does it feel being back home, Lox?" Michael asked.

"Weird." He glanced down at the china he was eating from. "I'm not used to living with such expensive things."

"Where does Neci live?" Cathy asked.

"Around," Lox said vaguely. "Much more low key than us."

Thomas shot him a look that Emily didn't understand before he turned to Sally. "Amazing dinner, did Greta cook it?" Thomas wiped his mouth with his napkin.

"No, we let Greta go," Sally responded.

Thomas froze. "Why?"

Sally glanced at Emily. "Emily was having a difficult time at school before she went to Osaki. She wanted to fit in with the other kids, so we got rid of the hired help."

Thomas laughed. "How would she have a hard time fitting in when she was attending Patchinson's Academy?"

"We didn't send Emily to the private school. We sent her to St Mary's Secondary School."

Thomas dropped his napkin. Lox raised his eyebrows, but didn't say anything.

"Why did you send her there?" Thomas asked in a terse voice.

Sally dropped her cutlery and glared at Thomas. "She had lost her mother, her brother had run away, and her father had abandoned her; she didn't really want to endure all of the stares. Your family is high profile. Emily wanted to go to a normal school with normal people. So we tried to help her blend in."

Nobody spoke. Emily looked down at her hands, irritated by all of them. Why were they ruining her perfect family dinner?

"It's not a big deal," Lox said, breaking the tense silence. "I went to Patchinson's and I still ended up running away."

Emily snorted. Cathy, Michael and James laughed. Sally tried not to, but she smiled.

Thomas looked annoyed as he watched Sally. "So what else has been happening with Emily?" he asked, attempting to keep his voice light.

"She sees a counsellor twice a week and when she's at school she has the option to see one there."

Thomas slammed down his cutlery making everyone jump. "A counsellor? My daughter doesn't need to see a counsellor! Let alone two!"

Sally stood up. "I don't think you have a clue what your daughter needs."

"Sally," Michael said squeezing her hand.

"No Michael," Sally yelled, pointing at Thomas. "You left her! So don't you dare question how we raised her." She stormed out of the dining hall.

Thomas crossed his arms with a stony expression on his face.

"I've missed this," Lox said, finishing off the rest of his ice cream. "Nothing like family domestics."

Thomas sighed before placing his face in his hands. Everyone stared at him apart from Lox who was now cutting himself a slice of cake.

Emily felt a nudge in her ribs. She turned towards Cathy who hissed, "Say something."

"Like what?" Emily whispered back.

Cathy shrugged her shoulders.

"She didn't mean it Dad," Emily heard herself say. Everyone glanced from Emily to Thomas, including Lox.

Thomas rubbed his face. "But she's right," he said in a defeated voice. "I don't know you and it's my fault."

"Well. . . this is our chance to get to know each other, isn't it?" Emily said.

Thomas smiled. "I would love that."

"Technically it's my fault," Lox said, letting his spoon clatter on to his plate.

"It doesn't matter," Emily said firmly. "Let this be a new start for all of us."

"It really is great to have you back," Cathy chipped in, smiling at Lox and Thomas. "Mum just feels uncertain about what happens to us now."

"What do you mean?" Thomas frowned.

"You know," Cathy said, looking at the table. "This is your home. We're only here because you had gone. She thinks you want us out."

Thomas stood abruptly. "Is that what Sally thinks?" He shook his head. "You're all family. My family. Let me go and talk to her. I can't believe she thought I would do that."

He walked out of the dining hall. Emily sat in Thomas' chair as James asked Lox, "Are you happy to be back?"

Lox didn't answer straight away. Instead, he looked slowly around the room, taking in the familiar and unfamiliar objects that were placed around the house. He glanced at everyone sitting at the table, holding Emily's gaze a bit longer than the others, before he turned to James.

"Yeah, it feels good. Really good."

CHAPTER THREE

The Birthday Girl

Emily awoke with a sinking feeling in her stomach. She had slept terribly. The argument between Sally and her dad last night had echoed around her head as she slept. She understood where Sally was coming from, but couldn't she have held her tongue for a few more days? Emily rolled on to her side, hugging her pillow tight.

A gentle knock came at her door and Sally opened it. She looked sheepish as she came and sat on the edge of Emily's four poster bed.

"Is he still here?" Emily asked, sitting up.

Sally nodded before another knock came at the door. Thomas entered the room and looked surprised to see Sally, but he came and sat beside her. He was holding a rolled-up newspaper in his hand.

"Happy birthday," Thomas said, leaning forward and kissing Emily's forehead.

"Happy birthday darling," Sally said, squeezing Emily's hand. "And your dad and I are very sorry for yesterday.

We've spoken about it and today is going to be perfect for you."

"Okay," Emily said, smiling.

"Hurry and get dressed. Your friends will be here soon," Sally said, getting up. She nodded at Thomas and left the room.

"I thought you might like to keep this," Thomas said, handing Emily the newspaper.

Emily rolled it open and on the front page was the headline

HAPPY BIRTHDAY EMILY KNIGHT!

Emily gasped as she read the birthday wishes from celebrities printed in the paper. "Oh my gosh! This is crazy."

Thomas frowned. "Don't they do this every year for you?"

"No!" Emily exclaimed. "This is really cool."

"That's strange," Thomas said. "They used to do it for you and Lox when you were younger."

Emily placed the paper on her bed. "Maybe they did it more for you? It's not really a coincidence that they make a fuss about me because you're back, is it?"

Thomas scratched the back of his neck and looked around Emily's room. His eyes landed on a picture of Leah Knight by Emily's bed. He picked it up and his eyes softened as he studied his wife. Emily held her breath. She didn't want to talk about her mum today. Today was her birthday and thinking about her mum always made her feel sad. She wanted to be happy, just for one day at least. Thomas sighed and without saying a word, he put the picture back.

"Michael filled me in about Blade." He gave Emily a knowing look.

Blade was the ice man that had trapped Gabriel Thompson in the ice. He would have done so to Emily if she didn't have Julian Kena helping her.

"You had quite a year. I remember fighting Blade many years ago."

"You trapped him under the ice all those years ago, didn't you? Who taught you Hariem?"

"My uncle taught me when I was younger. Some of my fighting moves I got from the inscriptions on the wall. You know where they teach Foughtgon?"

"No way!"

"I would never have dreamt this would all come back to you, but like Neci, I should have finished the job once and for all. I won't make that mistake again. Now, when am I going to meet Tahama's son?"

"You know Julian's mum?" Emily asked, surprised.

"Of course! Tahama was in the Warrior competitions. She even beat Roberta once—don't tell Roberta I told you—and I knew her father well. You've seen Tainwo's house in the Village? Is Julian coming to your party?"

"He should be."

"Good. Michael said he has been meaning to invite the Kenas to dinner as a thank you?"

"Yeah," Emily said, looking at the newspaper. "But I don't think that's necessary. Julian knows how thankful I am, and we've been training and hanging out together all summer." Thomas raised his eyebrows and Emily laughed. "What?"

"That's exactly how Roberta and Jenkins started out, just 'training' together," he said, making air quotes. "And I was the third wheel."

"Whatever Dad," Emily said, playfully hitting him.

Thomas exaggerated the impact and fell of the bed as if he was knocked out. Emily threw back her head and laughed. She jumped out the bed and leaped on top of him, pinning him to the floor and he pretended to be in agony, pleading for her to release him. They were laughing so hard, they didn't notice that Lox was standing in the doorway, already dressed, staring at them with an odd expression. A mixture of admiration and. . . was it envy?

"I could hear you laughing from my room," he said, leaning against the door frame. "Happy Birthday."

"Thank you," Emily said, releasing Thomas.

He grabbed her around the waist and lifted her above his head, making her squeal. "Come on Lox, join in." Thomas said, throwing Emily up like she was a baby and catching her again.

Emily looked at the doorway but Lox was already gone. Thomas noticed and gently placed Emily down.

"I'm sure he just went to get ready for the party," Emily said, wanting to keep the playful mood.

"Yeah maybe," Thomas said, looking towards the door. "Actually, you should be getting ready, birthday girl." He flashed a smile before getting up and leaving the room.

The barbecue was already under way with Michael in charge of grilling the meat. A low key day was all Emily wanted and she was happy to see that a long table in the middle of the garden had been simply covered in a white table cloth, with platters of food, wrapped up in cling film. Jars of flowers had been added and presents Emily had received from family and friends at school were stacked at the end of the table. Emily looked up to the sky and she could see, floating above them, the security that Thomas had hired, to make sure there were no press intruders or unwanted warriors.

Emily was sneaking a sausage wrapped in bacon from under the cling film when the doorbell ring. She abandoned the food and ran to the door, almost knocking over the hired cook. Emily opened the door and there stood her best friends, Michella Kinkle, Wesley Parker and Jason Notting.

"Happy birthday," they chorused, each holding a present in their hands.

Emily grabbed them into one big hug.

"I have missed you so much," she said, meaning all of them.

"We have to," Michella said squeezing her.

Emily studied her friends. Michella Kinkle was a striking, lean-figured girl, with long black braids and brown eyes. She was an inch taller than Emily and they had been best friends since they met in the Warside changing rooms, trying on their school uniform two years ago. Even though Michella thought she was just an average warrior, Emily thought she was one of the smartest and honest people she had ever met and she happened to be dating one of the most beautiful boys Emily had ever seen in her life—Jason Notting.

Jason had grown over the summer, looking even more stunning than before, with his streaked blond hair, which now hung past his shoulders, clear blue eyes, tanned skin and muscled physique. To add to Jason's perfection, he was the smartest student in their year. Jason was telekinetic and was training with Emily in a secret elite warrior group ran by Roberta Taniana and Hubert Jenkins.

Lastly, Emily looked at Wesley Parker. A comely mixed raced boy with big hazel eyes and curly brown hair. Wesley never failed to entertain her. She was still angry with herself for not telling him how she really felt about him when she had the chance. She wished she could tell him how he was one of the only people who made her feel safe. He understood what it was like to come from a broken family, so she never felt she had to pretend. And when he smiled at her. . .

But it was too late. He was with Harmony Loving-Dale now.

"Guys, I said casual," Emily said, glancing from Wesley and Jason's shirts and trousers to Michella's white evening gown. "It's only a barbecue."

The three of them looked at each other.

"We wanted to make a good impression," Jason said in a low voice. "Is he here?"

Emily began to shake her head, then turned it into a nod. Michella squealed and started running her hands over her dress.

"Oh my gosh, oh my gosh," Wesley said looking excited and nervous at the same time.

Emily laughed. "Come on through, he's in the garden."

Jason marvelled at the extravagance of Emily's home. He was the only one of her friends to have never seen it and he practically drooled at the marble flooring and over-the-top décor.

"What's he like?" Michella asked Emily, whilst Wesley

told Jason the story about last summer, when Emily didn't breathe under water and almost drowned in her indoor pool.

"He's great," Emily said smiling. "You'll really like him."

"And how have him and Lox been together?"

Emily shrugged her shoulders. "They seem okay. Not overly friendly, but not aggressive either."

They walked through the hallway to the garden and Michella froze.

"What's up?" Emily said, staring at her.

"It's Thomas Knight. Thomas Knight is right there!" Michella pointed at him.

"Where?" Jason said and he gasped when he saw him.

Emily laughed. She knew her dad was a big deal, but it was weird for her to witness her friends' reactions to him.

Thomas was leaning on the wall beside the barbecue, laughing with Michael. When he saw Emily and her friends he beckoned them over.

"Come on," Emily said and when her friends didn't move, she added, "Be cool, okay? Just think of him as my dad."

They walked behind Emily. Michella kept fussing with her dress until Emily insisted that she looked fine. Wesley was dusting imaginary dirt off his shirt and Jason kept running his hands through his hair.

"Michael, Dad, these are my best friends—Michella, Wesley and Jason. Guys, this is my godfather Michael and. . . well, you know him already," Emily said, gesturing to Thomas.

"It's so great to meet you. We've heard amazing things about you all," Michael said, shaking their hands.

"You're Thomas Knight," Wesley said, staring at him with wide eyes.

"I am." Thomas laughed. "How are you all finding Osaki?"

"Amazing," Michella said, recovering quicker than the boys who were staring at Thomas as if in a trance.

"Osaki is something all right. Have any of you discovered any hidden powers?"

Michella blushed. "No, not yet, but Jason is telekinetic."

"Really?" Thomas said, looking at Jason with interest. "What's the biggest thing you've moved?"

Jason ran his fingers through his hair again. Emily was shocked it hadn't started to fall out yet.

"Err. . . w-well. . . on S-Survival Training—sorry I'm so nervous," Jason said.

"Don't be," Thomas said, placing a hand on Jason's shoulder and Wesley's mouth dropped open. "I'm just Emily's dad."

"Well. . . I . . . err. . . used my powers to stop Emily when she saw her moth—"

Jason stopped abruptly and Thomas looked from Jason to Emily in confusion.

"Emily saw who?"

Emily sighed. "I saw Mum at Mount Gregory, but it wasn't really her. We had to climb a mountain and defeat someone that we loved but it was just Uncle Jenkin's illusion. Jason stopped me from getting sucked into it."

Thomas stared at Emily and gently touched her cheek. "That must have been so difficult for you."

"Emily was great," Wesley piped in and Thomas looked at him surprised. "We had to defeat the illusion to complete the task and even though Emily struggled, she did it."

"That's some kind words you have to say about my

daughter. Thank you all so much for being there for her. I really appreciate that," Thomas said.

They all mumbled 'thank you' and 'no problem' but Michella was staring at Thomas intensely. "Can I ask you a question, Mr Knight?"

"Please just call me Thomas. What is it?"

"Can you beat Neci again?"

A silence descended upon them and Emily looked from her dad to Michella.

Thomas had his arms crossed over his blue t-shirt and was staring at Michella with a blank expression. Emily had no idea if he was annoyed or offended.

Suddenly, Thomas smiled, revealing his dimples. "I'll be surprised if I don't."

Michella grinned and Emily—not realising she was holding her breath—exhaled. They heard voices coming from the back of the garden. Lox, Cathy and James, were dirty and sweaty as they trudged through the grass, laughing and talking.

When Cathy saw Wesley and Jason, she immediately tried to wipe the dirt marks off her face, which only made them worse. Lox wiped his hands on his training kit and shook Wesley and Jason's hands in greeting. When he shook Michella's, Emily noticed she was staring at him as if hypnotised. Girls loved Lox Knight. Wesley nudged Emily and smirked, noticing it too. It obviously didn't register to Jason as he was still looking at Lox in admiration.

"I'm Lox," he said, finally getting his hand free from Michella's.

"They know who you are," Emily said impatiently. She was getting a little tired of this Lox effect.

"Have you been training?" Michael asked from behind the barbecue.

"Yep," Lox said, squeezing James until he giggled. "This lil' man has some skills. I honestly believe he has the warrior gene."

"Emily you should have seen me!" James gushed. "I was flying!"

"You were flying?" Emily asked shocked.

"Well, no. . . I mean Lox flew me around, but it was so cool. I wasn't scared at all."

"And what exactly were you doing, Cathy?" Emily asked, smirking at her.

Cathy flicked her blonde curls and said, "Training of course. I'm not afraid to get a little dirty."

She winked at Jason before she strutted off to the house. Emily scoffed and Michella tutted and stared after Cathy.

"You're not really one to talk are you?" Wesley muttered, low enough for Michella to hear. He glanced knowingly at the hand she was cradling and Michella dropped it by her side.

Sally came into the garden, wearing a long, black, maxi dress with Rosy and Yvonne in tow. When she walked past Cathy, she frowned at her dirty face and clothes. "I'm not even going to ask," she said to herself.

"Mum!" James hollered. "I trained today with Lox and Cathy. It was so fun!"

"That's great, honey," Sally said, ruffling his hair. "But why don't you take a quick shower and then tell me all about it? And you can show Xavier and Antonio when they come."

"Cool!" James exclaimed, running through the house,

leaving muddy streaks on the floor, which made Mrs Asha, their new house keeper, curse in Swahili.

"Lox, go clean up for me, please," Sally ordered. "And Michael, how's the meat going?"

"All ready," Michael said.

Michella's eyes lingered on Lox as he went into the house and Emily coughed loudly making her jump.

"Do not get sucked in," Emily hissed.

"What do you mean?" Michella asked innocently.

"To the Lox circus. Cathy already has a VIP seat."

"I don't fancy Lox," Michella laughed unconvincingly.

Emily raised her eyebrows but didn't respond.

Sally gestured at them to sit down and help themselves to food. Thomas sat down at the wooden table and Wesley and Jason looked at each other before running to sit down on either side of him.

"And there was me thinking it was my birthday," Emily said to deaf ears, as the boys were too busy listening to Thomas talk about training.

Michella was frowning at her hand. "I won't get sucked in. I mean he's really cute and a legend and—"

"You already have a boyfriend," Emily cut in. "That's what you were going to say next, right?"

"Of course," Michella said blushing. Avoiding Emily's laughing eyes, she helped herself to potato salad.

"Do you know what I would love to know?" Wesley asked, as soon as Thomas had stopped speaking. "How did you finally manage to find Lox?"

"What was that?" Lox asked.

He seemed to appear out of thin air and he sat down beside

Emily. Cathy and James were walking into the garden, talking animatedly with Roberta, Jenkins and their sons, Xavier and Antonio. Julian Kena was walking beside them.

"Look who finally decided to show up?" Roberta called over to Thomas, who laughed. He got up from the table and walked to Roberta with his arms wide open before he grabbed her, swinging her in a circle until she was laughing and begging to be put down.

"We have missed you, brother," Jenkins said, once he released Roberta.

"I have missed you too." Thomas hugged him. "Thank you for looking out for my family. Oh wow, look at Xavier! And who's this little man?" He waved at Antonio, who shyly hid behind his father.

"Hey!" Emily said, beckoning Julian over.

Julian waved awkwardly at everyone and Lox moved a seat over, so Julian could sit beside Emily.

"Sorry I'm late. Happy Birthday!"

"Thank you and my dad's been wanting to meet you."

Emily stood up and waved at her dad until she got his attention.

"Everyone, this is Julian Kena," Emily announced. "He was with me when we fought Blade in the ice room."

Thomas embraced a surprised Julian. He held him by the shoulders. "Thank you. You are a hero just like your grandfather."

"Oh thank you, Mr Knight," Julian said humbly.

"To Julian," Sally said, holding up her drink and everyone followed suit. Wesley did so reluctantly.

"Come on, everyone sit down and eat as much as you

want," Michael said. He brought over platters of freshly cooked meat to the table and everyone dug in.

Emily looked around the table, where everyone was in engrossed in their stories. There was so much laughter and intimacy, which was all Emily wanted for her birthday.

"Dad," Lox called across the table. "What were you and Wesley talking about earlier? I heard my name."

"Oh, Wesley wants to know how I found you," Thomas explained. "Do you mind?"

Everyone suddenly went quiet. Lox shrugged his shoulders, looking un-interested and continued to eat his food. James, who sat opposite him, was struggling to cut his steak. Lox grabbed his knife and cut the meat into small pieces for him. Emily saw that Sally had noticed and for the first time since Lox had returned, there was a warmth in her eyes.

"Well, where to start?" Thomas said, scratching his chin. "You all know that Lox is a very talented warrior and has won many competitions. From training Lox, I began to learn about his power. I can sense Lox anywhere. His power to me is so distinct but the problem with Lox is that he's very fast and gave me a heck of job."

Thomas smirked and Lox laughed. Emily looked from her brother to her dad in disbelief that they could even joke about what happened.

"I would sense Lox and go to him and he would be gone. He could sense me too. I would always be close, but not close enough. In the end, he actually came to me."

"Really?" Emily said, looking at Lox baffled.

"I told you I would stop running," Lox protested.

"I was actually training at your grandfather's house, Julian," Thomas said. "He is a great man and I was meditating in the fields when I sensed Lox so close. . . I thought I was dreaming. Then he was there when I opened my eyes. I can't even begin to explain that feeling, when you have finally found your child. I couldn't breathe. The beauty of the fields looked ugly compared to seeing Lox again."

Lox looked up from his plate and stared at his father.

Thomas's voice broke as he spoke. "I had promised my wife. I had left behind my baby girl to find him. I couldn't believe that after so long he was here. He was so grown up, so beautiful. . . a bit thin."

Everyone laughed, but Lox's eyes never left Thomas.

"And when he told me that it was thanks to Emily, Roberta, Jenkins and even his mother that he was ready to come home, I couldn't believe it. I was scared to believe that he really wanted to come with me because that's all I've thought about. No matter what I think of Neci, I'm so thankful that she didn't hurt my son and she trained him to be even more amazing than he already was. Then Lox told me about you." He looked at Emily. "About how feisty and awesome you are and I just felt like I could have my family again. I knew that Lox and I couldn't just waltz back in, and I knew the pressure that you had been under. Everyone had to see that we were back together but Neci had to be handled delicately."

"Sorry to interrupt," Cathy said, looking much cleaner in a fitted pink dress. "But how did you even get near Neci without her sensing you? Doesn't she have hundreds of warriors around her?"

"She actually doesn't," Lox said, to the surprise of everyone.

"People wouldn't just attack Neci. Her name alone creates fear but her power energy is insane. After I met Dad, we decided that I would go back to Neci and play it cool. Dad is telepathic, so as soon as I found out Neci's plans to have another announcement, I told him where to come. When Blade showed up, I knew that things were going to start moving quickly.

"I rose up my power level to cover up Dad's. None of them questioned why I was powered up like I was ready to battle. I guess they thought that I was being cautious. Dad caused a blackout and then they knew something was up. It happened so fast. There was so much going on. They all escaped but we eventually caught one."

"Who?" Jason asked.

Lox and Thomas smiled.

"Who?" Emily demanded, her heart racing.

Thomas and Lox looked down the table and Emily followed their gaze.

"Neci's right hand girl, Scarlett, and she isn't going anywhere," Roberta said.

CHAPTER FOUR

Growing Up

Everyone gasped.

"How? Where?" Emily asked in disbelief.

"I can't say the location," Roberta said. "But she's currently in a cell that we built, made of Masonka and Illiarn. Getting Scarlett is the best thing that could have happened."

"Sorry, what's Masonka and Illiarn?" Cathy frowned.

"Masonka absorbs power. So if Scarlett has a hissy fit and tries to blow up the place—she can't. The Masonka will only get stronger and if she tried to teleport, the Illiarn blocks it. There's no way to escape." Roberta grinned from ear to ear.

"That is so cool," James said.

"Wait, you have Scarlett, and Neci isn't on the war path?" Jason asked alarmed.

"Why has she gone quiet?" Julian asked. "She showed no mercy with Blade."

Roberta hesitated. "We don't know. When we took Scarlett we were ready for Neci to do something but. . ."

Everyone glanced at Lox who crossed his arms defensively.

"How would I know what her plan is? I was the one who ambushed them, remember?"

"So what are you going to do with her?" Michella asked.

"Question her. Find out what Neci is really up to. She hasn't cracked yet but she will," Roberta said confidently. "Everyone has their weakness. We just need to figure out what hers is, but the best thing is that Neci doesn't have a full army."

"So no war?" Emily said hopefully.

"No war yet," Thomas chimed in. "But it buys us time to keep training."

Emily tilted her head up to the clear, blue, August sky. Time. She prayed they would have enough of it to unlock what her full power could do when controlled. She wanted to see the positive of the situation. Scarlett was caught.

Neci's target was always the Five Warriors and even though she had murdered Five Warriors legend Niles Thompson, she still made Scarlett torment his younger brother Gabriel and forced him to release Blade from his icy prison. She deserved every pain that Roberta would certainly inflict on her but a niggling in Emily's brain kept drawing her back to the fact that Neci was planning something. They took Scarlett and Neci would certainly punish them for it.

"She wants to speak to you." Roberta watched Emily carefully.

"Why?" Julian demanded before Emily could even process what Roberta had said. "What could she even say to Emily that would be worth hearing?"

"I don't know. Emily's the only one she's asking for. I

thought she would want Thomas or even you Lox. What do you want to do?"

Emily could feel everyone watching her carefully. *What could Scarlett want with me?*

"Do you think I should?" Emily asked.

Roberta nodded. "I'll be with you the whole time."

"Can we discuss this later?" Sally suddenly said. "It's her birthday. Why don't you open your presents?" She sipped on her glass of red wine. "I'd love to see what you got Emily, Thomas." Sally drummed her nails on the table and smiled slyly at him.

"I'm sure you would," Thomas smoothly replied back. "Okay, sweetheart, I've been thinking really hard about what to get you and I. . . I just hope you like it." He handed Emily a silver envelope and Emily took it curiously.

"Hurry up and open it," Cathy said, trying to peer over Emily's shoulder.

Everyone looked on as Emily grinned, opened the envelope and pulled out a small card. Her eyes raced over the words and very slowly the smile disappeared from her face as she digested what it said.

"Well?" Cathy asked. "What is it?"

"I'm competing in this?" Emily asked, attempting to keep her voice light. Thomas grinned enthusiastically. "But Dad this is. . . I mean it's. . ."

"Do you like it?" Thomas asked, looking more excited than Emily.

"I thought. . . I mean watching it would have been cool. . . but to be a part of it?"

"Part of what?" Cathy asked trying to look at the card.

"The World Warrior Tournament."

There was a stunned silence. Lox dropped his cutlery that echoed across the garden and glared at Thomas. "You just can't help yourself, can you?" He pushed back his chair so that it fell with a bang on the floor before storming into the house.

"The World Warrior Tournament?" Wesley repeated in disbelief. "I mean, that's the world!"

Cathy took the card from Emily and read it for herself, her blue eyes growing wider and wider. "Only the best warriors in the world enter this. Does she stand a chance?"

"Of course she does," Thomas said, sitting up proudly. "She's a Knight."

Sally chuckled to herself, pouring more wine into her glass. "She isn't Lox."

"And what's that supposed to mean?" Thomas asked.

"She." Sally pointed at Emily. "Does not want to compete in that."

"Do you think it's the best time for this?" Jenkins asked.

"It's fine," Thomas snapped. "It's not until next summer. Emily is strong enough and Neci will be gone by then."

"But if she isn't," Roberta interrupted. "Then you're putting Emily into a dangerous situation for Neci to attack her or to study how she fights. Also, this is a lot of stress for her, I mean the Worlds, Thom—"

"Emily will be fine," he said with a finality in his voice. "Lox competed all the time and won."

Emily wanted to echo what Sally had said. *I'm not Lox.*

Thomas excused himself and walked into the house. Emily placed the card on the table and everyone looked at it in silence.

"Well, it's not really fine, is it?" Wesley said, looking around the table.

Emily groaned. "I can't fight in Worlds and I don't want to."

Sally drank her wine and snorted. "He's only thinking about himself."

"Sally," Michael hissed, moving the bottle away from her.

Sally shrugged and finished her drink.

The party deflated soon after that. Everyone kept shooting looks at the card like it was about to explode until Emily eventually placed it in her pocket.

Cathy took the kids to the indoor pool when they complained of being bored. Michael went to check on Lox and Thomas whilst Roberta and Jenkins were talking in hushed voices far away from everyone else. The only one who looked amused by the unexpected turn of events was Sally. She was sitting alone at the table, amongst platters of untouched food. It didn't help that she had drunk more wine than she could handle.

Julian tactfully excused himself from the party, claiming he had to help his mum.

"I'm sorry for all of that," Emily said.

"Don't worry about it," Julian said, hugging her tight. "I wanted to say earlier but you look really pretty."

"Thank you." She blushed as he released her.

His hand lingered a second longer on her waist before he turned away. She spotted Michella, Wesley and Jason near the barbecue and went over to them.

"Sorry that your party got ruined babe," Michella said.

"Let's go to my room," Emily said, massaging her temples. "I need to get away from all of this."

They hurried up the stairs and Jason collapsed on her four poster bed and let out a long sigh. "Well, that was awkward."

"You're telling me," Emily responded, sitting on the edge of her bed. "Does my dad really not see the issue with this?" She took the card out of her pocket and stared at it. "Going for the championship that he won, that Lox won. How can he even be thinking about this when we have Neci to deal with?"

"He did say he thinks Neci will be gone. Maybe he thinks you'll win," Michella said.

They all looked at her.

"Are you okay?" Wesley asked, raising his eyebrows. "There are hundreds of warriors. The best warriors! The elite!"

"Emily's a great fighter," Michella protested.

Emily snorted. "I have battled in a few Dojo matches. I've never really defeated any strong warriors without help. I don't know how Lox won when he was so young."

"Because Dad trained me every day, so I could keep up the family name," Lox said. He was standing by the doorway with his arms crossed, making his muscled arms bulge even more under his fitted shirt.

"Are you all right?" Emily asked softly.

"Yeah, he just annoys me. He made me do all that and look at how our relationship turned out. I get it, he's the all great Thomas Knight but this obsession of keeping the Knight name out there is his problem not ours."

"Couldn't you just not do it?" Michella suggested.

"You do know when you sign up to do Worlds, you can't back out?" Lox said and Michella gasped. "When you enter, you have to sign a contract, which Dad must have already

45

done for you because you're under eighteen. Besides, with Emily competing, the news will travel quick."

Emily groaned, putting her head in her hands. "Seriously? What was he thinking?"

"What happens if you lose?" Jason asked, sitting up.

"Lose? She can't lose." Lox laughed. "That isn't an option. Emily needs to win, so everyone can see what great genes Thomas Knight has passed on to his kids. Trust me, we're just the puppets."

"I thought you liked competing?" Wesley asked confused.

"I did," Lox said. "But I mainly did it to get his attention. Family isn't the number one priority for our dad."

"Lox, don't start," Emily said sharply. "Don't act like we're some baggage in his life."

Lox shrugged and closed her bedroom door. Michella grabbed a hold of Emily's hand and squeezed it.

"What if I do lose? Lox never lost," Emily said, already feeling defeated.

"Listen, you're strong and talented, you'll hold your own," Jason said.

"You have more faith than me."

"Let's stop talking about it," Michella suggested.

"You do know kids never enter Worlds, right?" Wesley said pulling out a pack of playing cards from his pocket. "Lox is the first and only one. There's going to be grown warriors fighting with years of experience against you."

"I was trying to make her feel better," Jason said, hitting the card packet from the bottom, so the cards shot up and sprawled across the floor.

"Hey!" Wesley elbowed Jason's torso.

"Stop you two," Michella snapped. "Pick up the cards and let's play a game."

Three rounds of Black Jack later, Emily was rolling on the floor in laughter as Wesley did his best impressions of the teachers at Osaki.

"No, that ain't right, Mr Waternham just does this whenever Emily speaks," Jason protested. He sighed loudly and rolled his eyes dramatically.

"I don't even know why he doesn't like me!"

"Because you don't breathe under water," Michella said.

"I did eventually get there. So glad I can drop stupid Water Studies this year."

"Same," Wesley said.

"I've got some one-on-one sessions with Jenkins to train my telekinesis," Jason said.

"Oh nice one! I'm actually gonna miss Flying class though. Easiest class to pass in exams." Wesley's stomach rumbled loudly and they all looked at him.

"How can you be hungry?" Michella asked, flicking her long braids over her shoulder. "I think I'm full till tomorrow."

"I'm a growing boy," Wesley protested. He looked at Emily hopefully. "Do you think there's any food left?"

"There should be. Hopefully we'll find my birthday cake somewhere."

They trooped down the stairs. The house was quiet. In the kitchen, Sally was slumped over the counter, with her mouth slightly open and drooling. A half-empty bottle of red wine was beside her. Emily felt Wesley stiffen. Without a word, she picked up the wine bottle and poured it down the sink.

"Sorry, she doesn't usually drink."

Wesley avoided her eyes and Emily cursed Sally in her head. She would get drunk in front of Wesley of all people.

"How is your mum?" Jason asked Wesley.

"She's back home from rehab and she's doing okay. It's good to have her finally home but it's weird as well. It's just seeing Sally like that. . ."

Emily glanced at Sally who was now unattractively snoring. Emily shook her hard on the shoulder.

"What? What?" Sally instantly woke up and looked around the kitchen.

"I think you should go upstairs," Emily said sharply, as she helped her up. "My friends are here."

"I'm fine," Sally said, swaying slightly.

"Mum?" Cathy walked into the kitchen holding a bin bag. Cathy spotted the empty bottle of wine and instantly grabbed Sally's arm. "Come on, you." She led Sally towards the stairs.

Emily opened the fridge and there in the centre was a heavily creamed, red-velvet cake. In loopy writing it read, 'Happy 15th Birthday Emily X.'

"Would your dad get mad if we just ate it?" Michella asked.

Emily picked it up and led them towards the table. "It's my cake and if they wanted us to eat together, they would have brought it out rather than argued."

She placed it on the kitchen table and the four of them surrounded it.

"Candles?" Wesley asked.

"Err, I think they're in that drawer by the sink," Emily responded.

"I'll get them," Jason said and he put his fingertips to his temple and stared intensely at the drawer. It slowly opened and a packet of pink candles floated out. Emily watched in awe as the candles flew over her head and landed perfectly in Jason's hand.

"I'm so jealous you can do that," Emily said.

Jason placed fifteen candles on the cake. "Wouldn't it be great if I could produce fire too?"

"It would, but we'll stick to regular old matches," Emily said, picking them up from the cupboard beside the stove.

She carefully lit each candle as her friends tunelessly sang, 'Happy Birthday.'

Michella clapped her hands and said, "Make a wish and make it count."

Emily closed her eyes and thought of a million different things to wish for. Winning the World Warrior Tournament, Ogragon keeping the Dojo Championship but one thing she needed was hope. Hope that they could survive Neci. So Emily made her wish and her friends whistled and cheered.

"Ooh cake! Can we have some?"

James, Rosy and Yvonne were standing in the doorway, in their wet swimsuits, looking excited at the huge cake in front of them. Emily rolled her eyes. They obviously had a sixth sense when it was time to eat dessert.

"Come on then," she said and they ran over, looking hungrily at the cake. "Where are the adults?" she asked James, who went to grab a piece of cake with his hand, but Emily slapped it away.

James shrugged. "Dunno, but Aunt Roberta is in the living room. Can I have a big piece?"

Once everyone had a piece of cake, Emily walked towards the living room. There wasn't any noise coming from it, but the living room door was closed, which was unusual. Emily opened it and Roberta was sitting on the couch staring blank-faced at the television.

Since Neci's warriors had taken control of the stations only Channel 47 broadcasted anything. Emily had no idea how they were still able to. She followed Roberta's gaze and saw a street full of protestors on the screen. They were holding signs that read, 'IT'S NOT OUR FIGHT' and 'NO TO WARRIORS.'

"What is this?" Emily asked, sitting next to Roberta.

"I knew this would happen," Roberta muttered.

"What? What's happening?" Emily asked urgently.

"They're rebelling. They're rebelling against warriors. They don't want to fight with us."

Ordinary people were marching the streets of London, shouting and waving posters. A blonde lady with messy hair and a checked shirt shouted directly into the camera, "Why are our lives at risk? Because those brutes can't control themselves. Get rid of warriors!"

Emily gasped. She'd only had one encounter last year with someone judging her for being a warrior, but to have an entire street of them. Did they not know not know how much danger they were in?

"Do they think we're the bad guys?" Emily asked surprised.

Roberta sighed. "They think all warriors are like Neci."

"But we're nothing like her!"

"We battle, we have powers; to them we're all the same."

"For goodness sake, can't they see that we're trying to protect them?"

"They're just scared, Emily," Roberta said sadly.

"They're scared!" Emily shouted. "Are they kidding me? We save their lives. You have personally saved their lives. Doesn't this make you mad?"

"They're scared that they're going to die for a war that really has nothing to do with them. I'm surprised that non-warriors have tolerated our need to battle for as long as they have, but we need to show them that we're the ones that will win. Without us, the bad warriors will kill them. We have a lot of lives to save."

"Yeah? Who's going to save us?" Emily said and she wasn't surprised when Roberta didn't answer.

The television screen was now showing a packed hall. They were shouting over one another and again Emily noticed the signs hung on the walls, 'NOT OUR WAR' and 'WE DON'T NEED A KNIGHT.'

"That's not what they were saying before," Emily said bitterly. "What happened to celebrating the glorious return of Lox and Thomas Knight?"

"Not everyone has turned against us," Roberta reminded her.

Emily took a deep breath. "I want to meet Scarlett."

Roberta didn't look the least bit surprised. "When?"

"Now? But you already saw this happening, right?"

Roberta smiled. "I did."

"Let me just tell my friends that we're popping out, then we can go."

CHAPTER FIVE

Overload

Emily and Roberta walked out of the front door. Emily looked up at the banners celebrating her brother and Dad. If they could see first-hand how dysfunctional the Knight family was, how much faith would anyone have in them?

They got towards the end of the Village and Roberta turned to a house that had been vacant for as long as Emily could remember. It was decorated just as beautifully as all the other mansions, with its cream coloured exterior and a perfect flower display by the door.

To Emily's surprise, Roberta pulled out a key and opened the door.

Emily grabbed her arm. "You left her here in the Village?"

"Don't worry, it's safe and no one will think to look for her here."

Emily stared at her in disbelief. "How can you leave her so close to us? You know what she's done to me, to Gabriel—"

"And I would never have done that if I didn't have it under control."

Roberta pushed open the door and the house had no furniture and no paintings. It was an immaculate empty space. Emily followed Roberta down the stairs and Roberta pressed a switch on the wall where a dim light appeared above them.

At the end of the corridor, Roberta walked into a small kitchen. She opened the fridge and pulled out a bowl of pasta covered in cling film. She put it into the microwave and caught Emily's confused expression. "I can't let her starve."

Emily tutted. "Why not?"

"Because she's valuable to us. She's valuable to you."

"What do you mean by that?" Emily frowned.

The microwave pinged. Roberta took the food out and placed it on a plastic plate with a fork. She filled up a cup with tap water.

"Do you think Neci would show us this same generosity?"

Roberta chuckled. "Oh, definitely not. Come on, let's go."

They retraced their steps and Roberta turned right into a corridor that Emily had missed because of the poor lighting. Roberta typed in a code on the side of the wall. A light flashed green and the door opened automatically. The strength of the Illiarn weighed down heavy on Emily's shoulders.

The lighting was a bit better in this room and Scarlett was sitting in a chair in the middle of it. For a prisoner, she looked in good shape. Her long, red hair was shiny and wavy down her face. Her skin didn't have the sunken look to it that Lox used to have. Emily noticed that she sat up straighter when she laid eyes on Emily. Her green eyes seemed to smile at her and Emily held back, not wanting to get too close.

Roberta approached her easily and handed her the plate of pasta and water.

"Thank you," Scarlett said, drinking back the water in one go before she put the cup on the floor and began to hungrily eat the pasta. "This is really good."

"You're welcome," Roberta said.

Emily looked from one to the other. "What is this? It's like she's your friend or something? She blackmailed Gabriel all year. She tried to get Blade to kill me. And you're feeding her pasta!"

A clatter came from the other side of the room, as Scarlett put her plate and fork on the floor.

"Thank you for coming to see me, Emily," Scarlett said softly.

"Why did you want to see me?" Emily challenged.

Scarlett smiled. "I just wanted to look into the eyes of the person that's going to change everything."

"What do you mean?"

Scarlett leaned back in her chair and stared at Emily amazed. "You have no idea who you are. "

"I know exactly who I am," Emily shot back. "I'm not evil like you. I don't threaten children like you. I don't stand beside a warrior that kills people for fun. You're disgusting. I want nothing more than to see your head roll on the floor. All of you that fight for her, I want to see you burn."

"Well, I'm not standing with her now, am I?"

Emily jerked her head back. She turned to Roberta, who avoided her eyes. Emily took a step closer to Scarlett.

"Only because you were captured."

Scarlett shrugged.

"You know, you haven't once showed any remorse for what you did," Emily said, marching up to Scarlett so she was standing right in front of her. "You have no idea the damage you caused to me and Gabriel. You threatened him, his family, you destroyed his home. What you did to him is unforgivable."

"I was just following orders," Scarlett said quietly.

"Where's your boss now?"

To Emily's surprise, Scarlett smiled. "Do you really think I was captured?"

"Of course you were," Emily snapped.

Scarlett stood to her feet and Emily stepped back. In that moment, she noticed that Scarlett wasn't tied up.

"Scarlett," Roberta said. "Sit down."

But Scarlett kept moving forward keeping her eyes on Emily.

"Come on," Roberta said, grabbing on to Emily's arm and hurrying her out of the door but Scarlett was right behind them and she grabbed Emily's hand.

"Hey!" Emily said, trying to pull her off but she couldn't.

They were standing just in front of the door and the air felt lighter without the Illiarn.

"Maybe I came here willingly," Scarlett said. "I can see it now." She held Emily's hand tight and Emily looked down and could see that her hand was slowly turning red. Then she felt it. Her hand was burning.

"Get off!" Emily said, trying to pull her hand away. "Aunt Roberta!"

"If you embrace it, it won't consume you," Scarlett said.

The heat was travelling up her arm. Scarlett was grinning as Emily groaned.

The burning was getting stronger and stronger. Emily

screamed and felt herself being pulled back. She stumbled to the floor. The heat seemed to linger on her arm.

Roberta was standing in front of her facing Scarlett. She could hear mumbled voices but she couldn't pick up what they were saying. Scarlett nodded her head towards Emily and Roberta whipped around. For a split second, Roberta looked afraid. Emily slowly stood up and Roberta rushed to her side, helping her up.

"Get back inside," Roberta ordered and Scarlett waved at Emily before walking back into the room, closing the door behind her, which instantly clicked as it locked.

"Let's go," Roberta said, leading Emily away from the door.

"Embrace it, Emily!" Scarlett shouted from behind the door.

Emily wanted to turn back. She wanted to understand what she was talking about but Roberta had a firm grip and led her up the stairs and out of the house.

"What the hell was that?" Emily yelled as Roberta locked the door. "What is she even talking about?"

Roberta was looking up to the sky, breathing hard. She looked down at Emily with her green eyes filled with tears.

"What's wrong?" Emily asked reaching out to her. Roberta grabbed the hand that Scarlett had held and it felt tender. Emily winced but Roberta didn't notice.

"This war is bigger than me, you, even your dad. We all have our roles to play. I thought I knew how this would go but the things I've seen. . ."

"What's my part in all of this?" Emily asked.

"Oh, Emily, there is just so much to it that doesn't make sense. You're so important but if I was to tell you everything. . .

it wouldn't pan out the way it's meant to, so I can't say, yet."

Roberta looked down at Emily's hand where Scarlett's heat was slowly fading. She rubbed her hand gently over Emily's skin. "It will all make sense," she mumbled under her breath.

"Am I going to die?"

"What?" Roberta looked up, alarmed, then she noticed Emily's gaze on her hand. Roberta shook her head. "No, she didn't do anything bad, I promise."

"What did she do?"

"Do you trust me?" Roberta suddenly asked and Emily pulled her hand away.

"You always ask me that!"

"I know," Roberta said blushing. "Because I ask so much of you and I know it's not fair. I've known you since you were a baby. Have I ever not come through for you?"

Emily shook her head.

"I love you like you're one of my own children. I would do anything to protect you. If you went against everything that everyone told you to do, I would understand. If you marched back into that house and choked the life out of Scarlett, I wouldn't blame you. But I'm asking you for the last time to trust me. Trust me about Scarlett, about any instructions that I give to you, because we're all going to have make sacrifices, some more than others. If you can trust me, despite all of the confusion, we can win this war."

Everything felt muddled in her head. Emily didn't understand why nothing could ever be straightforward. It was like everyone was talking a language that only she didn't understand. She looked up at her dad's handsome face on a flag that was blowing back and forth. Roberta wrapped an arm around her shoulders. Emily leaned into her, breathing her familiar sweet smell.

"Did you see my dad beat Neci?"

Roberta squeezed Emily's shoulder. "I believe that Thomas can beat Neci but do you know what?"

Emily looked up at Roberta.

"Sometimes the unlikeliest people are the best heroes."

"Do you think?"

"Oh definitely." Roberta kissed the top of Emily's forehead. "Now let's get back to your party." Emily scoffed. "Or salvage it. I need to find your dad, but Emily, you cannot tell anyone about Scarlett's whereabouts, okay?"

"Why?"

"I think everyone would react the way you did. That she is too close to home, but I need her here." Emily hesitated. "I would never have brought her here if I didn't need to."

"I know," Emily eventually said. "Okay, I won't tell."

It was a few days after Emily's birthday and she wished she could rewind to when she felt excited that her family was back together. Lox was still annoyed with Thomas and everyone could feel the tension in the house. Sally was mortified by how drunk she had been at the party and kept apologising. When Cathy questioned why she had drunk so much, Sally blushed and refused to answer, but Emily knew it had something to do with her dad.

Emily felt as though she had a massive arrow pointing at

her, flashing in neon lights, highlighting that she was keeping a huge secret from everyone.

One afternoon she found herself standing outside the abandoned house where Scarlett was. The heat that Emily had felt when Scarlett touched her was now gone. *What did Scarlett do to me? What did she mean by 'embrace it'?*

Emily wished she could get into the house and question Scarlett herself but only Roberta had the key. Emily hadn't seen Roberta since her birthday. She was tempted to tell someone about what was going on but she didn't want to break her promise.

Emily was sat in Michella's garden with Wesley and Jason. They were going to Sia's Avenue to visit the Warside store. Emily wanted new baht shoes for school, and Wesley and Jason both needed new uniforms and Dojo kits, as they had outgrown them over the summer. Wesley was also planning to meet up with his girlfriend, Harmony which Emily wasn't looking forward to. She didn't want to be the spare part between two couples.

Usually, Mrs Kinkle would drive them, but because they were fifteen and had their FLY cards—which allowed them to fly outside of school—Michella had persuaded her to allow them to go together. Mrs Kinkle wasn't too keen but she gave in when they promised they would only be an hour and would call once they got back to Emily's house.

Michella stood and brushed the grass of her legs. "So are we going?"

"Yeah, let's get a move on," Emily said, also standing to her feet and picking up the disguise she'd brought to wear.

"Maybe you should have some form of bodyguard," Wesley suggested. Emily shot him a disgusted look and he quickly added, "Or not."

"Not," she replied. "That would only draw more attention."

"Can you imagine if Thomas was at Warside waiting for you?" Jason said and they all laughed.

"It would be awful." Emily put on a short, black wig, a baseball cap and sunglasses. "Complete pandemonium. I just want to get in and out without drawing any attention."

It was worse than they'd imagined. When they landed at Warside, Thomas *and* Lox were standing at the entrance.

"What the?" Emily said, marching up to them.

People were walking in and out of the building. Thomas and Lox were getting a few curious glances but no one had actually approached them. . . yet.

"What are you doing here?" Emily hissed, dragging them both by the arm, away from the entrance. "Why are you only wearing sunglasses? You're not even trying to blend in."

"We wanted to help you shop." Thomas looked at Emily up and down. "I like your disguise. Cathy told me what to look out for."

"He wanted to help you shop," Lox pointed out, crossing his arms. "I came to make sure he didn't do something stupid like take pictures with fans and draw attention to us."

"Why would you want to help me shop?" Emily asked confused.

"I have missed out on so much and I wanted to share this moment with you." Thomas squeezed Emily with one hand.

"That's nice Dad but you're not even in disguise. I just don't like drawing attention to myself if I don't need to."

"I told you that she wouldn't be happy," Lox said matter-of-factly.

"Here, Mr Knight," Wesley said, taking off his blue baseball cap and handing it to Thomas.

"Ah, thank you, and please call me Thomas," he said, placing the cap on his head.

Jason stood in front of Lox and studied him. "I don't think he looks too bad."

Emily turned to Lox. He looked less conspicuous than Thomas. Lox was wearing sunglasses, light jeans and a grey checked shirt, with his Afro hair back in a slick ponytail. Emily rarely saw Lox in anything but torn baggy, black clothes, so he didn't look as recognisable, but she still felt it wasn't good enough.

"We'll be good, we promise," Thomas said earnestly, pulling his cap down further. "You won't even know we're here."

Warside, as usual, was packed with students and parents buying uniforms and Dojo kits before the school term. Emily was on edge thinking of the commotion if she, Thomas and Lox were spotted. She was so distracted that she didn't notice Harmony Loving-Dale and walked straight into her.

"Sorry," Emily said as Harmony squinted at her.

Harmony looked as pretty as ever with her long blonde hair twisted into an elaborate bun.

"Emily? Is that you?"

"Ssh," Wesley said, putting his arm around Harmony's shoulders. "She's in disguise."

"Oops sorry," Harmony said. She tiptoed and kissed Wesley on the cheek. "I've missed you."

"Sorry, I just saw something over there," Emily lied before walking off.

"Who are those guys?" she heard Harmony ask as she watched Thomas and Lox follow Emily.

"Err, bodyguards," Wesley said quickly.

Michella and Jason went off to find Dojo kits and Emily headed towards the baht shoes. She picked out a black pair to try on and sat on the nearest seat.

Thomas sat next to her grinning. "This is fun, isn't it?"

Emily glanced at him and thought it wise to not respond.

"I haven't been in here for years," Thomas continued, not caring that he was having a one-way conversation. "Not since Lox needed his first baht shoes. Remember Lox?"

"Ssh," Lox and Emily said simultaneously.

"Dad, don't say his name please," Emily whispered.

Thomas tutted and folded his arms. Emily tried on the shoes and they were the right fit. As she put back on her trainers, Thomas picked up the baht shoes and stood.

"Where are you going?" Emily asked.

"I'm going to pay for the shoes. I'll try not to embarrass you," he said sarcastically.

Emily sighed as he walked off.

Michella, Jason and Wesley (minus Harmony) found them a few minutes later, and they were each holding Warside shopping bags.

"Where's Mr K?" Wesley asked.

"His gone to pay for the stuff. Where did Harmony go?" Emily asked, trying to sound nonchalant.

"She's meeting up with her parents," Wesley said.

"I can't wait until this whole shopping trip is over," Emily said, glancing towards the checkout. "Where is he?"

"He has been gone awhile," Lox said, following her gaze. "Maybe I should go and look for him?"

Before Emily could respond, Thomas appeared looking cheerful, minus the baht shoes.

"Didn't you pay?" Lox asked.

"The nice man at the desk said he would wrap them and bring them over," Thomas said proudly.

Emily's heart skipped a beat. "Why would he do that?"

And as if on cue, a short man with a bald head and beard came over holding a shoe box containing Emily's baht shoes and a credit card.

"Thank you very much for your service, Mr Knight. I have given you a discount as we appreciate your custom."

"Please call me Thomas," Thomas said, accepting the shoe box.

"Thomas Knight?" a fat lady with a bad blonde perm said. She was standing next to them and she quickly dug through her purse and pulled out her phone. "IT'S THOMAS KNIGHT!"

"Thomas Knight?"

"Where's Thomas?"

"He's here? Where?"

"Good job," Lox said, frowning at him.

"Lox, it's not a big deal," Thomas said. A second later he realised his mistake and covered his mouth, but it was too late.

"Lox Knight is here!" someone shouted.

Everything happened so quickly. They were closing in on them from all sides, taking pictures and talking over each other. Someone grabbed the wig of Emily's head who automatically grabbed it back.

"It's Emily Knight!" a young man shouted. "Give me that." He pulled harder on the wig. "I can make some serious money off this."

"Let go!" Emily yelled, pulling the wig so hard that the man fell face first to the floor.

"I'm sorry," Emily said to the man, but her words got lost in all the shouting.

Thomas pulled her towards him and she felt herself being lifted into the air. The sounds were muted and everything blurred into one. She closed her eyes, holding him tight.

Thomas squeezed her hand and whispered, "You're okay now."

Emily opened her eyes and they had teleported back to Legends Village, outside their home. Lox had hold of her friends.

"I knew this would happen!" Emily yelled.

Thomas scratched the back of his head, "Look, Emily, this is what happens when I go out."

"All I wanted was to get some school stuff with my friends."

"Do you think I'm not going to go out in public with my kids because of some fans?" Thomas argued. "I think we should look into security for you."

"No way! Can't Lox just be around?"

"Lox?" Thomas scoffed. "Lox needs security as well. He has a massive target on his back."

"He is right here," Lox snapped.

"We're getting security and that's that," Thomas said before marching towards the house.

"I'll try and talk to him," Lox said before following Thomas.

"He's being protective," Michella said gently. "He's just being a Dad and. . . he hasn't been for years, so let him do this."

"I wish he could ask me what I want rather than tell me," Emily said, kicking the gravel on the floor.

"Shall we go to mine?" Wesley suggested. "Nan will make us lunch and everyone can cool off."

"Good idea, I'm just texting Mum," Michella said, taking her phone out of her pocket.

Emily looked back at her house. She couldn't face another argument with Thomas. "Yeah, let's do that."

CHAPTER SIX

Fame

They flew to Wesley's house in silence and landed outside to raised voices that could be heard coming from inside.

Wesley's face instantly hardened. "Wait here," he instructed before going inside the house.

"What do you think's going on?" Emily asked.

"I'm not sure," Jason replied.

A minute later, Wesley stormed out of the house with his face red and his hands in fists.

"I'll be the judge of that!" he shouted, over his shoulder.

"Wesley, please," a female voice called, but Wesley kept walking, striding past everyone.

A second later, a beautiful, willowy woman with dark brown skin and brown eyes stood at the door. She had long, black dreadlocks almost touching her waist. "Wesley!" the lady yelled. She looked surprised when she spotted Emily, Michella and Jason and hurried back into the house.

"Lorraine looks good," Michella commented. "I haven't seen his mum in years."

"That's his mum?" Emily asked. She had never met his mum before as she had been in rehab.

"I think Wesley is still adjusting to her being back," Jason said.

"I'll go check on him," Emily offered. She ran after him and caught Wesley turning the corner. "Hey," she said softly.

"She just comes home and expects everything to be how it was before!" Wesley yelled, kicking the wall. "It's like she doesn't understand how we felt being abandoned by her."

"I understand," Emily said, gently holding on to his arm. His face was red and he was breathing hard. "I get how you feel. Just calm down and let's talk through this, okay?"

"Okay," Wesley said rubbing his face.

"Come on," Emily said, linking arms with him.

There was a park opposite his house. Emily sat him down by the nearest bench. "What happened back there?"

"She hasn't been back to the house in a while and obviously things have changed. I don't even know why I snapped at her. All she did was move the tables and chairs round but it was just the fact that she hasn't been here and she assumes she can be the mum again and it's not that easy. We need time to adjust, you know?"

Emily nodded. "I know. There's a massive adjustment at my house too and it's hard because you're happy they're home but you also feel—"

"Weary? Like anything you do will trigger them?"

"Yes!" Emily said. "That's it! What if Lox gets upset and decides to leave, will Dad leave too? What's your mum's trigger?"

Wesley scoffed. "Being a mum. What she doesn't get is

when she couldn't handle life and started drinking, I had to step up to protect Cammie because she's my little sister. When Nan came to look after us, Mum fully checked out. It was like she felt that we were good so she could go on one. When she finally went to rehab, I felt such a weight off my shoulders and the three of us have been fine. Now she's back and I feel like if she can't be our mum full time then we don't want her." Wesley tilted his head back and sighed.

"You know Michella made a comment to me. She said that my dad was just being a dad. They know they haven't been around but maybe we just need to give them more time to figure it all out and hope they don't let us down."

Wesley stared at Emily. "That's what you're doing?"

Emily nodded. "I've wanted him back for years and I know you don't speak about your mum loads but I'm sure you missed her?"

"Yeah I did," Wesley said. "It's just. . . going to take time."

"And try and be patient. Actually, let's both be patient with them. Deal?"

"Sometimes I wish I could pick my family. Just a normal one," Wesley whispered.

Emily had never thought that one of her friends would feel the same way she did. The pressure to be the one to 'fix' the family. It was a burden that was too heavy at times. Emily was so distracted by her thoughts that it took her a second to realise that Wesley's hand was brushing against hers. Without saying a word, she held on to it, interlocking her fingers with his own.

Emily was sitting at the dining table eating breakfast. Channel 47 could be heard in the next room. Sally was sitting opposite Emily. Her grey eyes looked alert. Sally cleared her throat and everyone looked at her.

"I was just wondering, what are the arrangements for today? Usually I drive Emily to school and pick her up but I don't know if you want to. . ." she trailed off and looked at Thomas.

Thomas looked effortlessly handsome in a black training kit. He looked up from his newspaper and said, "Well, I was looking into a security team that will accompany her to school."

"Great," Emily muttered.

"In fact everyone was going to get security," Thomas continued, ignoring Emily.

"What?" Cathy said, looking annoyed. "No one said we would need security." She looked accusingly at Sally, who looked surprised.

"But Lox persuaded me not to. He pointed out that he'll be visiting Osaki as he has work to do with Mr Davon and I'm in and out of the house so I can keep an eye on everyone. Plus all of the cars now have an emergency button whose signal will come straight to me." Thomas held up a small black device. "This will beep if anyone presses it."

"Thank you," Emily mouthed at Lox, who smiled back at her. She glanced at the clock and quickly finished her toast. "So how am I getting to school?"

"What exactly are you doing at Osaki?" Cathy asked Lox, with her eyebrows raised.

"In time you'll find out, beautiful," Lox said, winking at Cathy who blushed. Emily rolled her eyes.

"Sally can take you to school as usual," Thomas said. "I did wonder if you wanted to board at school this year?"

Emily shook her head. "It can get too much sometimes with people just wanting to ask me questions and stuff. Now you're both back I think it will draw even more attention to me."

"I've got to get a move on but don't worry Dad, this year Emily will be more than safe. I'll watch her every move." Lox grinned at her.

Emily frowned. "You don't have to do that."

"Have a good day," Thomas said. He opened up his arms and Emily ran into them. He kissed her forehead and squeezed her tight.

"Breaking news, Professor Eugene Elwood is missing," the TV blared from the living room.

Thomas frowned and hurried to the TV with Emily right behind him. A brunette with big, blue eyes was speaking and Thomas grabbed the remote and turned up the volume. All Emily could see was a house covered in ice.

"You may remember from years ago that Professor Elwood is best known for creating a solid-able version of Reviving Water nicknamed the R Cap. He supplied it to warriors but when they sold out, people started rioting, so Professor Elwood refused to make any more. But he famously gave them to The Five Warriors in their life or death battle against Neci. Some claim Professor Elwood was the true hero of the battle because if it wasn't for him, it is uncertain whether The Five Warriors would have been victorious.

"Professor Elwood has been missing since the early hours of the morning. His secretary found the lab he was working at in a distressed state. The police are investigating this matter. Professor Elwood is a widow and his only child, Hayley-Elizabeth, is staying with relatives. More news to come after this break."

"Blade," Emily muttered and everyone looked at her.

"That ice man did this?" Sally asked and Emily nodded. "How terrible."

Thomas didn't say a word. He sank to the couch with his head in his hands.

Emily stared at the profile picture on the screen of Professor Elwood. If Neci had him captured and he was providing them with limitless R Caps then it didn't matter how hard they trained, they wouldn't stand a chance.

The journey to Osaki was sombre. Emily couldn't stop thinking about Professor Elwood's home. It took her back to the ice room where she had met Blade. Emily shuddered.

"What is going on?" Sally stopped the car and leaned over Emily to look out of the window. Emily gasped when she saw it packed with students and parents, pushing each other and yelling, whilst taking pictures on their phones. "It's complete pandemonium."

Sally pushed the car door open. Emily followed suit and watched in disbelief. She searched the crowd, but couldn't see Michella, Wesley, or Jason.

"Emily!" Lisa Fowler, a cute blonde haired girl in Ogragon, ran up to her, looking excited. "I can't believe he's here!"

"Who?" Emily asked confused.

"Lox! Lox is here!" Lisa squealed.

Emily forced a smile. Of course it was Lox causing all the mayhem, she should have guessed.

"It's only Lox," Emily said to Sally, who laughed.

"Obviously!" She hugged Emily tight and whispered in her ear, "Keep your head up."

Emily squeezed her back. "I'll see you tonight."

Once Sally drove off, Lisa linked arms with Emily and dragged her towards the crowd. "You have to get me closer to Lox."

"No, Lisa," Emily said, brushing her off.

"Please!" Lisa said, standing in front of her with her hands clasped. "I have loved your brother for years and Jason's hard-to-get game is really getting on my nerves."

Emily scoffed. "First of all, Lox is way too old for you and Jason is going out with Michella. He isn't playing a game, you weirdo."

Lisa gasped. "Since when have they been together?"

"There you are." Wesley was beside her, holding on to his suitcase.

Michella and Jason were approaching them, walking hand in hand and Lisa spotted them and stormed off in their direction.

"I can't deal with all of this today!" Emily yelled over the noise.

Wesley was looking at the crowd in awe. "Do you know what's going on?"

Before Emily could answer, she spotted Lisa from the corner of her eye, standing with her hands on her hips, pointing accusingly at a terrified Jason.

Emily grabbed Wesley's arm. "Come on."

They got close enough to hear Lisa shout, "You said you're a Jew?"

"I am," Jason replied innocently.

"And you said you can only date Jews. So what happened? She's converted or something?"

Jason had the good decency to blush. "Yes. . . I mean no, err. . ."

Lisa looked at Michella up and down before storming off. Emily watched her until her blonde hair disappeared.

"Just ignore her," Emily said as Michella hugged herself. "She's just jealous."

"Guys, look at Alice," Wesley said, pointing at the school doors.

Alice Archinia was in mid-conversation with Lox. Her hand kept touching his and anything he said, she seemed to find hilarious, flinging her head back with laughter.

Emily couldn't deny that Alice was a striking girl, with pale skin, shoulder length, white-blonde hair, green cat shaped eyes and high cheekbones. The granddaughter of Five Warriors legend, Cecil Archinia and ex-reality show princess, Alice felt like she deserved more of the spotlight in their elite fighting group than Emily. They now had a civilised relationship, but Emily wasn't holding her breath that it would last.

Emily folded her arms and watched Lox being drawn into Alice's charming ways, seeming unaware to the frenzy it was causing amongst everyone.

"She is such a fame junkie," Michella said. "Doesn't Lox realise she's only trying to make herself relevant again? I can't believe I used to be a fan of hers."

The noise level was at an all time high. Emily spotted Gabriel Thompson, with his dark hair and glasses, walking beside his friend Jasper Jones. She couldn't believe the transformation of Gabriel. From last year to now, it was clear that the weight of Scarlett's blackmail to release Blade had made a massive difference in him. He walked with a presence and this time you noticed him for all the right reasons. She wished she could tell him that Scarlett was their prisoner.

"That's Emily Knight."

Emily looked behind her to see a group of students she didn't recognise shooting her shy glances.

Some of the students started nudging each other as a mixed-raced girl with light brown skin, curly black hair, small eyes and a slim frame, hurried past everyone with her head down. It was Professor Elwood's daughter, Hayley-Elizabeth.

Finally, Laton Chin, the deputy headmaster, opened the front doors and stood in front of the students in his beige training kit. He always looked immaculate with his slicked back hair and cool exterior. He allowed Lox and Alice to enter inside before instructing all of the students to go to the dining hall. The first years had to stay outside, where they would be placed into one of the six teams at the Osaki Training School: Ogragon, Berbinin, Linktie, Pentwon, Mentorawth or Jenkint.

"Come on," Jason said, grabbing his suitcase and leading the way into the school.

Emily picked up one of Michella's suitcases and followed Jason. All eyes were on Emily when she walked by. The first years were still excited and seeing Emily only heightened that. They began to take pictures and call out her name, only stopping when Laton Chin raised his voice and told them to be quiet.

"*Fire,*" a small voice said in Emily's ear.

"What?" Emily said, looking at the ginger-haired girl to her right, who was staring adoringly at her.

"Are you talking to me?"

Emily shook her head. "Sorry. . . I thought you said. . . never mind."

Shaking her head, Emily walked through the front doors. She could have sworn she heard someone.

"Oh, it's so good to be home!" Wesley said, running up to the grandfather clock and hugging it.

"Loser," Tanya Frank said, shooting Wesley a dirty look, that was echoed by her two friends, chubby Ola Ade and acne-prone, Fiona Corn.

Tanya Frank was a slim-built girl with mid-length brown hair and what Emily thought were dark, menacing eyes. Emily and Tanya had never seen eye to eye. Tanya thought Emily was overrated and Emily thought Tanya was a cow.

"How was your summer, Emily?" Tanya asked, sneering at her. "What does one do when their rich daddy comes home?"

"Get lost," Emily said wearily but Tanya followed her.

"Us normal warriors are trying stay alive and not get killed in an upcoming war. You know the war that's really about killing your family?"

"Tanya, we've been at school for five minutes!" Michella shouted. "Just back off."

"Ooh." Tanya laughed. "That's the brave talk that comes

when you're protected by the Knight inner circle, but what are you going to do, Michella, when Emily gets killed by Neci?"

"Don't rise to it," Wesley said at the same time Emily lunged for Tanya.

Jason grabbed Emily and held her back.

"Do you want to repeat that?" Lox appeared beside Emily and stared coldly at Tanya.

Some of the students had stopped walking, eagerly waiting to see what was going to happen next.

Tanya took a step back. She bumped into Ola.

"Nothing else to say?" Lox asked, with his eyebrows raised.

Tanya shook her head and quickly hurried off with Fiona and Ola right behind her.

"I can handle Tanya," Emily said to Lox, crossing her arms.

Lox laughed. "Oh, I know that, but I was just trying to stop you getting suspended from school. She's a piece of work."

"That's one way of putting it," Wesley said. "We could all use a permanent break from her."

The students around them, losing interest in what could have been an entertaining fight, headed into the dining hall.

"I don't believe it," Lox said in disbelief and Emily followed his gaze to see Niles Thompson floating towards them.

"You know you're only getting this much attention because I'm dead, right?" Niles joked.

Niles was a teenage ghost and the youngest of The Five Warriors. He was murdered by Neci in the same battle Thomas had won. Emily always felt extremely intimidated around Niles. Last year, he had trusted her to look out for his little brother, Gabriel. The guilt still hadn't left Emily. She felt that if she had tried harder with Gabriel, Blade wouldn't have escaped his ice prison and this war wouldn't be happening. On top of that, Niles was gorgeous. It was a punishment for all the females at Osaki that one of the hottest boys at school wasn't alive.

"Hey man," Lox said grinning. "Someone's gotta take it."

Niles laughed. "Good seeing you. Have you seen Cecil yet?"

"No, I'd love to see the old man. I met his granddaughter though." Lox and Niles shared a knowing look and both burst out laughing.

"We'll find him after. Mr Davon wanted me to grab you, to talk about. . ." Niles trailed off when he noticed Emily, Michella, Wesley and Jason eavesdropping on the conversation.

"Oh, hey Niles," Emily said, in mock surprise.

"Gosh, we didn't even see you there," Wesley added and Michella nudged him. "Not because you're dead—I mean because we weren't paying—sorry, just ignore me."

"Let's walk and talk," Lox suggested. He squeezed Emily's shoulder as he walked past.

"I never thought Niles and Lox would be happy to see each other," Michella said.

"Why?" Emily frowned.

"Because Neci killed Niles and then Lox ran away with her. You would think Niles would hold a grudge or something."

"I never thought about it like that," Emily said, watching Lox and Niles banter like brothers.

They left their suitcases in the hallway with the other students' and entered the dining hall. Emily stopped walking so suddenly that Michella, Wesley and Jason bumped into her.

A. BELLO

"Oh. . . my. . . gosh," Emily said slowly, as she looked around the room.

The dining hall was covered in colourful banners reading 'Thank you Thomas and Lox.' Emily felt hundreds of eyes stare at her as she stood at the doorway. It was like she wasn't even part of the family.

CHAPTER SEVEN

The Five Warriors

They grabbed seats at their usual table. Michella's older brothers, Warren and Pete, greeted them enthusiastically.

"You know, this should be us," Warren said, pointing to himself and Pete. "We're the ones with two professional Dojo players as family members and two future ones." He pointed again to himself and Pete. "Where are our banners?"

"Not sure why anyone would celebrate you two," Michella said.

"See, this is why Madison is our favourite little sister," Warren said and Pete laughed.

"Shut up, Warren," Michella snapped.

"Always a party when you're around, sis. Are you loving the Knight takeover, Emily?" Warren asked

"Best day ever," Emily said with a forced smile.

It took Emily a moment to notice the group of students hovering around their table, pretending to engage in conversation, just so they could stand closer to her. They kept glancing her way, hoping to catch eyes with her.

"You know what, we should have gotten some form of victory for defeating Alan Fair last year!" Pete said irritated. "That was a true David and Goliath battle."

"You would think so right?" Warren agreed. "We're so unappreciated here."

"Guys, no more snake surprises, please. I don't think Emily can take it," Wesley joked and Emily blushed.

The last thing she wanted to remember was Wesley kissing Harmony to distract her from seeing the snake that Warren had brought out on to the pitch during their Dojo match. Emily had seen the kiss and blown up parts of the stadium, knocking a few people out. Michella always referred to it as her 'jealousy-filled fireball.'

The dining hall was filling up quickly. Emily saw Julian Kena walk in, looking handsome in his school uniform, talking animatedly with some of his friends from Mentorawth. He stopped mid-walk when he noticed the banners. Julian immediately looked around the hall and spotted Emily. He said something to his friends before heading over to her.

"Hey," he said.

Emily stood up and hugged him. She felt like there was a spotlight beaming brightly on them. The whole school knew that they had fought Blade and rescued Gabriel together last term.

"How are you doing?" He watched her intensely, oblivious to the stares.

"Not the best way to start back at school," she admitted. "Did you see Hayley-Elizabeth's house?"

Julian nodded. "It took me right back to that ice room. I feel for her. I heard that Lox is here?"

Emily nodded and pointed at the ceiling. "His own little welcome home party. He only went to Osaki for what? Two seconds?"

Julian laughed. His long black hair was hanging in a plait over his chest and Emily had an urge to touch it.

"Any time you need to talk, you know where I am."

"Thank you." Emily smiled.

Julian gave her one last squeeze, before he walked off. Emily took her seat and caught eyes with Violet Hijen and Sydney John from the Ogragon team and they gave her the thumbs up.

Violet mouthed, "Get it, girl."

Throughout the day, first years entered the room and sat down at various tables. They all seemed to have the same reaction. They were surprised and excited to see the decorations celebrating Thomas and Lox Knight, then they would immediately seek out Emily.

"I bet the first years would make you a banner if you asked," Wesley teased and Emily playfully elbowed him.

From where she was sitting, Emily could see Gabriel Thompson looking uncomfortable as the students sitting at his table were blatantly staring at him. On the other side of the room, Alice Archinia was surrounded by a crowd of adoring students who were hanging on to her every word. Whilst Hayley-Elizabeth Elwood had her head down in an attempt to avoid the curious stares.

Laton Chin walked through the dining hall with the headmaster Mr Davon, who was wearing a blue training kit. His silver, blonde hair was pulled tight into a low ponytail. Following him were the teachers: Master Zen, who taught

81

Foughtgon class, where the students learnt how to battle and create fireballs; red-haired Ms Macay, the flying teacher; petite Amity Roshi, who taught Meditation; Mr King, looking excited for once, the complete opposite to how he usually looked teaching History; Mr Waternham, the scowling Water Studies teacher; Roberta Taniana, Hubert Jenkins and the ghosts, Cecil Archinia and Niles Thompson. Even though Emily saw them all the time, she still felt a shiver of excitement seeing the Five Warriors together.

"O-M-G! They're here!" One of the first years on their table shouted when she saw Roberta, Jenkins, Cecil and Niles.

"Where's Thomas Knight?" someone asked on the other side of the hall and everyone cheered.

"I don't know how their little hearts can take it," Wesley said grinning. "I'm shocked no one has fainted yet."

Mr Davon stood at the top of the dining hall, in the centre, with Roberta and Jenkins on either side of him. Roberta looked stunning in a fitted black dress with red heels showing off enviable legs. Her long, wavy black hair hung down her back and she smiled beautifully at everyone.

"Why is she so hot?" Pete sighed.

"I know right," Warren said wistfully.

"What was that?" Warren's hot-headed girlfriend, Summer Wind asked, with her arms crossed over her chest.

"Nothing, babe," Warren said, looking at the floor.

Roberta's husband and fellow Five Warriors teammate, Jenkins, was a tall, handsome man who could easily be a model. He wore a fitted white training kit over his athletic built and he waved at everyone around the room.

"Good evening and welcome first years to the Osaki

Training School," Mr Davon said and the hall fell silent. "If you have any problems at all finding your way around, please do not hesitate to ask a teacher. I would like to remind everyone that flying and fireballs are not permitted around the school. If anybody is interested in playing Dojo, all of the teams apart from Mentorawth are currently looking for Fighters and Distracters, so please see their team captains. As you can see by the decorations in the hall, today we have a reason to celebrate!"

The hall erupted into loud cheers. Mr Davon smiled and waited for them to hush before continuing. "But before I introduce our guests, I would like to publicly honour two very brave warriors. Last term, they rescued a fellow student, and fought a highly trained warrior who was under Neci. Can we please give a round of applause to Emily Knight and Julian Kena!"

A shocked Emily sat frozen in her seat as everyone cheered.

"Stand up," Jason said.

When Emily didn't move, she felt a force push her up. Jason had his hand on his temple and was encouraging her to smile. In contrast, Julian was on his feet embracing the cheers and attention.

"I won't go into great detail, but I'm sure you all know the story," Mr Davon continued. "I am so proud and thankful to both of you. You're the perfect example of what it means to be brave. Thank you Emily and Julian."

Emily sat back down with flushed cheeks.

"Better than any stupid banner," Wesley said and Emily smiled.

"Today, we have two special guests here at Osaki," Mr

Davon said. "I'm sure you all know who they are. One is the youngest warrior champion of all time, with exceptional battling skills. He made a great sacrifice for us all and the other is the leader of The Five Warriors—"

Whatever Mr Davon said next got drowned out by the screams and cheers from the dining hall. Emily, Michella, Wesley and Jason looked at each other surprised.

"He's here? My dad's here?" Emily questioned, looking around the hall.

The students were on their feet, staring at the doorway. Mr Davon was still talking, but Emily couldn't hear a word, and then Lox walked into the dining hall, followed by the one and only, Thomas Knight.

The noise in the hall was deafening. Thomas and Lox looked like clones as they walked through the dining hall in matching black training kits. Everyone on Emily's table was cheering and clapping. In a daze, Emily followed suit.

Thomas waved as he walked through the dining hall and some students started crying, a few fainted. Many were trying to touch them but it was like there was a force field around them so no one could even get close.

Emily didn't know how to feel. It was one thing Lox turning up, then all of the banners, and now her dad was here. She didn't understand why she was never in the loop.

She watched her dad lapping up the attention, waving and blowing kisses. Then he looked right at her. He gestured for her to come towards them, but Emily shook her head. They all wanted to see Thomas and Lox. She understood that, they were legends after all, but it still made her feel like a spare part.

It seemed like forever before they made it to the top of the dining hall. They stopped to greet all of the teachers. When Thomas stood next to Roberta, Jenkins, Cecil and Niles, the noise was indescribable. Students were shoving each other trying to get a picture of The Five Warriors. Warren and Pete flew out of their seats to get a closer look, even though flying outside of lessons was banned.

"Just look at them," Michella said, with her hands clasped and her eyes were shining. "This is historic."

Even Emily had to admit that seeing them together was surreal. The Five Warriors symbolised hope.

"Thank you so much for that amazing reception," Thomas said to loud cheers. "Lox and I are very humbled by the love everyone has shown us. I came here today because the Osaki Training School is such a special place to The Five Warriors. It's where we formed and trained and made lifelong friendships. I want to ask every single one of you students, whether you're just starting today, or you're in your last year, to train as hard as you can, so that we can fight united when this war happens. We can beat Neci once and for all!"

Everyone applauded him, then the girls got hysterical when Thomas stepped back, leaving Lox front and centre. He was standing casually with one hand in his pocket.

"Just to echo my dad, thank you so much for today. I never got a chance to train at Osaki for long, so it's very cool to be here. I know there are people out there who are confused by my actions, and I all I can do is apologise. By leaving Neci, I've hindered her plans for the war, but please realise that it's still coming," Lox added, and the hall quietened down. "Neci will come for us with everything she's got, but my departure

85

has given us a bit more time to prepare and when she strikes, we will be ready. I used to think my actions only affected my mum, Dad and Emily, but now I see that it's so much bigger than us, and in time I hope I can earn your forgiveness."

Thomas clapped him on the back and Emily could see the girls melting.

"History has been made today," Mr Davon said. "To have all of these legendary warriors under one roof is incredible and we have an amazing opportunity for all of you. Lox Knight will be running a one-off training session for those that want to push themselves the extra mile. Lox is unique because he is the only warrior to be trained by Thomas Knight and Neci, and I have no doubt that his knowledge will be life changing. It's based on a first-come, first-serve basis for all students. Sign-up sheets will be at breakfast inside each team's living room tomorrow morning. Now, let's give a big cheer to Lox Knight, Thomas Knight, Roberta Taniana, Hubert Jenkins, Niles Thompson and Cecil Archinia!"

Emily clapped loudly along with the rest of the hall.

"Fire," a voice whispered in Emily's ear.

"Huh?" Emily said to Michella, who frowned at her.

"What's up?" Michella asked.

"Did you say something?" Emily yelled over the noise. Michella shook her head.

"Let's eat!" Mr Davon announced.

The atmosphere throughout the meal was electrifying. For once, no one was interested in eating. They were trying to get Lox and Thomas's attention, where they spent breakfast walking around the hall, taking pictures and signing autographs. Emily tried to eat, but the attention she was receiving made her self-conscious. When her dad came close to her table, Emily excused herself and hurried out of the hall.

She stood in the hallway and immediately felt better. She slowly walked up the stairs passing the 'Osaki Wall of Fame.' She paused before retracing her steps to study the pictures of famous and successful warriors who had attended the school.

One of her favourite things to do at Osaki was to check if there were any new additions to the wall. She was proud to see that her old Dojo captain and Michella's eldest brother, Lenny Kinkle had been added, wearing the London FlyAways Dojo kit. Emily then looked at her dad and Lox's pictures. It wasn't the first time she wished she was with them on the wall. . .

Emily sat up and shook her head. She felt dazed as she rubbed her eyes but quickly jerked her head back. Her hands were boiling hot. She stared at them but they didn't look any different than usual.

How did I end up on the floor?

She slowly heaved herself up and leaned on the wall with the pictures of her family. She felt exhausted, as if she had just completed a Dojo match. Slowly she made her way back down to the dining hall and sat back at the table, feeling lightheaded.

"Where did you go? Your dad was asking for you," Michella asked.

"I just needed some air," Emily replied, pouring herself a huge glass of water and swallowing it down. She poured herself a few more and felt a little bit better. She picked up her fork and began to eat the cold food.

Dessert followed next and Emily helped herself to a huge piece of chocolate cake. As she was eating, she spotted a balloon floating around the room with Thomas Knight's smiling face printed on it. Laughter filled the hall as the balloon was bounced around to different tables. Someone hit it at Emily and she hit it back, so hard that it soared to the other side of the room, bumping into Alice Archinia's head. She swiftly turned around and flashed Emily an annoyed stare, even though Emily mouthed, "Sorry."

Mr Davon stood up at the front of the hall. "I hope you all have enjoyed your meal—"

"Fire!"

Everyone looked at the doorway at Kenan Taydon, a fifth year from Jenkint. He ran up to Mr Davon and yelled, "There's a fire upstairs on the second floor!"

CHAPTER EIGHT

Rise Up

In a second, everything changed.

Yells, screams and shouts filled the dining hall. Students ran out of the door, wanting to see the fire. Mr Davon flew over the students' heads, shouting at everyone to stay in the hall, whilst the teachers struggled to keep everyone under control.

Before Emily could even take in what was happening, Thomas Knight had teleported to her side.

"Is she here?" Emily asked, holding tight to her dad.

Thomas shook his head. "I can't sense her. Stay right here, okay?"

Thomas teleported and was instantly replaced by Lox.

"Neci's not here," Lox said. When Emily looked at him uncertainly, he added, "I would know."

"If she's not here, why are you protecting me?" Emily asked, looking around at the commotion.

Ms Macay grabbed the leg of one student who was up in the air, and dragged him back down, shouting words that Emily couldn't hear.

Lox stared out into the distance. His handsome face blank as he watched the frantic students and teachers. "Because I don't know who is."

The noise level was so loud that Emily couldn't hear herself think. Everything was a blur and she could see the frightened faces of the first years who were huddled together. She could hear Lox in the distance asking her if she was okay. Emily closed her eyes, wanting to block everything out. A second later, she felt the heat on her face. Her eyes snapped open, her heart was racing and she searched for the fire, but she was surprised to see the sun blazing down on her.

"Oh wow," Michella gasped, bending down to pick up the sand and letting it run through her fingers.

The dining hall had transformed into a beach. The ceiling was a clear, blue sky and Emily could smell the sea. The room was filled with laughter. Students were lying on the floor, or on their knees with their heads turned up to the sun. A beach ball was bouncing around the room from one end to another.

"Very cool," Lox said, staring up at the top of the dining hall where Jenkins was looking out at the illusion he had created.

The fire seemed to be forgotten by the students. Michella, Wesley and Jason were laughing with each other as they fell on to the warm sand. Lox's eyes were closed and his face was raised up to the sun with a small smile on his lips. Emily took that chance to slip out of the dining hall.

No one noticed her standing out in the hallway and looking up at the staircase. She could hear raised voices. The closer she got to the second floor, the stronger the smoke got. She covered her mouth and nose with her school uniform and went to take another step when she heard her dad's voice say, "It could have been anyone."

Emily stopped. She strained her ears trying to catch more of the conversation.

"But why would they do this here?" Roberta asked confused. "An empty corridor?"

There was some mumbling that Emily couldn't hear, then Niles spoke loudly over everyone. "This is a sign to us. To everyone here!"

Emily frowned. *What was he talking about?*

The smoke was creeping into her lungs. She desperately wanted to cough, but she held it in.

"We need to sit down and think this through. Let's go to my office," Mr Davon suggested and eventually their footsteps faded away.

Emily stayed as still as she could, until she could no longer hear them, and then she spluttered unattractively. She hurried along the corridor and gasped when she saw the damage. The Osaki Wall of Fame was destroyed. The glass that framed the pictures was shattered, burnt images were spread over the floor, and there was a massive hole in the wall. Emily looked around distraught.

Who could have done this? She bent down and picked up a damaged picture. It was of Lox. *I was standing here.*

Emily stumbled back away from the wall. Suddenly, she felt cold. The same place that the fire had caused the most damage was where she had been standing earlier on. Emily looked around her. The dark shadows in the corridor looked like they were moving. Without hesitation, she sprinted down the steps back to the dining hall.

Emily was breathing hard and she rubbed her sweaty palms on her school uniform. She looked around the beach for her friends and she spotted Wesley brushing sand off himself. When he looked up, he looked straight at her and Emily waved her hands, signalling him to come over. He nudged Michella and Jason. Without a word, Emily led them to the Grandfather clock, which they hid behind. She told them what she had witnessed.

Michella gasped. "Who could have done that?"

"I don't know," Emily said. "But isn't that weird that I was just there?"

Did I do this? Emily shook her head. *No, I couldn't have. . . but how did I end up on the floor?*

"Are you alright?" Michella asked, gently touching Emily's shoulder and Emily jumped.

"Sorry—yes, just shaken up."

"It couldn't be Neci, could it? I mean, if Neci was ready for war, she would come in with an army, not just destroy a wall, right?" Wesley asked.

"It could have been a message from her. It was a wall with our families' faces on it," Michella pointed out, gesturing at herself and Emily. "All of those people on the wall had done significant things. She was trying to say something."

"It might be a student doing it. You know, supporting her like Gary Coles did last year," Jason suggested.

"Jason, don't say that." Emily shuddered.

"Look, let's not panic," Michella said to Emily. "You have so much protection this year that no one will be able to hurt you. The Five Warriors are here! And Lox. They will keep you safe."

Emily didn't respond. Why, if she was so protected, did she feel so vulnerable?

"Come on, they're going to bring out some ice cream," Wesley said. He placed a hand on Emily's lower back and guided her to the dining room.

They sat back down in the sand and Emily couldn't help but look around at all of the students. There were hundreds of them and there was no way to know what their motives were.

Emily glanced at Tanya Frank and Alice Archinia. They were both talking animatedly with their friends, not paying any attention to Emily. She looked next at Gabriel Thompson, who was talking with his friend Jasper Jones. Gabriel looked relaxed and friendly, and it was hard to believe that he was the same person that had led her to Blade last year. Emily then looked at Hayley-Elizabeth Elwood. She was lying on her side, propped up with her elbow. She looked relaxed as she talked to one of her friends.

"I did think of her," Michella said, following Emily's gaze.

Wesley and Jason looked over.

"But who would she be blaming for her dad's disappearance? Thomas? He'll most likely be the one to save him," Jason said.

Michella brushed the sand off her hands. "I just think she's someone we should keep an eye on."

Hayley-Elizabeth's friend, who was facing their direction, spotted them watching and nudged her. Hayley-Elizabeth looked at them over her shoulder and Emily quickly turned away.

Thomas and Lox came to find her a few hours later and Emily was grateful that it was a half-day at school. She didn't want to stay at Osaki any longer than she needed to. She waved goodbye to her friends, who were still lying on the sand, and Thomas teleported her home.

Emily noticed that Thomas and Lox seemed more tense than usual. They kept shooting annoyed glances at each other when they thought she wasn't looking. Throughout the rest of the afternoon, when one of them would walk into a room, the other would leave. Emily watched their behaviour in silence.

She walked around the house unsure of what to do with herself. She spotted today's newspaper with a picture of her and the headline 'KNIGHT TO COMPETE AT WORLDS' on the kitchen table.

"Great." Emily hurried to page six to read the article and was surprised to find a picture of her, Lox and Thomas at Warside.

Emily scanned the article, hoping to find any indication of who else was competing at Worlds but there was only a quote from Tyson Hart, who had won two years ago: 'Yes, Emily maybe as strong as her brother Lox, but who has seen her battle? I don't know if she is up to the Worlds standard.'

Emily threw the newspaper on the floor and thumped the table. It was one thing her thinking that she wasn't good enough, but another to see someone else's opinion in print for the whole world to see.

She glanced out of the window and saw Lox training in the garden. His bulging muscles and toned torso had a gleam of sweat, as he punched and kicked the air. A few seconds later, Thomas walked into the kitchen whistling to himself. He winked at Emily and poured two, tall glasses of homemade lemonade and walked into the garden. As Thomas got closer to Lox, Lox glanced at him before he bent his knees and soared into the air. Emily's mouth dropped open at Lox's obvious rudeness and Thomas was rooted to the spot as he looked up at the sky.

Emily walked to her dad and put an arm around his waist. She took one of the glasses from him.

"He can get his own drink," she said, before she clinked her glass against his.

Thomas sighed. "I told him not to fly. It's not safe. . . and the press—"

"He'll be fine," Emily said, guiding him back towards the house.

"What's this doing there?" Thomas muttered, noticing the newspaper with pages spilled over the marble floor.

Before Emily could answer, the doorbell rang shrilly and the housekeeper, Mrs Asha, went to open it.

"Oh, that must be Jenny," Emily said, putting her empty glass on the table.

Thomas frowned. "Jenny? Who's Jenny?"

"My counsellor."

Thomas snorted. "Oh, the counsellor."

"Whose name is Jenny," Emily said sharply and Thomas tutted. "I don't know why you have a problem with me seeing one. If you want her to go, you can tell her yourself."

"Fine!" Thomas said, slamming his glass so hard on the table that it broke and scattered over the floor, making Emily jump back.

Emily insisted on clearing up but Mrs Asha shooed her away and took the dustpan and brush out of her hands. Emily was five minutes late for her session. She couldn't find her dad anywhere and she wasn't sure if Jenny was still at the house. A part of her hoped she wasn't. She was apprehensive about what her dad would have said to her and how upset she would be.

"Emily! Happy belated birthday," Jenny said cheerfully, handing her a card. "How was your party?"

Confused, Emily sat down on the chair opposite Jenny. Jenny Li was a petite Chinese woman, with long, auburn hair and she had been Emily's counsellor for many years. Sally had found her at a time when she felt that Emily's anger issues were out of control.

Jenny liked to see Emily at least twice a week, but when Emily was at Osaki, she was to report to Ruth Walker if she felt overwhelmed. Emily loved Jenny like a big sister and understood that Jenny's job was to help her understand her emotions, but sometimes, Emily just wanted to be angry and she wished Jenny could understand that.

"Did my dad speak to you?" Emily asked slowly.

"Yes! Ah, I could barely speak! Thomas Knight is gorgeous," Jenny gushed before she put her hand over her mouth. "Sorry, is that weird for you? We just spoke for a bit and look!" Jenny showed off Thomas's loopy signature on her pale arm.

"So he didn't shout?" Emily pressed on.

"No, of course not. Why would he?" Jenny smiled prettily. "He's such a gent."

"Mmmm," Emily said, thinking of the broken glass.

"How was your party?"

"It was okay."

"Good and how are you getting on with Lox?" Jenny sat with a pen poised and Emily's bulky file on her lap. "Is it weird having him home?"

"It's cool and we're getting on fine. I think Michella has

a crush on him though. Actually so does Cathy, Lisa from school—you get the picture? It kind of annoys me."

"Why?"

"Well..." Emily hesitated. "I just got Lox back. I'm not ready to share him yet."

Jenny smiled. "I get it. How about your dad? Is it fun having him back?"

Emily snorted. "Fun isn't the word."

Emily went on to explain about Thomas and Sally's conflict and Thomas's birthday present.

"I just feel like he doesn't know me at all and he's angry with Sally because she keeps pointing it out." Emily looked down at her hands. "I was so mad at her for giving him a hard time. I was scared he would disappear again, but she's right. She knows me better than he does. What was he thinking entering me into Worlds?"

"He just needs time to adjust," Jenny said. Emily shrugged and played with the sleeves of her school uniform. "Are you sleeping okay?"

"Sometimes but I still have nightmares. I still see ice, Blade, fire and Neci. I wonder if my dad has nightmares about the stuff he experienced?"

"Why don't you ask him? Don't you share with him how you're feeling?"

"Not really," Emily said, looking at her hands. "I just wish I could be brave like him."

"You're brave! You're one of the bravest people I know. You're not Thomas Knight and no one wants you to be. You're your own person."

Emily looked out of the window at the picture-perfect

Legends Village. "Everyone says that. . . I don't think they mean it."

"I mean it," Jenny said softly, drawing back Emily's attention. "I gave you an assignment a while back. To go under water in the pool. Have you done it yet?"

Emily shook her head.

"After what happened with Blade, it's important that your fear of water doesn't get any worse."

"Okay," Emily said, getting up. "Let's give it a go."

The indoor swimming pool was warm when Emily stepped into it. Jenny wanted her to try and go under the water, just for a few seconds. Emily closed her eyes and felt herself sinking under. The warm water rushed over her face.

She opened her eyes and she was back under the ice and suddenly she felt like her throat was closing and the panic was rising in her chest. She began to thrash in the water that felt so cold, forgetting that she could breathe under water, and just when she thought she was going to drown, strong hands pulled her up by her shoulders and Jenny wiped her face with her hands.

"You're okay, you're okay," Jenny said, hugging her shaking body.

Emily was coughing violently. It took a while for her eyes to refocus.

"I was back. . . the ice. . ."

"Ssh, it's okay," Jenny said softly. "Come on, let's get you dry."

Emily was in her bedroom, sitting on her four poster bed, wrapped in a thick towel and a bath robe, when Sally came into her room.

"Jenny called me. Do you feel better?"

"Yeah better," Emily replied. Her throat ached and her voice sounded hoarse to her ears.

"Lox told me what happened today at school."

"Just some silly kids," Emily said, trying to sound nonchalant.

Sally sat on the bed beside her. She stared at the bright duvet, deliberately avoiding Emily's eyes.

"I've been meaning to say that I'm sorry for your birthday and just for my behaviour in general, especially towards your dad."

"It's okay. I get it."

Sally looked up at her surprised. "You do?"

Emily nodded. "You feel like I won't need you as much, like Dad has swooped in and is trying to take over, when you've been in charge for years. You're annoyed that Dad is acting like he knows me so well when he obviously doesn't and you're scared that we won't be a family anymore."

Sally raised her eyebrows. "Wow. Am I that transparent?"

Emily laughed, which made her throat ache even more. She reached over and grabbed Sally's hand. "You're the best parent I have ever had. I honestly couldn't be without you. We're family and we always will be. Yes, I'm glad my dad is back, but I know he needs time to know who I am, so we both need to help him rather than get annoyed with him for doing silly things. . . like entering me into Worlds so I end up on the front page of the paper, which is the last thing I want."

Sally rolled her eyes. "He has a lot to learn."

"He does but there's loads I need to learn from him. I don't feel like I have a choice in anything anymore." Sally went to protest and Emily shook her head. "I don't, not really and I need to be the best warrior that I can be, so I can protect you and the family. I have to fight and I have to win." Sally squeezed her hand tight. "I'm sick of not sleeping well. I can't even go in the pool without thinking of Blade, but I have the strongest warrior in the world that sleeps downstairs and another that has been trained by Neci down the hall. Dad and Lox are the best people to teach me everything they know, so I will be ready when it's time."

"You'll definitely be ready," Sally said confidently.

"I won't be if I keep sitting here feeling sorry for myself." Emily stood to her feet. "Are Lox and Dad here?"

"Yeah, they're downstairs."

"Can you get them to meet me in the garden? Whilst I get dressed?" Emily asked.

"No problem," Sally said, standing up.

Emily quickly changed into jeans and a t-shirt and brushed her wet hair out of her face. She stared at herself in the mirror, practicing her stern face so that her dad and Lox would take her seriously when she spoke to them. When she was satisfied, she ran down the stairs. She could see from the staircase that Lox and her dad were standing awkwardly in the garden with Sally between them, her hands on her hips.

As she got closer, she could hear Sally hiss, "That girl is relying on you, so get it together!"

Emily stepped on to the fresh grass and the three of them turned to her with plastered smiles on their faces.

"Sally, can you excuse us, please?"

"Of course," Sally said, winking at Emily when she walked past.

"Sally mentioned you wanted help with something?" Thomas asked.

"You are one of the best warriors to exist," Emily said to her dad. "And you are one of a kind." Emily stared at Lox, whose face remained blank. "You have trained with Neci and Dad. Dad, you have fought Neci and won. So, the way I see it is, you two are my best bet."

"For what?" Thomas frowned.

"To train me!" Emily said impatiently. "I need to be one of the best too! I have to beat all of these warriors who are trying to kill me. I can't afford to pretend this isn't happening anymore."

"So what exactly do you want to learn?" Lox asked. His light brown eyes looked amused.

"Everything! Your special attack moves, the way Neci fights, how to tap into my hidden power, how to control my powers better. I want the best of the best type of training."

Thomas and Lox glanced at each other before looking back at Emily. Emily crossed her arms and waited. This wasn't the response she was expecting. She thought they would be ecstatic that she wanted to train this hard.

"I don't think you know what you're letting yourself in for," Lox eventually said, scratching his hair.

"What do you mean?" Emily asked defensively.

"He means this isn't Osaki," Thomas said.

"If you want the raw training, it's going to be the hardest thing you've ever done, and it will take time to get the results you want," Lox explained.

"And you think I can't handle it?"

"I heard about your Survival Training last year," Lox

said and Emily looked away. "I know you found a bit of camping difficult and climbing a mountain was really hard for you, wasn't it? You say you want to be this amazing warrior, right? Yet, you can't breathe under water, which is basic training–"

"I can do it now!" Emily yelled.

"Really? Cause you almost drowned in the pool ten minutes ago! You panic over the simplest things. You lose control easily. You doubt yourself and you find the easiest things the hardest to do. Am I lying, Dad?" Thomas avoided Emily's gaze and looked uncomfortable. "Dad, isn't that what Niles, Cecil, Roberta, Jenkins, pretty much everyone, said to us?" Lox challenged.

"I risked my life saving Gabriel Thompson. Are we all just going to forget that happened?" Emily shouted.

"Look Emily, I want you to train hard and be one of the best. I know you can, which is why I entered you into Worlds despite what everyone has said. You have it in you," Thomas said. "There are a lot of things you have to work on, but you're my daughter and of course I'll train you."

Emily gasped. "You mean it?"

Thomas nodded. Emily broke into a huge smile and ran over to him and hugged him tight. "Thank you, thank you, thank you."

Lox snorted. "I'm not helping."

"Why?" Emily asked.

"Because you need to step it up first," Lox said. "I can teach you all that Neci has taught me, but you need to prove to me that you're ready."

"And how am I meant to prove that?"

Thomas raised his eyebrows at Lox and to Emily's surprise he laughed.

"You're not," Thomas said in disbelief.

Lox smiled. "I definitely am."

"What?" Emily said, looking from one to the other. "What is it?"

"I'm going to enrol at Osaki," Lox declared.

CHAPTER NINE

Powering Up

"I don't understand how Lox coming to my school acting like a student is going to help!" Emily said, throwing her hands in the air. "I can see what's going to happen already. The girls will fall in love with him, the guys will adore him and he's going to get annoyed at the attention—"

"Emily," Thomas said in a warning voice with his eyes closed.

"—then he's probably going to run away again just to irritate everyone—"

"Emily, I'm training," Thomas said, opening one eye which he used to stare directly at her.

"Oops, sorry, I'll be quiet," Emily promised, putting a hand over her mouth.

They were sitting deep in the garden, where they were surrounded by so many trees that Emily could only see patches of the sky, which was a beautiful mix of pink, purple and blue.

Thomas was sitting cross-legged with his hands resting

on his knees. He was allowing Emily to watch him train and had warned her to pay close attention. Thomas was breathing slowly in and out and Emily bit her lip hard, trying to resist talking again. She looked around the garden. It suddenly was very quiet. The birds that were chirping seemed to have disappeared. Emily went to say it to her dad, but she noticed the deep frown line in his forehead and then she felt it. His power energy was slowly rising.

"Wow," Emily whispered, as she watched the branches and stones that were surrounding them vibrate and float into the air. The trees beside her were creaking loudly as they slowly uprooted from the ground. All through this, Thomas Knight was completely still with his eyes closed.

Emily's head turned with every sound. She couldn't believe that her dad was creating all of this. The wind even seemed to get stronger, blowing Emily's hair into her face. The wind howled so loud that Emily had to cover her ears and before she knew it, the trees were rocking from side to side. The branches and stones were now above her head. They were circling, going faster and faster, making her dizzy. Emily ducked her head into her lap, shielding her face, still blocking her ears. She was praying for it to end. She gritted her teeth as she felt the wind hit her hard from either side. She felt a hand on her shoulder.

"It's over," Thomas said.

Emily looked up and Thomas was smiling down at her. Emily dropped her hands and looked around the garden. Everything was still again.

"What was that?" Emily asked slowly.

"That is called powering up."

"Powering up?"

"It's building up your power so that you're ready to battle. Haven't you learnt that at school?" Thomas asked.

Emily shook her head. "I would have remembered learning that. It's a bit scary."

"Yeah it is. When I first learnt it, I thought it was the weirdest thing," Thomas explained. "It took me ages to understand it, but now when I see others doing it, it really fascinates me, seeing all of their energy. It will be interesting to see what your energy will create."

"A whole lot of mess I'm sure!"

Thomas laughed. "You'll be fine."

"So is that what you will have to do against Neci? Do your opponents leave you time to power up?"

"If they want a good fight they do. Neci and I will only battle at one hundred percent. Last time she powered up, she knocked Cecil back a few metres." Thomas laughed. "That's when we knew we were up against someone special." He stretched out his arms.

"Do you really think Neci's special?"

Thomas looked at her surprised. "Of course! Whatever anyone thinks of Neci, she is a very talented warrior, and from what I have heard she trained herself. You don't think that's special?"

"It's kind of impressive," Emily said. The idea of praising Neci made her uncomfortable.

"Do you want to try powering up?"

"Err. . . how?"

Thomas smiled. "Close your eyes and relax. The main aim is to draw out as much power as you can."

"So if I'm in the middle of a fight I need to sit down and close my eyes to power up?"

Thomas laughed. "No, you can do it standing up as well. This is a good way to learn though, until you feel more in control. Right, close your eyes and think about a person or a situation that made you angry."

Scarlett was the first person that came into her mind. Scarlett attacking her and Sally last year on the way to school. Scarlett blackmailing Gabriel and forcing him to release Blade. Emily could feel a heat in the centre of her chest.

"That's it." She could hear her dad's voice but it sounded far away. "Now focus your energy. You want it to travel through your whole body."

Scarlett grabbing her so tight that she felt like her hand was on fire. The heat seemed to travel to her arms, to her hands and Emily closed her fists tight. The last thing she needed was any fireballs shooting out. Emily flinched as she felt a whooshing sound past her ear. She tried to focus but the sound was getting louder.

She opened her eyes and her dad was a few metres away from her shielding his face. Emily whipped around when she heard a loud creaking sound and saw one off the trees bending back to its original position.

"I did that?" Emily asked surprised.

Thomas began to clap loudly. "Yes! That was a very good first try. It was much more controlled than I was when I first did it."

"Really?" Emily said, jumping to her feet. She was surprised at how energised she felt.

"You feel good?"

"Yeah I do. What's next?"

Thomas smiled, showing off dimples and straight, white, perfect teeth. "Catch me."

And he disappeared. Emily closed her eyes, trying to sense his energy, but she couldn't. Frustrated, she opened her eyes, but she couldn't see anything because of all the trees. Emily bent her knees and flew up, landing on all fours on a thick branch. She looked down trying to see a glimpse of him. A swift of wind passed Emily's left ear and she shot off, knowing that was her dad. For a split second, she thought she saw something dark flash past her. Emily soared after it and was now out of the trees and in an open space. She gritted her teeth. She still couldn't see him. She looked down and there he was, standing in the garden, casually looking up at her. Emily flew down towards him and he teleported.

"Give me a break!" Emily yelled.

"No way," Thomas shouted, appearing high above the trees, before he disappeared again.

Emily bent down to put on her baht shoes and winced at the pain that shot through her back. She didn't manage to catch him, but her body took the hit from the fireballs he threw at her. She had been in agony all night, not managing to sleep.

Thomas apologised again when he saw her limping in the morning. "I thought there was Reviving Water in the house."

Sally laughed as she helped Emily put her shoes on. "Where would I buy that? From the local supermarket? Come on you or you'll be late for school."

Emily was seated in History class with the Ogragons and their teacher Mr King who was wearing a bowler hat with his training kit. He was staring at the ceiling. The Ogragons were too busy chatting about the fire and they only stopped when Mr King sighed so loudly that it interrupted their conversations.

"As entertaining as it is hearing you all talk about the wretched fire, I have a lesson planned for today."

"That's a first, sir!" Wesley shouted from the back, making everyone laugh.

"Ha ha," Mr King said in a deadpan voice. "Now, where are your History books?"

The class looked blankly at him. They never seemed to be needed in class.

"Why do I bother?" Mr King said to himself.

"You don't usually," blonde haired Daisy Atam said innocently, and Mr King shot her a sharp look.

There was a knock on the door and Lox came into the room, wearing the Osaki school uniform, but the sleeves had been ripped off, exposing his bulging muscles. He had a decoration of tattoos on both arms from his shoulders to his wrists.

"Oh my," Sydney John said looking at Lox appreciatively. Everyone looked at Emily.

"What are you doing here?" Emily asked.

"Hi Mr King, did Mr Davon tell you?" Lox said ignoring Emily but Mr King was looking at Lox like he was one of his fans. "Sir?"

"Yes, of course," Mr King said, flashing a rare smile. "Just find a seat."

"Err hello? What are you doing?" Emily said as Lox sat in the seat behind her.

Lox smiled. "Learning."

"You're in the wrong class for that," Wesley said under his breath.

Mr King was scurrying through his bag. He took out a flask and had a quick gulp.

Michella raised her hand and Mr King pretended that he didn't notice.

"Mr King, Michella has a question," Lox said.

Mr King looked up and grinned.

"He's smiled twice in one day," Wesley muttered. "Is he actually drinking alcohol in class?"

"Yes, Miss Kinkle?" Mr King asked, in an unnaturally concerned voice.

Michella raised her eyebrows at his tone. "I have my History book. What page are we starting on?"

Mr King stared at her blankly as if not understanding the question. He took his time putting the lid back on his flask, turning it slowly. "Well," he eventually said. "We are going to—"

He paused and looked at Jason, who was one of the few who had his History book. Jason was leaning over his desk, with one elbow propped up, and his chin resting in his hand. With his other hand, he was doodling on the cover of his book.

"Mr Notting is going to explain to us what we have learnt so far. I need to err. . . test. . . yes, test! I need to test your knowledge."

"What knowledge?" Jason asked, sitting up in his seat. "I thought you had a lesson planned?"

"Get up here," Mr King hissed, glancing over at Lox who looked baffled.

Jason had half his hair brushed back into a bun which showed off his sharp cheekbones. He walked to the front of the classroom, unaware that Lisa Fowler had leaned forward in her chair, twirling her blonde hair around her finger, looking lustfully at him.

"Right, so... we... err..." Jason glanced over at Mr King who was not so discreetly sipping from his flask again. Jason opened up his History book and flicked through the pages. "So we have... sir, we haven't learnt anything!"

Jason slammed his book shut, making Mr King jump and spill his drink down his training kit.

"Oh, look what you've done!" Mr King hollered. And with that, he huffed and stormed out of the classroom, slamming the door behind him.

"And he's back," Wesley said satisfied, leaning back on his chair, with his hands behind his head.

Lox's mouth dropped. "What the hell just happened?"

"That is how Mr King teaches," Jason said, sitting back in his chair. "A lesson planned. Why did I even believe him?"

"Finally he's gone. Now let's get on to more important things," Danny June said, his usual Afro in neat cornrows. "How good was that beach? I even got a tan—look." He held out his arm for everyone to see.

The class began to talk over one another and Emily turned around to Lox, who was getting up from his chair.

"Where are you going now?" Emily asked.

Lox looked around the room. "There's no teacher. I'm going to find a class where I can actually learn something."

Emily watched him leave the room and Violet came and sat on her desk.

"I know he's your brother, but he's dead sexy. I literally can't even breathe when I'm around him."

"Yuck, he's too old for you," Emily said, pushing Violet who squealed as she fell off the table.

"I would actually learn History for him," Nicky Johansen said and she and Violet high-fived each other. "Where's he gone anyway?"

"To find a class that is doing work," Emily said.

"He might get lost!" Violet exclaimed, looking concerned and Emily rolled her eyes.

"We should help him," Lisa Fowler chipped in and before Emily could tell them to leave it, all of the girls had gathered their stuff and run out of the room.

Michella laughed. "Can you imagine his face?"

"Hopefully that will be the last class he's in with me," Emily responded.

But the next lesson, Lox followed Emily down the stairs to the basement of the school to Foughtgon class. The girls were trailing behind him in a lovesick daze and the boys were enviously watching.

Emily was unhappy that no one had bothered to warn her that she would have another shadow all day. She sat on the wooden floor. Lox hadn't even taken a step in the classroom before he was surrounded by Berbinin students hurrying to get his autograph. Lox's smile looked strained as he signed the arms of excited students. Ambria Appleton had a poster of Lox in mid-battle that she pushed in his face.

"This isn't going to get annoying," Emily muttered.

"To be fair, he doesn't look like he's enjoying it," Jason commented as he watched Lox.

"What did he think was going to happen? He'll blend in?"

The students were so distracted with the presence of Lox Knight that they failed to notice Master Zen teleport into the room. There was a smile on Master Zen's withered face when he saw Lox.

"Come, come," Master Zen called to the class, who reluctantly came over. Lox hovered near the back. "Welcome back third years. I hope you had a good summer. We're going to do something a bit different today. Lox come over please."

Lox walked to the front of the class with everyone, besides Emily, looking at him in awe.

"I want you to help me today. Can you please show the class Disc?"

"Sure," Lox replied easily. He clenched his fists and closed his eyes. "Disc."

Nothing happened straight away but then the Reviving Water in the buckets rippled. Lox's arms were positioned outwards, but not in the usual fireball position, where the palms were touched to form a 'V' sign, instead Lox's hands were flat. In the middle of his hands were two yellow beams. Lox touched his hands, so the beams formed together and he spread his arms wide so the beams stretched. Lox then put his arms above his head and the beam was flat.

"So cool," Michella whispered.

Lox shot the Disc forward. The students ducked as it flew over their heads and sliced into the Masonka wall, cutting it in half, but the Masonka wall heaved forward and then reformed, sucking it in.

The class applauded loudly and Lox bowed. He hadn't even broken a sweat.

"Depending on how powerful you are determines how much of an impact the Disc will create. It can leave a scratch or cut someone in half. Who taught you how to do that, Lox?"

Lox hesitated for a second. "Neci."

A few people gasped and most looked surprised. Emily didn't understand why. Everyone knew Neci trained him.

Master Zen nodded knowingly. "It's not an easy move to learn but it would give you a great advantage in the war to come. Let's all give it a try. Everyone find a space facing the Masonka wall."

Emily rubbed her sweaty palms on her training kit. She always got nervous when they were learning new moves. She could never forget her first Foughtgon lesson when she learnt how to do a Baby Ball. She was mortified that she was the only one in the class to not have achieved it, especially with Five Warriors legend, Niles Thompson watching her. It took her many late nights of practising before she was finally able to do it.

Now, there were more eyes on her than ever before and it didn't help that Lox was teaching. She positioned herself in front of the wall, in-between Jason and Wesley, who looked a lot more excited than she felt.

"Everyone power up," Lox instructed. The third years looked at each other confused.

"My dad taught me how to do it," Emily whispered to Wesley.

"Shut up! Was it hard?"

"More scary to be honest."

Lox turned to Master Zen. "They don't know how to power up?"

Master Zen shook his head. "Only fourth years and over are taught it."

"Right, okay, it will still work but it just won't be very powerful. All of you close your eyes, keep your hands out in front of you and think about the beams that you saw. Very clearly say Disc."

Emily closed her eyes and thought about the beams in Lox's hands.

"Disc," she said and instantly she felt her hands burning.

"Now merge the two beams together and then open your hands out wide," Lox instructed.

Emily opened her eyes and two small beams sat in the middle of her hands. She slowly moved her hands together, afraid that the beams would disappear. They touched and fused into one. She opened her hands out wide so the beams were stretched out. She gasped when she saw the Disc in her hands.

"I'm doing it!" she squealed.

Lox walked over to her and nodded in approval. "Okay, now slowly move your hands above your head. Don't lose your power."

Gritting her teeth, Emily followed Lox's directions. He made it look so simple, but she could feel the heat and the heavy weight of the Disc. Her hands shook as she tried to steady it. One of her legs buckled and she quickly caught herself.

"Lock your knees. Good—now throw it with as much force as you can. The more force, the more impact," Lox said.

Emily moved her arms behind her head and threw her Disc as hard as she could. It hit the Masonka wall, but it was nowhere near the impact that Lox had. Emily dropped to her knees with beads of sweat dripping off her forehead.

Master Zen brought over the buckets of Reviving Water and Emily grabbed on to the closest one and drunk until she felt her energy come back.

"That was really hard!" she said, looking up at Lox, who was standing over her.

"I know, but you get used to it."

Wesley collapsed beside her after throwing his Disc, which had done much better than Emily's.

"Pass us that," he said, gesturing at the water.

"You did better than I thought," Lox said, as Wesley dunked his head into the bucket.

"So you'll train me?" Emily asked eagerly.

Lox raised his eyebrows. "We'll see," he said before he went to check on the other students.

CHAPTER TEN

Her

During lunch, Ms Macay, the flying teacher, discreetly handed Emily a note. She opened it and it was from Mr Davon requesting she come to his office immediately. Emily looked up to where the teachers usually sat and noticed Lox, who was a second ago sitting beside Amity Roshi, the Meditation teacher, was now nowhere to be seen.

"I'll be back in a bit," Emily told her friends.

"We'll save you some dessert," Michella said.

Emily walked the familiar route to Mr Davon's office. She knocked on the door that read 'Mr Davon - Headmaster' in gold lettering, until she heard him say, "Come in," and she opened the door.

Emily was surprised to see Lox, Thomas and Roberta in the office.

"Dad," Emily said, running into his open arms and giving him a big hug.

"Hello, baby," he said, kissing her forehead.

"Hey, Aunt Roberta," Emily said, hugging her next.

When she pulled away, she noticed Roberta's strained expression. "Sit down, Emily."

"What's going on?" Emily asked, noticing the sombre atmosphere.

Mr Davon cleared his throat and gestured for Emily to take a seat in the spare chair. She sat and looked from one face to the other.

"We have received unfortunate news," Mr Davon said looking grave.

"What is it?"

Mr Davon nodded at Roberta who said, "I saw a vision of Neci with an army, much bigger than we thought."

Emily gasped. "How much bigger?"

Roberta shook her head. "Thousands. She's also got warriors looking for Scarlett. Whatever happens we have to keep Scarlett away from Neci."

"Is the army the people she microchipped last year?" Emily asked.

Roberta nodded. "She's been a busy girl."

"I didn't see it for myself but there's a device that controls the microchip," Lox explained.

"And how do we stop it?" Thomas asked.

"Find the device, which is likely on Neci or get the chip out of anyone that has it," Lox said.

Thomas stood to his feet. "We have to rescue Professor Elwood. We can't let her get her hands on any R Caps. If she has the R Caps and she's controlling people, we've pretty much lost this. I've got lots of warriors ready to fight with us but to take on this many, I think we will need more help."

"Whatever you're planning to do, I'm coming with you," Lox said, staring at his dad.

"What? Are you leaving again?" Emily asked surprised.

Thomas walked over to her and gently cupped her face. "You're safe with Lox—"

"No!" Lox said, standing up. "I just said I'm coming with you. I can help."

"You need to protect your sister," Thomas replied. "And the whole family, so I need you here."

"We all need to help," Mr Davon said, leaning forward in his chair. "Including Lox and all the young people we have been training in the elite group. We will need all hands on deck if we want to stay ahead of her. We have a strong team of young, talented warriors. We need to step up their training."

"Mr Davon, I think it would help if you did an appeal," Roberta said. "A lot of warriors trained here and they respect you. They will stand with us."

"That's not a bad idea, Roberta," Mr Davon said.

"But we shouldn't televise it," Thomas said. "Neci can't see what we're up to. Mr Davon, I think it would be best if you spoke to people face to face. Are you able to leave Osaki in the hands of someone else for a while?"

Emily couldn't believe what she was hearing. She had just got her family back and now she was going to lose them again because of Neci. Everything bad that happened to her was always because of Neci.

Emily put her hand to her chest and rubbed it. Her chest felt unusually hot and tight like someone was squeezing her.

"Fire," the same voice she had heard before, spoke loudly into her ear.

"What?" Emily said aloud, looking around the room.

"Fire."

"Who keeps saying that?" Emily asked and everyone looked at her.

"Saying what?" Roberta asked carefully, studying Emily closely.

"Fire."

"Stop it!" Emily yelled, covering her ears.

"Darling, what's wrong?" Thomas put a hand on her arm but quickly withdrew it shaking out his hand. "Ow! Your skin is boiling."

"Are you hot, Emily?" Roberta asked slowly with a strange edge to her tone.

Emily leaned over. Her breathing came out hard and heavy. Her heart was racing. Sweat was dripping down her back. Her school uniform felt stuck to her body. She swung her hands back and forth in front of her face trying to cool herself down.

"Drink this." Roberta was kneeling beside her. She helped Emily to hold on to the bottle of water and she tipped it back so the cold liquid raced down her throat, cooling her overheated body. "Better?"

Emily nodded. She could feel the tightness in her chest easing off. She still felt hotter than usual but it was manageable.

Roberta gently brushed Emily's hair off her forehead and whispered, "It will be okay."

"You didn't hear the voice?" Emily whispered back.

Roberta leaned in closer to her so Emily could smell her floral perfume. "What did it say?"

"Fire."

"No, I didn't hear that," Roberta said calmly, as if Emily had asked how the weather was. "Only you can hear her."

Roberta gave her a knowing look.

"How do you know that?" Emily questioned.

"You okay?" Lox asked, appearing by her side.

"Yeah," Emily said weakly. She drank down more of the water but kept her eyes on Roberta, who sat back in her chair.

"I know you're upset that Dad's leaving but I'll stay with you, alright? No need to freak out," Lox teased.

"Oh come here," Thomas said, pulling Emily into a tight hug. "You feel much cooler now. You shouldn't get yourself into such a state, sweetheart. I'll be back before you know it."

"Yeah, of course," Emily said. She watched Roberta over his shoulder.

Who is her? Who is speaking to me?

"And in the meantime, I can train you," Lox said, interrupting Emily's thoughts.

"You will?" Emily asked weakly. Thomas was still holding her and she was glad that she had someone to lean on.

"Maybe not my level of training but we'll build up to it," Lox said.

Emily didn't care. She wanted to learn anything he could teach her.

"Jenkins and I can help recruit warriors. Can I leave my boys with Sally and Michael? I'll teleport into the Village to check in on everyone," Roberta said.

"Sounds good. Sally and Michael won't mind." Thomas kissed Emily on the forehead. "I'll be back in a few weeks, okay? Hopefully we'll get an army as big as Neci's."

"Fire."

Emily jerked her head away from her dad, hitting the back of her head against the wall.

"Emily! What's wrong?" Thomas asked, searching her face.

"I just need some air. See you soon, Dad," she said hurriedly before she walked out of the room, avoiding Roberta's piercing stare.

She closed the door and stood with her back against the cool oak doors, waiting. She couldn't hear anything. There was no more voice.

Home life was strange without Thomas around, but it was also very noisy with the addition of Xavier and Antonio Jenkins. Emily found it hard to focus on anything. They were bunking with James and the boys were determined to train James up (even though he had no powers) and a ridiculous amount of explosions came from their room.

Emily had never been more grateful for Jenny Li and their counselling sessions. It was the only way she felt she could have any peace in the house. She felt guilty for not telling Jenny about the voice in her head but she couldn't risk Jenny telling her dad or Sally and Michael.

Emily hadn't heard the voice since the day in Mr Davon's office. She couldn't forget the way Roberta had acted. It was as if she knew what Emily was talking about and who was talking to her but how was that even possible? Unless Roberta was the voice? Emily scolded herself. The voice sounded nothing like Roberta's.

Emily was grateful she had Dojo practice at school.

Something to distract her from all the weird stuff happening. After lunch, Emily left Michella, Wesley and Jason and walked towards the stadium. Dojo season was about to start and this was the first training session of the new term with Summer Wind as captain.

Right now, nothing seemed better than playing a fast game of Dojo. The idea of punching someone in the face and not getting into trouble for it was extremely appealing.

Dojo was a fun but hardcore game where two teams made up of Fighters battled it out until there was one Fighter left standing. Each team had three Distracters (who were usually female) and their job was to distract the opposing Fighters but Fighters weren't allowed to hit the Distracters. Emily was the only female Fighter on the Ogragon Dojo team.

Emily could hear the team before she saw them. They were a loud and opinionated bunch and Emily wondered how there was going to be any form of control since Lenny Kinkle had graduated. Lenny was an amazing captain but even he had struggled to control the rowdy Ogragon Dojo team.

"Oh, no Lox?" Warren Kinkle laughed when he saw her. "Michella said he's been stalking your sessions?"

Emily sat on the sand beside him. "I'm sure Lox has better things to do than watch your poor aim."

The team laughed.

"Do you know that's not a bad idea. Why doesn't Lox play for Ogragon?" said Raquel Davis, a pretty girl with many facial piercings and newly-dyed, cropped, blonde hair. "I mean, if he's going to be in all of Ogragon's lessons."

"Isn't he a teacher?" Jessie Kendaschi asked.

"You girls just want to drool over him. Where's our eye candy, eh?" Pete Kinkle asked.

"Hey!" Summer, Raquel and petite Rosa Martin said at the same time.

Rosa flicked sand in Pete's face and he yelled.

"Rosa! Come on," Pete said, dusting of his eyes.

"Okay guys, let's get serious for a second," Summer said, tying up her long, wavy, blonde hair into a messy bun that rested on top of her head. "We have got to sort this team out. Lenny has done us proud and is the new third Fighter for the London FlyAways. Representing us! And you all know that I'm the new captain." Summer smiled prettily and the boys booed her.

"I can't believe our own brother didn't make one of us captain," Pete moaned.

"Oh please, you both would be awful," Raquel said looking from Pete to Warren.

"I wouldn't say awful," Pete said looking hurt.

"You both brought a snake on to the pitch and stole another team's tactics," Emily said, reminding them of the trouble they had caused last year.

"Err. . . that was a genius idea!" Warren said, looking offended. "And we won."

"Because of me!" Emily said and Warren rolled his eyes.

"Lenny led us to the championships," Rosa said, with her hands on her hips. "He was the best and Summer will be great too."

"Thank you Rosa. I have some ideas. I think Raquel should be our lead Distracter so now we have a position for a new Distracter. Any suggestions?" Summer asked.

"What about Jason Notting?" Raquel said, winking at Rosa who laughed.

"I second that," Rosa squealed. "He is smoking hot. Shame he's younger than us."

"Shame he's my sister's boyfriend," Warren said.

Rosa stuck her tongue out at him.

"Be serious, we know guys aren't Distracters," Jessie said unamused.

"How uncool is that?" Summer said, crossing her arms over her chest. "What about equal rights?"

"You know Jason is telekinetic," Emily said. "It's a shame we don't have a position for a Fighter."

"You could always give up—" Warren began.

"Shut up," Emily said, cutting him off.

"Okay, let's get the word out," Summer said, glaring at Warren, who smiled sheepishly. "We are the reigning champions and we are not going to lose that on my watch. I'm open to a first year, as long as they're as talented as Emily was when she joined."

"Boo," the boys chorused when Emily did a mock bow.

"And in case you guys didn't know, Alan Fair is the new Linktie captain."

Everyone groaned.

"You sure you still want to be captain?" Warren asked and Summer gave him a dirty look.

"Just because you couldn't beat him fairly, doesn't mean I can't," Summer shot back at him.

"Oh snap!" Raquel said, clicking her fingers.

Warren pointed at Emily. "She's the only one that beat Alan but had to destroy the whole stadium to do it!"

"That's not—" Emily went to say but Summer placed her hands over her ears and yelled, "SHUT UP!" And everyone fell silent. "Now I feel sorry for Lenny dealing with us for years. Let's pair up and spar."

The practice was just what Emily needed to let off steam. Her head felt so much clearer after battling with her team mates and she couldn't wait for the matches to start. Under Summer's leadership, Emily was confident they could hold on to the championship.

CHAPTER ELEVEN

Lox's Training Session

Emily was sitting in the Ogragon team living room with Michella, Jason and Wesley. They were attempting to do a History essay that Mr King surprisingly sprang on them. Emily couldn't get her head around it, so she was waiting for Jason or Michella to finish theirs, so she could copy.

Wesley sighed loudly. "I can't believe they're still giving us homework. What use is all this in a war?"

Michella tutted. "Wesley, how are we going to learn if we don't do the work? Why are you even moaning? You're not even doing anything and don't you dare think you're copying my work!"

"Fine! I'll copy Jason's!" Wesley retorted. Jason raised his eyebrows and Wesley added, "Please, mate."

"Did you read the newspaper?" Jason asked, looking at Emily. "Thomas met with the Prime Minister and got his backing."

Emily nodded. "Yeah, it's good, but the protests are getting worse."

They fell silent. The protests were getting more and more press, highlighting how dangerous warriors are. They were getting so much attention that people such as Professor Elwood and Neci were no longer the forefront. It worried Emily how much support the protestors were getting. Not all warriors were dangerous like Neci.

"I just want a break from all this war stuff. I wonder if we're having a Revolution Night party this year," Jason said. "They've been pretty quiet about it." He handed his essay to Wesley who took it gleefully.

"I think a party would be great," Michella said. "I think that's all everyone needs."

"Speaking of what would be great," Emily said, eyeing Michella. "Would you consider following in the footsteps of your big sister?"

"What do you mean?"

"Being a Distracter. We have an opening on the team."

"Michella, that would be good," Jason said encouragingly, and Wesley nodded his approval.

"I don't know. . ." Michella hesitated.

"Come on, you'd be perfect and you can reign in your brothers for us, so it's like a double bonus."

"I'll think about it," Michella eventually said. She took a deep breath. "Actually guys, there's something I've been meaning to—"

"Jason! Your writing is embarrassing!" Wesley thrust the essay under Jason's nose. "What's that word there?"

Jason peered at it. "It says 'rising.'"

"It doesn't," Wesley said, writing it down.

Jason tutted. "Sorry, what was you saying, Michella?"

Michella shook her head. "Don't worry. . . maybe later." She looked at the floor.

"I can't wait for Lox's training session tonight," Wesley said. "Do you think it will be hard?"

"One hundred per cent," Emily replied, grabbing a pen to copy Jason's homework.

After dinner, Emily, Michella, Wesley and Jason headed to the Foughtgon room in the basement, where Lox was going to be running his session. The queue to get into the room was going around the corner and Emily didn't see how they were all going to fit in the space and battle. There was at least fifty students in front of them ranging from the first years all the way to the sixth.

She spotted Alice Archinia talking with Tanya Frank, Julian Kena and Gabriel Thompson near the front of the queue. Since Lox had warned Tanya off, she hadn't said a word to Emily, but Emily wasn't holding her breath. Once Dojo started again, Tanya would be back to her aggravating self.

When they were finally let in, Emily was surprised to see a wrestling ring in the middle of the room and Lox was standing inside it. He was swinging a baseball bat in his hand.

Buckets of Reviving Water was in the corner of the ring and scattered around the room were chairs, tables, dustbins, broken bottles and baseball bats.

"What is this?" Wesley asked, looking around the room. "Some kind of street fight?"

Everyone gathered around the ring looking confused or anxious, but Lox looked ecstatic.

"Thank you everyone for coming. I only want to train those who are serious about being the best warrior they can be for this war. People who are willing to battle Neci, and get seriously hurt in the process, even die. If you're having second thoughts, leave now."

Everyone looked nervously at each other, but no one left the room.

"Good," Lox said. "Tonight we are going to have what I like to think is a real battle. Inside this ring is sanctuary. This is where you stand when you have had enough, but outside the ring is where the fight happens. Sometimes it's not about your powers, it's about using what's around you." Lox teleported and picked up one of the broken bottles from the floor. "If this is lying around during a fight, you use it. Use everything."

He teleported again, this time appearing on top of a bin.

"This is one of the ways I was trained by Neci. It's all about the last person standing. Yes, the person next to you is your friend, maybe even your boyfriend, or girlfriend, but in this room, trust no one. Not even your family," Lox locked eyes with Emily, who stared back at him surprised. "Let's fight," he said before he disappeared.

"He's just expecting everyone to start fighting?" Michella asked looking from left to right.

All the students seemed to have had the same thought. Everyone was staring at each other nervously and no one made any move until a giant fireball flew across the room, hitting a fifth year girl in Pentwon in the chest, so that she fell back and hit the floor.

Emily suspected that it was Lox. A giant roar echoed around the room and the girl that was hit threw a fireball back across the room, which hit a fourth year boy in

Mentorawth in the back. Suddenly, fireballs were being shot all over the room and people were crashing to the floor in agony.

Emily ducked as a sixth year boy from Berbinin aimed a punch at her. She blocked it and punched him in his jaw and he fell flat on his back, completely knocked out.

"Emily, are you okay?" Michella asked, reaching for the hand that she had used.

Emily grabbed Michella's shoulders. "Grab a weapon and fight, okay? Don't hold back."

Michella nodded but she looked scared.

"Just imagine they're all me," Wesley joked, but even he looked nervous.

Jason kissed Michella on the lips before bending his knees and soaring into the air.

Emily grabbed a bin lid from the floor and used it as a shield when people shot fireballs at her. From the corner of her eye, she saw Lisa Fowler charging at her and Emily threw the bin lid at her, which hit Lisa's leg and she buckled. Emily ran to the corner of the room. She positioned herself with her legs apart and her arms outstretched. She shot a fireball, taking out all the students in her line of fire. She searched around for Lox, but she still couldn't see him, although the wrestling ring was filling up steadily with students.

Emily ran aimlessly through the crowd, trying to find some form of shelter to hide behind and ran straight into Harmony Loving-Dale. Harmony stumbled back and when she realised it was Emily, she looked relieved.

"Isn't this crazy?" Harmony shouted, looking around at the battles.

Emily formed a fireball in her hands, keeping her eyes on Harmony. When Harmony noticed it, she gasped.

"What—what are you doing?" she stammered. Harmony stepped closer to Emily. "Is this because I'm dating Wesley?"

"What?" Emily said surprised and her fireball disappeared.

"I've noticed since we've started seeing each other, you don't want to talk to me," Harmony said looking visibly upset. "Why? I did ask you before if it was okay for us to date."

Emily was stumped. This was the last thing she expected to deal with in the middle of a battle! Before she could even think of a response, Wesley ran past and backtracked when he spotted them.

"Everything cool?" Wesley asked, glancing from Harmony to Emily.

Harmony nodded and Wesley squeezed Harmony's waist.

There was something about that small gesture that caused a heat in Emily's stomach and before she could stop herself, she was thinking of Wesley kissing Harmony in the middle of her Dojo match. When Emily looked down, a fireball was sitting in the middle of her hands.

It seemed to happen in slow motion. Wesley went to stand in front of Harmony but she was grabbing his arm and turning around, like she was going to run. Emily shot her fireball and it hit Harmony in the middle of her back. She collapsed on the floor; her blonde hair sprawled around her.

Wesley ran to help her and Emily didn't wait around for his reaction, instead she bent her knees and flew as far away from him as she could.

"Emily!" Wesley roared.

Emily felt something strong hit her arm making her yell

out loud. Gripping her bicep, she turned around to look at Wesley but instead she saw Lox staring at her with his arms folded over his chest. The baseball bat he had used to hit her was falling to the floor. Emily ducked in and out of students and fireballs, trying to get as far away from him as possible. Suddenly the room was filled with horrified screams.

Bright yellow fireballs were being shot into the air, one after the other, knocking out students. Emily flew behind Alan Fair, a strong, hefty warrior from Linktie, and used him as a human shield, as he blocked the fireballs flying their way. From her position, Emily could see that it was Lox attacking everyone, but to her surprise, right behind him, Michella was creeping up with a Disc in her hand. She was biting her lip, the strain of the Disc was clear on her face. Emily couldn't believe Lox couldn't sense her.

Lox's fireballs were causing explosions around the room. His eyes were bright and a smirk played on his lips. Michella shot her Disc and it sliced across Lox's back in a perfect line. He screamed and dropped to the floor in a heap.

Emily shot off in the opposite direction before Alan could sense her behind him. She tried to shift her arm, but it hurt so much that she feared it was broken. She used her right arm to shoot fireballs at people blocking her way. She spotted Julian Kena to her left and she instantly flew the other way. The last thing she needed was to fight Julian with a useless arm.

There was a lot more space in the room, now that most of the students were in the ring. Fully healed from the Reviving Water, they were on their feet, cheering and shouting. Emily tried to scan the crowd for Wesley, but couldn't see him. She needed to avoid him too.

As Emily was flying, she realised that everyone was getting into a huddle. She stopped abruptly when she saw a chair floating in front of her. On either side of her was a broken bottle and a metal dustbin.

"Look, it's Jason," someone in the crowd said and Emily could just about spot his blond hair down below.

Jason was holding one arm outright and another at his temple. All of the weapons in the room, were floating in the air, aimed at somebody. Emily smiled. Now that was some power.

Someone in the crowd scoffed. "What's he going to do now? Just keep us here?"

Jason smiled and tilted his head to the left and then the weapons flew at them. Emily ducked, so the bottle and the bin missed her but the chair caught her hard on the head. Bright spots floated in front of her eyes and she could feel herself falling fast to the floor. She hit the ground on her injured arm and a sharp pain shot through her entire body.

Bodies and weapons fell nosily around her. Her head was pounding and when she opened her eyes, everything looked blurry, she could just about see the wrestling ring. Slowly, she used her good arm to drag herself towards it. Her vision was coming in and out of focus. She pushed unconscious bodies away with her strong arm.

Hayley-Elizabeth Elwood was sitting propped up against the wall with blood dripping down the side of her forehead. Her eyes were closed and she was groaning. Not too far from her, she could see Lox watching Jason closely. She had to warn him. Emily stopped and laid still on the floor. She gritted her teeth and raised her injured arm with difficulty, putting both her hands on top of her forehead, with her palms facing outward, she chanted, "Anyosingh, Anyosingh, Anyosingh."

Everything she had left in her was going into the huge, blood-red fireball in her hands.

"ANYOSINGH!" she screamed and she shot the fireball at her brother.

It hit Lox on the side of his torso and he went flying to the other side of the room, where he hit the Masonka wall. The baseball bat that he was holding fell out of his hand and clattered to the floor. Alice Archinia picked it up, raised it in the air and with a manic look on her face ran into the crowd of people.

Emily closed her eyes. She had sweat forming on her upper lip. She knew she was in a vulnerable position, but she no longer cared. She had no strength to move and the wrestling ring looked miles away.

"Emily?" a soft voice called close to her. "Don't move."

Emily opened her eyes, but it seemed to make the pain in her head intensify. She felt pressure on her legs and her heart started to race. She was a sitting target. Then Emily felt that familiar tingling sensation through her body as if she had just drunk Reviving Water. But she didn't just feel energised, the pain in her head also disappeared. Her arm felt usable again. Her focus was back—sharp and clear.

Emily pushed herself up, feeling like she hadn't even joined the battle yet and she gasped when she realised who was behind her.

"You can heal?" Emily cried.

CHAPTER TWELVE

Problems

"That's what I wanted to say earlier but then Wesley interrupted me."

Emily reached forward and grabbed Michella's hands, turning them over. They didn't look any different from before.

"Since when?"

"End of summer." Michella grinned. "Crazy, right?"

"Crazy," Emily echoed, carefully looking at her friend and noticing that she didn't look like she had been fighting at all.

A fireball shot over their heads and exploded not far from them. They instantly ducked and covered their ears.

"We need to move!" Michella yelled. "How are you feeling?"

"As good as new. Let's go."

Emily grabbed Michella's hand and guided her through the battle that was thankfully thinning out, when she felt something hard tug on her arm. Michella was on her knees with her eyes closed. Her hand dropped from Emily's and she fell to the floor. Emily ran to her side and gently shook her.

"Michella?" Emily put her ear to her chest and her heart

rate was slow. She had used too much of her energy. "No, no, no. Come on Michella! Talk to me."

She softly tapped the side of her face and Michella let out a low groan but didn't move. Emily looked around the room. The wrestling ring was too far and everyone was in mid-battle. There was no way she could get anyone's attention to help. Emily picked Michella up, wrapping her arm around her waist. Slowly, she dragged Michella towards the wrestling ring, stepping carefully over the broken bottles, bats and bodies on the floor.

"You're going to be okay," Emily whispered. "I'm going to get you in the ring where there's Reviving Water."

"Hey! What's wrong with her?" Pete Kinkle asked, as he ran up towards them with a gash on his forehead and a split lip.

"I need to get her Reviving Water," Emily said urgently but Pete didn't move. He was staring at Michella with a quizzical expression.

"Why does she look like she hasn't been fighting?"

"Err. . . she was hiding," Emily said, instantly regretting her words.

Pete stared at Emily confused. She didn't blame him.

"Hiding?" Pete looked around the room. "Where? There's nowhere to hide!"

"I'll explain later," Emily said quickly. "Look, she's barely breathing. We need get her over there, quick." She nodded towards the wrestling ring on the other side of the room.

"Give her to me," Pete said and he scooped Michella in his arms. "I'll stay with her." He looked Emily up and down. "And later you'll explain to me why you don't look you've been fighting either."

Emily hesitated and then nodded. Pete and Michella teleported and Emily noticed three pair of eyes staring at her: Lox, Wesley and Julian.

"Great," Emily muttered.

She stretched out her neck and cracked her knuckles. She knew she had the advantage over all three of them, as she was the only one who was fully revived. Emily looked from one face to the next, analysing who would be the best to attack first. What she wouldn't do for one of her emotion-filled giant fireballs to take everyone out.

Before she could do anything, Lox teleported at the same time as Wesley threw a Disc at Julian, who flew out of the way just in time. Emily closed her eyes and she sensed Lox before she saw him. She turned around and kicked her leg, but Lox caught it in his hands. He dragged her forward so she was hopping on one leg and punched her in the stomach making Emily double over. He grabbed the back of her head and pulled it down roughly on to his knee. Emily clutched her bleeding nose and stumbled. Lox swiped her legs and Emily fell backwards smacking her head on the floor. The blood from her nose was going down the back of her throat making her choke. She rolled to the side and coughed violently. Emily saw a shadow on the floor and looked up to see Lox.

He bent down and wrapped his hand around her neck, lifting her up. Emily scratched at his hands as he flew her to the other side of the room and slammed her against the Masonka wall. Emily groaned and Lox squeezed until Emily could barely breathe. She tried to push him off but he didn't loosen his grip. The blood from her nose trickled to her mouth; she could taste it.

"Come on! Fight back!" Lox shouted.

Emily wanted to but she could feel her body giving up. Over Lox's shoulder, Emily saw something in blue moving. She tried to focus and realised it was Julian creeping up behind Lox with a blue fireball in his hands. Emily's eyes widened and Lox noticed and peered over his shoulder.

Julian shot his fireball but Lox teleported. Emily tried to fly up, but the fireball caught her leg and she screamed. She instinctively tried to hold her leg, but as she reached for it, she turned to her side and fell. She was falling fast to the floor, unable to control her body when she landed heavily in someone's arms.

"I got you," she heard Wesley whisper.

Emily looked up at him. He had a swollen eye and a bruise across his left cheek. Emily pinched her nose in an attempt to stop the blood. He glanced down at her neck and grimaced at the red bruises that had formed.

"Wow. Lox doesn't hold back does he?"

They were flying slowly across the room and Emily could hear the cheers and shouts from the other students getting louder. Emily stared at Wesley in disbelief as she realised what he was going to do.

"Don't," Emily croaked. "Please."

"Lox said not to trust anyone," he said before he dropped her.

Once again, Emily was falling. She could hear hurried footsteps as the other students ran out of the way. Just before she touched the floor, she felt her body hover before she was slowly lowered. She could faintly see Jason's blond hair but everything looked blurry.

"Get her some Reviving Water quick," Jason said but his voice sounded far away.

Someone held on to her hand before everything went black.

Emily was seated in Ruth Walker's office, in a big comfy chair, listening to the soft gospel music playing in the background. Ruth was Emily's school counsellor and she was sitting opposite with Emily's file in her hands. She was a middle aged, large woman with dark skin and black hair pulled into a neat bun.

She was the only woman, apart from Roberta Taniana, to wear heels instead of baht shoes around the school. But whenever Emily came to see her, they were usually dumped by her feet.

Emily was starting to dread her counselling sessions now that Ruth and Jenny Li were in constant contact. Before she could get away with not talking if she didn't want to, but now she felt double teamed. If one of them couldn't get a response out of her, then the other would try and it would go back and forth, until Emily was forced to opened up.

As the word got out about Lox's training session, Lox was called to the deputy headteacher's office as Laton Chin was filling in for Mr Davon. Parents were outraged by the weapons Lox had supplied their children and also the brutal way in which he had attacked Emily. Laton Chin had announced during breakfast that any future training sessions with Lox were banned until further notice, much to the annoyance of the students.

"He's teaching us what it's like out there!" Warren Kinkle shouted to a round of applause.

Laton Chin held up his hands to silence everyone. "All students should feel safe during training at Osaki. I will review the session with Lox and if we can come to an agreement, maybe we can resume them."

Lox was aggressively poking his food with his fork.

"So Lox won the battle," Ruth asked, interrupting Emily's thoughts. "Who came second?"

"Wesley," Emily said, remembering how Julian had been dumped by the side of the wrestling ring by Lox and how the students pulled Julian in, even though he was telling them not to. It was clear to everyone but Julian that he wasn't able to battle anymore. He could barely see with his two black eyes. That only left Wesley and Lox, and Emily was amazed by how well Wesley had fought. He managed to get in some good hits at Lox, much better than Emily had done.

"How did you feel about Wesley doing better than you?"

"It didn't bother me," Emily said truthfully. "I was proud of him, but Lox mentioned that he wants Wesley to join our elite training group. He wants him to be on the frontline in the war with us."

Ruth peered at her over her glasses. "Does this upset you?"

"Of course! It's hard enough that we all have to fight in the first place, but then Jason coming on board last year—as much as he's talented—that's one of my best friends who's now a target. Wesley will be too and that's why I don't even want them to know about. . ." Emily stopped herself in time.

Ruth tapped her temple and smiled. "Michella and her healing powers."

Emily mentally kicked herself. She forgot Ruth was telepathic.

"So, you're scared that your friends will die? Do you not feel that they might die anyway? Whether they were on the frontline or not? Everyone you know will be involved in this war in some way."

"I feel like they would have a better chance of surviving by not being on the frontline. I know Michella's healing power will be a great asset to our team. I mean she'll probably save us all."

"Isn't that a blessing then?" Ruth asked, tilting her head.

Emily hesitated. "To an extent, but look at Professor Elwood. He hasn't even been found. No one knows where Neci is and this is all because he knows another way to heal us. Neci will take Michella if she finds out what she can do and I'm afraid that I can't keep her safe."

They fell into silence. Ruth stared out of the window which faced the stadium, where Berbinin were currently holding Dojo auditions. Emily knew Michella had told Wesley, Jason and by force Pete, which meant Warren probably knew too. It was only a matter of time before more people caught on, but it was hard to tell who was an enemy at Osaki. The wrong person knowing could put Michella in a lot of danger.

"You mentioned your fear of not being able to keep Michella safe," Ruth said, looking at Emily. "But have you ever thought that maybe Michella is meant to keep you safe?" When Emily didn't respond, Ruth closed her file and took off her glasses. "Michella is your life line. She could be the difference between you surviving this war or not. She could help Thomas beat Neci, but her powers need to be trained, just like all our powers do, or it could end up being a curse to her. It's up to Michella if she wants to be on the frontline, but I can't help but think that it's more than a coincidence that her powers have come through when they're most needed."

Emily knew better than anyone what a hindrance it could be to not control your power. She shuddered when she remembered how Michella was barely breathing after she had healed her.

"You're right," Emily said and Ruth nodded in agreement. "I don't want her killing herself trying to help others. She needs training from the best. I'll let Lox and my dad know—well, when he gets back."

"How have you been sleeping? Jenny Li says sometimes you dream of the ice room." Emily nodded. "Have you walked down Knights Row?"

Emily shook her head. "I assumed it would be sealed off."

"The suit of armour that activated the door has been removed. It might help walking down it, realising that it's no longer scary."

"I guess I'll give it a try," Emily said, thinking it was the last thing she wanted to do.

Ruth smiled. "Thomas is back now. He's in the Ogragon team room waiting for you."

"Seriously?" Emily jumped up. "Can I go?"

"One second—is there anything else that I need to know about?"

Emily's excitement faded. She hadn't heard the voice telling her to make a fire for a while, but she quickly erased that thought before Ruth tried to read her mind. Emily shook her head.

"Okay, you can go," Ruth said and Emily ran out of her office faintly hearing Ruth shout after her, "I'm here if you need me."

Emily ran down the corridor and up the flight of stairs, weaving through students, who tutted at her when she accidentally pushed them. She reached the Ogragon room and opened the door to find Thomas Knight sitting on an armchair surrounded by, what looked like, every Ogragon student. They were hanging on to his every word. Thomas looked up when the door opened.

"Ah, here's my favourite girl! Excuse me everyone," Thomas said, getting up from his chair. He jumped over the students easily and picked Emily up and swung her around.

"Dad." Emily blushed as everyone watched.

"Oh, am I embarrassing you?" Thomas teased, putting her down. "I told you I wouldn't be gone too long."

"It was still too long," Emily said, crossing her arms. "Did you sort everything?"

"Kind of," Thomas said. He looked at the red marks on Emily's neck and his jaw tensed. "I heard Lox had fun at training."

"I'm a tough girl," Emily said.

"Yeah, you are, but that's not the way I would have trained everyone. I guess Lox can only train the way he has been taught."

From the corner of her eye, Emily saw Michella and Wesley come into the living room. Thomas also saw them and he hurried over to a surprised Wesley who grinned widely when Thomas put his arms around him.

"I heard you came second to my son? That is incredible!"

"Thank you," Wesley said, looking ecstatic.

"We can definitely use you and you—" Thomas pointed at a confused Michella. "What you can do is amazing."

"How do you know?" Emily and Michella asked at the same time and Thomas frowned.

"What do you mean? It was pretty obvious." When they all looked blank Thomas added, "One minute Emily is out for the count, the next second she's ready to fight. You have countless energy throughout the whole battle, but then you faint once you've healed Emily."

"But how do you know all of that?" Michella asked, still looking confused.

"Lox, of course. He saw everything." Thomas placed a hand on Emily's shoulder and gently squeezed it. "I cannot wait for this fight to happen. Neci's not going to know what's hit her."

CHAPTER THIRTEEN

The Elite Team

The next day, before breakfast, Emily found herself standing in the middle of Knights Row, staring at the suits of armour. Her heart was racing and her hands were sweating so much that she had to wipe them on her school uniform. She had almost asked Julian to come with her but she stopped herself at the last minute. She had to prove to herself that she was brave enough to face her fears.

Only some months ago, she has been dragged down here, barefoot and in her pyjamas, by Gabriel Thompson in disguise. Emily closed her eyes. She remembered first laying eyes on the ice room and being struck by the beauty of it. Not knowing that Blade was underneath the ice waiting for her.

She hesitantly walked closer to the knights, and gently touched their hands to double check none moved. They stayed perfectly still. Even though nothing happened and Blade was somewhere with Neci, Knights Row still freaked her out.

Emily made it to breakfast just as food was being served. She didn't have much of an appetite. Ms Macay approached her table and told her, Michella, Wesley and Jason to stay behind in the dining hall once breakfast was over.

As the students left to go to their lessons, Emily could see Gabriel Thompson, Alice Archinia, Julian Kena and Lox.

"I'm guessing we're having a training session," Emily said.

Michella's eyes widened. "Right now?"

"What? I just ate three stacks off pancakes!" Wesley said, tapping his bloated stomach.

"Is that all you can think about?" Michella snapped and Wesley recoiled. "Sorry, I'm just nervous."

"It will be fine," Jason said, grabbing her hand.

Mr Davon, Thomas, Cecil, Niles, Roberta, Jenkins and their sons, Xavier and Antonio walked into the dining room, followed by a baffled looking Jessie Kendaschi, and they beckoned everyone to come closer.

Jessie stood beside Emily. "What the hell is this?" he asked from the corner of his mouth.

Emily smiled. "Don't worry, you'll love it."

"Thank you for staying behind," Mr Davon said, beaming at them. "As you can see, we have some new additions to our group—Wesley Parker, Michella Kinkle and Jessie Kendaschi, all from Ogragon."

Everyone clapped for them. Jessie looked suspiciously from one face to the other.

"The reason we've asked you to join our elite team is because you have displayed great fighting ability. Some of you have incredible hidden powers. Jessie can create and manipulate fire, Michella can heal, and Wesley came second to Lox during his training session."

"Heal?" Julian said, staring at Michella. "Very cool."

"What's the biggest thing you've done with your fire?" Lox asked Jessie.

"I can turn my fist into fire," Jessie replied and Lox's eyes lit up.

Everyone looked at Lox to elaborate on his fascination.

"Oh, you know Neci. . . she's scared of fire."

"She is?" Jessie gulped. "Does that mean I have to fight her directly?"

"Don't worry about that," Mr Davon said, smiling at him. "I feel this is a great team of warriors that can make the difference in us winning over Neci. I don't want you to feel pressured to fight with us, but I do believe that your input makes us stronger."

"Sorry sir," Jessie said, putting up his hand. "You want *us* to fight alongside the Five Warriors against Neci?"

"Yes, Jessie," Mr Davon said, looking amused.

Jessie glanced at Xavier and Antonio. "And they're fighting too?" Everyone nodded. "But they're just kids! We're kids and you want us to take on Neci? I thought that was his job?" He nodded at Thomas.

"Jessie, you do know that Neci has a team of very talented warriors by her side?" Roberta explained. "That's not counting those who were microchipped by her last year. And you think Thomas is meant to take care of her and all of them?"

Emily couldn't help but think that Jessie would have reacted way better with prior warning. He usually was so cool that seeing him shaken highlighted how real the situation was becoming.

Jessie ran his fingers through his blond hair. "I just don't know about all of this."

Thomas and Mr Davon glanced at each other. Thomas walked to Jessie and stood in front of him.

"What you can do, none of us here can do. We would never have asked you to train with us if we didn't think you could handle this. Trust me, Neci will be frightened of you!"

"But I can't do this," Jessie said, looking desperately at Thomas. "I might die!"

"Well, we all might die," Alice snapped, crossing her arms over her chest.

"Not helping, Alice," Niles responded.

Cecil shot his granddaughter a sharp look and she fell quiet.

Thomas sighed. "Look, if you don't want to, we can't force—"

"He has to do it," Lox interrupted. "We need him."

"Just give him some time," Thomas said wearily.

"There is no time!" Lox argued. "I'm sorry that this is being thrown at you but this was thrown at everyone. We need you to fight and as much as they think you have a choice, you really don't. If Neci knew what you could do, she would—" Lox stopped abruptly.

The colour from Jessie's face had completely gone. He looked like he was going to faint any second. "She would what?" Jessie asked in a whisper.

But Lox shook his head and didn't say anything else.

"She would kill you," Alice said and when Lox glared at her, she shouted, "What? Someone had to say it."

"I need to sit down," Jessie muttered and Emily grabbed his arm and led him to a chair, where he instantly slumped down and placed his head in his hands.

"I don't think I want to be here either," Michella whispered when Emily came back.

"He's in shock," Emily said reassuringly. "Jessie's a great fighter. He'll be more than fine and so will you."

"We have been securing ties with other warriors," Mr Davon said. "We are fortunate that we have a lot of support, but we still need more. It seems like Neci is easily replacing her warriors that we sent to S.U.D.W." Mr Davon turned to Julian. "I need you to speak to your grandfather. I have asked Tainwo to come out of retirement to help fight and he refused. I didn't mention that you were fighting because I didn't want him to feel that I was pushing him into a corner, but I now need you to get him on board."

"I'll try," Julian said, scratching the back of his neck. "He can be very stubborn."

"What we need to do is take out Neci's key warriors one by one so Neci is left alone. When we fought her she didn't have anyone by her side so it makes me wonder why she needs help now." Thomas looked around the room. "Maybe she's more scared than we know, but we need to find her. No one knows where she is."

"That's all for now," Mr Davon said. He swept his arms outwards and the tables and chairs, apart from Jessie's, flew back to the side of the walls. He walked to the corner of the room with Cecil and Niles floating behind him. A clear barrier appeared in front of them. It reminded Emily of the protective glass that surrounded the audience during the Dojo match. "Now, Jenkins, if you could?"

The dining room slowly transformed and within seconds they were standing outside. The ceiling resembled the dark sky, with a few stars shining brightly above them, giving off a dim light. A gentle breeze blew around them. Jessie slowly stood up and looked around in awe.

Antonio ran up to Emily and grabbed her hand. Emily looked down at him and Antonio pointed in front of them and asked, "Who are they?"

"Oh no," Michella gasped, taking a step back.

Emily caught her breath when she saw Neci, Scarlett and Blade.

"They're not real, they're not real," she chanted to herself.

She knew Scarlett was captured and Neci and Blade would have come into Osaki with an army but she found it hard to convince herself because they looked so real.

Blade, who she had battled last year with Julian, was wearing a long white cloak over his tall and toned frame. His long brown hair fell over his shoulders and his cold blue eyes bored into them. Scarlett was effortlessly beautiful with her flame red hair and full red lips. She blew a kiss at Gabriel, who she had blackmailed last year to help release Blade from his prison. Gabriel let out a loud roar and lunged for her. Wesley caught him and held him back, muttering into his ear, but Gabriel's eyes never left Scarlett.

Emily couldn't stop staring at Neci. There was a power about her that radiated around the room. She was wearing her trademark black cloak and white mask. Emily wondered why she hid her face all the time.

"Hello Lox," she called softly across the room.

They all looked at Lox, whose fists clenched. Neci noticed and laughed. Her laugh put Emily on edge.

"Lox, are you sure you're standing on the right side?"

"It's not real," Jessie Kendaschi said aloud, with his eyes squeezed tight.

Antonio let out a whimper and Emily held his hand tighter. Xavier stood next to his brother in a fighting stance. Emily couldn't understand how a child so young could be so fearless.

"It's okay," Emily said, kneeling down to hug Antonio, and then she saw a flicker of concern in Neci's eyes.

Alice must have seen it too because she yanked Antonio's arm and pushed him towards Neci.

"What are you doing?" Emily yelled, trying to reach for him, but Alice was beckoning him forward.

"That's your mummy there, she's not going to hurt you."

Neci raised out her arm and shot a fireball that just missed Alice, who jumped back and Antonio sat down, opened his mouth and cried. Emily groaned when the pink bears Antonio conjured popped up all over the room.

"Now you've done it," Xavier said angrily. He ran up to his brother and put his arms around him, but it only seemed to make Antonio more agitated.

The bears were growling and each step they took made the ground shake. Antonio was crying noisily, thumping his small fists on the floor and the only way for the bears to calm down was if Antonio controlled them.

"Where did these come from?" Wesley asked, watching the bears prowl around the room.

"Antonio is an illusionist. We have to shoot at them and they'll disappear," Julian instructed. "Cheers Alice for making this harder!"

"I didn't think she would shoot her own son!" Alice retorted.

"You have to think of her as Neci and Neci doesn't care how old Antonio is," Lox said calmly. "I'll get Antonio. Don't hold back. Attack them all!"

Lox slid on the floor and picked up Antonio, who instantly wrapped his arms around Lox's neck. They teleported just as Blade shot an icicle at them.

Emily ran straight for Neci, who stamped on the floor which promptly broke apart. The ripple effect travelled towards Emily and she jumped high to avoid it. Neci met her in the air and kicked Emily in the stomach.

Wesley grabbed Neci around the neck and held her tight in a choke hold, but Scarlett was behind him, holding a fireball in the palm of her hands. She shot it at the same time Emily screamed, "Nooo," but Jessie had teleported in front of Wesley and caught Scarlett's fireball.

A surprised Scarlett stopped and Jessie shot the fireball back at her, which hit Scarlett in the face. She flew across the dining room and hit her back on the wall, falling into a clump on the floor.

Gabriel went after Blade, punching him in his torso. Blade shot an ice beam at Gabriel's arm, which instantly froze. Gabriel used his other arm and shot a giant fireball at Blade, which knocked him into Julian. Julian kicked him in the back and hit him with an 'Anyosingh' fireball.

Blade shot another ice beam, but as he fell, his ice beam travelled around the room. It hit Alice in the chest, as she was destroying the pink teddy bears and she froze in mid-punch. Xavier caught her before she hit the floor and placed her icy form as far away from the battle field as possible.

"What do I do?" Xavier cried.

Emily turned when she heard his voice and shouted, "Use your fireball to thaw her out."

Xavier nodded, but his hands were shaking so much that he couldn't produce a fireball. Emily bent her knees to take off, but Neci ran up to her and caught the back of her ponytail, yanking her backwards. Emily clawed at her hands, but she wouldn't let go. Neci swung Emily around the room in a circle and Emily held on tight to Neci's wrists. Neci let go and Emily went flying. Everything was such a blur that she had no time to block the fireball Neci shot at her. It hit her in the stomach and she fell on to the floor landing hard on her recently healed arm.

"It's okay," she faintly heard Michella's voice as she placed her hands on her.

Emily bit her lip when the pain shot up her arm. A few minutes later the pain gradually went away. Not one hundred per cent healed but manageable.

"Thank you," Emily said, standing to her feet. "You're not going to pass out right?"

"No, I didn't heal you fully."

Emily looked around the room. Alice was now half released from her icy prison with Xavier and Jessie helping to thaw her out. Jason was holding Blade in mid-air as Julian lunged for him. Wesley was injured on the floor whilst Gabriel, whose arm was free from the ice, dodged Scarlett's attacks. There were only a few pink bears growling around the room, but where were Lox and Antonio?

"Where's Neci?" Michella asked, looking around wildly.

Emily couldn't see her anywhere. Michella noticed Wesley and ran to help him. The ground began to shake. Emily lost her balance and fell. She looked up and saw sparks flying out of Neci, as she powered up. Her power was so strong that it made Scarlett's fire flame, in the middle of her hand, burn out. Alice crashed against the wall, breaking the remainder of the ice.

"Stop her Jason!" Michella screamed.

"I'm trying," he yelled back. "She's too strong."

Neci's fireball was getting bigger and bigger. The floor was noisily breaking. Someone shot a fireball at Neci, but she caught it and added it to her already huge fireball. If she shot it, they would all be wiped out. The sharp icicles that Blade had shot across the room during the battle was now flying around, making everyone duck.

An evil smile was plastered on Neci's face and she held the fireball over her head. Scarlett and Blade appeared beside her, adding their fireball to hers. The fireball turned from yellow to white to red.

Suddenly, there was an army of Neci's, each holding a red fireball in their hands, surrounding a surprised Neci, Scarlett and Blade. Emily was completely thrown. She looked around to see who was doing it and then she noticed Antonio Jenkins, standing still underneath them, with his eyes closed. He didn't seem to be affected by Neci's energy at all.

Neci looked at her replicas, then to Antonio and everyone else, as if deciding who to shoot her fireball at.

All the Necis shot their fireball at once, but one stood out. It was bigger and brighter than the rest; hidden amongst the Necis was Lox. Neci, Scarlett and Blade were hit from all directions and their screams echoed around the room, but to Emily's horror, Neci still had enough control to shoot her fireball. Lox teleported and caught it with both hands, but the fireball was pushing him back. He gritted his teeth and strained to push it. Emily flew up and joined him.

The fireball was heavy and hot; even with Emily and Lox working together, it was too powerful. The rest of the elite team raced over to help them.

Alice, with what little energy she had left, teleported to the other side of the room, grabbed Antonio and teleported him away from harm before she collapsed on the floor. Scarlett and Blade were both knocked out but Neci, although injured, was still standing.

Jason held his hands out and managed to keep her still. "I can't hold her for long. Shoot!"

"Push," Lox commanded.

Together they pushed forward Neci's fireball and it travelled rapidly across the room, exploding into a blinding light as it hit her. The impact of the fireball exploding rebounded back on them. Emily landed face down on the floor, breathing hard. Bodies were scattered everywhere and then she heard the voice, loud in her ear, *"Fire."*

"Go away," Emily said covering her ears but then she yelped. She looked down at her hands and they both had small red fire flames in the middle of it. Emily shook her hands, but they wouldn't disappear.

She looked over at Neci, who was slowly sitting up. The fire flames seemed to have a life of their own as they flew from her hands towards Neci but to her horror, Michella was walking across the room and she was in the firing line. Lox saw and he teleported and appeared directly in front of Michella taking the hit in the chest before falling to the floor at Michella's feet.

CHAPTER FOURTEEN

Secrets

"Lox!" Michella cried, reaching out to him.

Emily looked down at her hands. *Did I just do that?*

"I don't know what happened," Michella said, looking hysterical.

Everyone was looking at Lox, but Neci was now on her feet and staring at Emily.

Mr Davon, Cecil and Niles who had been watching the battle from the corner, surveyed the damage they had done.

"Not too bad," Cecil commented.

Emily looked back at her hands, turning them over slowly, but there was no evidence that she had created fire.

"Impossible," Wesley said, when he saw Neci and now Scarlett and Blade standing up. "We gave everything we had."

"But did you?" Niles questioned. "You wasted warriors by having two of them help Alice, when all you needed was Jessie to melt the ice with his fire flame. He could have done that in seconds. Alice, you should have ignored the bears as they would have disappeared over time when Antonio had calmed down and was more in control. More of you should have gone for Neci, as she is the hardest one to beat. It should have never gotten to a place where she had time to produce such a huge fireball! Emily, are you even listening?"

"Yes," Emily lied, looking up.

"If Lox and Antonio hadn't created that illusion and attacked, every single one of you would have been knocked out," Niles continued. "And as you can see, Neci, Scarlett and Blade are still able to fight and that is without the help of a healer. Lox, how are you feeling?"

"I'm okay." He stood to his feet. "I had to try and stop Scarlett's fire flame."

Emily looked at him surprised. She could have sworn he had seen her shoot it.

"Lox, I do think you could have given them more guidance," Cecil added. "Seeing as you know these warriors. Although, it was very smart of you to stay hidden until the last second. You managed to preserve your energy and saved everybody."

"Thanks Cecil," Lox said, glancing at Emily and looking down at her hands.

He knew. Emily hid her shaking hands from sight. She didn't understand what had happened. In that moment, she had created fire and had shot it with no control.

"Do you guys have anything to add?" Niles asked Neci, Blade and Scarlett.

Neci transformed back into Roberta, Blade into Thomas and Scarlett into Jenkins. Roberta took off her white mask and wiped her forehead with the back of her hand.

"It could have been better," Thomas said. "Did you see

how Jenkins was fighting? And yet he still kept up his illusion. That's the level of control you all need. Did you notice how controlled Antonio was standing in Neci's power? But none of you was protecting him. He was so focused on creating the Neci illusions that if we were really these warriors and attacked him, he would be dead."

Xavier put his head in his hands and Antonio, completely oblivious, looked ecstatic to see his parents and kept patting Xavier on the back saying, "Look, look they're here."

"He's so little. How can he even do that?" Wesley asked in disbelief.

"Alice. Don't you ever use my son as bait. Ever." Roberta glared at her.

"Sorry," Alice mumbled, turning red.

"I think that's enough for today," Mr Davon said, with a strained smile. "Why don't you all head to your team rooms? There's Reviving Water just outside the dining room door."

Thomas took a step forward towards Emily, but she quickly hurried out of the hall, avoiding everyone's eyes. She grabbed a bottle of Reviving Water and drank it down. She couldn't help feeling defeated. She had no idea it would be this difficult and that was only fighting three of them. What were they going to do with an army?

"Hey, wait up Em," Jason called and Emily reluctantly stopped. She saw Michella and she guiltily hid her hands behind her back.

"That was pretty fun," Jessie said, looking more upbeat than he did during the training.

"Fun?" Michella screeched, as they walked up the stairs.

"That was the scariest thing I have ever done. That fire came from nowhere. Thank God for Lox."

"I just can't believe they were still standing," Wesley said shaking his head in disbelief.

They entered the Ogragon living room and there were a few first years lounging around. Jessie went straight to his bedroom and Michella suggested they go to her room for some privacy. Emily collapsed on Violet Hijen's bed, that was closest to the door, and stared up at the ceiling. Someone was making her create fire. . . but how? And who? She had no idea how she could explain what was going on without being taken into S.U.D.W.

"Is everyone still coming tomorrow to the twins' birthday?" Michella asked from her bed.

Wesley groaned. "That's tomorrow? Why are you only reminding us now?"

"I sent an invite! And don't act like your sister isn't talking about it non-stop."

"Is your mum picking us up tonight?" Jason asked and Michella nodded.

"Can we just take a second about Lox's fascination with Jessie. Anyone else notice that?" Wesley asked, sitting on the floor, with his back against the bed.

"I did but didn't he say that Neci is scared of fire?" Jason said.

"Yeah, she is," Emily said, sitting up. "Apparently something happened to her in her childhood."

"What?" Michella said. "That's terrible."

Wesley snorted. "You know we're talking about Neci, right?"

"That's probably why she's crazy," Emily said.

"But why wouldn't Scarlett be in charge if she had something Neci feared?" Wesley asked and they all fell silent. "Unless Neci has something on her?"

"I asked Lox that once and he said you can't be scared of something you can control or something like that," Emily said.

"Maybe Scarlett just isn't strong enough to beat Neci, even with her fire ability," Jason suggested.

"But what happens if Neci beats everyone? She's now number one and what next?" Michella questioned. "There will always be a warrior better."

"And why does she wear that mask?" Jason asked. "I want to see her face. I wish we knew more about her. I mean Neci can't be her real name."

"It's not. Her name's Rose," Emily said without thinking. The three of them looked at her surprised. "Blade told me, when Julian and I were rescuing Gabriel. Blade's real name is Max."

"Rose and Max?" Wesley scoffed.

"What else do you know?" Michella asked intrigued.

"Blade said something about Julian's grandfather teaching them how to do light beams."

"No way!" Wesley said shocked. "Tainwo trained them?"

Emily shrugged. "I don't know, that's what he said. Maybe that's why Tainwo doesn't want to fight them."

"I wonder. . ." Michella said slowly. "If we could find out more information. We could probably ask Lox—"

"No!" Emily said loudly and they all stared at her. "I mean, you know how funny he gets." The last person she wanted to talk to was Lox. She knew that he had seen her throw the fire flames and he would want to question her.

"We could look in the library," Jason suggested. "There must be loads of stuff about Neci. She must have a family somewhere."

"There's a library?" Emily and Wesley asked at the same time.

Jason and Michella glanced at each other.

"You're joking, right?" Jason asked and when Emily and Wesley stayed quiet, he added, "This is our third year at Osaki! It's next to the sick bay."

"Well, I'm always knocked out when I go to the sick bay, so I must have missed it." Emily looked at Wesley. "What's your excuse?"

Wesley sighed. "I wish I had one. You're absolutely serious that there's a library here?"

Michella rolled her eyes. "Come on, I'll show you."

They made their way back down the stairs and out of the front doors of Osaki. They walked along the path by the sick bay and right next to it was a building that Emily had never noticed, even though it had a library sign in big, bold letters.

"Well, I'll be damned," Wesley said.

It wasn't that busy, but there were a few sixth years working. Jason grabbed a table whilst Emily and Wesley followed Michella. It was the coolest library Emily had ever seen. The walls were covered in murals of famous warriors either posing or in mid battle. Of course, The Five Warriors were there, behind the librarian's desk, standing in a clump and smiling. Michella certainly knew her way around the library. She went to a section packed with autobiographies.

"Do you think Neci wrote one?" Wesley asked confused.

"Of course not." Michella tutted, as she looked along the aisle of books. "But I remember seeing a book that related to Neci. . ." She pulled out an old, hardback book and handed it to Wesley. "Go and check this out please." When Wesley didn't move, she added, "The desk Wesley—at the front."

"Oh, okay," he said, when he noticed it and walked off.

"Sometimes I worry about him," Michella muttered.

They joined Jason at the table and they could hear Wesley arguing loudly with the librarian.

"I just said I don't have a library card. I didn't even know this place was here!"

Michella rolled her eyes. "I'll go and help him."

"Jason, can I ask you something?" Emily said as soon as Michella was out of earshot.

"What's up?"

Emily sat down opposite him. "Hypothetically speaking, is there a way that you can hear someone talking to you, but in your head?"

"Like telepathy?"

Emily frowned. "Oh, I thought telepathy was being able to hear other people's thoughts?"

Jason shook his head. "You can also put thoughts into other people's heads. There are techniques to block telepathy because Gabriel said he did."

"But can telepathy actually make you do what they're telling you to do?"

Jason frowned. "I don't know. I guess if they were really strong they could."

"Oh, okay," Emily said, then quickly changed the subject

before he could ask questions. "There are Dojo auditions today. I wonder who's going to join Ogragon?"

Jason frowned at her. "Is there something you want to tell me?"

"No," Emily said innocently.

"Because if there is anything. Anything at all, you know you can tell me, right?"

"I know," Emily said, looking at the table.

"I don't want to hear about another Blade situation where I had no idea what had been happening," he said in a stern tone, which made Emily look up.

The weight of the secret she was carrying seemed to feel heavier. She beckoned him to come closer. He leaned over the table. His blond hair brushed her face.

She whispered in his ear. "That fire that happened on the first day back at school. I think I did it."

"What?" Jason shouted, jerking his head back. He was so loud that everyone in the library, looked over at them.

Wesley and Michella, who were on their way back towards their table, stopped in mid-track. Jason looked around the library, aware that he had made a scene. Emily was already on her feet.

"I'm sorry," Jason said to her. "Emily don't—"

"I'll be late for practice," she said, heading towards the exit, brushing past a confused Michella and Wesley.

Emily made her way to the stadium for the Dojo trial. She was early, but she didn't care. She needed to get away from everyone. Seeing Jason's reaction showed her how crazy she sounded. *Maybe I am crazy?* Emily stared at her hands, which felt frozen because of the cold.

As she got closer to the stadium, she could see someone leaning against the wall with their arms crossed. Emily slowed down when she noticed it was Lox. He beckoned her over at the same time Emily took a step backwards.

"You can't avoid me," he said.

Defeated, Emily walked as slowly as she could and Lox looked unimpressed.

"I'm not avoiding you," Emily lied.

"Of course not," Lox replied, once Emily was stood in front of him. "You just had to hurry out of training. Now are you going to tell me why you shot fire flames at Michella? And how the hell can you make fire flames in the first place?"

Emily stayed silent. She didn't want to tell him about the voices because then he would tell their Dad and Mr Davon, and Emily was scared of what might happen to her.

"Do you remember that time last year when I tricked you into meeting me in the forest, and Roberta and Jenkins tried to read your mind? You stopped them from hearing your thoughts. How did you do that?"

Lox looked at her perplexed. "What has that got to do with anything?"

"How did you block them?" Emily asked, ignoring Lox's question.

Lox uncrossed his arms. "Why do you care?"

"Because—" Emily started, then she stopped. Lox looked at her expectantly waiting for her to finish. "No reason, I just think it's something I should learn."

They stared each other out. Emily tried to keep her face as blank as possible.

"You're hiding something from me," he said confidently.

"I'm not," Emily responded, not breaking eye contact.

"You are a liar," he said, walking towards her, making her walk back. "And I'm going to find out exactly why you're lying to me."

Emily's face hardened. "Well, what about you? You're hiding something."

"No, I'm not." Lox laughed.

"You have never said one thing about what it was like with her."

Lox smiled. "Why don't you tell me your secret and I'll tell you mine?"

"You first," Emily retorted.

"Nope." Lox held out his hand. "We can even shake on it and I promise I'll tell you whatever you want." Emily hesitated. "Come on."

Emily reached for his hand.

"Hey Emily," Summer called from behind them. Emily dropped her hand and Lox stared hard at her. "Oh. . . and Lox! Are you helping us with the Dojo trials?"

The rest of the Ogragon Dojo team were behind Summer. Rosa went beetroot red when she saw Lox.

"Yeah, I might stick around," Lox said, casually putting his outstretched hand into his pocket. "Need to finish my chat with Emily first."

"Sorry, did I interrupt?" Summer said frowning, looking at both of them.

"It's fine," Emily said, before Lox could comment. "It can wait."

"Cool, okay we have about twenty people that have signed

up, but more might turn up. Let's set up guys," Summer said, leading the way into the stadium.

Once they had all disappeared, Lox said to Emily, "We'll finish this conversation at home," before he walked into the stadium.

Summer was a hardcore captain. Emily was surprised by the intensity she showed, putting the potential team members through their paces. She was getting through them quickly and they were soon down to only two girls. One of the girls threw up during the process and Summer dismissed her without any sympathy.

"Summer!" Rosa said, giving her a hard stare as she fetched water for the girl.

"We don't need people who don't have the stomach for it," Summer said stubbornly, crossing her arms over her chest.

"And I thought my brother was crazy," Pete said.

Summer shot him a dark look. "There is no way I'm giving up my spot as Distracter for a girl who throws up over blood! What kind of warrior is that?" Summer looked unimpressed as she watching the girl stumble out of the stadium.

"You're not being cool," Raquel said, with her hands on her hips.

"We are not losing the championship on my watch," Summer said angrily. "Right, who's left?"

A shy girl with glasses and red hair was hovering nervously in the middle of the pitch.

"Oh great," Summer muttered before she turned to Emily looking hopeful. "What about Wesley? He came second to Lox, so I wouldn't even audition him."

Emily shook her head. "There's no way Wesley can be a

Distracter. . . wait, were you going to give away my spot as a Fighter?

"No!" Summer said, but she turned red.

"She's kind of pretty," Jessie said, looking over at the red head. "Maybe if she lost the glasses."

"Hey, it's not all about looks you know," Raquel said hotly.

Warren laughed, but quickly stopped when all three girls looked at him.

"What do you think, Emily?" Summer asked, keeping her eyes on the girl.

"Let's see what she's got," Emily said, glancing at the stands where Lox was sitting and watching her.

"Hey! What's your name?" Summer barked and the girl jumped.

"Amaya Ethans. I'm in my first year."

"Do you need those glasses?" Summer asked.

"N-no," Amaya stammered. She removed them and put them in her pocket. Without the glasses, Emily could see her bright blue eyes.

"Okay, Pete and Jessie, I want you to battle, and Rosa and Amaya distract," Summer instructed.

Amaya nodded, but she still looked nervous. Emily gave her an encouraging smile and Rosa flew over, took her hand and led her to where the boys were preparing to battle. Emily hoped Amaya was a dark horse. There was no way she was giving up her spot as a Fighter.

Thankfully, she was right. What Amaya lacked in technique, she made up for with speed. She literally was everywhere and Jessie and Pete were clearly getting irritated, especially when Rosa shot a fireball at Amaya, who rebounded it, so it flew towards Pete, and it just missed his arm.

"She's good," Emily said to Summer.

"She's okay," Summer said in a flat voice.

"She's the best we've seen today," Raquel said forcefully. "Come on Summer! I've got homework."

"Fine," Summer said reluctantly. "Hey!" They stopped their battle and Summer beckoned them over. "Amaya, I'm going to give you a shot."

"Oh my gosh, thank you," Amaya squealed and Summer held up her hand to silence her.

"You are the second first year to ever join the Ogragon Dojo team after Emily. My Distracters are the best girls around and we are the champions. So don't mess up."

"I won't, I promise," Amaya said, with her blue eyes shining.

"Come on, let's spar," Pete said, leading Amaya and the rest of the team to the other side of the stadium. Summer hovered beside Emily and sighed.

"How do you feel about giving up lead Distracter?" Emily asked.

"Rubbish. Sometimes I hate the rules of Dojo. I hope I made the right decision becoming captain."

"You did," Emily said, nudging her. "You'll be a great first Fighter and Amaya will turn out to be amazing. Who knows, she could be a future captain one day."

"Hmmm," Summer said, looking unconvinced. "Speaking of captains, I was thinking that when I leave I would most likely give the team to you or Jessie."

"Really?" Emily said, surprised she was even considered.

"Of course. Next year will be our last year for the majority of the team. I could give it to Jessie and then when he leaves, he could give it to you, so you both have a shot. You're a strong leader, but it depends. . ." Summer trailed off.

"If I'm still alive?" Emily said in a jokey voice.

Summer's eyes suddenly welled up and she hung her head, hiding her face behind her blonde hair. A startled Emily turned away, knowing that Summer would hate her witnessing her vulnerability.

"I'm okay," Summer said in a small voice and when Emily looked back at her, the only tell-tale sign was that her eyes were red. "It just sucks so much that Neci wants to steal everyone's future. I've found mine and if anything ever happened to him. . ."

Her eyes wandered over to Warren who was laughing loudly with Jessie.

"Well, we'll just have to beat her then," Emily said and Summer held her arm.

"You know we will fight with you all the way, right? You're our girl and there's no way anyone's going to stop me getting a shot at Neci, even if it's one fireball before she blows me up."

Emily hugged her tight. She felt Summer resist at first, but then she relaxed when Emily squeezed her.

"You're not so tough after all," Emily teased.

"Excuse me!" Summer said, raising her eyebrows.

Emily smiled. "It's refreshing to meet a girl that's not on the Lox love boat."

Summer pulled away from Emily and glanced over at Lox. "It's tempting. He is beautiful."

Emily pushed her away. "Don't start."

When the others had finished training, Emily saw Lox gesture at her to come over, but she was saved by Michella, who was standing at the entrance of the stadium, waving her arms wildly to get Emily's attention. Emily flew down towards her and when Lox noticed he bent his knees to take flight.

"Lox!" Rosa called and Emily glanced back to see Rosa hovering in front of him, talking animatedly, as he watched Emily over her shoulder.

"Emily, you would never believe—hey!" Michella said surprised, as Emily gripped her arm and hurried her out of the stadium.

"Sorry," Emily said, nervously checking over her shoulder. "Trying to get away from Lox."

"Why?" Michella asked.

"Oh just family stuff," Emily said vaguely. "Let's go sit by the koi pond."

They sat on the curved bridge, watching the colourful, exotic fish dart to and fro. Emily insisted that they sat under the huge tree with the pretty pink flowers, that hung over the bridge, making it harder for Lox to spot her.

"What's up?" Emily asked, taking in Michella's excited face.

"I found something about Neci. So, apparently, after her grandparents were killed she was sent to live with her aunt in London."

"What was her name?"

"Janet Moore. Hopefully, if her aunt is still alive we could find her and speak to her."

"Good idea. Any insight into Neci would help."

Michella clasped her hands together and looked up at

the grey sky. "I can't wait for all this to be over. I just want everything to go back to normal."

Emily glanced at Michella. She didn't want to admit that she had no idea what normal was anymore.

CHAPTER FIFTEEN

The Army

"Hey, what you reading?"

Emily looked up from where she was sitting by the oak tree. She had gone to the library with Michella after Dojo practice and stumbled upon a book detailing special gifts a warrior could have.

"A book from the library." She budged over so Julian could sit beside her.

"A bit cold to be sitting outside," Julian said.

"I wanted to know more about special gifts. You know, how fireballs are made from our energy?"

"Yeah," Julian said. "That's why everyone has a different colour."

"Right, so I was looking into fire and apparently if you have that gift, you could walk into a massive fire and not get hurt. You could even turn into fire."

"Wow," Julian said. "Can Jessie Kendaschi do that?"

Emily shook her head. "Not that I know of but maybe Scarlett can."

Julian gently nudged her. "Remember Scarlett can't harm us anymore."

Emily smiled weakly but didn't respond.

"Oh, I've been meaning to tell you, I spoke to my Grandad."

"Oh cool, what did he say?"

"I'm going to visit him over Christmas and hopefully I can persuade him to join us."

"Julian, that would be huge."

"Well fingers crossed." He glanced at his watch. "Come on, lunch is going to start."

Emily folded a page in the book and placed it in her school bag before they walked in a comfortable silence towards the dining hall.

"Catch you later," Julian said, when his friends waved him over.

"See you."

Emily walked into the dining hall, as someone grabbed her arm.

"We need to talk," Jason said urgently. He was staring at her as if he was just seeing her for the first time. Emily discreetly shook her head.

"Not here," Emily hissed.

"Hey." Wesley appeared beside them. "I'm starving."

"Me too," Emily said, avoiding Jason's eyes. "I need food after Dojo."

"How was it?" Wesley asked, walking beside her.

"We found a first year. I think she's good but Summer's on the fence about her."

Emily could feel Jason's eyes boring into hers and she deliberately sat at the end of the table, where thankfully Wesley sat next to her. Jason looked stumped for a second before he sat opposite her, beside Michella.

"Can't wait to see the new team in action. How's Summer as captain?" Wesley asked.

"Good," Emily said, piling salad on her plate. "She's basically Lenny, and I think once the boys stop taking the mick, she'll really shine. Amaya—that's the new girl—is petrified of her!"

"I wouldn't want to be on the end of Summer's wrath. You alright, Jas? Your man bun too tight?" Wesley teased.

Jason was so focused on Emily that he hadn't filled his plate. Emily glanced at him and immediately looked back down.

"Huh?" Jason said, eventually looking away from her. "What did you say?"

"Aren't you hungry?" Michella asked, passing over the dim sum.

"Sorry, just got stuff on my mind," Jason said, taking the bowl from her.

In the middle of lunch, Mr Davon stood up. "Can I have everyone's attention, please? The Dojo season will commence next week followed by our annual Revolution Night party, straight after the match. I think this is the perfect time to celebrate warriors who fought for change. The first Dojo match will be between Linktie and our reigning champions, Ogragon."

"Get in!" Warren Kinkle shouted over the loud applause and cheers in the dining room.

"You might actually get to fight Tanya this time," Michella said to Emily.

"I hope so," Emily replied, glancing over at where Tanya Frank was sitting. She had a huge smile on her face.

"I need to talk to you," Jason blurted out to Emily.

Michella frowned at him. "Why are you acting so weird?"

"Now, please," Jason said, standing up.

A few people were staring at them. Emily glared at Jason as she stood to her feet and walked away from the table. They walked past Tanya Frank who sneered at Emily.

"I've been waiting to beat you up for years," Tanya said.

Emily laughed. "You'll still be waiting."

They finally made it out of the dining hall and Jason crossed his arms. "Why did you run out like that earlier?"

"Because of the way you reacted," Emily said. "I know it sounds crazy and I sound even crazier for saying it. Do you know why I didn't tell you about Blade? Because I told Michella first and she didn't believe me."

"Oh come on, I'm allowed to react! You didn't even give me a chance to say anything else. Look, I don't think you should battle against Linktie."

Emily snorted. "Don't be stupid."

Jason shook his head. "I'm not joking. What if this fire happens during the match? You can't control it."

"So you're going to take that bullet and tell Summer I'm not going to battle?"

"This is serious," Jason said urgently, grabbing on to her arms. "Why is this happening to you?"

"I don't know but Roberta does."

"Roberta?" Jason asked surprised. "How? What did she say?"

"She told me to embrace it."

"But why?" Jason frowned, running a hand through his hair. "None of this makes sense."

"I don't know. Ever since I saw Scarlett things have been—"

"You saw Scarlett?" Jason hissed. "When?"

Emily sighed. "I wasn't meant to say anything. It was on my birthday."

"What did she say?"

"Just random stuff. It was all weird and she grabbed me. . . sorry I know I'm not making any sense."

"Lately, nothing has been making sense."

"Please don't tell anyone else," Emily begged.

Jason groaned. "This is Blade again! We shouldn't be keeping secrets from each other."

"I wasn't meant to say anything about Scarlett and this whole thing that's happening to me. . . I'll figure it out."

Jason rolled his eyes. "How are you going to do that?"

"Please, Jason. Just don't say anything. I'll talk to Roberta."

Jason sighed, rubbing the back of his neck. "I won't say a word but talk to me. Please don't shut me out."

"I won't," Emily said, hugging him, and over his shoulder she could see Lox standing by the front doors of Osaki watching them.

Emily spent all evening avoiding Lox. She insisted she had homework that couldn't wait and she had to help James with his science project.

"Emily, dinner," Sally called from downstairs.

Emily was just about to say she wasn't hungry, but her

stomach said otherwise. She reluctantly dragged herself out of bed and headed down the stairs.

The dining table was laid out and Emily sat next to James, who immediately started digging into his pasta. Lox arrived a few minutes later and deliberately sat opposite Emily.

"Where's Thomas?" Cathy asked, cutting her chicken.

"He should be—ah there he is," Sally said, as Thomas strolled into the dining room, holding a case of water.

"Sorry, everyone," Thomas said. "I think Roberta and Jenkins left us some Reviving Water." He placed the case down on the floor. "Wow, the food looks great."

"Isn't that stuff expensive?" Cathy asked, pointing her fork at the Reviving Water.

"Very," Thomas said. "It's so hard to get that people are charging a ridiculous amount for it."

Michael glanced at Emily. "Not hungry?"

"Oh sorry," Emily said distractedly, picking up her fork.

"Dad, what did you think of today's training?" Lox asked, studying Emily carefully.

Emily dropped her fork and it clattered nosily to the floor. The housekeeper, Mrs Asha appeared straight away.

"No, it's fine. Sorry," Emily said picking it up.

"Very good," Thomas said. "That Jessie kid is pretty amazing. I saw some really interesting things today."

"Me too," Lox chimed in. "Things I can't even begin to explain."

Emily glanced at Lox and pushed her chair away from the table.

"I don't feel well," she announced.

"Oh no," Sally said at the same time Lox said, "Sit down."

Thomas shot a quizzical look at Lox. "If she's not feeling well, she can go and rest."

Lox laughed easily. "She's fine. Sit down."

Emily hesitated and slowly sank to her chair.

Cathy looked from Emily to Lox. "Is everything okay?"

"I think you need to ask her," Lox replied, nodding at Emily.

"I really don't feel well," Emily moaned, resting her head on the table.

"What's wrong, sweetheart?" Thomas asked, getting out of his seat. He kneeled beside her and rubbed her back.

"Why don't you tell everyone what happened today at training?" Lox said.

Emily sat up. "I don't know what you're talking about." She mouthed "Shut up" to him, but he ignored her.

"Or I can." Lox shrugged. "During training today, Emily shot a fire flame at Michella, and considering Michella is her best friend and Emily doesn't know how to do a fire flame, I find that very odd."

"What?" Thomas asked alarmed, standing to his feet. "You did that?"

"Why did you shoot at Michella?" Lox asked.

"Oh, just leave me alone, Lox!" Emily snapped.

"That's enough!" Sally said, slamming the table hard, making everyone jump. "We are having dinner. I don't want to hear all of this whilst I'm eating!" Everyone fell silent. "Now, let's finish our food, then we can discuss this properly."

Lox's mouth hardened and he stabbed into his food.

After dinner, Sally sent Rosy, Yvonne and a reluctant James

out of the room. She waited for Mrs Asha to go home before she rounded on them.

"So, what is going on here?"

"I told you, Emily created a fire flame—"

Sally held up her hand. "Emily can speak for herself, Lox."

"Emily?" Thomas asked. "What's going on?"

Emily took in everyone staring at her. Waiting. She felt her mouth dry up. "Can I have some water?"

"No!" Lox shouted. "Stop stalling."

Cathy reached out her hand and held on to Emily. "Please, tell us."

"I don't know. I just don't feel like myself. Sometimes my powers do things that even I don't know how or why. I don't know how I created a fire flame. I did once around two years ago. It just happened. I was aiming for Neci and Michella walked past as soon as I shot it. I wasn't trying to shoot her. Why would I shoot my best friend?" She looked at Lox.

Eventually he shrugged but his eyes still looked suspiciously at her. Thomas sat back in his chair looking satisfied. Emily breathed a sigh of relief, hoping she had convinced them.

That night, Emily tossed and turned. She had been lying on her side attempting to fall asleep and had only shut her eyes for a few minutes when she heard loud voices. She opened her eyes and was still. She could definitely hear chanting and yelling. She sat up. Something was happening in the Village.

Emily hurried out of bed and looked out of her window.

She gasped when she saw what looked like an army in black walking through Legends Village. Some were running, whilst others were flying. The glow from their fireballs created un-natural shadows across their faces. One of the warriors shot a fireball randomly at one of the mansions. It belonged to an elderly legend called Marashi Ali and to Emily's knowledge, he was inside the house.

Emily turned and ran out of her room breathing fast. She had to get her dad quickly. The hallway was dark and she tripped over one of Rosy's dolls. She almost screamed when she bumped into something solid. Lox put a finger to his lips before pointing to the window at the end of the hallway that had a better view of Legends Village. They ducked under the window and peered out. There were hundreds of warriors heading their way.

"This is Neci, isn't it?" Emily asked, looking up at Lox who nodded but he kept his focus to the window. "Why are none of the warriors fighting back?"

"They're waiting for a signal from Dad."

"He knows they're here? I was running to get him."

"He sensed them miles away," Lox said.

"Emily?" James was standing in the middle of the hallway in striped pyjamas. He rubbed his sleepy eyes. "There are some people outside."

"I know," Emily said, running up to him. "It will be okay. Go and wake everyone and stay hidden, yeah?"

"Is something bad happening?" James asked, looking more alert.

Emily debated whether lying would be the best option but what was the point? He would figure it out soon enough.

"Yes," she said and James stared at her with wide green eyes. "Go." She nudged him and James ran, disappearing into the darkness.

"Emily? Lox?" Thomas called.

"We're here," Emily said, trying to keep calm. "What do we do?"

"We need to get everyone downstairs to the underground safe room. All the warriors are ready to go on my signal—"

"What underground safe room?" Emily asked confused.

Thomas looked at her bewildered. "The safe room," he repeated slowly.

"We have a safe room?" Emily asked.

Lox sighed. "We haven't got time for this conversation."

"But how did I not know about it?"

Even in the dark, Emily knew Lox was rolling his eyes at her.

"Lox," Thomas said turning to him. "Take everyone downstairs and then teleport to the back of the mob. Let's try and diffuse the situation. Attack only if necessary."

"I'm on it," Lox said, running past them.

"What can I do?" Emily asked, eager to help.

Thomas hesitated. "I want to try and calm the situation and I can't risk you shooting fire flames at them."

"I won't," Emily promised. "I mean. . . I'll try. I'll try really hard."

Thomas put a hand on her shoulder. "Okay, follow me."

Thomas opened the front door. The smell of fire hit Emily hard. Thomas held her hand and pulled her outside. The warriors in black stopped moving when they laid eyes on them.

Emily could hear her breathing loud in her ears. She trailed her eyes around the Village, seeing all of the legendary warriors outside of their houses. Some were dressed in pyjamas like herself and others in training kits. They were outnumbered by an enormous amount.

CHAPTER SIXTEEN

The Takedown

Roberta, Jenkins and their children, Xavier and Antonio, walked over to them. They were dressed in dark training kits. Thomas and Jenkins greeted each other with a handshake and a one-armed hug whilst Roberta stood next to Emily. She didn't look the least bit fazed by the attack.

"Did you see this coming?" Emily asked and Roberta nodded her head.

"But this doesn't look right." Roberta said, staring at the warriors. "I saw a lot more people than this."

"More?" Emily asked with her eyes wide.

"I'll be back," Roberta said before she teleported.

"Where has she gone?" Thomas questioned.

The warriors in black were looking up at the sky, from left to right, with their bodies poised ready to fight.

"Where's Roberta?" Emily overheard one of the warriors say.

"I think that they think Roberta has teleported to attack them," Jenkins said slowly.

"Well, where did she go that was so damn important?" Thomas snapped.

Jenkins didn't respond but he caught Emily's eye. She had gone to Scarlett.

"I wanted to avoid a fight." Thomas continued. He turned to Emily. "You ready to put that training into use?"

Before Emily had a chance to respond, one of the warriors was squaring up to a young woman who played Dojo for England called Kerry Rome. Her trademark giant Afro framed her pretty face. The warrior was screaming something at Kerry whose face suddenly hardened and instantly there were ten versions of her lined up in a row.

"Kerry," Thomas warned.

The Kerrys had their hands in fists and slowly the ground around them rumbled. Some of Neci's warriors lost their balance and toppled to the floor.

"Kerry, don't!" Thomas shouted but the ten Kerry's charged towards the mob.

"Go! Go!" Thomas commanded, sprinting into the crowd, and all of the legendary warriors ran forward to join the battle.

Neci's warriors let out a loud roar and started to run in different directions. A giant fireball came soaring towards the Knights' house but Jenkins caught it and threw it back at a group of Neci's warriors, who fell as the fireball knocked them out.

Emily took a step forward and felt herself being tugged back. A frantic Cathy, wearing a short nightie, was holding on to her.

"I can't find Yvonne! She got scared and ran."

"No, no, no," Emily said, searching the crowd. There were so many people, she could barely make out anyone.

"YVONNE!" Cathy screamed.

"Get back inside, I'll find her," Emily promised, pushing her towards the door.

She saw her dad knock out four people with one punch and a group of Neci's warriors were staring into space with a dreamy expression, as they were trapped in one of Jenkins' illusions. Lox was being ambushed by five warriors and at one point he seemed to have fallen to the floor. Emily felt her stomach drop. Suddenly, the five warriors on top of him soared into the air. Lox shook his head and charged back into the battle. And then she saw her. Yvonne was in her bright pink pyjamas, standing in the middle of the battle, clutching her teddy bear and crying.

"Yvonne!" Emily screamed as she ran towards her.

"Ahhh," a giant bear of a man charged at her and Emily skidded on the floor, kicking his ankle, so that he toppled over with a loud thud.

She ducked and dived under punches and fireballs. Yvonne had buried her head in her teddy bear and was curled up into a small ball. A fireball flew over Emily's head, heading in Yvonne's direction. Emily sprinted and leaped into the air, catching the fireball and throwing it over her shoulder. She had no idea where it landed but it exploded loudly a few seconds later.

"Yvonne," Emily said gently. Yvonne peeped at her from behind her teddy bear with a tear-streaked face. When she realised who it was, she jumped into Emily's arms and wrapped her small frame around Emily's body, clinging tight.

"It's okay," Emily said soothingly, rubbing her back. "Let's get back home."

"It's too loud," Yvonne said, pulling a face.

Bodies were sprawled on the floor, mansions were on fire, the few decorations left celebrating Lox and Thomas were going up in flames, there were battles in the air and blood was splattered everywhere.

Legends Village was a war zone. The house looked so far away that Emily didn't see how she could get Yvonne there safely. She shifted Yvonne, so she was on her back and Yvonne's arms were around her neck.

"Do not let go of me," Emily instructed, before she started to run.

The shouts, scream and explosions made Yvonne jumpy, so Emily had to grip her extra tight. It was much harder to avoid the battle with someone else to worry about. She could see their door number. . . so close. . .

Yvonne screamed and Emily could feel her being pulled away.

"No! Bad man!" Yvonne yelled, hitting the warrior in the face with her teddy bear. He lost his balance and Emily spun round and kicked him in the stomach so he doubled over.

"Good job!" Emily called to Yvonne.

She was almost at the house, when she felt something heavy on her leg.

"I've got her!" A man screamed with a manic look in his eyes. "I've got Emily-oof!"

Emily kicked him in the mouth and the warrior fell backwards to the floor. She sprinted towards the house, looking back over her shoulder, but he was out cold.

Emily opened the door and Sally let out a small cry when she laid eyes on Yvonne. Yvonne ran into her arms and Sally sunk to the floor on her knees and howled.

"Hi Mummy," Yvonne said, patting Sally's hair. "I hit the bad man."

"Go back to the safe room," Emily said, hurrying to the door, eager to join in the battle.

"You're not leaving us?" Sally asked. Her eyes were red and wet.

"Is she back?" Michael asked, walking towards them in his pyjamas.

"Daddy!" Yvonne squealed and Michael scooped her up.

"Was that Yvonne?" Cathy asked, holding a sleeping Rosy in her arms with James walking beside her.

"You need to go back to the safe room," Emily said frustrated.

A loud bang went off outside the door making everyone jump.

"Please stay with us, Emily," James said, visibly shaking.

"We're all scared," Cathy said. "And that safe room is so far underground, you feel like you can't breathe."

"I have to help," Emily said. "Stay in the dining hall and keep the lights off."

She hurried back outside, shooting a fireball that took out everyone in front of her. The sound of helicopters made her look up. The paparazzi had gotten wind of what was happening and were taking pictures from up above.

Emily ran into the mob, fighting as many people as she could. It was clear that they had taken out most of Neci's warriors. The few left were walking away from the Village in a daze. Emily rubbed her aching knuckles as Lox hurried over to her.

"Come on, let's go back inside. Jenkins will sort the rest."

They hurried back to the house followed by Thomas, Roberta and her children. Emily caught Roberta's eye and she responded with a slight nod. Scarlett was still hidden.

Thomas clapped Lox on the back and the two shared a genuine smile with each other.

"You did great out there," Thomas said, hugging Emily.

Emily smiled. She was glad that her powers had behaved for once.

"Here," Lox said, throwing a bottle of Reviving Water at Thomas and Roberta.

Thomas opened his bottle and drank from it. He lowered the bottle and opened his mouth to speak, but no sound came out. Thomas clutched his throat and his eyes rolled to the back of his head before he fell with a loud thud to the floor. His head hit the marble hard and his Reviving Water gushed over the floor.

"Dad!" Emily rushed to his side.

"What's happened to him?" Lox cried, kneeling down and feeling his pulse. "It's weak."

"Someone get Jenkins," Roberta yelled.

Michael ran from the room and out the front door.

"Oh, Dad," Emily said, burying her face in his chest. She could hear a dull heartbeat and his body felt hot to touch.

"What happened?" Jenkins asked, hurrying into the room.

"We don't know," Roberta said, rubbing her face. "Are the hospitals safe?"

"Not tonight," Jenkins said, pacing the room.

Cathy ran out of the room and reappeared with a pillow that she gently placed underneath Thomas's head. She held his hand and rubbed it gently. "He'll be okay?"

"Why can't we take him to a hospital?" Sally questioned.

"The battle, everything that's happened tonight. It's not safe for him or for us. Someone did something to the water and I think they may have poisoned it," Roberta said, looking out of the window. "Neci sent those warriors and we don't know if she's out there watching us right now."

"Poison? Then he definitely needs a hospital," Cathy argued.

Jenkins appeared in the dining hall and Roberta turned to him and froze. Her eyes looked glazed over and she was staring into space.

"Mummy?" Antonio whimpered, trying to hold on to her hand but she didn't react.

"It's okay," Jenkins said, with his eyes on Roberta. "She's just having a vision."

Roberta blinked and looked confused for a split second before she shouted, "We have to leave. There are more warriors coming!"

"We should stay and fight," Lox argued but Roberta shook her head.

"There's too many and we won't be able to take them all on—not without any Reviving Water."

"What about my dad?" Emily asked.

Jenkins picked Thomas up. "Where can we go that's safe?"

"We can go to Michella's house," Emily said quickly. "She's home this weekend. She can heal. She lives on Bridge Street."

"I'm going to grab some trainers," Cathy said, running out of the room.

"Okay, I'll take him there. I'll come back as soon as I can," Jenkins said before he teleported with Thomas in his arms.

"Okay let's go. Lox take the kids," Roberta said, grabbing on to Sally and Michael.

"Come on, guys," Lox said, scooping up the sleeping kids. "You all have to hold hands. . . where's Cathy?"

"She went to find her trainers. Go, I'll find her," Emily said running out of the room.

"I'll be quick," Lox promised.

She ran through the house and could hear yells and screams from the Village. She ran to the nearest window and gasped when she saw hundreds of bodies over the floor and more people walking towards the house.

"Cathy!" Emily hollered, running up the stairs. She heard a thud coming from her bedroom and Emily walked slowly towards it. She opened the door carefully and peered into the dark room. "Cathy?"

The windows smashed and two people in white masks soared into the room. Emily yelled and quickly shut the door. She ran down the stairs and into the kitchen, where a frying pan was swung at her head and she ducked just in time.

"Emily?"

"Cathy?"

"I went to get some shoes but I heard a noise."

"There are people in the house," Emily said. "We have to get out."

"What?" Cathy said, looking pale.

Emily opened the kitchen cutlery drawer. In the back was

a sharp knife that they hid from the kids. She handed it to Cathy, who shook as she took it.

"Don't hesitate to use it, okay?"

Cathy nodded, but she was shaking so much that she dropped the knife and it clattered loudly on the floor.

"Did you hear that?" a deep voice said from outside the door.

"Get down," Emily hissed, pulling Cathy's nightgown. They were hidden behind the kitchen island.

Cathy pressed her back against the island, clutching the frying pan to her chest. She closed her eyes and whispered a prayer under her breath. Emily peered out from behind the island and was surprised to see two soldiers in black, walk into the kitchen, holding rifles.

Why were soldiers working for Neci? Emily thought. She held her breath as they crept around the kitchen. Emily opened her hand and formed a small fireball.

One of them walked around the island with their gun aimed and Emily jumped out and shot her fireball, hitting the person in the stomach, so they flew to the other side of the room.

Emily caught eyes with the other warrior and she noticed he had a glazed look, like he wasn't all there. Emily took a step towards him. The soldier raised his rifle and fired at Emily. She jumped up into the air and shouted, "Anyosingh," and the fireball shot through the kitchen wall, making a giant hole, taking the soldier with it.

Emily walked over and grabbed the fallen rifle. She had never held a gun before and it felt heavy and uncomfortable in her hands. Someone grabbed on to her shoulder. Emily swung around and hit the soldier on the chin with the end of the gun, so he staggered backwards.

"Get away from her!" Cathy screamed, whacking the soldier hard across the head with the frying pan until he fell.

Emily broke the gun in half and dumped it on the floor. They walked into the dark living room. Emily looked up the stairs to see if there was anyone there. It was silent.

"Okay, let's go," she whispered. She took a step forward when the windows shattered behind them and more people in black flew into the kitchen.

"Run!" Emily pulled Cathy up the stairs. They ran along the corridor and Cathy yelped as her bare feet scraped against the broken glass. Loud voices surrounded them and footsteps were running below and above them. Emily turned back and bright lights flashed in her eyes.

"This way," Emily said, pulling Cathy down another staircase that led them to the other side of the house.

They ran down the stairs. The wall in front of them burst open and dust flew everywhere. Emily placed her hand over her mouth. They turned and ran the other way. Emily threw a fireball behind her and a second later, there was a huge explosion. They ran up another flight of stairs to an empty corridor and ran quickly across it.

"Out the window!" Emily shouted.

"The window?" Cathy screeched.

"Stop!" a voice commanded as four people appeared in front of them holding rifles. They shone bright lights into their faces and Emily and Cathy squinted as they tried to see.

Emily put a hand in front of her face and stood protectively in front of Cathy. "Did Neci send you?"

"Arms down or we'll shoot."

"Where is she?" Emily yelled.

"We'll give you three seconds to put your arms down. One—"

"Cathy, stay behind me!"

"Two."

Cathy whimpered behind her.

"Three."

Emily ducked her head and put her arms across her face in an 'X' shape bracing herself for the bullets that were going to fly at her. She heard them shoot. She waited. Nothing.

Emily slowly lowered her arms and she watched in disbelief as a bullet aimed straight at her heart was floating in mid-air as if stuck.

"No way," Emily said in disbelief.

"How is that possible?" Cathy asked, looking from behind Emily.

The men looked bewildered before the guns they were holding vibrated and burst into small pieces. They yelled as the metal hit them across the face and the bullets fell nosily to the floor.

Emily and Cathy walked backwards, keeping their eyes on the men, before they bumped into something solid. A familiar blond boy was standing with his hand to his temple and his arm outstretched, facing the men.

"Wesley, Michella—NOW!" Jason yelled before pulling Emily and Cathy down to the ground.

Fireballs shot down the corridor, hitting the men and they fell face down to the floor.

"It's safe," Jason said, helping them both up.

"Thank you," Cathy cried in Jason's arms. "Thank you so much."

Wesley jumped over the fallen men and Emily ran over to him. She fell into his arms and hugged him tight.

"We saw your house on the news. We came straight away," Wesley said. "If anything had happened to you."

"Stop hogging her!" Michella said, pushing Wesley away. She pulled Emily close.

"My dad is sick," Emily said. Her voice broke on every word.

"Oh no, but he'll be fine, I promise," Michella said, with a confidence Emily wished she had.

Emily's eyes widened. "We took him to your house! We have to get you back quick to heal him."

A stampede of footsteps ran across the floor above them. Emily could hear glass shattering.

"They're all over the house," Emily said looking up.

"Come on, let's get out of here," Jason said, heading towards the nearest window. Suddenly, his knees gave way and he caught himself before he hit the floor.

"What's wrong with him?" Cathy asked tearfully.

Michella held on to Jason's hands and closed her eyes.

"Don't," Jason said weakly.

"Ssh, we need you better," Michella said.

Cathy wiped her wet eyes. "Look what they've done to our home."

Emily could sense the warriors getting closer. She walked slowly away from her friends and down the dark corridor, listening to every creak and every breath. There was a few of them walking just as slowly towards her. Emily stopped. She could feel her heart racing and her breathing getting faster and louder. The attack, her dad getting poisoned, getting shot at. Neci. It was always Neci.

Fire.

Emily closed her eyes and felt the heat pour out of her hands. This time she wasn't afraid. She hovered above the ground with her hands in front of her. Two fire flames appeared in the middle of them. She saw a glimpse of a pale-faced man, who gasped when he saw her, before Emily's fire flames soared through the corridor, catching on to the warriors, who screamed as they were devoured by the fire. The floor turned a mix of red and orange and the flames rose up high. Emily watched the flames dance.

"Emily, move!" Michella screeched. She pulled roughly on her arm but she jerked her hand back and held it protectively as if she had been burnt. "We need to go now. The house is on fire!"

"Are you serious?" Wesley yelled back. He broke the window with his elbow and the glass shattered over the floor. Jason stared concerned at Emily.

Michella held on to Cathy and they bent their knees and soared out of the window, up to the clear black sky. The cold air hit Emily's overheated body, cooling her down. From up high, she could see that the fight was far from over. Warriors fighting Legends.

Cathy let out a choking sound before covering her mouth and crying.

Mansions were broken, trees were on fire. There was smoke and bodies everywhere. And then she spotted him, in mid-battle, in the midst of the chaos.

"Is that Julian?" Emily gasped. "We can't leave him."

"You've already fought tonight and Jason's too weak. You need to come back to my house and rest," Michella said.

"I'll help him," Wesley said and Emily looked at him in disbelief.

"Thank you." Emily went to hold his hand but he flinched as their skin touched.

"Why are you so hot?" he questioned, looking at her hands.

"Really, Wesley, you think this is a good time to flirt!" Michella snapped and Wesley stared at her confused.

"Can we go please?" Cathy begged, with tears running down her face.

"I'll stay and help. I'll be fine," Jason said when Michella went to argue.

Emily and Wesley locked eyes.

"Be careful, please," Emily said. "I can't. . . if anything happened to you. . ."

He smiled at her and gently pushed her. "Go."

"Let's go heal your dad," Michella said.

Emily squeezed Cathy tight, praying that they weren't too late.

CHAPTER SEVENTEEN

Aftermath

They landed on Michella's doorstep twenty minutes later. Emily placed Cathy down on the floor and she instantly hugged herself tight, looking up at the sky. She hadn't stopped shaking the entire journey.

"We're safe here," Michella said gently but Cathy didn't respond.

Michella shot Emily a concerned look before opening the front door. Emily winced as she walked. Her right calf was bleeding and covered with cuts. Cathy's feet looked worse. She hadn't complained once about the pain even though her face was deathly white. Cathy gritted her teeth and limped to the living room. Emily hobbled in after her but she couldn't see her dad anywhere.

"Baby," Mrs Kinkle said, holding out her arms for Michella.

"The boys are coming," Michella said as her mum hugged her tight. "We saw Julian Kena from school in the battle."

Emily and Cathy both ran to Sally and hugged her. Sally

leaned back and looked them up and down. "Look at all these cuts!"

"Where's Dad?" Emily asked and Sally shook her head sadly.

"We got here but Michella was gone so they took him to a healer called Seven."

Michella gasped. "I'm sorry. I just saw your house on the news and we just came—"

"It's okay love," Sally said kindly. "You weren't to know. Thomas will be fine. Apparently, Seven is one of the best healers."

"They're in our house," Cathy said, with tears falling down her eyes. "They tried to kill us. They had guns and they shot at Emily. I thought we were going to die."

Sally wiped the tears from Cathy's face. "The important thing is that you're safe. Oh sweetheart."

Cathy collapsed on her shoulder and cried nosily.

"Your leg," Lox said, appearing next to Emily. He bent down and looked closely at it. "Come and sit down."

"Is Roberta with Dad?" Emily asked, not moving.

"I think so."

She wrapped her arms around herself and took a deep breath.

"Emily," Mrs Kinkle said softly. Emily could see her walking towards her through the reflection from the window. "Come, sit down and get warm."

She gently pulled Emily and led her towards the couch. Pete and Warren immediately stood up and looked around like they didn't know what to do with themselves.

Emily suddenly felt so tired. There were too many people

in the room. She felt like her head was buzzing and all she wanted was for everyone to be quiet. A tear fell down her face and then another. Emily sniffed and tried to wipe them away quickly but they were falling faster than she could catch them.

"Here," Michella said, wrapping a blanket around her. She noticed Emily crying and gently pulled her towards her.

"I can't lose him again."

"You won't," Michella said, holding Emily tighter.

It didn't seem possible that her heart could take any more. She had only just got her dad back. The idea of him dying made her heart feel like someone was squeezing it tight. A low moan escaped her mouth.

"Your leg must be hurting loads," Michella said, mis-reading her pain. She held on to Emily's leg who instantly felt the pain disappear.

"Thank you," Emily said.

"I'll go and do Cathy."

"What are you doing?" Cathy panicked when Michella put her hands on her feet and closed her eyes. Cathy looked at Emily bewildered and then a second later, she looked surprised and then relieved. Cathy looked at her feet in amazement. "Thank you."

"Wow, that is some gift," Sally said looking at her in awe.

There was an insistent knocking on the door and Michella jumped up. "That must be the boys." She ran out of the room.

Emily could hear muffled voices and a second later, Wesley and Jason walked into the room with Julian Kena, who had a swollen lip that was bleeding and a huge bump on his forehead.

"Bring him to the kitchen," Pete instructed.

Julian's mum, Tahama, walked with her head down, looking like she had aged years in the last hour. She had pink rollers in her hair and a violent red gash across her cheek.

"Come and take a seat," Sally said, leaving Cathy's side and helping Tahama to the armchair.

"Thank you," Tahama whispered. She clutched Sally's arm tight, surprising her. "Legends Village is ruined. They have destroyed everything. They came in black with guns and were... look what they did to my poor boy."

"We're all safe now," Sally said, holding Tahama.

Lox stormed out of the room.

"Where are you going?" Sally called, but he had already shut the front door.

"Who was that?" Mrs Kinkle asked, walking into the living room.

"Lox," Michella replied. Mrs Kinkle looked like she wanted to say something else, but Michella shook her head.

"Right," Mrs Kinkle began. "I think a good rest will do everyone some good. Now, where to put everyone?"

"Jackie, we couldn't possibly intrude even more," Sally said, standing to her feet. "Michael and I will find a hotel for the kids—"

Mrs Kinkle waved her hand. "Oh, don't be silly! There's plenty of room. Janette and Lenny are away and Mike and Madison are at Wesley's house, so we could surprise them with a party." Mrs Kinkle sighed and continued. "I think that will have to be delayed. Right, the little kids are all sleeping in the spare room. So, Sally, you and Cathy can go in Janette's room, Lox and Michael can go in Lenny's room.

Emily, you bunk up with Michella, and Tahama and Julian in the twin's room."

"What about Jason and Wesley? I want them to stay close," Michella said. "They might need me to heal them."

"Michella, you'll wear yourself out healing everyone!"

"I know, but just in case," Michella said. "Please Mum."

Mrs Kinkle massaged her forehead, "Okay, I'll call their parents. Maybe they can sleep on the couch. The last thing we need is Lorraine getting frantic."

"Just talk to Wesley's grandma," Michella said. "She'll deal with it better."

"I have to get Julian to the hospital," Tahama said standing up but her knees gave way. Sally caught her just before she hit the floor.

"Let's sit you down," Sally said gently.

Tahama reminded Emily of a deflated balloon.

"What he needs is a good night's sleep," Mrs Kinkle said. "Besides, he'll get better treatment with Nurse Hilda. We can take the kids back to Osaki tomorrow. They'll be safer there and you all can stay here until Legends Village is safe."

"Thank you," Sally said looking weary. She rubbed her tired eyes and sighed. "Have you got anything to drink?"

Mrs Kinkle smiled. "I think we could use some rum. Come on Tahama, it will do you good."

Tahama wiped her face with the back of her hand, and with the help of Sally, they followed Mrs Kinkle out of the room.

Michella peered into the corridor and watched them go. "Right, I'm going to heal Julian."

"Michella," Emily said, gripping her arm. "Maybe don't overdo it?"

"I'm fine. You two should go upstairs and rest." She walked out of the room.

Emily stood up on her healed legs. "You did well back at the house."

"I've never been so scared in my life," Cathy said, looking at her with huge blue eyes. "That was Neci's army? Is that what it will be like from now on? People just attacking us?"

She wished that she could tell her that it would get better, but Cathy always knew when she was lying.

"I just want you guys to be safe, so she can't get to you."

"And what about you?" Cathy asked, holding Emily's hand. "You should be safe as well."

"I thought having Dad back would make me feel safer." Emily sniffed, brushing away the tear that ran down her face. "I just. . . I just feel like I have no control over anything, not even my own thoughts."

"You know, once Neci's gone, everything will be perfect. Neci won't be able to hurt you anymore."

They sat in silence for a few minutes and Emily couldn't help but wonder, what was Neci's next move?

"Let's get some rest," Emily eventually said, pulling Cathy up to her feet.

After directing Cathy to Janette's room, Emily walked to Michella's and gently closed the door behind her. Her body ached all over. She rubbed her tense neck, moving her head slowly from side to side. What she needed was a hot bath to soak in, but she didn't want to ask Mrs Kinkle for anything else. She had done so much for them already.

Emily looked around the pretty room and felt an ache for her own one. All their stuff was gone. Every memory of her mother was probably wiped out and now Lox had walked out on them—again.

She quickly undressed, dumping her clothes by the side of Michella's bed. She opened her drawers and found a pair of clean pyjamas. She knew Michella wouldn't mind, so she put them on.

The door opened slightly and Emily shouted over her shoulder, "I borrowed the grey ones."

"It's me."

Emily turned and Wesley was standing by the door. He had a bandage around his left hand and he looked exhausted.

"Where's Michella?"

"She's resting downstairs. Julian's almost healed, but she started to get weak so we told her to stop." He closed the door softly behind him. "How's your dad?"

"Jenkins took him to someone called Seven."

Wesley looked at her surprised. "Seven? I've heard of her. She's a healer. . . an amazing one, but I thought she retired."

"Hopefully she can do something. What happened?" She pointed to his bandaged hand and Wesley smiled and held it up like he had won a prize.

"Punched a guy whose face, I swear, was made of steel."

Emily laughed. "Thank you for helping Julian."

Wesley shrugged like it was no big deal.

Emily reached out for his injured hand and carefully held on to it. She felt a tingle as their skin touched. She wished she could take the pain away from him. She looked up and Wesley was staring at her. He moved closer, so she could see the green and brown in his eyes.

With her other hand, she reached out and softly touched

the side of his face, running her thumb slowly down his cheek. Wesley grabbed her hand and kissed it softly and in that moment, her mind went blank. She forgot about the attack, her dad, Lox—everything but the person in front of her. She wanted everything to pause so she could be in this moment forever.

Wesley sighed, breaking whatever connection they had. "We can't."

Emily pulled her hand out of his grasp. "I know." She sat on Michella's bed and Wesley sat beside her.

"I just wish you had told me... about how you felt about me," Wesley said.

Emily looked down at the beige carpet. "You know I like you."

"But I needed to hear it," Wesley said, reaching forward and lifting up her head. "I needed you to tell me."

"I know," Emily said. "I wish I had."

Wesley smiled sadly. "Shall we get some sleep? Michella's staying with Jason so I'll stay with you... if you want me to?"

"After tonight I'll be glad for the company."

They awoke the next morning with Emily's head on Wesley's chest and Wesley's arm around her. The duvet was sprawled over them. Emily slowly stirred and lifted her head. She rubbed her cheek that had been on the zipper of Wesley's hoodie and she could feel the imprint it had left.

She looked around the room and it took a while to remember why she wasn't in her bedroom. Then it hit her. The attack last night, her dad being poisoned and Lox disappearing. She glanced at Wesley, who was sleeping with his mouth slightly open.

Emily swung her legs and got out of the bed. She leaned over and pulled the duvet over him and Wesley sighed in his sleep. It dawned on her that despite everything that had happened, she didn't have any nightmares last night.

She could hear people talking downstairs and when she walked into the living room, she saw the kids watching a cartoon whilst eating pancakes. Cathy was sitting on the couch and she looked up when she saw Emily.

"Did you sleep well?" she asked.

"Yeah, you?"

Cathy shrugged.

"Where's everyone else?" Emily asked.

"Michella and Jason are in the kitchen, Julian is still asleep, the parents are hungover and I'm not sure where Wesley is," Cathy said.

"Oh, he's upstairs in Michella's room," Emily said.

Slowly it dawned on Cathy and her smile made Emily laugh.

"Don't start!" Emily said.

"Did you kiss?" Cathy sang.

"No!"

"Yeah right."

"I swear nothing happened. Any news on Dad?" Emily asked.

Cathy shook her head. "But Lox came by, well, I think it was him because there are bags in the corridor from the house."

"You're joking," Emily said, hurrying into the corridor

where she saw bin bags, piled on top of each other. She bent down and opened one up and took out one of James's t-shirts. She peered through the rest of the bags and it was an assortment of clothes and shoes. They still looked in good condition.

"Where did he go now?" Emily asked, walking back into the living room.

"Maybe to Thomas? I haven't seen Roberta or Jenkins yet, but they'll have to come get their kids, right?" Cathy asked.

"Yeah they'll be back. Are you going to be okay with me staying at Osaki?"

Cathy hugged herself. "I just wish Thomas was here to protect us."

"Lox will be around."

"I just wish he didn't always run off," Cathy moaned.

"Me too." Emily waited a beat. "Is it just me that thinks he's mental to have gone back to that house by himself?"

"We know Lox is unpredictable. I can't believe we're homeless. . . and all my makeup is gone." Cathy winked to show she was joking and Emily smiled and shook her head.

"I'm going to check on my friends."

"I'll keep the kids glued to the TV. At least they seem unaffected by what happened."

Emily walked to the kitchen to see Jason flipping pancakes and Michella cradling a cup of tea in her hands.

"Hungry?" Jason asked.

"Starving," Emily said truthfully, sliding into the seat next to Michella, who yawned.

"I'm so exhausted. Do you know when we're leaving?"

Emily shook her head.

Jason handed Emily a plate stacked with blueberry pancakes. "That was such a crazy night. I haven't seen Wesley."

"He was still sleeping," Emily said, biting into the pancakes. "Mmmm, this is so good. How's Julian?"

"He's alright. I just think the sooner we get to Osaki, the better," Jason said.

"Did you see Lox?"

Michella blew into her hot tea. "I haven't—oh morning, Julian."

Julian was hovering by the doorway looking better than the night before. Emily pulled out a chair for him and he smiled gratefully. He walked slowly over to them, lowering himself gently into the seat.

"Some night," he said. There was a slight bruise on his forehead.

"Did you recognise anyone?" Emily asked but Julian shook his head.

"They didn't care that we were kids. They would have killed us if they had the chance," Julian said.

"Neci's a coward," Michella spat and they looked at her. "If she wants to kill us, she should come and do it herself. Not send her army and poison Thomas to make us weaker. She shouldn't underestimate us." She pushed back her chair and stood up. "I'm going to wake up the parents. We need to get back to school and start training."

Emily bit another piece of her pancake before it dawned on her that Michella could go to her bedroom. She stood up abruptly and the boys looked at her.

"I left something upstairs," she said hurriedly before rushing out of the room.

The bedroom door was still closed and she sighed in relief. She had no idea what Michella would say if she realised Wesley was in her room with her. It wasn't like they were doing anything, but Emily knew how it could look. Emily opened the door and Wesley was on his side still sound asleep. She smiled and gently closed the door behind her. . .

And screamed when she saw Lox standing against the wall with his arms crossed and a black coat over his shoulder.

Wesley jumped up awake, kicking the duvet off. "What's going on?" He looked wildly around the room. "Oh." His eyes landed on Lox. "Hi."

"You scared me," Emily said with her hand on her chest, staring at Lox. "Where have you been?"

"So this is what you do when I'm not around?" Lox asked, looking from Emily to Wesley. He had a bandage wrapped around his arm and dark circles under his eyes.

"We didn't do anything," Wesley said, shaking his head. "We just fell asleep."

"In the same bed," Lox said in a stern voice.

Wesley gulped and Emily looked down at the floor.

"Nothing happened," she mumbled.

They stood in an uncomfortable silence.

"I'm going to see Dad. Do you want to come?" he finally said.

"What? Yes, of course," Emily said. "When are we going?"

"Now," Lox said. "I'm sure Wesley won't mind telling everyone where we've gone."

"No, not at all," Wesley said jumping out of the bed.

Lox looked up to the ceiling, muttering something under his breath. Emily noticed that his fists were clenched. Wesley must have to because he pulled on his jeans over his basketball shorts in record time.

"We'll wait for you before we go to Osaki," he said to Emily before rushing out of the room.

She could feel the anger radiating off Lox and she nervously ran her fingers through her thick hair.

"Nothing happened," she repeated. "Stop being all big brother about it."

Lox looked at her from the side of his eye and Emily stared at him defiantly. He opened his mouth, but instead of speaking, he let out a deep sigh. He held out his hand. She grabbed hold of it and they both teleported.

CHAPTER EIGHTEEN

Seven

The sharp cold hit her first. Emily gritted her teeth as the strong wind blew around her. Lox handed her the black coat and she quickly put it on over Michella's pyjamas, fumbling with the buttons.

They seemed to be in the middle of nowhere. All she could see were miles and miles of fields. Lox looked unaffected by the cold in his light leather jacket and he pointed up ahead before he began to walk.

Emily followed directly behind him, using his body as a shield against the wind. She was confused as to where her dad could possibly be. She wanted to ask Lox but the wind was howling nosily.

Suddenly she saw a house amongst the trees. It looked tiny, like it could be blown away at any moment, but what she found strange was that the trees around the house were swaying dangerously but they never touched the house. Emily remembered seeing her dad train and the way nature reacted to it. It wasn't the wind. This was someone's energy.

The closer they got to the house, the harder it was to walk. Even Lox had to shield his face and push through. Emily wrapped her arms around his waist and allowed him to lead the way through the energy field. Up close, the house looked ordinary. The door even had a little knocker in the shape of a woodpecker.

Lox reached and pulled it back before releasing it. Emily wondered how anyone would even hear it over the noise but when the woodpecker's beak touched the door, a loud 'dong' echoed throughout the house and four warriors dressed in black appeared around them, each holding a fireball in their hand. Emily caught her breath.

"State your name," one barked.

"It's okay," a soft voice carried from inside the house. "Bring them in."

The fireballs disappeared. One of the warriors opened the door and Lox glared at him before walking through. Emily hurried behind him. As soon as the door shut, the sound of the howling wind was gone.

"Am I glad to see you two," a tired looking Roberta said, grabbing them in a big hug. "How are you feeling? How are my boys?"

"Good, everyone is fine," Emily said, looking around the house. Everything was white, with splashes off green from the huge plants in the corner.

"How is he?" Lox asked when she let them go.

She shook her head. "He's through there." She pointed at the door behind them and Lox immediately went to it.

"Is he dying?" Emily asked in a quiet voice.

"No, sweetheart," Roberta said holding on to her hands.

"He is getting better but very slowly. Seven is doing her best."

Emily nodded but her eyes were burning. A sound escaped her and she felt like she was choking.

"Hey, hey, it's okay," Roberta said rubbing her hands. "Come on, let's see him."

But Emily couldn't move. She didn't want to see her dad lying there helpless.

"He's fighting it and hearing your voice will help him. Have faith, Emily," Roberta said gently.

She led Emily though the door. Emily peered anxiously around Roberta to see a man that looked like her father lying on a bed in the middle of the room. His skin was grey and his eyes were closed. There was a breathing mask attached to his face connected to a monitor that beeped every few seconds.

A slim lady with a maroon headscarf was standing over him with her hands on his torso, whispering something under her breath. Lox was sitting beside her with his hands clasped tight together like he was praying.

Emily picked up Thomas's hand. It was dry and rough.

Seven glanced at her but didn't stop chanting. She sounded like she was saying a prayer in Arabic. Emily studied her and was surprised to see how youthful she looked. She had clear light brown skin and huge almond eyes with long black eyelashes. She was wearing a white tunic and white loose bottoms. Emily could see dark hair peeping out from underneath her headscarf.

A few minutes later, Seven stood to her feet and without a word, she left the room. They watched her leave and Emily pointed at the door that slammed behind her.

"Where is she going? She's meant to be helping him."

"She's been trying to cure Thomas since we arrived," Roberta said rubbing her eyes. "We don't know why it's not working."

"Dad, come on, please wake up," Emily said urgently, squeezing his hand.

She didn't know what she expected when a great healer like Seven wasn't getting any results, but she was still disappointed when Thomas didn't react.

"You look exhausted," Lox said gently, evacuating his chair and leading Roberta to it. "Where's Jenkins?"

"At Legends Village," Roberta said, pushing her hair off her face. "They're clearing it up. They're going to start rebuilding it and someone had to be there to check our houses. He left a few minutes before you guys showed up."

The door opened and Seven appeared holding a jar with a clear liquid in it. She handed the jar to Emily. "Smell."

Emily looked at it wearily but took a sniff. "I can't smell anything."

Seven smiled but it didn't reach her eyes. "Exactly, but if you were to drink it, you would end up like your father." She screwed on the lid. "That is Rainium. Someone put that in the Reviving Water that Thomas drank."

Roberta gasped and Lox's mouth dropped.

"But you can cure him right?" Emily asked.

"I don't have the cure," Seven said, looking at the floor.

"What?" Lox shouted standing to his feet.

"I. . . I don't understand," Emily said looking from Seven to Roberta. "They said you're the healer and you could save him. You have to save him!"

"I'm sorry. I can't do it," Seven said and Emily's hand flew to her mouth.

Lox yelled and punched the wall creating a huge hole and Roberta buried her face in her hands. Emily looked at her unconscious father and all the years she had missed out.

He will never wake up.

Emily's shoulders shook and her chest heaved as her eyes welled up. She felt a light touch on her shoulder.

"I can't do it, but there is someone who can," Seven said. "The only person with the cure."

"Who is it?" Lox demanded walking up to her.

Seven shook her head gravely. "He has been missing for months and no one knows where he is. Professor Elwood can make the antidote. He is the one who can save Thomas."

"But he could be anywhere!" Emily protested. "He could already be dead. He could be—"

She stopped abruptly when she saw Roberta. Lox and Seven noticed too. She was staring into space with a vacant expression on her face. She was completely still as if she was frozen. Emily looked at Lox who put a finger to his lips. They sat silently as Roberta was trapped in her vision. A few seconds later she blinked and took in a deep breath. When she exhaled, a smile spread across her face.

"I saw the Professor chained up in a room but he's alive." Roberta looked at Lox. "Remember Blade covered his house in ice? So I think the Professor is with Neci."

"She's not in any of the usual spots," Lox said. "Even the farmhouse is empty."

Roberta groaned.

"You went to find Neci?" Emily asked in disbelief.

"After she poisons my dad, damn straight I went to find her," Lox snapped.

Roberta began to pace the room. "We need to find her quickly, before she does anything to Professor Elwood." She stopped suddenly. "Seven, how long does he have?"

Seven sighed. "It's hard to say. He is healing because of me, but the poison is attacking him also. As long as I keep fighting against it, I can keep him stable, but we need the antidote as soon as possible."

"Where could Neci be?" Roberta punched her fist in her hand.

"She doesn't have a secret hideaway or anything?" Emily asked staring at Lox.

Lox shook his head.

"It's just weird that you've been around her for so long and you don't know where she could be."

"If I knew her every move, don't you think I would have said something by now?"

Emily shrugged and Lox gripped her arm.

"Hey!" she cried.

"You listen to me, yeah. I came back for you! I'm not protecting Neci, okay? At some point you need to accept that I'm on your team."

"I know. . . sorry," Emily said, shaking her head.

Seven coughed gently making the siblings jump. "If I may? It would be best if you both go back to Osaki. There's not much you can do for your father except train. I will do my best, but you must support each other. Remember, we all have a common enemy."

Emily hung her head. She felt like she was losing control

of everything and the one person keeping her dad alive had to listen to her and Lox shouting at each other.

"I'm sorry," Emily said at the same time as Lox.

"Seven, has Channel 47 announced anything about the attack?" Lox asked.

Seven turned and walked towards a door that Emily didn't notice when they arrived. She looked over her shoulder and said, "Come," before opening the door.

"I'll stay with him," Roberta said.

Emily glanced at Lox before following her. They entered a lounge that had beige couches, white flowers and a TV attached to the wall. Seven was fiddling with the buttons on the television.

"I'm sorry, I never use this room."

The TV came to life and Emily gasped when she saw Legends Village. The mansions were gone, the trees were burnt and dead, and there was a greyness that seemed to float around the Village, taking away its beauty. The news reporter pointed to a building and was saying something into his microphone.

"Oh dear," Seven said, fiddling again with the television and the volume blared in the room.

"—we don't know where the Knight family are," the news reporter said. "As of yet, no warrior has been charged for the attack in Legends Village. Witnesses say that the attackers came dressed all in black but there was no sighting of Neci when the attack took place. There have been six casualties and fourteen people taken to hospital."

"Six," Lox repeated in dismay. "I wish they would say their names."

"People will ask about Dad at school," Emily said.

"No one can know," Seven stressed, looking from Emily to Lox. "Tell them he has left the country to recruit warriors. The only thing we need to find out is where Neci is keeping Professor Elwood."

"Wait—doesn't the Professor's daughter go to Osaki? Hallie-Elizabeth?" Lox said.

"Hayley-Elizabeth," Emily corrected. "And I don't think she will know where her dad is."

"But she'll want to help find him, right?" Lox asked.

Emily looked at Seven, who nodded. "It's worth befriending her."

"I'll try," Emily said. "I'll find out what she knows."

"How was he?" Sally asked, when Emily and Lox returned.

Everyone was in the living room waiting anxiously.

Emily shook her head sadly. "Seven can't heal him."

"What? Why not?" Michella demanded.

"She needs an antidote and guess who has it?" Emily said.

"Neci?" Wesley asked.

"Sort of," Lox replied. "Professor Elwood has the cure and we think Neci has the Professor."

"You're kidding me," Jason said, putting his head in his hands.

"I can't believe this is happening," Cathy said tearfully. "What do we do?"

Lox glanced at Emily. "We thought it would be a good idea if Emily befriends Professor Elwood's daughter. Maybe she knows something about this antidote. We can't let her know that Dad is sick but if we knew where his lab was, maybe there's a clue. . ."

"And what if she knows nothing?" Sally asked, rising from her seat. "And we don't find the Professor, then what happens?"

Lox fell silent.

"We can't afford to think like that," Emily said, glaring at Sally. "He is not allowed to die and leave us!"

"I know, honey, but—"

"No!" Emily yelled. "We will find the Professor, he will heal Dad and then we will take care of Neci. Whatever it takes—we'll do it." With that she stormed out of the room. She walked down the corridor and leaned against the wall, holding her hand to her chest, forcing herself to breath slowly.

"How long does he have before he dies?" she heard Mrs Kinkle ask.

"Seven couldn't tell us, but she's fighting the poison and the poison is fighting her. One of them is going to win," Lox said.

People were talking over each other and Emily strained to hear what was being said. Someone was racing up the stairs and Emily looked up at the ceiling as the footsteps walked above her.

"I have some contacts I'm going to chase up to see if they know where Neci currently is," Lox said. "Jenkins and Roberta are tied up, Mr Davon is helping to get more warriors on board. I spoke to Roberta and I'm going to run the elite team but we agreed that Emily will be in charge when I'm not there."

"Don't you think that's too much for her?" Julian asked.

"Maybe, but it will be good for her," Lox said. "I just need to find a way to tell her."

Cathy snorted. "Good luck with that."

Late that afternoon, when everyone was upstairs packing to return back to school and Emily was seated alone at the kitchen table with a lukewarm hot chocolate in front of her, Lox came to sit opposite her.

"I already know," Emily said and Lox raised his eyebrows. "I overheard earlier and I'm not doing it."

Lox leaned back in his chair and smirked. "Why?"

"I'm not a good leader," Emily said simply. "There's no way I can help them with their powers and teach them how to battle. I don't even know how to help myself half the time. My training with Dad was. . . limited. I don't want to be responsible for them. If they die, it will be on my hands. So count me out."

Lox leaned forward, resting his chin on his clasped hands. "You have no idea what you're capable of, do you?" he said softly.

Before Emily could respond, Lox placed his hands on the table and pushed himself up.

"I'll train you. I'll help as much as I can with the elite team, but there will be times when I'll be away. We need allies. When I'm gone, you will make the decisions." He held up his hand as she went to argue. "If someone isn't working hard enough during training, you tell them off. If someone is disobedient, you sort it. You will make bad decisions but also great ones. As long as you do what you think is right, it will work out. That's what a leader does."

He walked behind her, leaned down and kissed her on the forehead. "I'll always have your back."

He grabbed her cup of hot chocolate and swallowed it down in one gulp.

"Hey!" Emily said, when he placed it back on the table.

"Get your stuff. We're leaving for Osaki in ten."

CHAPTER NINETEEN

Michella

Emily arrived at Osaki with a suitcase full of what was left off her things. After a heated discussion with Sally, it was decided that Emily would stay at Osaki until further notice, but Emily was livid. She wanted to stay with her family, who were going to live with the Kinkles for the time being. The idea of being away from them right now gave her an anxiousness that wouldn't go away. But she was outnumbered. Lox, however, was allowed to come and go as he pleased, which irritated her.

"Can I speak to you?" Lox asked Emily. "In private?" he added when Michella, Wesley and Jason stopped as well.

"We'll catch you in a bit." Jason waved and Emily watched her friends walk towards the front doors.

Michella entered Osaki first so she didn't notice the fourth year girls that pounced on Wesley and Jason, touching them on their arms, looking sympathetic. Emily scoffed. Her house was burnt down, not theirs!

"I'll be gone for a few days," Lox said.

"Where are you going?" Emily asked, wishing he would stay with her.

"Roberta, Jenkins and I are going to speak to some warriors abroad. Hopefully they'll help us against Neci, but first I'm going to the Village to check about the house. Then I'll get security for the Kinkles and check in on Dad." Lox rubbed his face looking exhausted.

"Why don't you rest for a bit?" Emily suggested, but Lox shook his head.

"Find Hayley-Elizabeth and see if she has any clues about Dad but be smooth about it. We don't want her getting suspicious about you asking."

Emily nodded before she dropped her suitcase and wrapped her arms around him. Lox stumbled back. It took him a few seconds to hug her back, squeezing her tight.

"I'll see you soon," Lox promised.

When Emily walked into Osaki, she saw Michella standing in front of Jason with her arms crossed while he was looking sheepishly at the floor. Michella poked him hard in the chest before walking into the dining hall with Wesley behind her.

"Let me guess—she wasn't a fan of the girl club around you?" Emily said.

"Definitely not."

"Hey, Emily!" a voice called, disrupting them.

Harmony Loving-Dale ran towards them with her blonde hair in twists. To Emily's surprise, Harmony grabbed her in a tight hug. When she pulled away, she looked at Emily sadly with her huge blue eyes.

"I'm so sorry to hear about your house."

"Thanks," Emily said, looking away. A wave of guilt washed over her. Just the night before she had fallen asleep in Wesley's arms.

"You guys are so brave! I don't know what I would have done if that happened to me. Where are you staying?" Harmony asked.

"I'll be at Osaki, but my family are at Michella's for now. Hopefully it won't take them long to re-build everything."

"And how's your dad?" Emily froze and Harmony looked at Jason uncertainly. "I mean with everything that's happened?"

"Oh, he's fine. . . I mean not fine," Emily said when Harmony frowned. "He's, you know, just dealing with it the best he can."

"Right. . . so is he here today?"

"Not today," Jason said, placing a hand on Emily's shoulder. Emily felt her eyes welling up and quickly wiped them away.

Harmony opened her mouth and then closed it. Emily could tell she wanted to ask more, but Harmony being Harmony simply smiled and said, "I'm here if you ever need to talk."

"Yeah, thanks," Emily said, forcing a smile. As soon as Harmony was gone, Emily sighed. "Is it going to be like this all day?"

"Worse," Jason said. He linked arms with her. "Come on, let's get some food."

Emily would have thought that years of being under scrutiny would have prepared her for the looks she would get in the dining hall, but it didn't. Every move she made, she could feel hundreds of people watching her. She wanted to get up and go to her room but she knew that would make her more of a topic of discussion. Students she didn't know came up to offer their sympathies about her house, followed closely by 'where's Thomas and Lox?' Emily kept glancing at the teachers who were at the front of the hall. It was strange and unsettling to not have Mr Davon watching over them.

By the end of the meal, she had a throbbing headache and couldn't wait to bury herself under the covers.

"Emily," Michella said nudging her.

Emily stopped massaging her temples and followed Michella's gaze. Hayley-Elizabeth Elwood had walked in late to dinner. She looked how Emily felt. Her hair was unbrushed, her training kit looked as if it was tied up in a hurry and her face looked paler than usual. She sat beside one of her friends and they bent their heads in a whispered conversation.

"What's her friend's name?" Emily asked.

"I think Pete and Warren know her. I'll find out," Michella said. "Why was she late to dinner?"

"I wonder what she knows," Emily said, watching Hayley-Elizabeth carefully.

"Surely she can't know where her dad is. She would tell someone wouldn't she?" Michella said.

"Depends what Neci's offering," Emily replied.

"What you lot talking about?" Wesley asked, with a mouthful of ice cream.

"So gross," Michella said, pulling a face.

Wesley smirked.

"Look at Hayley-Elizabeth," Emily said nodding towards her. "We were wondering why she looks all messed up and who's she talking to."

"Nia Idris," Jason said. They all turned to look at him. "Don't ask how I know that."

"Oh, I want to know," Michella said, glaring at him.

Jason blushed. "She asked me out a few weeks ago."

"Bro!" Wesley said, going to pat him on the back.

Michella hit his hand away. "Don't 'bro' him!"

Emily kept her eyes on Hayley-Elizabeth and Nia, and as if she could feel her staring, Hayley-Elizabeth turned her head and glared back at Emily.

Emily awoke to voices whispering around her. She opened her eyes and she was in the Ogragon girls bedroom. The bright sunlight came seeping through the giant window by her bed, giving the illusion that it was a warm day, when in fact it was freezing. To her right she could hear Violet Hijen say, "But how do we ask her?"

"Just be subtle," Nicky Johansen hissed back.

"I am subtle!" Violet shrieked.

"Ssh," all the girls said.

Emily sat up and instantly the room fell silent. She rubbed the sleep out of her eyes.

"Hey," she said croakily.

"Oh hey," Sydney John said, glancing at Violet. "How are you feeling?"

Emily shrugged. "Okay." There was an awkward silence. "Girls, if you want to ask me something then just ask."

Suddenly they were shouting over one another as they ran to Emily and squeezed themselves on her bed.

"Neci burnt down your house?" Lisa Fowler asked. "How did you escape?"

"Are you homeless?" Violet asked, tilting her head to the side. "Ow!"

Nicky had elbowed her side. "No dummy, she's rich! How can she be homeless?"

Violet rolled her eyes. "Err, because her house was burnt down."

"Hey!" Sydney said, clapping her hands, and the girls looked at her surprised. "Be more sensitive." She smiled at Emily. "We're just glad you're okay."

"Of course we are!" Violet said. "And Lox too. . . where is he by the way?"

"So subtle," Nicky said, shooting her a look.

Emily looked past the girls and noticed that two people were missing.

"Where's Michella and Daisy?"

The girls shrugged their shoulders.

"The Daily Steward said that Neci set fire to your house," Sarah asked, with her eyes wide. "Is it true?"

"We think she sent her army to do it but she wasn't there herself," Emily said.

"So what happened?" Violet sat on the edge of Emily's bed with her legs crossed, leaning forward.

Emily explained about that night, trying to remember as much of it as she could. By the end the girls were looking at her horror-stricken.

"Damn Emily, you're so brave." Nicky said.

"You could have died," Sarah said, grabbing her hand.

Emily squeezed it back. "I'm fine, we're all—" She wanted

to say they were all fine, but at that point all she could see was her dad lying still in Seven's house. "We will be fine," she eventually said.

They got dressed for breakfast and Emily kept glancing at Michella's bed wondering where she had got to.

She walked into the Ogragon living room and Wesley was sitting in an armchair, bent over, writing on a piece of paper.

"Morning," Emily said, sitting beside him.

"Where's Michella?" Wesley demanded. He flicked the piece of paper, which Emily could now see was their Meditation essay. "She told me to meet her here before breakfast so she could help me with this."

"I don't know. I woke up and she wasn't there. Maybe she forgot."

Wesley looked at her bewildered. "When does Michella ever forget about homework?"

"Good point," Emily mumbled. "She'll be at breakfast. Where's Jason?"

"He went down already." Wesley touched his rumbling stomach. "I'll finish this later." He stuffed the essay in his bag and they walked down to the dining hall together. "How are you feeling?"

"You know. . ." Emily shrugged and Wesley nodded.

They walked into the noisy dining hall to find Jason at their usual table, eating cereal whilst reading the sports section of the newspaper. Michella was nowhere to be seen.

"Hey," Emily said, sliding beside him.

"Morning," Jason said, smiling at her. He looked over her shoulder. "Where's Michella?"

"That's what I want to know," Wesley said, grabbing a piece of toast. "She was meant to help me with my homework."

"She wasn't in the bedroom when I woke up," Emily said, pouring herself a cup of tea.

Jason glanced at them both. "Do you think she's okay?"

Emily nodded. "Yeah, she's probably with her brothers or something."

"No, she's not." Jason pointed at the table on the other side of the room where Warren and Pete Kinkle were having a mini food fight with their friends with no Michella in sight.

"Now I'm freaking out," Emily said, looking around the room. "Do you think something happened to her?"

"Li whoa," Wesley said with a mouth full of toast.

"Huh?"

He swallowed. "Like what?"

"I don't know," Emily said, standing to her feet. "But something feels off. I'm going to look for her."

"Yeah, I'll come," Jason said, pushing back his chair.

They looked at Wesley who hadn't moved.

"I'm coming, I'm coming," he said, buttering another piece of toast.

They hurried out of the dining hall and stood by the giant grandfather clock.

"Maybe she felt ill and went to the sick bay?" Jason suggested.

"Let's go check—hold on, wait." Emily ran back to the dining hall and peered in. She couldn't see Daisy Atam anywhere.

"Daisy wasn't in bed either and she's not at breakfast," Emily said as they walked out of the double doors. "Michella might be helping her with something."

"It better not be her homework," Wesley muttered.

Emily shielded her eyes from the bright sun and looked around the grounds but it was practically empty. At a far distance, she could see something yellow.

"Should we split up?" Jason asked.

Emily squinted her eyes as the yellow thing moved closer. It was someone running. Someone with blonde hair.

"Daisy?" Emily called. Without hesitation she ran towards her with Jason and Wesley on her heels.

As they got closer, Emily saw that it was definitely Daisy Atam. Her face was bright red and her signature pigtails were coming out of their hair bands. She ran straight to Emily and grabbed her arms. She looked close to tears.

"What the—" Wesley said, looking at her up and down.

"I saw them! She took her!" Daisy said, gripping Emily hard.

"Who?"

Daisy held her hands to her head. "They were arguing but I couldn't hear everything. Michella said your name." She looked straight at Jason, who jerked his head back.

"What? Arguing with who?" Jason asked.

"Professor Elwood's daughter!"

"Daisy, listen to me," Emily said gently. She held on to Daisy's hands. "You need to calm down and tell us what happened."

"Remember how Roshi taught us in Meditation class to breath when we're stressed?" Wesley said. He inhaled deeply and exhaled with a loud sigh. "Come on, try it."

Daisy took in a small inhale.

"Bigger," Wesley instructed. "Do it with me."

Daisy's chest rose and fell. Emily gently brushed away the

hair that was stuck to Daisy's forehead. Emily was trying her best to stay clam even though her heart was racing. Daisy, who always walked with a bounce in her step, looking scared made Emily nervous.

"Thank you," Daisy said to Wesley, who shrugged like it was no big deal. "I didn't want to wake the girls in our room so I was catching up on some homework by the koi pond. I wasn't there long when I saw Michella. I was about to call out to her but I realised she was walking away from Professor Elwood's daughter—what's her name again?"

"Hayley-Elizabeth," Jason said.

"Yeah, so Hayley-Elizabeth was holding her arm and shouting at Michella. I thought she was going to ignore her, but then Michella stopped walking and shouted back at her and that's when I heard your name." She glanced at Jason. "Then Haley-Elizabeth went and grabbed Michella's hand and placed it on her arm and held it there. I couldn't see what was happening so I started packing my bag to see if Michella was okay but then Hayley-Elizabeth was looking at her arm like. . . there was something special about it. The next second, Hayley-Elizabeth and Michella disappeared."

"They teleported?" Wesley gasped.

"Yeah and I was just running up to the school to tell Laton Chin. Why would she teleport her? We're not allowed to use our powers outside of lessons. And why would she shout your name?"

"I can only think that Michella was annoyed about her mate Nia asking me out," Jason said.

"Okay, listen to me," Emily said gently. "Don't say a word to anyone."

"What?" Daisy said bewildered. "Shouldn't I report it to a teacher?"

"Not yet," Emily said quickly. "I want to talk to Nia."

Daisy let out a small whimper. "Do you think Michella's okay?"

"She better be," Jason said fiercely before Emily could respond.

"She will be," Wesley said defiantly.

"Go get some breakfast," Emily said, guiding Daisy towards the school with one hand on her back. "We've got this. Trust me."

Daisy nodded weakly. "Let me know if there's anything I can do."

"Just don't tell—not yet," Emily said and Daisy nodded.

They watched her walk back to the school. Jason looked like he was ready to fight someone, Wesley buried his face in his hands and Emily breathed in deeply, trying to calm down her racing heart. She wasn't sure if she was angry or scared but every second counted in getting Michella back.

"Did you see Nia at breakfast?" Emily asked the boys.

"I didn't notice," Wesley said walking back towards the double doors.

"If she's there, we need a plan. We can't just walk into the dining room and grab her," Emily said.

"Just say we need to talk to her outside," Wesley replied.

"Do you think she'll know that we know?"

"WHO CARES!" Jason suddenly roared making them jump. "I'm giving her one chance to tell us the truth."

"Jas, cool it," Wesley said.

"If anything has happened to her," Jason said through gritted teeth.

"We'll find Michella before anything can happen to her," Wesley said. "You need to calm down."

Jason slumped over as if all of his energy had disappeared. "What if this is Neci?"

Emily knew it had something to do with Neci because she had Hayley-Elizabeth's father captive but hearing it aloud made Emily feel like she wanted to throw up.

"Look, let me do the talking with Nia," Wesley said, looking from one to the other. "In fact, you both go wait by the big oak tree."

"Are you mad?"

"No way!"

"If she sees either of you, she won't talk," Wesley snapped and they fell silent. "You look like you're going to murder someone." He looked at Emily. "And knowing you and your lack of control half the time, you probably will. I'll bring her over and I'll do the talking, okay?"

"Cool," Jason said harshly.

Wesley raised his eyebrows at Emily who tutted and crossed her arms, hating the fact that he was right.

"I won't be long."

Emily watched him run towards the school before disappearing inside. If Neci had Michella, she had no idea how they would get her away from her, or if they even could. Even the idea of being so close to Neci gave Emily chills.

"Come on," Jason said, scuffing his foot on the floor. "If he sees us standing here, he's going to be annoyed."

They walked in silence to the oak tree. Emily ran her

fingers through her hair. *Where was Neci?* Lox had said she wasn't at the farmhouse, wherever that was.

"We have to tell Roberta," Emily said but then she groaned. "She's gone away for a few days with Lox and Jenkins."

"As soon as that girl tells us where they've gone I'm going to get Michella," Jason declared.

"But Jas—"

"You don't have to go," Jason snapped, making Emily recoil. "But my girlfriend is in danger and I'm not going to leave her."

"We love her, too," Emily argued. "You're acting like we don't care. If this is Neci, we need more people. This isn't a suicide mission."

Jason glared at her. "No one's here for us! Mr Davon, Thomas, Lox, Jenkins, Roberta—they're all gone!"

Emily fell silent.

Jason gasped. "Is that Hayley-Elizabeth?"

CHAPTER TWENTY

Hayley-Elizabeth

Emily turned around and could see Wesley walking beside Nia and Hayley-Elizabeth, whose arm he held in a tight grip. It looked as if he was pulling her forward. As they got closer, Emily could see how scared she looked.

Hayley-Elizabeth had a massive scar on her left cheek that was oozing blood on to her white training kit. Nia was playing nervously with her hands.

"Where is she?" Jason asked Hayley-Elizabeth, who unsuccessfully tried to release her arm from Wesley's grip. She stared back at Jason with hard eyes.

"Where is she?" Jason repeated, taking a step towards her.

"Hayley, just tell them!" Nia yelled, looking close to tears.

Instead, Hayley-Elizabeth turned away from Jason and looked at the floor with her mouth set. Emily stepped in front of Jason so she was face to face with her. Hayley-Elizabeth looked up. Her bottom lip was trembling.

"What did you do with Michella? I'll give you one chance to tell me the truth."

Hayley-Elizabeth gulped. "I was trying to save my dad," she said in a small voice.

Emily frowned. "What's that got to do with her?"

She stayed silent. Emily was about to ask again but she saw Wesley subtly shaking his head. He mouthed, "Wait."

"I was trading her for my dad," Hayley-Elizabeth eventually said. "I saw what Michella could do during your brother's training session. I saw her heal you and I know Neci likes warriors with special gifts."

"You took her to Neci!" Emily yelled and before she could think, she charged at Hayley-Elizabeth dragging her to the floor, where she punched her hard across the face. A dark bruise instantly appeared on her jaw. Emily drew back her arm and Wesley grabbed it.

"Stop!" Wesley yelled. "Help me, Jason!"

It took both of them to get Emily off. Students walking to their next class, nudged each other excitedly. A few started to run towards them to get a closer look at the fight.

Emily was breathing heavily as the boys held her back. Nia ran to Hayley-Elizabeth's side and gently pulled her up. Hayley-Elizabeth was crying.

"I just want my dad back. I just miss him so much."

"We're on the same side," Wesley hissed, glancing up at the crowd that was drawing closer to them. "You don't think we want the Professor back too?"

"I'm sorry."

"I need to get her to the sick bay," Nia said, wrapping her arm around her waist and Hayley-Elizabeth leaned on her.

"Where did you take her?" Jason roared.

"I'm so sorry," Hayley-Elizabeth cried with tears running down her eyes.

"Where is she?" Emily yelled. "Just tell us."

"The farmhouse," Wesley said. He shook his head looking confused. "Did I just say that?"

Hayley-Elizabeth frowned. "How do you know that?"

"I-I don't know," Wesley said to himself. He rubbed his hand over his head.

"Is she there?" Jason asked and Hayley-Elizabeth nodded. She took a sharp intake of breath and clutched her jaw.

"They can't be," Emily said, glancing at Wesley, who kept shaking his head. "My brother checked."

"They're underneath it," Wesley said.

Nia glared at him. "How do you do know that? Are you working for Neci?" she demanded.

"Don't be an idiot!" Jason shouted.

"Well how does he know then?" Nia demanded, pointing at Wesley.

Emily and Jason glanced at each other. Emily had no idea how Wesley knew this information or what was wrong with him. He was walking back and forth, muttering under his breath and shaking his head.

"Wes. . . you okay?" Jason asked, placing a hand on his shoulder and Wesley jumped.

"What?" he asked confused. "You're talking at the same time."

"Who is?" Emily asked bewildered.

Wesley shook his head aggressively in response.

"Look, she's told you everything," Nia said, shooting Wesley a wary look. "I have to take her to Nurse Hilda."

"She better have," Jason said, staring Hayley-Elizabeth up and down.

With the help of Nia, Hayley-Elizabeth slowly walked away, with a small crowd watching them.

"What is up with you?" Emily hissed, rounding on Wesley. "You're acting so weird."

"I heard her. Loud in my head," Wesley said slowly.

"Who?"

"Michella." His large, hazel eyes were filled with worry and Jason gasped. "How is that possible?"

"Emily?" Julian Kena ran past the crowd that were wandering off. "What happened?"

Jason shot Emily a look that she knew meant, can we trust him?

"We need his help," Emily said. She could see Wesley massaging his temples from the corner of her eyes. *How could he hear Michella?*

"With what?" Julian asked frowning.

"Michella's been taken to Neci," Emily said in a low voice.

Julian's eyes widened. "Are you serious?"

"Very," Jason said. "We're going to get her today."

"Tonight," Wesley corrected, looking more alert. "We can't just walk out of Osaki in broad daylight, can we?"

Julian shook his head. "Wait, hold on a second. You're all going to Neci?"

"We have to. She knows that Michella can heal. I don't know what she will do to her, but Michella isn't safe," Jason explained.

"I just need a second," Julian said, holding both hands to the side of his face.

"I think we need Gabriel too," Emily suddenly said. "He can teleport us in and out."

"Can he handle that after Blade?" Wesley asked, crossing his arms.

"I don't know!" Emily snapped. "Can any of us handle what we've been through?"

"Alice?" Julian asked raising an eyebrow and Emily shook her head.

"She's a loose cannon, so no. Jessie—we can use him."

"But if we use Jessie, don't you think he'll tell Warren and Pete?" Jason asked.

"I don't know. Should they come? Warren and Pete can be unpredictable but they're strong and Michella is their sister." Emily rubbed her face. "I don't know."

"You're in charge of the elites remember. Whatever you say goes," Jason said.

"I say no to Warren and Pete but Jessie and his fire—"

"Call me crazy but I don't remember Jessie even being that excited to join our team," Julian said.

"That's true," Wesley replied.

"I think between us five we can get Michella out and maybe even the Professor," Emily said hopefully.

"I hate to point out the obvious," Wesley said looking at everyone. "But what about asking Lox to help us."

"Lox is away with Roberta and Jenkins, remember?"

"You're joking!" Julian said. "So it's just us?"

"Just us," Emily said. "But I think if we think of a good plan, we can do it."

"It would help if we knew where the farmhouse was," Wesley said, kicking a pebble by his feet.

Emily groaned. "How are we going to figure that out?"

"I know where it is," Jason said, to the surprise of everyone.

"How?" Wesley asked.

"Michella and I were doing lots of research on Neci," Jason explained. "That day we were looking in the library—" He glanced at Emily. "I found a lead there and we just kept searching but. . . oh crap!"

"What?" the three of them asked.

"I can't remember if I gave Michella all the notes we made. Come on."

He led the way back inside Osaki and headed towards the staircase.

"I'll go get the others," Julian suggested. "Where should we all meet?"

"Ask Laton Chin if we can have a training session. He'll give us a room where we won't be disturbed," Emily instructed.

"Good idea," Julian said. "I'll ask for the dining room. See you in a bit."

The three of them hurried up the busy stairs. Emily glanced at the Osaki Wall of Fame that was now fully restored. Students were moving from one class to the next and Emily was aware that they should be going to History. She hoped Mr King was his usual elusive self and wouldn't notice that the four of them were missing.

Jason led them through the Ogragon living room and towards the boys' room. Emily paused for a second. She had never been in their room before but when she walked in she was surprised to see it was a mirror image of the girls room, with 'BRAVE' inscribed into one of the walls. Their room was painted a sky blue rather than the sunny yellow the girls had, plus they had a view of the grounds rather than the stadium.

Wesley hurried past her and began gathering jeans and t-shirts from the floor and quickly stuffed it into his wardrobe. Emily caught his eye and smiled.

"Would have made more of an effort if I knew you were coming inside," Wesley said, sitting on his bed. He patted the space beside him and Emily sat.

"I appreciate the quick clean up. So what did you mean that you heard—"

"Come on, where is it?" Jason said as he emptied his school bag on the floor.

Notebooks and essays fell out and Emily couldn't help but think about her bag, which had a quarter of the school work.

"Yes!" he suddenly yelled, holding a sheet of paper up in the air.

"That's it?" Emily asked standing.

"Well, some of it. I think Michella took the rest. I'm just going to check her room to see if her bag is there."

"Do you want me to—"

But Jason had already left.

Emily sighed and sat back down next to Wesley, who wrapped his arm around her, pulling her close. For a brief minute, she rested her head on his chest and closed her eyes, forgetting about everything. . . and then she remembered.

She pulled away and stared at him. "You heard Michella? In your head?"

Wesley quickly glanced at her before staring at his hands and nodded. "It's like she was right here," he said quietly.

"Maybe you're telepathic!" Emily said excitedly. "That could be your hidden power."

"I don't know if I'm telepathic or not, but it was definitely her. She sounded so scared. She just kept telling me where she was and to help her."

Emily bit down on her lip hard. "Listen." She turned Wesley's head so it was facing her. "If you hear her again, embrace it, okay? Don't fight what's happening to you. Try and talk back to her."

Wesley laughed sadly. "It's kinda freaking me out."

"Yeah, these powers can do that to you."

"I spoke to Harmony," he said and Emily raised her eyebrows.

"Oh?" she asked, trying to sound nonchalant.

"I told her we need to talk."

"Are you breaking up with her?" Emily asked and Wesley nodded. "Do you think she knows what you want to talk about?"

"When has 'we need to talk' been followed by anything good?"

Emily placed her hands in her lap.

"You changed your mind about me?" he asked gently. "Now that I hear voices?"

Emily playfully nudged him. "I just don't want anyone getting hurt."

"Me neither, but it's not fair to her if I like someone else," Wesley said.

"So I think I have all the notes," Jason said walking back in. He knelt on the floor, putting the sheets of paper in front of him.

Emily and Wesley walked over to him.

"Talk us through it," Wesley said.

"Michella and I read loads of interviews and memoirs about Neci. There was one from a man who taught Neci at school and he mentioned a place called Necises Green."

"Neci from Necises Green?" Emily said doubtfully and Jason nodded.

"Sounds similar, right? I think she got her name from there. We researched Necises Green and there was a fire years ago where two people died—May and Jack Moore. Apparently warriors had come and set their house on fire but their granddaughter had survived. Her name was Rose Moore."

"No way," Emily whispered.

"So we looked up Rose Moore and there was all this stuff from people saying they went to school with her, and how she only hung out with one person. They confirmed that Rose was a warrior."

He pointed at an article that read 'YOUNG WARRIOR ATTACKS AUNT' alongside a picture of a large white lady.

"That's her aunt, Janet Moore, who said her niece Rose went crazy because she was getting bullied. She knocked her out and when Janet woke up Rose was gone, along with another local boy called Max Jacobs."

"Max Ja—" Emily's eyes widened. "You mean Blade?"

Jason nodded.

"This is mad," Wesley said, picking up the article.

"There are some reports that said the farmhouse was restored, and get this, people said they couldn't get close to the house because they felt something was blocking them, like it was haunted or something. One person described it as a strong power, like a force surrounding the house."

"You are brilliant," Emily said looking at Jason in awe.

He blushed. "Michella helped too. It just all connects. I think we have to go to Necises Green and find the farmhouse. That's where Michella is and hopefully the Professor."

"You're making it sound so simple," Wesley said, placing the article back on the floor. "There will probably be hundreds of warriors protecting Neci."

"We're not going to fight her. I want us to avoid her at all costs. We just need to get in and find them without attracting any attention," Jason explained.

"We're practically bringing a squad with us!" Wesley snapped.

"Listen I'm getting Michella with or without your help."

There was a tense silence. Jason was noisily packing the articles back in his bag and Wesley had his arms crossed and was staring out of the window.

If we could just get to the farmhouse but have eyes watching us, just in case anything happens. . .

"I have an idea," Emily said and the boys looked at her. "We can get Gabriel to teleport us there and Julian and Jessie can be our lookouts. No fighting if we can avoid it. Maybe Jessie could set off a fire somewhere. We know how Neci hates fires so I'm sure that will attract attention."

"How would they even signal to us if there's a problem?" Wesley asked.

"Well, they could tell you. You know, telepathically?"

"What?" Jason asked, looking at Wesley surprised. "How long have you been telepathic?"

"I'm not...I mean, I don't know," Wesley said frustrated. "Maybe I can just hear Michella's voice. You can't put all of that pressure on me."

"Have you got another idea?" Emily demanded.

Wesley crossed his arms and didn't answer.

"Why don't we try it now?" Jason said, getting to his feet. "Can you hear what I'm thinking?"

"No, I can't!" Wesley yelled before storming out of the bedroom, slamming the door behind him.

"Maybe he's not telepathic," Jason said.

"I think he is. He's just scared." Emily sighed. "Let's find the others."

CHAPTER TWENTY-ONE

The Plan

They found the elite team gathered in the dining hall, talking quietly amongst themselves. Julian was standing in the middle, using hand gestures to explain his story. Gabriel Thompson was running a hand through his thick, black hair. Jessie Kendaschi had his arms folded and was staring at the floor, nodding along to whatever Julian was saying. Emily was glad to see Wesley amongst them, looking annoyed, but at least he was there. To Emily's surprise, Alice Archinia was leaning with one foot propped up against the wall and she was staring at Emily amused.

"Hey," Jason called and the boys stopped talking.

"Is he for real?" Jessie said, pointing a thumb at Julian.

Emily nodded. "And we're rescuing Professor Elwood too. We're going tonight."

"Whoa! He only said Michella," Jessie said staring accusingly at Julian.

"Do we need the Professor?" Gabriel asked quietly. "I know that sounds bad but can't we do that another time?"

"Trust us, we need him," Jason said.

Emily slipped next to Julian as the boys rounded on Jason.

"What is Alice doing here?" she hissed. "I said not to bring her."

Julian sighed. "It's my fault. I forgot to tell Gabriel not to tell her. She might be helpful."

"Shouldn't we ask Roberta or Jenkins to sort this out?" Gabriel asked, looking worried.

"They're away," Emily said, standing tall, with all eyes on her. "Look, we've been trained to be leaders, heroes, whatever you want to call us. One of our team members has been taken and we have to get her back. Roberta left Lox in charge of us and Lox said that when he isn't here, then I'm in charge. And I say we're going tonight."

"You're in charge?" Alice drawled, stepping forward. Emily gritted her teeth. "I don't take orders from you."

"Yes, you do," Emily said, crossing her arms. "If you don't like it, you can leave."

"Well," Alice said, looking around the group smirking. "I think Miss Emily here has something to tell the group, don't you?"

Emily's stomach dropped. "What do you mean?" she said, trying to keep the tremor out of her voice. She hated the way Alice was smiling at her.

"Your little secret." Alice continued, and Jason looked at her in alarm. "So you're not going to say anything?"

Emily felt a bubbling deep in her stomach.

"Okay, I'll guess I'll say it," Alice said, clearly enjoying herself. She paced slowly up and down. "You're entering The World Warrior Tournament, aren't you?"

Jessie gasped. "You're competing in Worlds?"

Emily didn't know if she wanted to laugh or cry. She had completely forgotten about her birthday present.

"Yeah," Emily said, shrugging like it was no big deal.

"A little bird told me you entered yourself. Funny how you didn't tell your teammates all about it. Didn't want the competition, did you?" Alice said, with her green eyes shining.

Now Emily wanted to laugh. "Actually, my dad entered me."

Alice scoffed. "Why would he do that? You've got no chance of winning."

"That's rude, Alice," Gabriel protested.

Emily walked up to Alice and stood in front of her. "I have a much better chance than you will ever have and next time you want to question me, you need to remember that I'm running this, not you. So, stay in your lane or get out."

"Oh snap," Wesley said under his breath.

"You're so full of it," Alice spat.

"Come on, try me," Emily goaded. "Maybe you forgot how I beat you up last time?"

A flash of panic crossed Alice's eyes. Emily smirked. *Oh she definitely remembered.*

"Ladies, ladies," Julian said, stepping in-between them, forcing them to take a step back. "As entertaining as it would be seeing you fight it out, we have to work together and focus. Alice, are you going to help or not?"

Alice pursed her lips. "How exactly do you expect us to get Michella away from Neci alive?"

"And Professor Elwood, apparently," Gabriel said. "And

what do we do if Blade is there? I don't want to get trapped in the ice again. I still have nightmares about that night."

"We have a plan," Jason said.

Emily could barely eat the food on her plate. Everything was dry in her mouth. She glanced at Jason and Wesley; they were mirroring her exact movements. Julian, Jessie and Gabriel were a few seats down looking solemn. If anyone found it strange that they were all sitting with each other, no one commented. Alice was on the next table along and Emily could hear her loud voice carrying across the dining room. She seemed to be the only one unaffected.

Emily wasn't sure if they were being reckless with their plan or acting exactly as they'd been trained.

If this goes wrong. . .

Emily shook her head to erase the thoughts. They had one shot to find them. Rescuing one person was going to be a challenge but two was going to be a miracle.

"Hey, did Warren tell you?"

Emily turned to see Summer Wind behind her. Emily caught her breath. *Did he know Michella was missing?*

"About Dojo?"

"Oh Dojo," Emily said with a sigh of relief and Summer gave her a funny look.

"What else would he be telling you about? Our match has been moved to tomorrow at three."

If I'm alive. Emily shook her head.

Summer frowned. "You okay, Em?"

"Yeah, sorry I. . . err. . . just have a headache. Tomorrow's cool."

"Okay," Summer said slowly. "Maybe get an early night. Catch you tomorrow."

She walked off and Emily rubbed her face.

"I swear sitting here is driving me crazy. I need some air."

"Me too," Wesley said, throwing down his fork by his untouched food.

"Let's go," Jason said, pushing back his chair.

"What did you tell Summer?" Jessie asked, looking up.

"I'll see her at the match, you?"

"I said I would take a rain check." Jessie smiled. "She wasn't impressed."

"At least it was more accurate than mine. We're just going for a walk," Emily said before the three of them left the dining hall.

The cold air made Emily feel instantly better. They walked in silence across the grounds. The only sound was their feet hitting the crinkled leaves. Wesley was in front heading towards the forest. Emily stopped, remembering a cold, dark night like tonight when she had met Neci for the first time.

Wesley must have sensed her hesitation because he turned around and asked, "You don't want to go in?"

If I can't go in the forest at night because of a memory, how am I going to face her?

"I'm okay," Emily said. Taking a deep breath, she followed Wesley into the forest, with Jason behind her. "But let's not go too far."

"Here's a good spot," Jason said, pointing to where the floor seemed the most flat with fewer branches. He sat down and looked up at the stars. "Do you think Michella can see the sky?" He laid down with his hands behind his head. "I hope she can."

"Me too," Wesley said, laying down also.

Emily, although not keen to sit on the dirty floor, laid down with them. As she looked up at the sky and the darkness surrounding her, Emily felt surprisingly calm. She felt like they were in their own little bubble and nothing could get to them. They were invisible.

"I knew Alice didn't know about your dad," Wesley said eventually. "I couldn't hear her entire thoughts but I heard 'tournament' and I just knew."

"Is it weird? Hearing people?" Jason asked.

An owl hooted in the distance. A rustling noise beside Emily made her jump but it was just Wesley moving around to get more comfortable.

"Yeah, it freaked me out—still freaks me out. That wasn't the first time. I heard my mum a few days after you guys saw her. I could hear all the things she wanted to say to me but she couldn't." Wesley sighed. "I mean she probably could have but I was too mad to listen to her, but hearing her talk about how sorry she was and how much she loved me and Cammie, it just. . . I don't know. I wasn't mad at her after that."

"Maybe you're just hearing from the people you want to protect the most?" Jason suggested.

I wonder if he hears me? Emily thought but she was too scared to ask, in case he said no.

"There might be something in that," Wesley said. "Look guys, If I die tonight—"

"Don't Wesley," Emily said.

"If I die," Wesley continued. "My mum will relapse. I know she will. The thought of Nan and Cammie dealing with all of that again just hurts, you know. Just look after them for me."

"No one is dying," Emily said fiercely, grabbing on to Wesley's hand in the dark. He didn't respond but he squeezed it.

"Doesn't it feel like we're in some weird spiral and we can't get out? Everything feels broken," Jason said while Wesley rubbed his thumb in a gentle circle on Emily's hand. "I don't feel scared, which kind of freaks me out. I feel angry. The thought of anyone hurting Michella makes me want to kill someone."

Wesley chuckled. "Sounds like you're in love."

Emily turned her head to Jason but she could only see the outline of his face in the dark.

"You think?" he eventually asked.

"Definitely," Wesley said.

"You ever been in love, Wes?"

Emily could hear her breathing loud in her ears. She was aware that Wesley was still holding her hand, moving his thumb across her skin and every single nerve was alert.

"Yeah," Wesley said and Emily wished there was a spotlight on him, just so she could see if he was looking at her. She waited for Jason to ask with who but he didn't say anything.

Was it me? Emily felt a pain in her heart. She knew if Michella was here she would challenge Wesley on who he was talking about. She wanted her best friend back.

"It's weird, just us three," Emily said.

Jason groaned. "It sucks."

"That's a strong statement," Wesley said. "I mean it's way more peaceful." Emily and Jason burst out laughing. "You know damn well Michella wouldn't be lying here on the floor. Emily is because there's no one to back her."

"Shut up," Emily said still laughing.

"We can do this, right?" Jason said anxiously and instantly the laugher stopped.

"We can do this," Emily said confidently, ignoring her racing heart. "We have to."

"Let's head back," Wesley said sitting up and dusting the leaves of his training kit. "The others will be panicking."

He held his hands out to Emily who grabbed on and Wesley pulled her up.

"Bring it all in guys," Wesley said, with his arms open wide.

Jason laughed and Emily rolled her eyes but they all held tight on to one another. Emily closed her eyes and silently prayed. *Please let us come out of this alive.*

There was a dim light in the Ogragon living room and they were talking in hushed voices to avoid waking everyone up. The group was ready to go to the farmhouse, but there was one person missing.

"Is she even coming?" Emily asked annoyed.

"She said she would," Julian said. "You know what Alice is like."

"We'll leave her behind if we have to," Jason said, abruptly getting up and pacing around the room. The closer it had gotten to midnight, the more anxious he seemed.

There was a light knock on the door.

"Finally," Emily said, getting up to answer it.

Alice Archinia was dressed in a tight-fitting, black jumpsuit with a black mask over her face.

Emily stifled her laughter. "What's up with that?" She pointed at the mask.

"I don't want her to see me."

"The whole point is that she won't see you because you'll be hidden."

"Well, forgive me if I don't want to take any chances," Alice snapped.

She walked into the living room and Emily could hear Wesley say, "Lord, help us," as he looked up to the ceiling.

"Okay, let's go over the plan one more time," Emily said, looking around the room. "Gabriel, you're going to teleport me and Jason, Alice you'll teleport Julian and Wesley, and Jessie you can meet us there. When we go into the farmhouse, you guys will keep a lookout—"

"I think I should go in with you," Julian said. "To even out the odds. So two of us can get Michella and the other two can find Professor Elwood."

"Err—" Emily looked at Jason and Wesley and Jason nodded. "Okay sure. Gabriel, if anything goes wrong you teleport back to Osaki and get help."

"Got it," Gabriel said, looking more confident than Emily had ever seen him.

"Jessie use your fire only if you need to create a distraction. We will know to get out of there ASAP and Alice. . . just stay alert."

Alice ripped off her mask, threw it on the floor and glared

at Emily. "That's all I get? Stay alert. Where's my role in all of this?"

"Your role is to keep an eye out and make sure we don't die!"

"Ssh," Jason said, glancing at the bedroom doors. "Alice we already went over this."

"You let Julian come in, so why can't I?"

Emily threw up her arms exasperated. "You just said you didn't want her seeing you and now you want to go into the house?"

"If things go wrong and Jessie uses his fire to cause a distraction and Gabriel teleports back here to get help, what exactly do I do?"

Everyone fell silent, until Wesley said, "You find a way to contact Lox and tell him to rescue us."

"I don't know what Neci will do when she seems him," Emily said. "He did betray her."

"Emily, he is the only one that Neci might listen to," Wesley said. "It's a last resort."

"I agree," Jessie said from the couch.

"Me too," Gabriel said.

"We get in and we get out," Emily said, speaking over everyone. "Let's go."

Necises Green station, as expected, was deserted. There was a dim light shining and they were surrounded by seemingly endless trees.

"This is creepy," Alice said, hugging herself.

Every time the wind blew, the trees created different shadows, making Emily agitated. She couldn't help but feel that Neci knew they were there and was waiting for them.

"Where do we go?" Emily asked Jason, who was holding a map. He traced the path with one finger.

"That way," he said pointing left. "It's a straight road until we see a bridge."

"Can't we fly?" Gabriel asked.

Emily shook her head. "They might sense us. It's best to walk."

The only light they had was the glow from the moon. Emily kept her wits about her, looking from left to right and up at the sky. An owl hooted and they jumped.

"We're a mess," Wesley said, watching the white owl who stared back at them from a tree with its large, amber eyes.

The bridge was in the distance. They were closer to the farmhouse, closer to Michella, but as they walked to the bridge, the air felt thicker and walking required more effort. It seemed to be colder and the wind was howling. It reminded Emily off when she went to Seven's house.

Emily signalled to keep going and she bent her head, walking towards the bridge. As she stepped on it, she felt a force pushing her back. She gritted her teeth and gripped the side of the bridge to keep her balance. Suddenly, Emily felt a firm hand on her shoulder. She tried to see who it was but instead she felt herself floating. All the sounds around her muted and a few seconds later, she landed heavily on the floor.

"Thanks," she said, looking at Jessie.

"No problem," he said, looking back at the bridge. "I didn't see how else we were going to get through that."

"Good thinking."

They waited as Gabriel and Alice teleported the rest of them through the force field. Julian's hair had unravelled from its neat plait and Wesley stumbled as he landed on the ground.

"No wonder they think it's haunted," Wesley said, dusting off his jeans. "At least we're through."

Jason ran a hand though his untidy hair. "It's only going to get worse."

They walked further up the road and Emily gasped when she saw the sky covered in bright lights. She could make out huge vehicles slowly driving along the fields.

"Are those tanks?" Alice's mouth dropped open.

Julian was staring up at the sky. "The trees," he suggested. "Fly up."

Emily bent her knees and flew up, balancing on a thick branch. From her height, she could see, not just tanks, but what looked like hundreds of people marching back and forth. Some had long rifles against their shoulders and others were holding fireballs in their hands. She could make out a quaint building—the farmhouse.

"Lox said nothing was here," Emily said confused.

"She has an army!" Wesley said, glaring at Emily, as if it was her fault. "What are we meant to do now?"

"Are those guns? I can't see." Gabriel took off his glasses and wiped them on his shirt. He put them back on and swallowed. "Yep, those are guns."

"So what's the plan?" Julian asked Emily.

Emily watched the hundred-man army, who would kill them in a second.

"I-I," she stammered.

"What are we going to do?" Jessie asked.

Emily wished she could answer them but she couldn't. All she could see was the army down below. She had no idea how they could get to Michella. She bent her head, taking in deep breaths.

Don't lose it, don't lose it, she said over and over again.

"I have an idea," Alice said confidently and Emily stared at her surprised. "There's no way we're getting in that building, so Jessie, I think you should create the biggest fire you can that way." She pointed to her right. "Then, I will go down there just for a second—"

"That's crazy!" Wesley said.

"Listen! They will see me and I'll teleport. I'm fast, they won't be able to catch me. I'll keep re-appearing so they follow me. Gabriel, you get Emily, Wesley, Jason and Julian as close to the house as you can. Don't teleport them in because we don't know where Neci is. Then come back here to the trees. If Jessie and I aren't back within ten minutes, figure out a way to get Lox here."

"That's not a bad idea," Julian said, staring down at the army. He looked at Emily. "What do you think?"

Emily caught Alice's eye and Alice gave her a small smile, so quick that anyone could have missed it, but Emily didn't. For once, she was grateful to have Alice with them.

"It's good," Emily said, finding her voice. "We have to move as quick as possible."

"What if someone sees them by the house?" Gabriel asked.

"We need to blend in," Jason said. His eyes were on the army. "Let's go steal some clothes."

CHAPTER TWENTY-TWO

The Rescue

They landed silently behind the tree closest to the farmhouse. As soon as their feet touched the floor Gabriel teleported back to where they were originally hiding. There was a faint light coming from the side of the farmhouse but they weren't close enough to see inside properly. Not far from them was an army that was a mix of adult men and women and a few teenagers of all different races and sizes. It was obvious to see who were warriors and who had most likely been threatened by Neci to fight for her. What struck Emily as odd was that they all had a vacant look, as if they weren't really there.

"There he is," Jason whispered.

Opposite them, deep in the trees, was the biggest fire Emily had ever seen. Jessie had made it rise so high that it looked like the sky was on fire.

"What are you waiting for?" a short man with a Mohican came striding out from the side of the farmhouse.

Emily, Jason, Wesley and Julian huddled closer together to avoid being seen.

"That's Dion," Emily said. His gold tooth caught the light and glistened. "He can manipulate time."

"Just what we need," Julian groaned.

Dion was heading towards the army who were still marching and driving the tanks as if nothing had happened.

"THOMAS KNIGHT!" Dion roared, pointing towards the fire and the tanks came to a holt.

The marching soldiers stopped instantly and turned their heads a towards the fire. Emily caught her breath.

Dion bent his knees and flew up into the air and the warriors amongst them followed suit. Soldiers came out of the tanks, holding rifles. The non-warriors cocked their guns and held them tight in their hands.

"LET'S G—"

Emily gasped. Alice was floating in front of Dion with a smirk on her face. Dion's mouth fell open and Alice waved her fingers before she teleported.

"W-What?" Dion stammered looking around for her. He clenched his fist and yelled, "Maggie, get out here!"

"Yes Alice!" Wesley said quietly.

A small white lady with frog-like eyes ran out from one of the tanks. Emily remembered how Maggie had attacked her that night in the forest when she was trying to get her and Lox to safety. Everything in her wanted to grab her curly hair and choke her.

"What can she do?" Julian hissed.

"She can heal," Jason said, with his jaw clenched.

"The fire," Maggie said, pointing at the flames that were spreading rapidly amongst the trees. "We have to sort it before she comes back."

"Didn't you see her?" Dion hissed and Maggie stared at him blankly. "Alice Archinia is here! She teleported right in my face."

"How?" Maggie asked alarmed with her big eyes bulging. "Are there more of them?"

"I don't know. Find her!"

Maggie nodded and teleported.

"Did you hear that? Neci's not here," Julian said. His eyes were shining bright.

The news should have made her feel better but instead Emily felt even more jumpy.

"If she's not here then where is she?" Emily asked.

Dion flew towards the flames with the warriors behind him, except for four teenagers who had taken a step and couldn't move any further.

"Come this way," Jason said, with his fingers on his temple. "Do not make a sound."

The four people walked vacantly towards them, holding their guns tight.

Emily and Wesley grabbed them and pushed them to the floor as Jason held them still. Julian quickly took off their black hats and jackets which revealed a fitted white t-shirt underneath and a small bulge in their arm.

"That's the chip Neci puts inside people," Emily said, gently touching it. It felt hard under their soft skin.

"Can't we take it out?" Julian asked, as he put on a black jacket and buttoned it up.

"We can't rescue everyone today!" Wesley snapped. "We'll sort out the chips later."

Emily buttoned up the fitted black jacket and pulled the

hat down as low as she could. It dawned on them that they didn't have any rope to tie them up with.

"Tell Gabriel to come and take them," Emily said turning to Wesley who stared back at her like she was crazy.

"How?"

"With your. . ." She tapped her forehead.

Wesley sighed. "I already said—"

"Just try!" Emily argued. "We can't leave them out here."

Wesley closed his eyes and after a second, he said, "It's not working."

"How do you know?" Emily crossed her arms.

"Do you see Gabriel here?" Wesley asked, dragging out each word.

"Guys stop!" Julian said sharply. "Let's get them into one of the tanks. We needed to get in the farmhouse about five minutes ago."

"Stand up," Jason commanded and the teenagers stood up. "Walk to that tank in front of us. Get inside. Don't move or speak."

Like robots, they marched to the tank in single file. The boy leading the way got to the door and was struggling to get it open.

"He is going to get us killed," Wesley said, running a hand over his head.

Emily leaned forward ready to run and grab the door open when a loud boom came from the far right. She prayed that wasn't Maggie catching up with Alice. Emily sprinted to the tank door and flung it open.

"Come on, come on," she said, watching them move painfully slowly into the tank.

When they were finally in, she leaned her back on the door, breathing hard for a few seconds.

It's now or never, she thought.

Emily nodded at the others and they ran to the farmhouse, keeping themselves pressed against the wall as they got closer to the dim light shining from the side of the house. Emily led the way. She was conscious of every noise they made when they walked over the crinkled leaves and how loud her breathing was. Neci wasn't at the farmhouse but she could be back any second. With Dion and Maggie occupied, that only left the iceman Blade, and he was a warrior Emily never wanted to battle again.

The door was wide open and there was a flight of stairs. They walked in with their eyes slowly adjusting to the light. The house was tidy and clean with dated, floral wallpaper. There was a large beige couch with a small coffee table and a vase of fresh red roses. The fireplace was boarded up. On top of the cabinets were pictures of an elderly man and woman with a small dark haired girl. Emily peered at the picture closely. *Was this Neci?*

"I didn't expect it to look like this," Wesley said, staring up at the ceiling fan. "Are we in the right place?"

Jason had his hand on his forehead with his eyes closed.

"You okay?" Emily asked.

"Yeah, I just have a headache from using my powers."

"How do we get underground?" Julian asked, looking around the room.

"There must be a secret door or something," Wesley said. "Start pushing things on the wall and see if anything moves."

The boys began to gently press against the walls, whilst

Emily gazed around the room. Everything looked perfect. How could someone like Neci have grown up somewhere so lovely? Emily had been expecting somewhere cold, dark and dirty with cobwebs. She had always pictured Lox growing up that way, not somewhere that was a home.

Emily took a step towards Jason and heard a crunch under her foot. She looked down at the broken pen and bent to pick it up. That's when she noticed that there was a small bump under the patterned dark brown rug. She ran her hand across it.

"Guys, I think I found something."

Emily walked to the edge of the thick rug and pulled it to expose gleaming wooden floors. She walked to where she'd seen the bump and there was a small button that was a little bit darker than the floor.

"This must be what Hayley-Elizabeth was talking about," Emily said.

"Everyone ready?" Julian asked, who looked so confident and strong.

"Let's go get our girl back," Wesley said, stretching out his neck from side to side.

"Remember, we get in and out as quick as possible," Jason said. "I'll lead the way. In case anyone sees us, at least I can hold them back for a bit."

"Maybe I should go first," Emily suggested.

Jason shook his head. "I'll be fine. Press the button."

She pressed the button and gasped when a piece of floor raised high above them, exposing a dark circle below. It was too dark to see if there were any stairs or if anyone was waiting for them.

"Follow my lead," Jason said. He was holding a small yellow Baby Ball in his hand. He held it over the hole but the darkness swallowed up the light. "See you down there." And he jumped.

"Emily, you go next," Wesley said and before she knew it she was in his arms hugging him tight. Over his shoulder, she saw Julian looking at the floor.

"I'll see you in a bit." She let go of Wesley and ignored his surprised expression when she hugged Julian next. "Be safe," she whispered before pulling away.

Wesley was staring at them both with a hard stare. Emily peered down the hole, trying to get a glimpse of Jason's Baby Ball but there was nothing. She closed her eyes, took in a deep breath and jumped. The cold wind rushed past her and the black tunnel seemed to go on forever. She controlled her speed, so she wasn't going as fast as she could. She wanted to make sure she was prepared for what was at the bottom. Emily could faintly see a small ball of light that got brighter and brighter.

She landed gracefully on the white floor, where she saw Jason surrounded by a group of men dressed in black with their hands held high as if they were surrendering. Their guns were floating in the air but facing back at them.

Jason had beads of sweat trickling down his forehead and his face was turning a bright shade of red. He shot a quick glance at Emily and very quickly nudged his head. Emily charged forward knocking two people to the floor. She punched one in the face and he was instantly knocked out. The other person threw back his leg to kick her and she grabbed it, yanking him forward as he yelled, "No, no, no!"

She jumped on to his stomach, pressing her feet into his abdomen and he cried out in pain. Emily looked over her shoulder and saw Wesley and Julian were attacking the others.

In the middle of the room, Jason was kneeled over on all fours. Emily ran over to him, wrapping her arm across his back. She gently lifted up his head and he had turned a strange greyish colour.

"Come on." Emily dragged him to a corner away from the fight. He pressed his head against the wall and closed his eyes. His face was drenched in sweat.

"My head," Jason mumbled. "My head is spinning."

"Here, put your head between your legs," she said. Jason gave her a strange look. "Trust me, it works."

His blond hair flopped forward as he leaned over. His strong back was moving slowly up and down.

Emily rubbed his back in circular motions. "That's it. Just breathe deeply—in and out."

One of the men flew beside Emily and hit his back on the wall before collapsing in a heap by her feet. She glared at Wesley who looked sheepish.

"My bad. My aim was off."

Julian was walking around the lifeless bodies. He picked up the guns and examined them before breaking them in half and scattering the black pieces on the floor.

"You alright, Jas?" Wesley asked, kneeling in front of him.

Jason nodded. "Using my telekinesis just took more out of me than I thought. Help me up, man."

He leaned on Wesley who helped him to his feet. He looked better but not his usual self. Emily bit her lip. They didn't have any Reviving Water—actually no water at all—and within the first ten minutes of being underground, Jason had already lost half of his energy.

"What happened?" Emily asked.

"They were waiting for us as I came down. I instantly took their guns away and that scared them. They didn't try to attack—they're not warriors."

"Wish we had kept one awake so they could take us to Michella." Wesley nudged one of the men with his foot, who didn't move.

"Come on," Emily said. "We have to be quick."

They walked towards the corridor that thankfully had better light. They couldn't hear any sounds and Emily kept her hands in fists, ready for anyone who was going to attack them. They ducked when they saw a door with a window.

"Wait," Julian said. He slowly stood up and peered through the window. He gasped. "Check this out."

Emily stood up and looked. The room was empty apart from monitors and computers flashing different colours. There were screens showing different parts of the farmhouse. Every few seconds the screens would change showing another room. Blade, the iceman appeared on the screen. He was in a room, standing over a table covered with huge pieces of paper with handwriting on it.

She glanced at Julian who looked just as shocked as she was.

"He can't know we're here," Emily said urgently.

"There they are," Wesley suddenly said.

On one screen, it looked like a laboratory and a man that resembled a much skinnier version of Professor Elwood, was pouring a liquid substance into a test tube. The screen next to it showed Michella sitting hunched up against the wall with her eyes closed.

"Okay, how are we doing this?" Emily asked, not tearing her eyes away from Michella.

"I vote we get Michella first and then the Professor," Wesley said.

"We need to split up," Jason argued. "We'll save more time and then we can get both of them."

"We're stronger together," Julian said. "And no offence but you needed us back there with those people and they weren't even warriors."

Emily placed her hand on the window wishing she could get them both. One was her best friend and the other could save her dad's life. Emily squinted her eyes as she watched Michella. Her shoulders were shaking and her head was pressed to her chest.

"I think she's crying," Emily said softly and the boys instantly pressed their faces against the glass. "Right, we're getting her first and then the Professor."

They hurried down the corridor as quietly as they could. A flashlight shone towards them and they quickly pressed themselves against the wall. Emily held her breath until the flashlight disappeared and the footsteps died away. She signalled to the boys to keep going. They came to a turning. One side was another corridor and the other had stairs that led to a floor below.

"Which way?" Jason asked.

"I don't know," Emily said, running a hand through her hair. "Maybe it's—"

"She's downstairs," Wesley said. "She told me she's downstairs."

Emily grabbed his hand and squeezed it.

They crept down the stairs and there were voices below. Emily peered over the banister and could see two people in deep discussion. Emily held up two fingers to the boys, who nodded. Julian pointed at himself and made a hill motion with his hand.

"What?" Emily mouthed and before she knew it, Julian had jumped over the banister.

Emily, Wesley and Jason looked at each other alarmed before they hurried down the steps after him and all Emily could hear were yells and moans.

When they got to the bottom of the stairs, the two warriors were on the floor, knocked out, and Julian was massaging one of his knuckles.

"I think she's that way," Julian said as if nothing had happened. He gestured further up and Emily sprinted, with Wesley and Jason right behind her.

Michella was locked behind a cell with bars separating them from her. Her long braids were covering her face and she was hugging herself in her dirty training kit. Emily bent to her knees, gripping the bars tight.

"Michella," she said softly.

Michella peered out from behind her braids and gasped when she saw her. Emily noticed that she didn't have a single mark or bruise on her.

"Emily?" Michella hurried towards her on all fours. "Oh my gosh," she added when she saw Wesley and Jason. "How?"

"Don't worry. We're getting you out."

Michella shook her head sadly. "I've tried. The bars are too strong."

Emily stood up and stared at the bars. She could see that a few were slightly bent so they weren't made out of Illarn. She rubbed her hand on the top and wrapped her hands around two of the bars. She gritted her teeth and pulled. At first it seemed like nothing was happening, but slowly the bars were moving towards her, bending into a 'V' shape. Emily slowly walked backwards, pulling as hard as she could, then she pushed one bar to the left, so there was a gap in the middle.

"Whoa," Wesley said in awe.

Emily bent over with her hands on her lap, breathing hard.

"Can you get through?" Jason asked and Michella nodded.

She slowly stood up and turned to the side, where there was just enough space. She fell into Jason's arms and he squeezed her tight, spinning her around.

"How did you find me?"

"Daisy told us and Wesley heard you," Jason said.

Michella stared at Wesley. "How?"

Wesley shrugged. "I think I might have telepathy."

She ran to Wesley, hugged him tight and kissed him on both cheeks. "I prayed that someone would hear me. Thank you."

"We couldn't leave you here," Emily said when Michella went to hug her. "Did they hurt you?"

Michella pulled away. "They put something in my drink that made me black out. When I woke up they wanted to see how much I could heal. . . and I did after every attack. They said Neci was coming to see me."

"I'm so sorry this happened to you," Jason said, squeezing her hand.

"Neci's not here yet," Wesley said.

"Shall we get the Professor?" Julian asked.

"You came too?" Michella said, hugging him. "Who else is here?"

"The whole crew—Gabriel, Jessie and Alice," Julian said.

"Alice?" Michella said looking so surprised that it made everyone laugh.

"Mich, where's the laboratory? We saw the Professor on a screen," Wesley asked.

Michella shook her head. "I haven't seen it but it must be upstairs. I'm the only one down here."

They hurried up the stairs and back to the corridor. They had only walked a few steps when it went pitch black. A red fireball soared through the darkness and hit Emily in the chest and she fell back, knocking her head on the floor.

There was a sudden explosion of bright lights, fireballs and screams. Someone roughly pulled her up by the arm and held her tight around her waist. She was flying so fast that everything looked like a blur. The air was thick with smoke and her head was thumping. She felt herself flying up but she couldn't see a thing. She fell on to the hard wooden floor, landing on her arm. She winced and slowly used her other arm to pull herself up. She was back in the farmhouse living room.

Michella, Wesley, Jason, Julian were next to her on the floor, struggling to get to their feet. Opposite her was a red-faced Alice and Jessie was sporting a black eye. They were being held back by Dion and Maggie, who both had raw scratch marks on their faces. Blade was standing beside them in a long white cloak and behind them was a figure in all black. She wasn't wearing her trademark white mask, but parts of her face was hidden behind a black scarf. Her piercing dark eyes narrowed in on Emily, who caught her breath.

CHAPTER TWENTY-THREE

Repercussions

"Hello Emily," Neci said. "And friends." She took her time glancing over all of them and stopped at Michella. "Oh, I see you got out. Blade?"

And before they could do anything, Blade shot ice beams at their legs that travelled to their torso freezing them in place. The cold seemed to seep through Emily's clothes all the way to her bones.

"I just didn't want you doing something stupid like trying to run." Neci smiled. "Now this is a good surprise to come home to. Fresh warriors and an Archinia and a Knight."

Dion and Maggie laughed. Neci shot them a cold stare.

"How did they get in here?"

Dion and Maggie instantly stopped laughing.

"He created a fire to distract us," Dion said, gripping Jessie tighter who groaned in response.

"So only Blade sensed them here?" Neci said and Dion and Maggie hung their heads. "And what about you?" Neci turned to Alice, who glared at her. "How's death treating your Grandfather?"

Alice went to lunge for her but Maggie pulled her back by her hair, making Alice fall to the floor.

"You see, I have a problem. I don't know where Scarlett is and I can't help but feel that one of you knows." Neci stared at Emily who did her best to keep her face as neutral as possible.

Emily's teeth chattered as she glanced to her left and noticed that Wesley had his eyes closed. It was only then that she noticed that Gabriel wasn't with them. It took Neci only a second to move and she was in Emily's face, with her hand around her neck. Emily gasped as Neci applied a light pressure.

"It would be so easy, wouldn't it?" Neci whispered.

Emily could feel her heart pounding loudly in her ears. *Come on.* Emily prayed to hear that voice, the one that made the fire flames appear, but nothing happened.

Emily winced and Neci smirked. She inhaled deeply. "I can smell your fear."

Emily forced herself to lock eyes with her. She could see the burn marks that her scarf was trying to hide.

"I can't wait till my Dad cuts your head off," Emily hissed back and Neci tightened her grip, making Emily choke.

"Where's your daddy now?"

"Lox!" Michella cried.

"Lox?" Neci said, letting go off Emily.

Emily felt like everything was moving in slow motion. Neci turned around with her eyes wide. Lox was opposite her in his leather jacket, his eyes fixed on Neci. There was a moment, when Neci stared at Lox the way Emily remembered her mother staring at her. It was a look filled with longing.

A look you gave to someone that you cared for deeply. It happened so fast that Emily questioned if it was real. She blinked and Neci was looking amused.

"Look who's returned home," she said, slowly clapping her hands.

"Let them go," Lox said forcefully.

Neci laughed. "And why would I do that?"

"Because your battle is with Thomas, not with them. They're just children."

"Just children he says!" Neci said and Blade, Maggie and Dion laughed. "I've seen what these *children* can do. They're valuable to me."

Lox took a step forward. He still looked calm and in control but Emily noticed that his left hand was clenched. "I won't let you harm them."

"I'll kill her before you even know what I've done."

Lox sprinted and grabbed Neci's hand and wrap it around his own neck. He held her hand in place with his own. "Kill me."

"No, Lox!" Emily screamed.

"KILL ME!" Lox roared. "You kill her, then you kill me. Do you understand?"

"I raised you," Neci spat. "I taught you everything. Treated you like you were my own son and you betrayed me for him!" Her face was contorted in an ugly sneer.

"For her," Lox said, glancing at Emily. "I would do anything for my sister, even walking away from you."

"I found you all those years ago because I knew who you could be. I knew you were better than him, better than being his shadow. I gave you everything you desired and more, you know that. We said we would destroy Thomas Knight together." Lox looked down at the floor and slowly lowered his hand. "And then you betrayed me and went back to him." Neci walked past Lox, purposely barging into him. "I know you took Scarlett, so I'll keep fire boy here and I'll kill you, your sister and her friends."

Emily stared across the room. Alice was on the floor and Jessie was looking right at her. He opened his hand quickly and in the middle of it was a fire flame. Emily knew what she had to do.

"I know where she is!" Emily yelled and everyone stared at her. "Scarlett. I know where she is. Just let us go."

"You don't know anything," Lox snapped. He shot her a look that screamed 'Shut up,' but Emily shook her head.

"I promise, I'll tell you everything." Emily glanced at Jessie, whose eyes were closed.

"You're making it worse!" Alice said, glaring at her. "Stop lying."

"I'm not," Emily argued. "I'm the only one who knows."

Alice scoffed. "You don't know anything."

"Emily, shut up!" Lox roared.

"No! I'm telling the truth. Please! Jason." Emily looked desperately at him. He looked even paler from being in the ice. "You know that I know where she is. Remember I told you?"

To her surprise, Jason was shaking his head in response.

"At school. I told you," Emily argued.

"I don't know what you're talking about," Jason said, through clenched teeth.

"What? Why are you lying?" Emily asked.

Neci watched her with a blank expression but her eyes

were shifting around the room, trying to judge who was telling the truth.

Suddenly, Jessie burst into a ball off fire. Dion stumbled back, shielding his face. Alice punched a distracted Maggie across the jaw and kicked her in the stomach.

Neci looked like she had seen a ghost. She was frozen to the spot. Before Blade could make a move, Lox shot a fireball at him that hit him in the stomach. Lox threw another fireball at Emily that hit the ice with a loud boom. Emily shut her eyes as the pieces of ice flew to her face. The fireball made enough room for Emily's right hand so she was able to create her own fireball, which she held against the ice and it started to melt.

Jessie walked purposely towards Neci. He aimed a fire flamed punch at her and Neci ducked. Jessie walked past her and the closer he got to Emily the more the heat radiating off him made the ice melt. Jessie walked past everyone trapped in the ice and placed his hands around them. The ice instantly melted into a river of water.

"Wow," Emily said.

Jessie was surrounded by fire.

Blade helped Neci to her feet and stood protectively in front of her. He stretched his arms outright. Jessie faced Blade and formed his hand into a 'V' and shot his fire at the same time Blade shot his ice. Emily stumbled as the fire and ice met with a deafening boom.

Lox and Alice teleported to them at the same time Julian cried, "Look out!"

Neci was floating above them with her black cloak bellowing behind her. In the middle of her hands was a black killing fireball. Bright white sparks were shooting out of it.

"Jessie come on!" Emily shouted.

"Go!" Jessie said, over his shoulder. "Quickly."

Emily tried to run to him but Lox grabbed her around her waist.

"No, stop! Jessie!"

Everything felt muffled. She felt like she was floating. The farmhouse was disappearing before her eyes. Lox had teleported her away leaving Jessie behind with Neci and her warriors.

They landed on the soft carpet in Mr Davon's office. Mr Davon watched them appear from behind his desk with Gabriel and Roberta standing beside him. They ran over to them at the same time Emily slapped Lox across the face.

"How could you?" she screamed.

Lox placed his hand over where she had hit and gently rubbed it.

"What happened?" Roberta said, standing in-between them. "Where's Jessie and Jenkins?"

"Jenkins?" Michella asked confused. "We never saw him there."

"He was distracting Neci's army with an illusion," Lox said. "I didn't see him after I got inside."

"And Jessie?" Gabriel asked.

Emily glared at Lox. "He was fighting off Blade and Lox left him behind."

"Neci was going to kill us!"

"She's going to kill him!" Emily argued.

"Can someone explain what happened?" Mr Davon said, standing to his feet with his hands on the table. "What I would like to know is what you were doing in Neci's house in the first place? When Gabriel came back to the school and we were contacted to come back I couldn't believe what I was hearing."

Emily gulped. Mr Davon walked around the desk and stood with his feet apart and arms crossed over his chest, glaring at them.

"Who authorised you to do this?" he demanded.

Jason took a step forward. "It's my fault, sir."

"No, it's not," Michella said, pulling him back by his arm. "It's Hayley-Elizabeth Elwood's fault. She saw that I could heal when Lox was training us and she wanted to trade me for her dad. Neci refused and kept me as a prisoner. These guys—" Michella looked at each of their faces. "They saved me."

"Michella, I am aware of what happened to you as Gabriel told me on his return. I am sorry to hear that Hayley-Elizabeth would do such a thing but my question is, who authorised you all to go? Why were we not informed of this?"

"It was all me," Jason said, ignoring Michella's protests. "I wanted to get Michella straightaway. I told them I would go by myself if they didn't come with me."

"I said we should go," Emily said. "I made the call and it was wrong."

Mr Davon switched his glare to Emily. "Am I right in understanding that you're in charge if none of the adults are here?"

"Yes."

"And was it your idea to involve everyone in your rescue mission to get Michella?"

"I did, but—"

"And you led them all to Neci's house without letting a responsible adult know?"

"I. . . I messed up," Emily said, looking at the floor.

"You were irresponsible, reckless and did not make a good judgement." Each word Mr Davon said seemed to hit Emily hard in the chest. "You're meant to be a leader, yet showed no leadership skills. Instead, you took your friends to the house of the most dangerous warrior alive and left Jessie behind."

"That wasn't her fault, sir," Wesley interrupted. "Jessie was keeping Blade from trapping us in the ice again and Neci was coming at us with a black fireball."

Emily blinked quickly, willing herself not to cry.

"Sir, if I wasn't so stubborn Emily wouldn't have—"

But Mr Davon held up his hand to silence Jason. "Emily still made the call."

"Mr Davon, may I say something please?" Julian Kena asked and Mr Davon nodded. "We've been taught to work as a team and to back each other. Yes, Emily was in charge but we still chose to go with her to rescue Michella, so we're all to blame here."

"I'm not to blame," Alice said.

"It was your idea!" Julian argued.

"I didn't suggest to go. Now can everyone finally see what I've been saying for ages? When this elite team first started, I said Emily wouldn't make a good leader. You only chose her because of Thomas Knight. Well, I was the one who offered solutions once we got there. Emily didn't have a clue what she was doing. I distracted Dion, Maggie and a whole army. I did all the hard graft. Even when they captured Jessie, I was still trying to fight. She didn't even try and get the Professor. . ."

Emily could hear sounds all around her. It felt like she wasn't even in her own body. Everyone was looking at her, accusing her of messing everything up and the worst thing was, she knew they were right. She knew she could never be the leader they wanted her to be.

"I tried, okay!" Emily screamed, drowning out Alice. "I try my best all the time and it's never good enough for anyone. Jason was ready to go by himself, what was I meant to do? Just let him? And you're saying I should have told someone? No disrespect Mr Davon but no one has been here. I've been left to be in charge of something I don't want to be in charge of, and I've said time and time again that I'm not a leader and no one listens to me! I've fought beside Jessie in Dojo for a few years now so I knew what he was going to do. I distracted Neci to give us a chance and it worked. No thanks to you, Jason, for not backing me when I asked."

"I'm sor—" Jason began.

"Whatever," Emily said, cutting him off. "Jessie wasn't meant to be left behind and Alice, if you want to be in charge so badly, then do it. Because I'm so rubbish, right? Well, guess what? I agree. I'm not doing this anymore."

"That's not true, Emily," Michella said. "We don't blame you."

"Yes you do. Didn't you blame me last year for Gabriel?"

Michella jerked her head back. "I apologised for that."

"So? Like everyone else, when it goes wrong it's my fault and I'm sick of it."

"Look, I think everyone needs to calm down," Roberta said, walking towards Emily who backed away from her.

"If it wasn't for your stupid secret—"

"Emily," Roberta said in a warning voice. "You need to calm down."

"I don't need to do anything and I especially don't need to fight alongside people who don't care about me."

Roberta raised her eyebrows. "You honestly think none of us care? Everything we do is to protect you. You should remember that."

"That's a lie. All you do is lie to me, and until you want to tell me the truth, I don't want to speak to you ever again."

Roberta opened her mouth but no words came out.

"Emily, I think you need to go and rest," Mr Davon said. "It's been a rough few months and understandably you are overwhelmed. Perhaps think about taking a break from Dojo—"

Emily laughed and Mr Davon looked at her surprised. She had forgotten all about her Dojo match tomorrow. "I guess they'll blame me because Jessie isn't there, right?"

She caught eyes with Lox who was silently watching her from the corner, before leaving the office, slamming the door behind her.

It was cold and dark. Emily shuddered under the big oak tree. All she wanted was to be home with her family. What she would do to have one of Sally's warm hugs and she knew Cathy would understand what she was going through and would know the right things to say. In the morning, she would figure out a way to get back to them. She wasn't allowed to fly alone but she didn't care anymore. If that was the only way to get home, she would do it.

She didn't want to go back inside, even though she was hungry and tired. A part of her wanted to punish herself for allowing the rescue to go wrong. Since her dad was poisoned everything had gone downhill. She had no idea how she was going to explain to the Ogragon Dojo team about Jessie. Just thinking about it made her feel sick to her stomach.

She watched a black silhouette walk slowly towards her and she could tell, even in the dark, that it was Lox. The guilt had crept in and she felt like rubbish for hitting him. He had come to rescue her and she hadn't even thanked him for it.

"Can I sit?" Lox asked and Emily scooted over.

He sat down letting out a heavy sigh. "I'm sorry for leaving Jessie, that wasn't what I wanted. But she would have killed us Emily. You do know that?"

"I'm sorry for hitting you," Emily said in a small voice. "I'm sorry I didn't tell you what we were doing. Thank you for coming to save us. How did Gabriel get in contact?"

"He went to one of the teachers who called Mr Davon but I was with Jenkins. You should thank Wesley. He was in my head telling us to come."

They sat in a comfortable silence. Emily wished so badly that their dad was with them.

"I'm sorry for not rescuing Professor Elwood," Emily said breaking the silence. "I thought we would have more time. Michella was crying. . . I just messed up."

"Hey, I get it," Lox said.

"Is Uncle Jenkins okay?"

"Yeah, you know him. If he hadn't distracted Blade and the army, we would have been in serious trouble. Emily, you know we need to go back to the farmhouse, right? Dad will die if we don't get the Professor and we have to get Jessie. . . if he's still there."

"I don't think I'll be any use," Emily said sadly and Lox nudged her.

"Stop that. We all make mistakes."

"It just feels like everything is always my mistake." Emily shuddered from the cold and without a word, Lox took off his leather jacket and placed it around her shoulders. "Thank you." She breathed in his familiar scent.

"You don't really know where Roberta is keeping Scarlett, do you?" Lox asked and Emily could feel him watching her carefully.

Emily shook her head. "I was just saying whatever."

She had no idea why she was still protecting Roberta, especially when she was clearly hiding something. Deep down Emily knew Roberta would only do something this drastic to protect them but she just wished she could be trusted to know what it was.

"I was thinking of our sessions we spoke about. Me training you? If you're still up for it," Lox said.

"For real?"

"Yeah, we'll start after your Dojo match. Do you want me to talk to Summer about Jessie?"

Emily shook her head. "I'll sort it."

"I think Michella's brothers know what happened. I saw her talking to them. Listen, I know you feel like no one is backing you but I'm always backing you, okay?"

"I know." She looked up at the starry sky, lost in their blinking lights. She just wished more than anything that for one day she could be a normal kid and not Emily Knight.

"I miss Dad," Lox suddenly announced and Emily looked at him surprised.

"Me too. Can you take me to see him soon?"

"Yeah and Mum. . . we should go and visit her as well."

Emily nodded not trusting herself to speak. She hadn't been back to her mum's graveside in years. She wished she was here, the real her, not the illusion Jenkins had created in the past. Her mum was the only glue that her family had. They had been broken ever since she died.

"Let's visit her before everything. . . you know," Emily said, knowing that Lox would understand what she meant.

Lox found her hand in the dark. It was rough against her skin. "I promise."

CHAPTER TWENTY-FOUR

Ogragon vs Linktie

Emily awoke before the rest of the girls in her bedroom and dressed quietly into her Ogragon Dojo kit, careful not to wake anyone up. She hadn't had much sleep and Michella had tossed and turned all night.

Emily had deliberately come into the bedroom once she knew everyone was asleep. She knew Michella would want to discuss what happened and that was the last thing Emily wanted to think about.

Emily looked out of the window at the empty stadium. In a few hours it was going to be packed with students and teachers. Everyone was going to ask where Jessie was. Should she just tell the truth?

Emily pulled on her baht shoes and walked into the living room. To her surprise, Wesley was sitting on the couch with his hands behind his head and his eyes closed. He sat up when he saw Emily. "Hey."

"Hi," Emily said, standing opposite him. "What are you doing up so early?"

"Couldn't sleep," Wesley said and only then did Emily notice the dark circles under his eyes. He looked Emily up and down. "You going to the pitch already?"

Emily nodded. "Do you want to come down with me?"

"I need to talk to Harmony before we have to do the commentary for the game."

"Oh, okay. Well I need to figure out what I'm going to tell the team," Emily said. "What are you going to announce?"

"The truth," Wesley said and then when he saw Emily's surprised face, he smiled. "Is it too early to hit them with that?"

"No, I just thought Mr Davon would have told you to give an excuse."

Wesley shook his head. "He just told me to say what I think is right."

"Anything else happen after I left?"

"Mr Davon said Hayley-Elizabeth has to go to counselling with that lady you see sometimes."

"Oh, Ruth Walker—yeah that's a good idea actually. I guess he can't expel her. She has nowhere to go."

"Exactly." Wesley waited a beat. "You didn't mean what you said yesterday, did you? About Alice taking over?"

"She can have it," Emily said, turning away.

"Emily, you know she can't lead this group."

"Well, neither can I apparently," Emily said with an edge to her voice.

"You know that's not true. We're all behind you."

"Maybe you are, but I can't say the same for all of my friends."

"Talk to Jason." Wesley stood to his feet and stretched

out, so his t-shirt rode up, exposing toned flesh. "He'll have a good reason why."

"Like what?"

Wesley held her gaze. "Trust me. Just talk to him."

Emily headed towards the door and paused. She looked back at Wesley. "How did you know Lox would come?"

"I didn't," Wesley said. "I just. . . I thought we were going to die and I kept speaking to him, hoping he would hear me. Then I heard him say he was on the way. I just need to train this telepathy more, so I feel like I'm more in control."

"Thank you. You saved us."

Wesley shook his head. "I just played my part, as we all did."

If we had all played our parts right then Jessie would be here, Emily thought.

"See you in a bit," she said before she walked out of the door.

Emily paced up and down the changing room, nervously tapping her leg with her hand. She could hear the Ogragon and Linktie team talking as they entered the stadium. Emily took a deep breath and stood in the middle of the changing room.

The doors opened and Warren and Pete came in. They spotted her and all Emily could see was two blurs running at her before they squeezed her tight.

"You have no idea how grateful we are," Pete said, pulling away and holding her shoulders. "Thank you for rescuing Michella."

"Yeah, of course," Emily said, off guard.

"I can't believe you went into the big bad wolf's house," Pete said.

"That's some gangster moves, Emily," Warren said looking impressed.

Emily smiled. "Some would say stupid."

"I'm not one to think anything is stupid," Warren said, winking at her.

The door opened again and the rest of the Ogragon Dojo team came in, talking loudly and digging out their kit from their school bags. The new first year Distracter, Amaya Ethan, was already in her too big Dojo kit and this time she had on contacts instead of glasses.

"Guys, I need to tell you something," Emily yelled over the noise.

"What's up, Em?" Raquel Davis asked, sitting on the bench.

Emily nervously wiped her sweaty hands on her legs. "I'm not sure if you heard about last night—"

"Oh my gosh—Michella!" Rosa said with her hands on her chest. "You are so brave to have gotten her."

"Three cheers for Emily!" Summer Wind said and the Ogragons applauded for her.

"No, stop!" Emily said loudly and the applause died out. "Please, just listen. Last night at Neci's house, there was a group of us that went and one of them was Jessie."

Summer looked around the changing room. "Where is he?"

Emily tried to blink away the tears but she couldn't. They raced down her face, coming to a stop at the tip of her chin, before falling to the floor.

"He was fighting off Blade, the ice man and then Neci

was going to shoot a killing fireball at us. Jessie told us to go but I didn't want to leave him. I-I-I'm so s-sorry."

Raquel gasped. "Jessie is with Neci?"

"I shouldn't have let her take him," Emily said in-between sharp breaths.

"Oh Emily," Summer said, hugging her tight. She soothingly rubbed her back in small circles. "It's not your fault. Besides, our Jessie is strong."

"Is there a plan to get him back?" Rosa asked.

Emily nodded. "And we'll rescue him. I promise."

"And he will be okay," Summer said. "I've known Jessie for a long time and he is one of the bravest people I know. If anyone can get through this it will be him."

"Do you think he's okay?" Warren asked.

"Oh, I pray that he is," Raquel said. "Babe, come here." Raquel hugged a tearful Emily before Rosa joined in, then Warren and Pete.

Emily heard Summer snap at Amaya to "Get over here" and Emily was squeezed by all of her team members.

"Alright, team," Summer hollered, separating herself from the team hug and clapping her hands together, drawing everyone's attention. "We've got to be practical for a second because we're one man down. Someone will need to battle more to make up for Jessie not being here."

"I want to do it," Emily said, wiping her wet face. "And can I go out in his place instead? It just makes me feel like I'm honouring him. I'll fight as many as I can."

"You sure?" Summer asked, raising her eyebrows. Emily nodded. "Okay, two minutes to get ready. Let's win this for Jessie."

"For Jessie," the Ogragon team echoed.

There was a knock at the door and Ms Macay, who refereed the match, poked her head around. "Summer, a minute please?"

Summer followed Ms Macay out of the room and Emily finished tying up her hair into a top bun. Amaya approached her shyly.

"I'm glad you're okay," she said quietly.

Emily smiled. "Thanks and remember—be fast and attack."

Amaya nodded. "I won't let anyone down."

"Guys, I didn't want to say whilst Summer was here," Raquel said, looking around the room. "But how the hell is she going to beat Alan Fair?"

"Who's that?" Amaya asked.

"Only the meanest, toughest warrior to play in Dojo," Warren said. "And we've never beaten him."

"That's not true. Emily did when she blew up the stadium last year," Rosa said.

"I didn't blow up the stadium!" Emily argued.

Amaya looked at her in awe. "You blew up the stadium?"

But before Emily could respond, Summer came back in looking solemn.

"They just told me and Alan Fair about Jessie. They're announcing it to the school that he's been captured by Neci before we start."

Everyone fell silent.

"Man, I really hope he's alright," Pete said. He wasn't looking at anyone in particular but Emily felt like it was addressed to her.

"He's a human fireball," Emily said and everyone laughed

breaking the sombre mood for a second, before they all fell silent again.

There was a round of applause in the stadium and Summer opened the door, so the sound intensified. "Let's go."

They walked in silence towards the sandy pitch and Emily looked up at the stands. She was always taken aback by how full it was. She could spot Lox sitting with the teachers and he waved at her. She waved back as Wesley announced, "And here comes the reigning champions, Ogragon, with a new line up. Led by their captain Summer Wind, we have the new lead Distracter, Raquel Davis, Rosa Martin, first year Amaya Ethan, Warren Kinkle, Pete Kinkle and Emily Knight! As we mentioned moments earlier, Jessie Kendaschi will not be competing today, so Ogragon will be one Fighter down."

The Ogragons stood opposite Linktie, who were dressed all in black. Emily stood next to Summer instead of her usual place as the last fighter, where she would have been opposite Tanya Frank. She caught Summer eyeing Alan Fair up and down. He seemed to have gotten even bigger than last year, which didn't seem possible.

"This is both Wind and Fair's first match leading their teams. . ." Wesley announced.

"I'm sorry about Jessie," Alan Fair said, speaking over Wesley and catching the two teams by surprise.

"Oh. . . thank you," Summer said, looking down the line at her team. "We appreciate that."

"Teams, on my whistle, fly up," Ms Macay said. She placed her lips over the whistle and blew so that it echoed around the stadium, which erupted in cheers.

Emily bent her knees and flew up in the air, hovering on the side.

"And they're off!" Wesley announced. "Wind has been the lead Distracter for Ogragon for years so I'm excited to see how she deals with Alan Fair, who we know is one tough Fighter. Fair's gone for a punch and Wind has ducked and elbowed him in the lower back. New Distracter, Amaya Ethan, has shot a fireball at Fair—he's dodged it but Wind has caught it! She's thrown it back—its hit Fair in the chest but it will take more than that to knock him out. Who are you backing, Harmony? Harmony?"

Emily looked up to the commentators box and tilted her head as she watched Wesley cover his mic and say something to Harmony, who then jumped to her feet and appeared to be shouting something at him.

"Right—so Harmony isn't feeling too well—"

"Don't talk for me, Wesley!" Harmony snapped.

For a moment, everyone seemed to have forgotten about the match and was looking at the commentators box. Ms Macay looked furious.

"Fair seems to be toying with Wind as he effortlessly dodges her kicks. But isn't that what guys do?" Harmony said. "They act like they want something but they really don't."

"Oh no," Emily said, putting her face in her hands as Warren and Pete laughed beside her.

A few girls in the stands clapped their hands for Harmony. Someone yelled, "Preach!"

Ms Macay bent her knees and flew to the commentators box. Emily tried to focus on the match but she felt like she was watching a car crash.

Harmony was red in the face, on her feet, pointing at Wesley, who was shaking his head. Ms Macay was going back and forth between them both. Harmony burst out crying and threw her mic on the floor, where the feedback echoed around the stadium, making everyone wince and cover their ears. Emily watched guiltily as Harmony ran down the stairs with her long, blonde hair behind her and out of the stadium.

"Sorry about that guys. . . so. . . err. . . okay, I guess I'm doing this by myself. Wind has kicked Fair in the stomach—he's toppled over—she's kicked him in the chin almost taking his head off. Davis has shot a fireball at Fair but Linktie Distracter, Lorlene Sims, has blocked it and now Davis and Sims are going at it. Ogragon Distracter Ethans can really fly! She's zooming all over the place, easily avoiding Linktie Distracters, Tan Matthews and Mary Ching. Ethan has grabbed Fair around the waist and speared him into the invisible wall, making the whole stadium shake."

Emily clapped for Amaya with the rest of the crowd before stealing a quick glance at Wesley, who seemed to have recovered.

"I think everyone is impressed with this Ogragon first year. The Linktie Distracters are blocking Fair, giving him time to breathe, but Ogragon aren't having it! Davis, Martin and Ethan have charged at the Linktie Distracters hitting them with a combo of punches—where's Fair? Oh no! Fair has teleported behind a distracted Wind and thumped her hard on the back—Wind is falling— Fair has shot a huge fireball—hitting Wind on the back of her legs—she's hit the ground—Ferguson Cloud, the flag flyer has raised the red flag—WIND IS OUT OF THE GAME! 1-0 TO LINKTIE!"

"No!" Emily yelled.

Emily watched as Summer rolled back and forth, clutching her leg until she was given Reviving Water. Emily looked up at Alan Fair, who was breathing hard but definitely still up for a fight.

"The next fighter up for Ogragon and taking Jessie Kendaschi's place is Emily Knight!"

The crowd roared for her and Emily flew to the centre off the pitch and faced Alan Fair. She grabbed on to Amaya who was beside her and Amaya looked at her startled.

"I messed up," Amaya cried and Emily shook her head.

"Avoid the Distracters and attack only Alan, okay?"

Amaya nodded vigorously.

Emily had faced Alan a number of times. He wasn't easy but she had to beat him or they could potentially lose all their Fighters to him, giving Linktie the win.

"For you, Jessie," Emily whispered before she charged at Alan with a punch, which he blocked with one hand. She drew her other hand back and threw an uppercut that hit him under the chin. Alan groaned, clutching his bleeding mouth.

"That's it Emily—she's not wasting any time and is hitting Fair with strong jabs—she's flown back and is that a. . . yes, an Anyosingh fireball that is charging at Fair—Lorlene Sims has jumped in front of it and taken the hit instead—she's touched the ground—the blue flag is up—SIMS IS OUT! 1-1 TO OGRAGON."

Emily didn't pay any attention. Whilst Alan was distracted looking at Lorlene, Emily flew behind him and grabbed both off his arms, locking them behind his back. Alan tried to pull his arms forward but Emily gritted her teeth and pulled hard.

"Now!" she yelled.

Amaya kicked Alan across the face, hitting his already tender jaw. She went to go again but Linktie Distracter Mary Ching pulled Amaya back by her ponytail and punched her hard on the face.

"Ethan is falling—a great start to this debut—what? She's back up!"

Amaya caught herself just in time and flew up.

"Yes, Amaya!" Emily heard someone shout from the crowd.

Emily placed her knees behind Alan's back and slowly extended one leg after the other, stretching his body forward as she pulled back his arms. Alan roared in pain.

"Had enough?" Emily shouted, pushing him even further.

A sharp pain on her temple made Emily see stars and she let go of Alan. Emily groaned and Tan Matthews watched her with a smirk as she held her closed fist. Emily slowly flew towards Tan, who began to fly away with her mouth open. Emily shook her head but it was throbbing and she felt hot. Very hot. Suddenly her Dojo kit felt too hot for her body and Emily squeezed her eyes shut.

"Something seems to be wrong with Knight—maybe the punch to the head was too much for her?" Wesley said.

Emily could hear people calling her name but it sounded faint and distorted. She touched her ears and they felt hot to touch. Someone pulled on her shoulder roughly and Emily spun around and punched them. She heard the audience gasp and Emily slowly opened her eyes. She was at the edge of the stadium, in front of the invisible wall and her hands were on fire.

CHAPTER TWENTY-FIVE

Fire Girl

Emily screamed as she shook her hands back and forth. Although protected, the students in front of her got out of their seats and ran. Emily spun around and everyone was staring at her. Someone was on the floor surrounded by people but she wasn't sure if Wesley had announced who it was.

Emily flew towards the middle off the pitch and the Linktie Distracters flew out of her way looking petrified. Raquel, Rosa and Amaya approached her wearily.

"I don't know what's happening," Emily said trembling.

This wasn't like the last time she had created fire. She hadn't heard a voice. Whatever heat was burning inside her was slowly cooling. It felt strangely pleasant.

"It's okay," Raquel said slowly, flying closer.

"Everyone's staring at me," Emily hissed.

"Well, you just punched Alan Fair in the face with a fist that was on fire!"

"I did what?" Emily asked alarmed.

The red flames were dancing around her hands and Emily was amazed that it didn't hurt at all. She touched her hands together and slowly pulled them apart leaving a trail of fire that made the audience exclaim, "Oooh."

"I thought only Jessie could create fire," Rosa said, coming closer but still keeping a cool distance. "This is amazing! Can you still fight?"

"Hell yeah, she can fight!" Raquel answered for her. "Can you keep those flames going?"

"I-I think so."

Raquel rubbed her hands. "Let's light them up."

Emily moved one of her hands over the sleeve of her Dojo kit but although she could feel a slight heat from the fire, it didn't burn her kit, not even a singe. Warren and Pete were watching her in awe whilst the Linktie Dojo team didn't look in any hurry to continue the match.

"That is what you call an unexpected turn of events," Wesley announced. "Ogragon are leading the way with 2-1 and it's time for Linktie's second fighter Craig Neon!"

Craig Neon was a tall, muscular, blue-eyed boy with a moustache and he was staring at Emily with his eyes wide, not moving an inch forward.

"Craig Neon is up next!" Wesley said again, this time sounding amused.

Some of the students laughed. Most were on their feet trying to get a better look at Emily's fire flames.

"Oi, Craig!" Warren Kinkle shouted across the pitch. "If you don't fight, you forfeit the match, mate."

The Linkties were talking to Craig who couldn't keep his eyes off Emily's fire flames.

"Is that true?" Emily asked Raquel, who was grinning from ear to ear.

"Yep, if he chickens out, we've won this."

"Ms Macay's coming," Rosa hissed.

Ms Macay was flying up towards them and for a second Emily thought she was going to be told off until she remembered producing fire wasn't against the Dojo rules but refusing to fight was. Ms Macay was talking with the Linktie Dojo team, who were looking furiously at Emily. Craig looked like he had been frozen. Ms Macay pulled out a microphone from her back pocket.

"Can the Ogragon and Linktie captains please come up?"

"Let's go and eavesdrop," Raquel said pulling Emily forward by her arm.

Emily noticed that Craig looked visibly shaken when she got closer. Summer appeared beside Ms Macay in no time. She caught Emily's eye and winked at her. Alan Fair, on the other hand, was talking aggressively to Craig but he had a fresh burn mark on his left cheek from where Emily had punched him.

"We are not forfeiting," Alan said forcefully.

"I think Craig really wants to," Summer said. "Or he can get smoked by Emily."

"Captains!" Ms Macay snapped.

"Remember last year when Tony got punched in the face by Jessie who used his fire? He said the pain was unbearable," Craig said, pointing at his teammate Tony Welsh. "I thought with Jessie not fighting we wouldn't have to worry about fire."

"We're still fighting, Craig," Alan said.

"Your funeral," Summer said, in a sing-song voice.

Ms Macay gave the thumbs up to Wesley and the stadium went crazy. She blew her whistle before her, Summer and Alan teleported.

Emily felt a stab of guilt for how scared Craig genuinely looked but she didn't even know how to get rid of the fire flames. Emily opened and closed her fists and her hands stayed alight. She flew to Craig, who tried to fly off but Raquel blocked him. He turned around and Emily punched him, landing her knuckles on his cheekbone, exposing raw skin.

Craig screamed and Rosa, who was hovering above them, shot straight down so her feet were on his stomach, forcing him to the floor. Just before they touched the ground she eased up and Craig slammed into the sand to thumping feet from the Ogragons.

"NEON IS OUT THE GAME! 3-1 TO OGRAGON!"

The whistle blew and Tony Welsh stepped forward. He glanced nervously at Emily's hands. From the corner of her eye, Emily spotted Linktie Distracter Mary Ching creep up on Amaya.

"Amaya!" Emily yelled but Mary had already grabbed her in a headlock. Using that distraction, Tony Welsh kicked Emily in the stomach and she toppled forward. He punched her across the face, whipping her neck to the side. Emily threw a punch back and Tony ducked before he head-butted her in the forehead.

Emily stumbled back, clutching her head in pain with her eyes half-closed. She could see Rosa charge at Tony but Distracter Tan Matthews kicked Rosa in the chin with her foot.

Emily shook her head and flew at Tony who teleported behind Emily and elbowed her on the side of her temple. Sharp bursts of pain exploded in her head. It was excruciating, every time she tried to open her eyes.

She could sense Tony coming closer to her. Emily pushed out her hands in front of her attempting to force him back.

"AAAHHHHH!"

Emily squinted and could see that Tony's Dojo kit was on fire!

"Knight threw two fire flames at Walsh and he is falling—someone better have some water to throw over him—but Knight doesn't look too good with all those hits to the head earlier," Wesley said.

She knew by the crowd's reaction that Tony had hit the floor and she heard Ms Macay blow the next whistle but Emily's head was pounding and she was finding it hard to focus. She could sense warriors surrounding her but she didn't know if they were Ogragon or Linktie.

Emily floated back with her eyes closed until she got to the invisible wall and swung her fire-covered hands back and forth in case anyone tried to attack her. There was so much noise and the smell of the fire from her hands was making her head feel worse.

"No!" she heard Raquel yell and a second later, Emily felt somebody fall on top of her and everything was muffled. She was falling in the dark with the wind whipping her face so for a few seconds she couldn't breathe, before she crashed hard on to the floor with sand filling up her mouth. A sizzling sound escaped from her hands.

A. BELLO

She felt herself being flipped over and water being forced into her mouth, before she started to choke. She sat upright and opened her eyes. Summer jumped on her.

"You are brilliant!"

Emily coughed and weakly said, "Thanks. Can I have some more Reviving Water?"

They sat on the bench, watching the rest of the match. Emily kept glancing at her hands expecting them to be on fire again, but they were back to normal, not leaving a trace of the fire abilities.

Summer was ecstatic, filling Emily in on what had happened. Tan Matthews had been hit by Amaya's fireball but she had fallen on Emily, taking her down with her.

"You know this will go down in the history books, right? It was bloody incredible!" Summer said, just as Linktie Fighter, David Blanc, landed by their feet.

"Yes!" Summer pointed at Alan. "We've won this, mate."

"Shut up," Alan said and Summer laughed and sat back down.

"They have one Distracter left and Tanya Frank. They have to beat Warren, Pete and all our Distracters. We've got this in the bag."

Tanya tried her best but she was no match for Warren's fireballs. She landed face first in the sand. Emily and Summer jumped to their feet, cheering loudly, as the final whistle blew.

"And the reigning champions Ogragon are the winners. We can all agree that was some match," Wesley announced.

"We did it!" Summer grinned and hugged Emily. "Oh I wish Jessie could have seen this."

"Me too," Emily said, hugging her back.

An hour later, Emily had changed back into her school uniform. Everyone was hurrying back to their team rooms to get ready for the Revolution Night party.

Emily sat on the bench and stared at her hands that had created fire. *How come I didn't hear the voice?*

She closed her right fist and opened it; there was a small red fire flame in the middle of it. She slowly moved her other hand through the fire flame and there was no pain and no burn marks.

"How is this happening?" Emily said to herself.

Everyone had always told her that she would have a hidden power—something that could give her an edge over other warriors. Maybe this was hers kicking in? But she never thought it would be fire. She thought of Jessie being surrounded by fire when they were at Neci's house and she wondered if it was something she would be able to do if she developed the powers.

Could Scarlett transform into fire?

Emily closed her fist and the fire disappeared. She wished more than anything that her dad had seen her battle today.

"Emily?" The changing room doors opened and Lox came in. "That was amazing."

"Thank you," Emily said, standing up to hug him.

"Do the fire flames hurt?"

Emily shook her head. "Can't feel it. I'm just so glad we won."

"Oh, they stood no chance with you guys. I'm going to head home—you coming?"

"Hello?" Wesley peered into the changing room. "You coming to the party?"

Emily slapped her forehead. "Oh I forgot about that."

"Stay," Lox said, smiling at her. "You deserve to have some fun."

"See you, Lox," Emily said before he closed the door behind him.

Wesley leaned against the door. "You continue to amaze me."

Emily smiled. "I don't even know how I did it."

"That's what makes you special," Wesley said, hugging her.

She rested her head on his chest listening to his heart racing and wondered if he could hear hers racing as well.

"What happened with Harmony?" she asked softly.

Wesley rested his chin on the top of her head. "I broke up with her this morning."

"You actually did it?" Emily asked, pulling her head back.

"I was just thinking about how I was going to be honest about Jessie during the match, but yet I wasn't being honest with her and it wasn't fair. It wasn't fair to you either. In hindsight, maybe saying it before we had to work together wasn't smart."

"You think?" Emily said, shaking her head.

Wesley laughed. "I just said that I didn't think it was working between us and she seemed to take it fine. She was very, you know, Harmony-like about it. That's why it threw me when she went off at me during the match. Anyway, I came to ask you something."

"What is it?"

"Would you be my date tonight to the Revolution Night party?"

"Really? I would like that. Actually I would love to be your date, Mr Parker."

"Why thank you, Miss Knight." Wesley grabbed her hand and spun her around, making her laugh. "Come on, let's get our costumes on."

Emily received a hero's welcome when she walked through the doors of Osaki. Everyone kept stopping her to tell her that she was the warrior of the match. Once she got into the Ogragon team living room, she was greeted by a round of applause.

"Our fire girl!" Summer said, who was dressed in a pink tutu with her blonde hair in a tight high bun.

"Thanks guys," Emily said blushing.

Her bedroom floor was covered in assortment of clothes from her roommates. This year, they had broken the tradition and weren't going in the same costume.

"You are something!" Nicky Johansen ran up to Emily and gave her a hug.

"Brilliant," Michella said. "Trust you to have such a cool power."

Emily laughed. "Says the girl who can heal." Emily walked over to her wardrobe, flung it open and stared at the rack of clothes. "I have nothing to wear!"

"The way you fought today, you should just go as yourself," Violet Hijen said, making everyone laugh.

"Oh my gosh, that's it!" Lisa Fowler said, with her eyes glistening. "We should all go as Emily."

"What?" Emily said, whipping round. "Oh no, don't do that."

"Yes! That's perfect," Sydney John said. "Like we're honouring you."

"But I don't want you to honour me," Emily protested but it fell on deaf ears.

"Let's find some red and orange material that we can wrap around her hands like they're on fire," Lisa said.

Michella looked at Emily amused. "No offence, but I'm not going as you."

"Please don't. They're insane."

"This is perfect! Now we can just wear our training kits," Sarah John said. "Thank God I don't have to wear heels!"

"I don't think Emily's comfortable with—" Daisy Atam began to say.

Sarah huffed at her. "Emily is fine with it! Come on Daisy, get in the Revolution Night spirit."

Emily put her hands on her hips. "Girls, I really don't want—"

"Where's your Dojo kit?" Lisa asked, cutting Emily off. Emily frowned and Lisa rolled her eyes. "You know, so I can look like I just won the match."

"You're crazy," Emily said.

There was a knock on the door and Emily couldn't be more grateful for the interruption. Jason and Wesley entered the room in the same black suits and sunglasses they wore every year. Emily could feel Jason looking at her through his sunglasses, but she deliberately looked the other way.

Nicky looked them up and down and tutted. "Ain't you got anything else to wear?"

Wesley popped his collar. "If it's not broke, don't fix it."

"It broke two years ago," Nicky said, making everyone laugh.

"Whatever," Wesley said. He peered over his sunglasses at Emily. "And who are you meant to be?"

Emily looked down at her school uniform. "Just. . . nobody." She grinned at a confused Wesley.

"And what are the Ogragon ladies going as this year?" Jason asked and Lisa blushed when he looked at her.

"We're going as our girl," Violet said, pointing at Emily.

"Huh?" Wesley said, taking off his sunglasses. "You're all going as Emily and Emily is going as nobody?"

"And I'm going as a fairy," Michella said. "I still have the costume from last time."

"You ready to go then?" Wesley asked Emily.

Michella looked back and forth between them. She slowly smiled. "Wait, are you going together?"

"Isn't he with Harmony Loving-Dale?" Violet said in what she thought was a whisper.

Nicky rolled her eyes. "Weren't you at the match? Didn't you see her run out?"

Emily grabbed her hair brush and ran it through her hair before coating her lips in gloss.

"Let's go," she said, ignoring Jason, as she grabbed Wesley's hand, leading him out the door.

The Revolution Night party was in full swing and Emily guided Wesley though the throng of people, who kept stopping her to say how great she'd battled earlier. They went to the food table and Emily piled her plate high. Wesley looked at her amused as she began to eat with her hands.

"You need a fork?" he asked, and laughed when Emily shook her head. She hadn't eaten for hours. She always felt ravenous after Dojo. "Are they really going as you?"

Emily swallowed. "Unfortunately."

"Well, you are the great Emily Knight."

Emily punched him in the arm. "Don't you start."

Wesley stole a hot wing from her plate.

"Hey," she said as he stuffed it in his mouth.

"Come on, let's dance."

To her annoyance, he placed her plate of food on the table, grabbed her hand and led her to the dance floor. She spotted the girls from her dorm with their red and orange coloured hands and led Wesley away from them, right next to the girls from Jenkint, where Harmony Loving-Dale glared at Wesley and walked in the opposite direction.

"I love this song!" Wesley shouted over the music, dancing vigorously, unaware of anything that had just happened.

"I can see." Emily laughed. "Good moves."

"You can't even handle all this," Wesley said, doing an elaborate high kick that almost knocked over a sixth year's top hat. "Oops."

Emily threw her head back and laughed loudly.

Wesley grabbed her hands and pulled her close. Time seemed to fly by and Emily was having the best time.

"I need a drink," she said, motioning a cup to her mouth.

"Cool," Wesley said, still moving his feet from side to side.

Emily walked to the food table and poured herself some iced water. She looked back at the crowd and next to her was a blond boy in a black suit and sunglasses.

"Let me explain," Jason said quickly before Emily could

speak. "I know I didn't have your back in there with Neci but I couldn't tell her where Scarlett was. I know where she is. Roberta told me everything."

Emily frowned. "She told you?"

Jason removed his sunglasses and looked at her sadly. "I spoke to her about the voices that you said was making you create fire. I wanted to know if she knew anything about it. . . if she could help. She tried to brush it off like it was nothing. I kept on at her and then she told me about Scarlett, about what's happening to you."

"What's happening to me?" Emily asked slowly.

"Roberta doesn't want you to know just yet," Jason said, leaning closer as someone had turned up the music. "She said she'll tell you when she thinks you're ready. I get what Roberta is doing and why, but on the flipside, I feel like she should have asked you if you were okay with it."

"Okay with what?" She put her drink on the table. "I thought maybe the fire was my hidden power."

Jason hesitated. "It is. . . kind of. Did you hear the voice earlier? Before your hands were on fire during the match?"

Emily shook her head. "It just happened and in the changing room I tried to see if the fire would come and it did."

It was only for a second but Emily saw the look Jason gave her. He looked frightened.

"Jason, is something wrong with me?" Emily asked.

Say no, say no, she said to herself.

"Not wrong," Jason said uncertainly. "Just. . ." He sighed and rubbed his face. "Talk to Roberta."

CHAPTER TWENTY-SIX

Crossroads

The snow was a few centimetres deep. Emily peered out of the hotel window; she could see Legends Village some metres away. She watched the snowflakes and felt like it was cleansing the area, wiping out any trace of the fire and allowing them to start all over again. For a second, she could almost forget the attack.

Her family had been staying at a hotel not too far from home. Sally and Michael felt they were getting under the Kinkle's feet especially with Christmas approaching. The house was still being re-built and thankfully the hotel they were at hadn't been damaged by the attack and was close enough that they could keep an eye on the building work. The only downside was the press were camped outside the hotel, bothering anyone and everyone to give them a statement.

Emily rested her forehead against the cold window and closed her eyes. The morning after the Revolution Night party Emily had asked Lox to tell Roberta to visit her. Roberta said she would but Emily was yet to see her.

She wondered if Jason was the only other person who knew. She didn't understand why Roberta was making him keep it a secret. Every time Emily questioned him on what she said, he would tell her that Roberta would explain.

Because they weren't staying in the Village, Emily couldn't go over to Roberta's house so the first thing Emily asked Sally, when she came down for the weekend, was to help her get in contact with Roberta. But Sally told her that Roberta, Jenkins and their boys had gone to Italy to visit her family for a few weeks. That was strange. Roberta usually went to Italy for a few days. Emily couldn't help but feel like Roberta was purposely avoiding her but why?

"You okay over there?" Cathy asked and Emily turned around to sit on the window seat.

"Yeah, was just watching the snow. It's so pretty."

"It is." Cathy came and stood next to her, hugging herself.

Emily glanced down noticing the shopping bags by Cathy's feet. "Where did you go?"

"Oh, I had to collect the delivery from reception. I passed Julian on the way."

"Julian?" Emily said surprised. "He's staying here?"

"Yeah, apparently a floor below. He looked shocked to see me. He asked if you were around to come over." Cathy smiled. "Door 99."

Emily grabbed her trainers and put them on. "I'll go and say hi."

"I'm sure you will," Cathy sang. "Dinner's in an hour."

Emily took the lift down a floor and walked down the corridor to door 99. Just as she was about to knock, the door opened. Julian's mother, Tahama, was wearing a thick fur

311

coat and black boots. She smiled when she saw Emily but her eyes looked tired.

"Oh Emily, good to see you. How is everyone?"

"Good," Emily said. "Off somewhere nice?"

Tahama pulled a face. "I'm off to see how the repairs are going on the house. I hate seeing it like that. So empty." Tahama shook her head. "I just can't get the attack out of my head. Anyway, ignore me." She forced a smile. "Julian's inside."

Tahama held the door open for Emily as she walked into the plush hotel suite. It was pretty identical to hers but not as big. Julian was sitting on the couch and he stood to his feet when he saw her.

"Hey, I didn't even know you were staying here," Julian said.

"Same. I just came down to visit for the weekend."

He hugged her before gesturing at her to sit down. "First time back?"

Emily nodded. "It's weird isn't it?"

"Very. I've been down a few time 'cause Mum is having a hard time after everything. My granddad is sorting the repairs so we're going to be here for a few more weeks before going to see him for Christmas."

"I think we all need to be around family right now," Emily said. "And how are you doing?"

Julian shook his head. "I can't believe I saw Neci. Like, she was in front of us, in the flesh."

Emily shuddered. "I know. I've seen her twice now and it's still horrible."

"Her power!" Julian said with his eyes wide. "I knew she was strong but man she is on another level."

"Between her and Blade—"

"Blade!" Julian exclaimed. "It was like a never-ending nightmare. I can't even believe that we got away from them. . . but Jessie." Julian glanced at her. "I can't stop thinking about him."

"Me too," Emily said, looking down at her hands. "I feel so guilty that we left him with that monster."

"We're going to get him back," Julian said. "You want a drink or anything?"

Emily shook her head and Julian got up and went to the fridge.

"You were amazing during the Dojo match," Julian said, leaning in the doorway with a fizzy drink in his hand. "Fire girl."

Emily smiled. "Thank you."

"But how did you do that?"

"Err. . . I'm still trying to figure that out," Emily confessed.

"Did you have fun at the Revolution Night party?" Julian came and sat beside her.

"It was fun actually. I needed that after the whole Jessie situation. What did you go as? I didn't even see you."

Julian slurped from his drink. "I didn't wear a costume this year. I just couldn't get into the party mood but I saw you though, with Wesley." Emily glanced at him and Julian was staring back at her. "Is that a thing?"

"We're not boyfriend or girlfriend but we do like each other," Emily said, avoiding Julian's gaze.

"I like you," Julian said and Emily looked at him. "I like you a lot."

Emily remembered the first boy she had really noticed at

Osaki was Julian Kena. There was a time she felt so shy to even speak to him! But over the past year they had gotten closer, especially after Blade. Julian was her first kiss.

"I thought you liked me too," Julian said softly.

Why was he so beautiful?

"I do like you." Emily rubbed her face. "I just. . . I don't really know right now what I want to do. Sorry, I'm just trying to be honest."

"I appreciate that." Julian gently wiped a stray hair from her face. "I don't think we have the luxury to not be honest." He squeezed her hand.

Emily glanced down at their hands and she didn't move her hand away.

Osaki was covered in tinsel and fairy lights. The huge Christmas tree in the dining hall was beautifully decorated and was so tall that the star on the top almost touched the ceiling.

Emily and Michella passed it as they went up the stairs to their bedroom.

"I feel like we haven't hung out together in a while," Michella said, jumping on her bed.

"It's been a rough few days, hasn't it?" Emily sat next to Michella.

"I just keep seeing Neci, Dion and Maggie. I healed so quick that the pain didn't last long but once they put me in the cell. . . I don't even know what they had planned."

"I'm glad we got you in time." Emily hugged her. "It was weird without you."

Michella smiled. "And how are you holding up with everything?"

"I feel like once we get Jessie and Professor Elwood, it will all work out fine. My dad will be healed and Jessie can teach me more about this fire power. We'll be united again."

Michella sighed. "I want nothing more but does it make me awful that I really don't want to go back to Neci's house?"

Emily shook her head. "I don't either. None of us do. It was so scary."

"I really thought we were going to die. I have never been so scared in my life. Oh I didn't even tell you. Yesterday Mr Davon said he wants me to train with him. He wants to test out my healing powers."

"That's cool!"

"I've never had one-on-one time with Mr Davon before."

"I'm sure whatever he teaches you will be amazing. Speaking of training, I'm going home before dinner because Lox is going to train me tonight," Emily said.

"No way! That will be fun."

Emily gave Michella a look and she laughed. "Fun isn't the word I'm thinking of."

"Lift the car."

Emily looked at Michael's black Range Rover and back at Lox. "What?"

Lox crossed his arms. "The car. Lift it."

Emily laughed but instantly saw that Lox was serious. "How?"

Lox raised his eyebrows. "Err. . . bend your knees, put your hands under the car and lift. You're telling me you've never lifted a vehicle?"

Emily threw her hands in the air. "Why would I have lifted a vehicle?"

Lox walked past her, bent down low, until his hands had a firm grip on the car and slowly stood to his feet, lifting the car up high above his head. He grinned at her.

"It's a good way to train. Here, catch."

"Don't," she yelled and instantly covered her head.

Lox placed the car down and sat on top of the bonnet. "I'm teaching you exactly how I was trained, so come on." He patted the car.

Emily walked slowly towards the Range Rover and gulped. Master Zen had made her break a tree with her head last term. She had seen stars and had a massive bump on her head but there was Reviving Water to heal her. There was none here.

Emily rubbed her sweaty hands on her training kit. She bent her knees and held on tight to the car. She took a deep breath and exhaled before she stood up, pulling the car up with her. When she saw she was doing it she almost dropped the car in surprise. Apart from a slight strain in her lower back, she couldn't feel a thing.

Lox peered over at her grinning. "Now, that's what I'm talking about!"

"Why is it so easy?" Emily asked confused, lifting the car up over her head.

"Because you're strong."

Emily waited to feel something from her body to remind

her that she was lifting a huge car in the air but she was fine. Emily bent her arms and lifted it back up again.

Lox rolled his eyes. "Okay now you're just showing off. We'll go bigger next time. We'll use trucks."

"Trucks!"

"Those big eighteen wheeler ones," Lox said with his arms stretched out wide. "Let's see how you get on with that."

When Emily and Lox walked into their hotel suite, Emily gasped.

"Who picked out the Christmas decorations? They look beautiful."

"I think Sally hired a company," Lox said. "It looks nice in here. I'm going to jump in the shower real quick."

As soon as he left, Sally walked into the living room, wiping her hands with a dish cloth. "How was training?"

"It was better than I thought it would be. This looks very cool."

"I wanted to go all out this year what with everything that happened and your Dad not being here."

"Well, thank you," Emily said hugging her. "I love it."

"And I wanted to make it special for Lox."

"Lox?" Emily frowned, pulling away from her.

"Yeah, I asked him what he did with Neci for Christmas, if he got any gifts and he just laughed. He said a new fighting move would be the present."

Emily couldn't imagine Neci presenting anyone with a gift wrapped in a bow.

"So what do you think I should get Lox for Christmas? I remember when your mum was here and Lox used to love all the presents."

"Maybe some clothes that aren't black?" Emily suggested and Sally rolled her eyes in response.

"There you are."

Emily, Michella, Wesley and Jason were walking through the grounds of Osaki when Tanya Frank stepped in front of them.

"Excuse me," Emily said, trying to get past her but Tanya stepped to the side blocking her, to the amusement of her friends.

"Move Tanya," Wesley said but Tanya smirked in response.

"I wanted to give you this," Tanya said, handing Emily the newspaper she was holding in her hand.

"She doesn't need to read that," Michella said, snatching the newspaper before Emily could take it. She pulled on Emily's jacket. "Come on."

Emily followed her in a daze and she heard Tanya shout, "Where is he then?"

"What is she talking about?" Emily asked and she saw Michella glance nervously at Wesley and Jason. Emily looked at the newspaper and reached her hand out for it.

"We should have warned you," Wesley said.

Michella gave her the paper. "Don't pay any attention to it."

Emily looked at the front page. "Where is Thomas Knight?" She flicked the pages to read the article. "They think. . . he's dead?"

"No one has seen him so people are talking," Jason said.

"What people?" Emily asked sharply.

"I've heard a few things said around school," Wesley confessed. "Just people wondering where he is."

"Like I need to deal with all this," Emily said, ripping the paper in two. "We're going to be late for class." She stormed off ahead.

Emily was barely listening in History class. Seeing an article about her dad being dead felt like a punch to her stomach. Seven was doing all she could to keep him alive but there was a strong chance he could die.

"Miss Knight?" Mr King was peering at her from under his trilby hat. "Did you hear what I just said?"

"Sorry. . ." Emily shook her head. "Can you repeat it please?"

Mr King sighed. "How did Kwame Adeyemi win the battle at High Rock against Lin Cho in 1986?"

Emily glanced down at her History book and back at Mr King. She had no idea what he was talking about.

"Transferring power from Cho," Jason hissed from the desk next to hers.

"He transferred his power," Emily said. "From Lin Cho."

Mr King nodded. "Good! Adeyemi had a special skill where he could absorb power from any of his opponents but he was also able to transfer his power. He is what you call a Somperu and that's why he was able to defeat Cho with her own special power—electricity."

"She could literally zap people?" Wesley asked. "Very cool."

"It is more than cool, Mr Parker," Mr King drawled. "Somperu is a rare skill. In fact there hasn't been a warrior known to have that gift since Adeyemi."

"Don't you love when he actually teaches us something?" Michella said, as they walked out of History.

"It actually was a good lesson for once," Jason said. He nudged Emily. "Are you still thinking about the newspaper article?"

"Yeah and my dad. . . just everything really."

A familiar figure was walking towards her.

"Is that Lox?" Wesley asked.

"He was down this weekend. Making me lift cars," Emily said.

"Err what?" Michella said, looking alarmed. "You're joking right?"

"I wish." Emily laughed. "I'll catch you guys later."

Lox walked through the busy corridor ignoring the excited students asking for a photo.

"Have you got another lesson?" Lox asked.

Emily shook her head. "Why?"

"I saw the newspaper and figured you might want to see Dad?"

"Yes please," Emily said. "When?"

"Meet me outside the front doors in five. . ."

The howling wind around Seven's house was always a struggle to walk through. Emily held on to Lox's jacket as she ducked her head. She could barely keep her eyes open as the wind hit her face. She could sense the warriors who surrounded her before she saw them but this time they greeted Lox like an old friend.

Once inside, Lox glanced at Emily and burst out laughing. "Your hair."

"Leave me alone," Emily moaned, pressing her hair down.

Still laughing, Lox led the way to Thomas's room and Emily nervously followed. She wanted to open the door and see her dad standing tall and back to normal. She would give anything to see him full of life again.

Lox held open the door and Emily's heart fell when she saw him still lying in the bed with wires crisscrossing over his body. Seven was hunched over him, her hands hovering just above his torso. She looked more tired than usual and Emily knew that the strain of keeping Thomas alive was getting to her.

"Hi Seven, any change?" Lox asked and Seven shook her head.

"Any updates on Professor Elwood?" she asked, keeping her eyes on Thomas.

Lox glanced at Emily. "Not yet but we're planning to go again after Christmas Day and rescue him."

"We are? Will Roberta and Jenkins be back?" Emily asked.

"They should be but regardless I'm leading the rescue and Alice will be second in charge, seeing as you gave her that power. I'm taking everyone from the elite group, including you."

"Oh, I don't know. . ."

"Look at him," Lox said gently. "He won't be here much longer."

Emily looked at Lox alarmed. "What do you mean?"

Only then did Seven look at Emily. Emily tried to hide her surprise at the dark circles under her eyes.

"He has a few months left at max," Seven said matter-of-factly and Emily gasped. "The poison is spreading. I'm doing the best I can."

"Would a second healer help?" Emily asked. "My mate Michella can heal."

Seven smiled sadly. "The poison will still spread without the antidote."

"I promise you, Seven, we will have the Professor here. Won't we, Emily?" Lox said.

Emily stared at her dad. He looked so small and weak. He couldn't only have a few months left. What would they do if he died? If she hadn't messed up the first time, he would already be fine. She couldn't afford to mess up again, but what if she did? What if he died because of her?

"I need some air," Emily said, running out of the door and into the living room, where she hunched over with her hands on her knees, breathing in and out.

"You'll be okay," a voice said behind her and Emily jumped.

Seven stood with her hands clasped in front of her.

"I don't want to mess it up," Emily whispered.

"You cannot judge yourself based on one mistake," Seven said. She walked towards Emily. They were the same height. "Your father needs you. Whenever you start to feel scared, remember that he would do the same for you."

"I don't know what I'd do if he dies. . ."

"Do not think like that. You can rescue the Professor. I have every faith in you, okay? You need to have faith in yourself."

"I'm trying to," Emily said in a small voice.

Seven smiled at her. "Keep trying. We all believe in you."

CHAPTER TWENTY-SEVEN

Christmas

On Christmas Eve, Emily and Lox set out early to visit their mother's grave. Emily didn't want Lox to know that she was nervous. She hadn't been back since the funeral and the only memory she had was that it had been heavy with rain, her dad was crying, and Lox hadn't been there.

Lox seemed to know the way to the grave easily which confused Emily. They both had a massive bouquet of colourful flowers that Sally insisted on paying for. Emily could see how proud Sally was that she was finally going to the cemetery.

"There," Lox said, pointing in front of him.

Emily took a deep breath and followed him, shifting the heavy bouquet from one arm to the other. She stood next to him and looked down at the marble headstone which read,

'In loving memory of Leah Nicole Knight.
Mother, Wife, Friend, Warrior.
Beautiful. Fearless. Wonderful.'

It was strange to think that she was standing on the soil that her mother was buried under. She shook her head. She didn't want to think of her mother under the earth. Emily bent her knees and lowered the flowers over the grave and Lox followed suit.

"Hey, Mum," Lox said gently and Emily glanced at him. "It's me. . . and Emily. We miss you so much." He stood to his feet. Emily shuffled nervously. "You don't have to say anything."

"How do you seem so comfortable when it's your first time here?"

Lox laughed. "This isn't my first time here! Why would you think that?"

"Because you missed the funeral and you were on the run."

"I was at the funeral."

Emily gasped. "No. . . you couldn't have. . . I looked for you."

Lox looked slowly around the gravesite before he pointed to a tree not too far from where they were standing. "I was in the branches."

Emily followed his gaze. It was so packed that day. So many people wanted to say goodbye to Leah Knight. Emily remembered looking everywhere for her brother. She had felt angry and heartbroken that he had chosen not to come but he had been hovering above them the whole time.

"I wasn't ready to come back, but I heard through the grapevine about Mum and I was just so mad at myself. I left her and she got worse. I was meant to come and see her." Blinking hard, Lox looked up to the sky. "I didn't leave my room for weeks after the funeral. That's when Neci told me about her grandparents and how they died. We spent the whole night talking about Mum and her grandparents. I think she thought I was going to go back home and I think she would have let me, but I couldn't imagine going back to the Village, to the house, without Mum." Lox looked down at her. "But I should have come back for you. You lost your whole family that day."

"Dad got really sad after Mum. I tried to help but I was only seven." Emily shrugged her shoulders. "He couldn't look after me. He could barely look after himself. I remember one day he seemed to have this light about him and I thought, finally, he's back. I was so happy. . . and then he told me he was leaving to look for you."

"I'm sorry," Lox whispered.

"It was Mum's last wish," Emily said. "I begged him not to leave me. I told him I would be alone and he said, 'Your godparents will move in with Cathy.' He just didn't understand that he could fill the house with a million people but without family I would always feel alone." Emily stared at Lox. "Do you ever regret it? Running away?"

"I regret not talking more to Dad about how I felt. How his actions affected me everywhere I went and I just needed to be in my own skin, but we could never have a conversation without us clashing. I saw how our relationship was affecting Mum. She was always torn in the middle and I hated myself for that. I'm just glad that she never knew that I went with Neci because she hated her guts!" Lox suddenly laughed. "I have no doubt Mum would have come for her if she knew I was there."

"What was she like before she got sick?" Emily could only remember her mum being tired all the time.

Lox smiled and his entire face transformed. "Amazing. She was my favourite person in the entire world. She was fun and smart and tough. To be with someone like Thomas Knight and deal with all that attention; she handled it like it was nothing. I loved when it was just me and her. I could talk to her about anything. She was so open and was always cheering way too loud at every battle." Emily laughed. "She would kick out the chefs so she could make her cinnamon buns. She didn't think they could make them as good as her."

"She always smelt like cinnamon," Emily said.

"Always! And she would do anything for us." He wrapped his arm around Emily's shoulders, pulling her close. "She would be so proud of you and who you've become."

"She would be proud that you came home," Emily said.

Lox smiled. "Yeah, she would."

Emily bent down so her face was close to the headstone and whispered, "I love you so much."

Emily tried to get into the Christmas spirit, but she couldn't stop thinking about her dad. Every second he was dying and she had one last chance to change that. If she messed this up, she would never forgive herself.

"Is the turkey too dry?" Michael asked Emily, peering at her over his glasses. His paper hat from the Christmas cracker was lopsided on his head.

"No, it's okay," Emily said, attempting a smile. She moved

a piece of turkey in the rich gravy before chewing it slowly but she had no appetite.

After dessert, everyone was lounging around the living room in a food coma. A Christmas movie that no one was paying attention to was playing. It was like there was an elephant in the room. No one mentioned Thomas, but his presence was sorely missed.

Emily was staring out of the window. The snow had settled, leaving a beautiful carpet of white. Emily took a deep breath. In a few weeks she would be back at the farmhouse with Blade and Neci. She just prayed they could rescue Jessie and Professor Elwood and that they wouldn't lose anyone else.

Emily was seated in an armchair opposite her counsellor Jenny Li with an ice pack behind her back. She was in agony. Lox was bored during Christmas so suggested that they should do more training. He wanted to test her fire abilities. Although she could create fire flames, she couldn't make the fire bigger.

"How does Jessie surround himself with fire?" Emily asked.

"Training," Lox said. "When we get him back, we can ask him to train you."

Lox then made her lift up two eighteen wheeler trucks. Although she had managed it, she felt the strain even more and when she woke up the next day, every muscle and joint was screaming. Not as loud as Sally did when she found out how they were training.

"I'm confused. Why would lifting trucks help you?" Jenny asked, during their counselling session.

"Strength training," Emily said, wincing as a sharp pain shot across her shoulders.

"Can't your friend help you? Which one is it again that heals?"

"Michella, and yeah she's coming over later."

Jenny scribbled something in Emily's file whilst Emily gazed out of the window. Now that the snow had cleared, it had left behind a grey mess with various footsteps that ran across it. She would be back at school in a few days, which meant that the second rescue mission was going to happen.

Emily couldn't shake the feeling that something was going to go terribly wrong. There had been no word of Neci, which always frightened her. At least when she was causing trouble, they knew where she was and what she was up to.

"What are you thinking?" Jenny asked softly.

"My dad," Emily lied, looking at the floor.

"When is he back from his travels?"

Lox had told her not to tell Jenny about what was going on, even though Emily protested that Jenny was practically family and she knew when she was hiding something. Lox didn't budge on his decision.

"Soon I think," Emily said, attempting a smile. "I just miss him loads."

"And nothing else has been happening? Anything troubling you?"

My dad is dying. Somehow I can create fire.

"Nope. Nothing."

Michella, Wesley and Jason came over to Emily's hotel later that day.

"Very nice," Wesley said, looking around.

After Michella had healed Emily's back, they hung out in Emily and Cathy's bedroom. Michella was laying on her stomach on Emily's bed with her feet on Jason's lap and Wesley was sitting on the floor next to Emily.

"I have something to say," Emily said, clearing her throat nervously. "I know we said no more secrets after Blade but I just didn't know how to say this." Emily took a deep breath. "I was hearing this voice telling me to create fire for a while and was feeling these weird symptoms. I felt my body burning up and then fire would come out of me. It felt like someone was controlling me."

"Controlling you?" Michella said alarmed, sitting up. "Did you recognise the voice?"

"It sounds familiar but I can't put my finger on it. It's definitely a female voice."

"You should have told us," Wesley said, looking hurt.

"I only told Jason."

"You knew?" Michella screeched and Jason blushed.

"It's not his fault," Emily protested. "I told him not to tell anyone."

"So, is that what happened during the match? You heard that voice?" Wesley asked.

Emily looked at her hands. "That's the weird thing, I didn't hear anything and when the fire came it felt almost natural to me. It doesn't make sense." Emily closed her eyes and blurted out, "Scarlett is in the Village. Roberta brought her."

"Shut up." Wesley jumped up in shock. "Please tell me you're joking?"

"You know the last house that's always empty? That's

where she is. I mean I think she still is. Roberta may have moved her."

"Why would Roberta do that?" Michella cried. "Is she trying to get us killed?"

"She's not. Don't worry," Jason muttered.

Michella laughed uncertainly. "And how do you know that?"

Emily and Jason locked eyes but neither of them said anything. Michella looked back and forth between them.

"Hello?" Michella snapped.

"I don't know what's going on with me, but Roberta does," Emily said slowly, turning away from Jason's glare. "She told Jason, but he won't tell me."

Michella hit Jason's leg hard. "Tell us!"

"I can't," Jason said looking pained. "I promised."

"So what?" Wesley said, crossing his arms. "Spill."

"No," Jason said forcefully and Michella jerked her head back surprised. Jason turned his gaze to the window signalling that the conversation was over.

They sat in a tense silence. Michella kept shooting dirty looks at Jason who refused to look at her. Wesley kept glancing nervously at Emily as if she was going to burst into flames any second.

"Anyone else hiding any secrets?" Michella asked, glaring at Jason who didn't respond.

Emily glanced at Wesley who was fiddling beside her.

"Me and Emily kissed!" Wesley said.

"Wesley!" Emily said surprised at the same time Jason said, "When?" and Michella said, "What did you say?"

"I'm sorry but I don't want to keep pretending like

something isn't here between us," Wesley explained, looking apologetically at Emily. "Especially with everything going on."

Michella smirked. "So that's why you broke up with Harmony."

Wesley nodded.

"You're dating then?" Jason asked uncertainly.

Wesley opened his mouth but then looked stumped. He looked at Emily confused.

"We're just. . ." Emily started but she didn't know. They hadn't had a conversation about it. Did it make sense starting a relationship in the middle of a war? Or was that a reason why they shouldn't wait to start one? And then there was Julian. "Seeing how things go," she eventually said and Wesley smiled satisfied.

"I hate to be the one to say it but what about Julian?" Michella asked. "I thought you liked each other?"

"I. . . I mean we. . ."

"It's okay," Wesley said and everyone looked at him surprised. "I know that you and Julian got close, especially after Blade. I just wanted to know if you liked me back. I think let's just see how things play out and what's meant to be will be."

"Wow," Michella said looking at Wesley in awe. "Very mature. I didn't know you had it in you."

"Shut up," Wesley said and Michella laughed.

"Thank you," Emily said gratefully.

She felt like her head was muddled up; Wesley being so understanding wasn't what she was expecting.

"Are we just going to ignore the fact that we're going back to the farmhouse?" Jason said. "I don't want to go back."

"Join the club," Michella mumbled.

"We'll have Lox and a better plan this time," Emily said confidently.

Michella gasped. "Wait, you're coming?"

Emily nodded. "But who knows what role Alice will give me. She'll probably leave me standing guard or something."

"We can't mess this up," Wesley said. "No matter what happens we need to get Jessie and the Professor. All these petty arguments need to be left behind."

"I'm not going to be left doing nothing because of Alice!" Emily argued.

"If I was you, I would just do what she says," Jason said and he held up his hand when Emily went to argue. "As much as we may not like it, we need Alice and if her bossing you about will make her feel better—therefore fight better—let her do what she wants."

Emily tutted and crossed her arms. Now she was seriously regretting giving that power to Alice.

CHAPTER TWENTY-EIGHT

The Sky Is On Fire

The first day back at Osaki, Mr Davon was seated at the far end of the hall with the teachers and Lox. Emily caught his eye and felt nervous to wave or smile after he had snapped at her in his office. Maybe Mr Davon sensed that because he gave Emily a warm smile, which encouraged her to smile back.

Emily sat at the table with her friends and poured herself a bowl of cereal. She was already over today. She had Meditation first thing, followed by Foughtgon class, two essays she had to finish because she hadn't done them over Christmas, and a training session with the elite team.

As she ate, she saw Ms Macay whisper something to Julian who looked surprised but then nodded.

What was that about? Emily wondered.

She didn't have to wait long, Ms Macay was walking towards her table in her red training kit that matched her hair.

"Stay in the hall after breakfast. Mission has been moved forward," she whispered before she walked off.

Michella dropped her fork that clattered nosily to the floor.

Emily looked at her friends. "She must have got that wrong, right?"

"Do you think forward means today?" Jason asked alarmed.

Wesley shook his head. "No way! We're not ready yet."

But as they stood in front of Mr Davon and Lox with the rest of the elite team after breakfast (minus Xavier and Antonio), Emily knew that it wasn't good news from the grave faces of Mr Davon and Lox.

"Roberta had a vision that the Professor is being moved this morning. We don't know why or where they're going but we need to go as soon as possible and rescue him," Lox said.

"What about Jessie?" Gabriel Thompson asked.

"You're rescuing him too. I do fear this will be our last chance to get them safely," Mr Davon said.

"Are Roberta and Jenkins helping us?" Julian asked and Mr Davon shook his head.

"They're still in Italy," he said, glancing at Emily for a second. "But you're all more than capable to make this rescue mission a success. Lox, would you like to explain the plan?"

Lox was wearing a black training kit and his Afro hair was pulled back into a tight ponytail accentuating his sharp cheekbones.

"I wish we had more time but we don't. If you see any warriors around, especially Neci's core ones—take them out."

"What do you mean by that?" Gabriel asked nervously.

"Do whatever it takes. Don't hold back on them because they will kill you and we already know that they don't care that you're kids. This is a rescue but it's also a survival mission and I would like us all to return back here in one piece. If you listen to my instructions, it shouldn't be a problem." Lox began to pace slowly with his hands behind his back. "I need three teams. Three of us will find Professor Elwood, three will find Jessie, and I need at least two of you keeping watch. To get Professor Elwood, I want it to be me, Julian and Emily—"

"Can I interrupt?" Alice said, with her hand in the air. "I don't think Emily should be rescuing anyone. She should keep watch."

Emily rolled her eyes, not the least bit surprised.

Lox looked at Emily and then back to Alice. "Why?"

Alice scoffed. "Because she was a complete mess last time. If it wasn't for me, we wouldn't even have had a plan! She's too big of a risk and I don't think it's smart to use her."

Jason who was standing beside Emily, gently squeezed her arm and whispered, "Remember, what I said."

"She's impulsive at the best of time," Alice continued. "And I would feel more comfortable knowing she was keeping watch, which is still an important part of the plan."

"Oh, is that right?" Michella argued. "You were offended that Emily left you to watch."

"But I did it!" Alice snapped back.

"So do it again," Michella growled, walking up to Alice.

"Hey!" Lox said, stepping in-between them. "That's not what we're going to do, okay? If we're fighting here, we're might as well just give ourselves up to Neci."

"Sorry," Michella said, crossing her arms and turning away from Alice.

"Sorry, but I stand by what I said," Alice said, with her hands on her hips. "I'm second in charge, right? Doesn't my opinion count?"

"Nope," Michella shot back and Alice glared at her.

Lox rubbed his hands across his face and sighed. "Emily, do you mind keeping watch?"

Everyone looked at Emily. Julian was subtly shaking his head and Alice's piercing green eyes zeroed in on her. Emily didn't know what to do. She knew this was her fault, giving away her power to Alice, and now she was paying for it. She wanted to fight alongside Julian and Lox, take out as many of Neci's warriors and find Professor Elwood but there was another part of her that was scared. As selfish as she knew it was, she didn't want to get blamed if at all went wrong. Maybe Jason was right. An angry Alice does fight better.

"I'll stand guard," Emily said to the surprise of everyone.

"Can I stand guard with her?" Michella asked.

"Okay, cool, so Alice, Gabriel and Jason, you find Jessie and Wesley and Julian you'll come in my team. Any questions?" When no one answered, Lox rubbed his hands. "Good, I'll give you ten minutes to get ready. Meet me by the big oak tree. Emily, a word?"

Emily stayed back as the rest of the team headed out of the dining hall. Julian gave her a sympathetic smile as he walked past her.

"You sure?" Lox asked.

Emily nodded. "I just want Dad to get better."

Lox wrapped an arm around her and kissed her forehead. "He will. I promise you."

They flew to the farmhouse in silence. Mr Davon suggested flying would save more energy than teleporting so many people. The curved bridge was in the distance and Lox signalled to them to keep going. Emily glanced down as they soared over it and she realised that being up this high, the energy surrounding the bridge didn't affect them.

After they had passed it, Lox pointed down to the floor. They landed behind the trees, where they had a clear view of the farmhouse.

"That's weird," Jason said frowning. "Where's her army gone?"

Emily followed his gaze and realised that it was deserted. The people, the tanks, everything apart from the farmhouse had disappeared.

"Are we too late?" Emily asked worried and Lox shook his head but he looked nervous.

"We can't be. Wait here—I'll be back." He teleported before they had a chance to ask him where he was going. Emily dug her hands in her pocket. She didn't like this one little bit. Lox was back a few seconds later.

"There's a helicopter behind the house and it's empty so they must still be inside the farmhouse. I can't sense many people though and I can't sense Neci."

"Where would she be?" Julian asked.

"I'm not sure," Lox said. "But stay vigilant because we don't know who's here." He looked carefully at all of them. "We all know what we're doing?"

Everyone nodded.

"You two take these just in case." Lox handed Emily and Michella a small radio each. Emily could faintly hear a news reporter. "Keep the volume low but listen to it. If Neci isn't here, then there may be a sighting of her."

Emily nodded.

"Let's go, team," Lox said.

Emily waved as they left her and Michella alone. Emily held the radio so tight that it was imprinting in her hand.

"Shall we walk around the back so we can see the helicopter?" Michella suggested as she placed the radio in her pocket.

"Good idea," Emily said.

They walked carefully through the trees, peeping through the gaps, but there was nothing to see. The white helicopter was huge up close with several bags leaning beside it.

"Let's grab one and see what's inside," Michella said just as the radio in Emily's hand came to life.

Emily twisted the dials trying to turn down the volume but she froze when she heard a shrill, female voice say, "Neci is here."

"Listen," Emily said to Michella, who took out her radio from her pocket.

The static made Emily wince. She slowly walked through the trees trying to get a good enough signal. She could only hear parts of the announcement.

"Neci is. . . iceman. . . so many. . . army. . . microchip. . . blank faces. . . robots are attacking. God help us."

The static took over the reporters voice and Emily looked at the radio confused. *Robots?*

"We have to tell Lox about Neci and Blade," Michella said at the same time a door swung open from the back of the farmhouse.

"Look," Emily said.

Dion was marching towards the helicopter, holding

Professor Elwood tight by the arm. As soon as they disappeared inside the helicopter, Maggie and Jessie left the farmhouse. Jessie's arms were in front of him and his hands looked like they were bound together. He was digging his feet into the ground as Maggie tried to pull him forward.

"Oh my gosh, they're there! Michella?" Emily questioned but Michella didn't respond. Emily glanced over her shoulder and caught her breath when she saw Michella staring at her with a vacant look on her face. Emily took a step closer towards her. "Michella?"

Suddenly, Michella lunged at her and Emily yelled and swiftly moved to the side. Michella looked like she was falling face first to the floor, but instead she did a roll and jumped back to her feet with two, red fireballs in her hand.

"What are you doing?" Emily asked but it was like Michella couldn't even hear her, like she was a robot.

"Robot, robot." Emily desperately tried to remember what the reporter said, then it clicked. *Does Michella have the microchip?*

Emily looked at Michella's arms but they were covered. Michella charged at her and Emily turned and sprinted through the trees, towards the helicopter.

Professor Elwood was looking solemnly out of the window of the helicopter but when he saw Emily, he banged his fists on the window and silently screamed. A second later, Dion's raging face appeared from another window.

Maggie and Jessie looked surprised to see Emily sprinting towards them with Michella on her heels. Jessie quickly recovered and elbowed a distracted Maggie hard in the face and she collapsed on all fours to the ground.

"Emily!" Jessie yelled.

"Oof." Emily fell to the floor as Michella's fireballs hit her hard on the back. The intense heat made Emily cry out. Her eyes started to water and through it she could see that the helicopter blades were slowly starting to turn.

Emily gritted her teeth and dragged herself through the dirt. A sharp pain shot through her temple. Emily rolled quickly, escaping the second kick from Michella. When Michella tried again, Emily caught her foot and pulled her forward so Michella landed on her back, hitting her head hard on the ground.

Emily crawled quickly, pinning Michella down, and sat on top of her. Michella was screaming and thrashing around like a wild animal, staring at Emily with a hateful stare. Emily used one hand to hold Michella down and the other to rip Michella's sleeve. She scanned her dark skin, trying to see where the microchip was, but she couldn't see anything. Emily ran her hand over her arm, making Michella scream even louder and just by her bicep she felt a small lump.

"What's happened?" Jessie asked, standing over her, with his hands still tied up.

"Get Professor Elwood! No, get Lox and the others. They're in the house."

"They're here? What's wrong with her?" Jessie asked.

"She's microchipped. I need to get it out." Emily glanced at Jessie's arms. "I think we both need something sharp."

Without a word, Jessie ran and Emily watched him approach Maggie who was still on the ground and he pulled something out of her pocket before running back.

The wind from the helicopter blades was shooting dust

into Emily's eyes and she could barely see Jessie. Emily felt something hard in her hands and Jessie pressed his arms close to her face. Emily gripped the rope before slicing it in half with the blade.

"I'll get the others and Professor Elwood," Jessie said.

"Do you have the energy to teleport?" Emily asked.

Jessie shook his head. "I'll run quick," he promised before he ran towards the farmhouse.

Michella wouldn't stop moving underneath her and was getting more and more aggressive.

"I'm sorry," Emily said before she thrust the knife into Michella's skin.

Michella's scream was drowned out by the noise of the helicopter. Her blood gushed over Emily's hand. Emily dropped the knife and was just about to put her fingers inside the gushing wound but Michella's skin was already healing over it.

"No, no, no." Emily scanned the ground trying to find the knife but Michella raised herself up into a sitting position and head-butted Emily hard on the forehead.

Everything looked like it was spinning as Emily fell backwards to the floor. She could feel Michella sitting on her and suddenly she couldn't breathe, as Michella's hands were wrapped tight around her neck. Squeezing.

Emily used her blood stained hands to scratch at Michella's arms, but Michella pushed down even more, making Emily gasp for breath. She gripped on to Michella's hands and with everything left in her she pulled. Very slowly, she could feel the pressure around her neck loosen and when there was a gap between Emily's neck and Michella's hands, Emily swiped her elbow across Michella's jaw and she fell, landing beside Emily on the floor.

Emily rolled to the side and dry retched as she massaged her bruised neck. The helicopter was hovering above her, swaying from side to side as if someone didn't have control over it. She could see bodies running out of the farmhouse towards her. Emily blinked rapidly. Everything looked like a blur.

Focus, focus, she told herself as she searched for the knife. The silver blade glistened and Emily grabbed it and plunged it again into Michella's arm but this time Emily worked faster. She dropped the knife and put her thumb and finger inside her arm, feeling around. Michella's skin was slowly starting to heal back so Emily punched her hard across the face, which slowed down the healing.

"Come on, come on," Emily said desperately.

Her finger bumped against something small and solid. Emily picked it out and held up a small metal chip. Emily placed it on the floor and rammed her fist against it, breaking it into small pieces.

Michella groaned as slowly her blood began to dry up and her skin started to heal. Emily wiped Michella's blood on her trousers, just as Wesley approached her.

"What the hell?"

"Stay with her," Emily said as she unsteadily stood to her feet. The pain in her head was even stronger.

She could see Jason not far from her, using his powers to hold the helicopter steady. Lox and Dion were on top of it taking blows out of each other, as Julian was flying a shaken Professor Elwood out of the helicopter.

Emily was breathing hard and she grimaced when she swallowed as it hurt so bad. In the distance, she could see a black ball coming closer and closer towards her.

What is that? Emily wondered.

There were electrical sparks flying out of it and it was glowing. As the black ball got closer, Emily saw Maggie charging towards with her, with a manic look on her face. The black ball was getting brighter and brighter. . .

"Move, Emily!" a voice yelled.

It took Emily a second to realise that it was a killing fireball and she bent her knees ready to fly up when a flicker of orange and red flew past her and Emily lost her footing. Jessie clashed into Maggie and a second later they were both up in the sky. Emily watched in awe as the sky turned a mesmerising mix of red, black, orange and yellow.

BANG!

Emily dropped to the floor and the last thing she remembered was how beautiful Jessie made the sky looked as he set it on fire.

CHAPTER TWENTY-NINE

Som

Emily opened her eyes and watched embers fall from the red sky and land beside her. Smoke was in the air. It filled her lungs and she sat up and coughed, wincing from the pain from her raw throat.

She looked around and saw her teammates had been affected by the huge explosion and were scattered around in various positions across the floor. The helicopter was on its side and had been slashed in half as if someone had shot a Disc on it. Somehow, the farmhouse was still in good condition apart from some rubble falling from the corner of the roof. Emily wondered what Neci would think if she came home to see her house alight for the second time.

Emily looked beside her to where Michella was but she wasn't there. Her heart raced as she looked around the battlefield and noticed that Jason, Professor Elwood and Lox were nowhere to be seen. Dion was still, face down on the floor.

Emily tried to get to her feet but her body refused to

co-operate. Everything was hurting. Emily looked back up at the sky in disbelief. Jessie and Maggie were nowhere to be seen.

Emily's attention was drawn to the left. A figure was flying towards them. A female with long, dark hair. Emily tried desperately to get to her feet but once again she couldn't move. She opened her fist and a small Baby Ball laid inside of it. Emily groaned, willing her body to give more but the Baby Ball refused to grow into a fireball. Her throat was on fire so Emily couldn't even shout to warn her team that Neci was coming. Emily gritted her teeth. She wasn't going down without a fight.

As the female warrior got closer, Emily realised it wasn't Neci—it was Roberta. Emily lifted up her arm and waved her hand back and forth. Roberta soared towards her, landing by Emily's feet.

"You're alive," Roberta said, running her hand over Emily's hair and pulling her close before kissing her on the forehead. She looked up at the sky. "I saw Jessie and Maggie, and then an explosion, but I couldn't see anything else in my vision."

"I'm okay," Emily said, holding her tight. "Some of our team have disappeared."

"Lox must have taken them." Roberta looked around. "He took Professor Elwood. I'm going to check on the others. I'll let Lox know I'm here and will get you all out of here."

She watched as Roberta stirred up her teammates, who seemed more shaken up than badly injured. They slowly got to their feet. Gabriel Thompson pointed at Dion, who was still on the floor and Roberta responded to him but Emily couldn't hear what was said.

Wesley and Julian walked over to Gabriel and Roberta.

Roberta seemed to be instructing them as they nodded along to whatever she was saying. From the corner of her eye, Emily saw Dion slowly stirring. Emily waved her hand manically at Roberta but she couldn't see her. A second later, Gabriel held on to Julian and Wesley and they teleported.

Alice Archinia was holding on to her arm and walking to Roberta who embraced her tightly. When she let go, Alice looked over at Emily who was taken aback by her expression. She was used to Alice being aggressive towards her but the look on Alice's face was. . . was it sadness?

"Come on body," Emily said through gritted teeth. She rolled herself to the side, so that she landed on her knees. "One-two-three."

She pushed herself up with everything she had and swayed as she tried to get her footing. She held on to her head wishing the throbbing would go away.

Dion was struggling to his feet. The side of his face was bleeding and he was shaking his head back and forth. Roberta and Alice were walking in deep conversation towards Emily.

"Hey," Emily tried to shout but it came out as a whisper. She took a deep breath and shouted, "Hey!" It was croaky but louder and it got Roberta and Alice's attention.

Emily pointed at Dion who was staring back at her. Roberta's mouth dropped. She sprinted towards Emily and Alice teleported.

Everything stopped. It was like someone had paused a movie. All Emily could see was Roberta with one leg in front of the other, a fist clenched, but not moving. Alice was standing beside Emily with her hands aimed at Emily's torso, Dion was staring at her. . .

The force of being pushed caught Emily off guard. She landed hard on the floor, scraping her chin on the ground.

"ALICE!" Roberta screamed before she shot a white ball—a killing fireball that hit Dion's chest. He died before he had even touched the floor.

Roberta ran to Alice and picked her up, burying her face in Alice's hair. Emily got to her feet, wiping away the blood from her chin and hurried over to Roberta who was crying loudly.

"I'm sorry, I'm sorry," Roberta kept saying over and over again.

Emily kept waiting for Alice to snap back something sarcastic but Alice didn't say a word. Emily touched her hand and jumped back when she felt how cold she was.

"I don't understand," Emily said, looking from a lifeless Alice to Dion.

"He froze time," Roberta said, wiping her nose. "That's his special power. He was going to kill you and Alice pushed you out of the way, sacrificing herself. " Roberta's green eyes locked on to Emily. "It was supposed to be me."

In the days following the second rescue mission at the farmhouse Emily had read every newspaper headline. Today's Daily Steward featured a flawless picture of Alice Archinia on the front cover with the headline R.I.P Young Warrior. The article went on to explain that Alice was the granddaughter of the Five Warriors legend, Cecil Archinia and she had the highest rated reality TV series, Life with Alice. Everything was about how beautiful and rich she was, but there wasn't many details about the rescue.

At the end of the article, there was a small part about Jessie Kendaschi's death and he may have killed Maggie but more details to follow. There was a sentence about Dion being dead but no information on who may have killed him.

Emily threw the newspaper down. She had refused to give any interviews to reporters but she hated that Alice was reduced to how pretty she was and Jessie was just a tiny paragraph. They were heroes who both sacrificed themselves for her. Emily rubbed her chest, wishing she could take away the pain that seemed to reside inside of her.

Why had they done that for me? Emily tormented herself, asking that same question at every moment. Jessie she could sort of understand. They were friends at least, but Alice. Alice didn't like her, so why would she save Emily's life over hers? Nothing made any sense.

Emily could hear the TV and the news reporter sharing that they had no news of Professor Elwood's whereabouts but sources had confirmed that he was alive, well and safe.

"Here you go." Sally sat beside Emily and handed her a cold glass of iced tea.

"Thank you," Emily said, taking it even though she wasn't thirsty.

"You're looking better," Sally said, stroking Emily's hair out of her face.

"Jenkins brought round some Reviving Water yesterday."

"That's good. I actually spoke to Jenkins today. We're going to go to Seven's house to see if Professor Elwood can wake up your dad. The antidote is ready. Lox is already there waiting for us."

Emily smiled. "Can't wait."

"Roberta wants to talk to you before we join them."

"Okay," Emily said, looking at her drink.

"Emily." Sally sighed. "None of this is your fault."

"Isn't it?" Emily asked, blinking away tears.

"It's not your fault," Sally responded in a firm voice and Emily wished more than anything that she could believe her.

Roberta was staying in the suite down the hall from theirs. She almost didn't recognise Roberta when she opened the door and was dressed in an oversized jumper and jeans with her curled hair tied messily in a bun on top of her head. Her usually perfect face had red blotches over it, like she had been crying for hours, which Emily was sure that she had.

She smiled weakly at Emily and stepped aside so she could enter. Emily sat on the plush cream couch and Roberta sat opposite her.

"I'm sorry," Roberta said, surprising Emily.

"For what?"

"Everything. I thought I was protecting you by not telling you certain things and I know that you think that this is all your fault, but it isn't, Emily. I promise you that."

"They shouldn't have done that for me," Emily argued. "I can't live with that on my shoulders."

"I understand—"

"No, you don't!" Emily snapped. "Because after Alice died, you said it should have been you. What do you mean? You would have left me and your husband and your kids—why would you that?"

Roberta pulled out her messy bun and her long black locks hung prettily around her face. She ran her fingers through them.

"Let me start at the beginning. I lied to you about Scarlett. I didn't capture her, she actually came to me. When Lox and Thomas appeared on TV, all of Neci's warriors went back to her, except Scarlett. She sought me out in the summer because she found out some information about Neci and she didn't feel safe. We all thought that Neci's vendetta was just against the Five Warriors but it's so much bigger than that. It's everyone. She is out to destroy every single warrior."

"I don't get it," Emily said slowly.

"You know about her grandparents being murdered by warriors who set fire to the farmhouse?" Emily nodded. "Since then, Neci blames all warriors for their death. She is very much scarred by what happened and wants revenge. Scarlett felt with her fire power she would be one of the first to go, once Neci had decided she didn't need her core team anymore. Neci chooses warriors who are special yet broken to be around her, but they are still much weaker than her. Scarlett is a Som. Do you know what this is?"

"Is that the same as a Somperu?" Emily asked. "I learnt it in History."

"No, Scarlett can only transfer her powers, she can't absorb power, but in doing so it will kill her. She wanted to transfer her fire power to me, but I'm not the right person to defeat Neci." Roberta gave Emily a knowing look. "And neither is Thomas."

Emily jumped to her feet. "You can't think it's me?"

"Emily, please—"

"You think I'm the one to defeat Neci? Why would you even think something so stupid?"

"I saw you," Roberta said quickly and Emily caught her breath. "I saw you create a wall of fire that surrounded you and Neci. I didn't see anyone else and I don't know what that means for the rest of us, but by the end of the battle, it was just you and Neci."

Emily knew the voice saying, 'Fire,' was familiar but she never thought it could be Scarlett. The day she met her, Scarlett had touched her and that's when Emily had felt that burning—the fire growing inside of her.

"So Scarlett's been in my head this whole time? Making me think there's something wrong with me. You've got it wrong. My dad is the one to fight Neci, not me."

"We got it wrong," Roberta said quietly. "We thought all this time it was Thomas. He defeated her once before so he can do it again but I'm not wrong on this. It's you. You're the only one who can defeat her. The only one who stands a chance. I didn't know how to tell you this information. I knew you would say no to Scarlett giving anything to you, so I had to put you in a space together so she could do it."

"This is a joke, this is a joke," Emily mumbled, with her hands on her head pacing up and down the living room.

Me? Defeat Neci? I can't even be in her presence without being afraid.

"Emily, please sit down," Roberta said.

"Why can't Lox fight her? You? Or Uncle Jenkins? Why would it be me? It doesn't make any sense."

"I'm sorry, I know this is a lot to take in. Please, sit down," Roberta said, gesturing to the couch. "Please."

Emily sat. She noticed her hands were shaking so she sat on them.

"When you started speaking about this voice you were hearing and the fire that happened at Osaki, I knew it was working. Scarlett said she would be able to help you control it by using her telepathy. She said once you desired it, that's when it would become part of you."

Emily shook her head. "But I didn't desire it."

"At the Dojo match, did you hear her voice?"

"No but I nev—" Emily paused. She had wanted the fire. At Neci's house, she had wanted the fire flames to come to her.

"I had to make sure that you were protected at all costs, so I told the elite team that our lives were dependent on you."

"My friends knew this whole time?" Emily asked surprised.

"They just knew that if we wanted to win this war we had to make sure you were safe. But my visions were strange and sometimes I saw Jessie and Alice fighting with us against Neci and other times I didn't, so I told them everything. And then Jason and Lox demanded to know."

"Lox knew too? And he didn't tell me?"

"Jason told Lox you were hearing voices. Please don't be angry with them," Roberta said. "I begged them not to say a word. Lox was furious with me. He told me to find another way but I can't see one. If I could, I would."

"But this fire—I can't do what Jessie did."

"Emily, I saw a wall of fire that you created. You just need to train your gift."

"I was going to ask Jessie to help me," Emily said sadly. "You said it should have been you that died—why?"

"That's why I haven't been around as much. I've been in

Italy spending time with my family because I was ready to die. I knew that you could end this whole war. Alice was meant to teleport back with the others but she was worried. She knew that this was where I was going to die. I saw myself fighting Maggie and Dion and Dion's fireball killing me. I didn't see Jessie doing what he did. I was trying to get Alice to go back to Osaki, but then Dion stopped time and. . ." Roberta trailed off, wiping her eyes with her sleeve. "She wasn't meant to do that. That was my job, but when we were talking she was reminding me that I had told everyone at all costs, we must protect Emily. I should have known that she was going to try something, but I didn't see it coming."

They sat silently. Emily was waiting for Roberta to laugh and say, "Only joking" or something along those lines.

"Neci couldn't know about Scarlett's whereabouts or what she had done. Jessie was never meant to be left behind. It was an awful situation but I swear I've never met a kid like Jessie. He is so incredibly brave."

"Yeah, he was," Emily said, sniffing back tears. Another person she wouldn't get to thank. "So, what happens now with Scarlett?"

Roberta smiled sadly. "She hasn't got much time left. Transferring her powers to you is killing her. Any day now she'll be gone."

"I knew she wasn't your prisoner. You were way too nice to her."

Roberta laughed. "I know! I've lost count of the times I made her my Mama's pasta. She's not actually a bad person. Neci's good at taking broken people and infecting them with her rage, thankfully Scarlett saw through that."

Emily took a deep breath and asked, "Does my dad know that he's not going to beat Neci?"

Roberta shook her head. "He got poisoned before I had a chance to tell him, but I don't know how he'll take it."

"I don't know either," Emily said honestly.

Her whole life she had been told that Thomas was the only warrior to beat Neci. People had said confidently that Thomas could and would beat Neci again.

Emily had believed all of them, without any doubt, and now she was being told that none of it was true. Like one of Jenkins's illusions, Emily was starting to see reality for what it truly was. Thomas Knight wouldn't end the war. . . she would. She wanted to cry, scream, punch someone, all at the same time.

Will he hate me? Emily bit down hard on her lip. She tried to put herself in her dad's shoes. Emily knew that if someone had taken her place in the most historic battle ever she would be jealous, annoyed and all the things she would hate her dad to think about her.

There was a loud knock on the door.

"Just checking to see when we're going?" Sally asked.

"You can't tell her," Emily said hurriedly. "Please don't tell anyone else about me and. . . just give me time."

"I understand," Roberta said, then in a louder voice, she yelled, "Door's open."

Sally peeped though and stared at Emily anxiously. Emily forced herself to smile and Sally visibly relaxed.

"Are you guys done?"

"Yes, I think we are," Roberta said, standing to her feet. "Let me just sort myself out."

"You're not going like that?" Sally teased and Roberta looked horrified.

"Got to always look the part." Roberta smiled as she headed towards her bedroom. "I'll be ready in fifteen."

Emily stood up and walked out of the door with Sally's arm wrapped around her shoulders.

"Good talk?" Sally asked.

"Insightful," Emily replied.

"Insightful is good!" Sally said. "At least now you have a better idea of everything, right?"

Emily glanced at Sally, wishing she could tell her what Roberta had said, but the words were stuck in her throat, so all Emily could do was nod. Sally smiled at her and kissed her on the side of her head.

CHAPTER THIRTY
Whatever It Takes

The first thing Emily saw when she entered Seven's house was Jenkins. When he saw her, he opened up his arms and Emily ran into them. He held her tight. There was so much about Jenkins that reminded her of her dad.

"I'm sorry," Jenkins said, pulling away from her.

"For what?"

"Not being around for you, what Roberta. . . saw." He gave Emily a knowing look. Sally was hovering around in earshot.

"It's not fair," Emily said quietly.

"I know," Jenkins said, rubbing her arms. "But we've got you and we're going to do whatever we can to help you."

"Roberta was going to. . ."

Jenkins smiled. "I know. Sacrifices have been made and will continue to be. We need to stop her no matter the costs. Hi baby." He greeted Roberta with a kiss, who had on perfect makeup and a fitted knee-length dress with high heels.

There was still a big part of her that felt like Roberta had got it all wrong. Emily knew she was strong, but she wasn't a match on Neci—whether she could create fire or not.

"The elite team are in the living room but let's go see your dad first," Jenkins said, guiding her towards his room.

"Sally, are you coming in?"

Sally shook her head. "We don't want to overwhelm him. You guys go on first."

Jenkins and Roberta led the way into Thomas's room. Seven was sitting beside him with her hands hovering over his body. She looked even more exhausted than the last time. Professor Elwood was a lanky, tall, white man with a black moustache and glasses. He was holding a cup of something steaming.

Lox was standing anxiously on the other side of the bed with one arm hugging his body and the other with his thumb in his mouth as he bit his nail anxiously. His eyes lit up when he saw them. "You made it just in time."

Professor Elwood was watching Seven closely. Emily didn't know what he was waiting for. The machine that Thomas was hooked up to started to beep more frequently. Seven nodded at the Professor who leaned over and opened Thomas's mouth, gently guiding in the cup of liquid.

Seven leaned back, wiping her brow. Jenkins reached down for the bottle of Reviving Water by her feet and handed it to her and Seven took it gratefully. That's when she noticed Emily was there.

Emily was surprised by the huge grin on Seven's tired face.

"Get ready," she said.

Emily watched her father. His skin was grey and he looked like he had lost so much weight. He seemed to have aged years.

Professor Elwood stepped away from Thomas once all of the drink had gone. At first it looked like nothing was happening. Emily kept looking from Seven to the Professor but their eyes were fixed on Thomas. Slowly, the colour in Thomas's skin started to turn from a dirty grey to a rich brown. Emily gasped as Thomas's eyelids flickered and then opened.

"Dad!" Emily burst into loud noisy tears.

Thomas's eyes slowly seared the room, taking in all of their faces. When he landed on Emily, he said weakly, "It's okay."

Emily ran to him, placing her head on his chest, listening to his strong heartbeat. Thomas put an arm around her.

"How are you feeling Dad?" Lox asked, standing by his other side.

Thomas gripped Lox's hand and kissed it. "Okay. I'm happy you're here."

"He's been here every day," Seven told Thomas whose eyes lit up. "He is a good boy."

Emily looked up, wiping her wet eyes. A tear fell from Lox's eye and Thomas placed Lox's hand on his cheek. It was the first time Emily had seen genuine love between them and it was enough to make her start crying again.

"Let's give Thomas a bit of space," Seven said delicately, glancing at Emily. "He will need to rest."

"Okay," Emily said even though she wanted to stay with him.

"Thank you Seven and Professor Elwood. Thank you, all of you." Thomas smiled.

They headed out of the room and Lox sat on the floor, with his back against the wall and his head in his hands.

Emily wasn't sure if he was crying. She glanced at Roberta and Jenkins.

"He'll be okay." Jenkins said. "Just give him a minute."

"Okay." Emily glanced once more at Lox, who hadn't moved, and went to seek out her friends. She heard them before she saw them. Emily stood by the door and smiled as Michella, Jason, Wesley, Gabriel and Julian were playing a fast round of Black Jack.

"In your face!" Gabriel said, so un-Gabriel-like, as he put down a Black Jack.

"I hate this game!" Julian moaned, making everyone laugh.

"Room for one more?" Emily asked and they looked at her.

"Emily!" Michella cried, reaching her first. She burst into tears as they hugged. "I'm so sorry. I didn't know about the microchip."

"I know," Emily said gently. "They must have done it when you were captured and you healed over it. It's not your fault."

"Lox said the chip can take a while to work. That's why I wasn't affected when you guys came to the farmhouse." Michella pulled away and looked at the floor. "Did I hurt you?"

Emily thought of the pain in her head and Michella's hands around her throat. "Just a bit, but it wasn't you."

"I can't believe that Alice and Jessie are gone. It feels unreal."

Emily nodded. Unreal didn't even sum it up.

"Do you think they'll come back as ghosts? Like Cecil and my brother?" Gabriel asked.

"I'm not sure," Emily said. "I guess it depends if they're offered the choice once they get to Par Bliss."

"I don't think I'd come back," Wesley said. "Not when Neci wants to destroy the world. I'd rather stay in Heaven."

"One hundred percent," Jason said.

"My dad's awake," Emily said grinning.

"Thank God," Julian said and everyone cheered. "Can we see him?"

"Maybe in a bit. He's just resting."

"Come join in," Michella said, leading her to the group.

"I have some news," Julian said. "My grandad will fight with us in the war."

"Amazing!" Michella said.

"And he wants us to come to his place and train with him."

"Are you serious?" Wesley said and Julian nodded. "Wow, training with Tainwo Kena. That's going to be very cool."

"Thanks for persuading him," Emily said.

"The least I could do," Julian replied.

They played a few more rounds of Black Jack but Emily felt like only a part of her was present.

Emily shuffled the cards in her hands. "I don't want to dishonour Jessie and Alice's memory by not telling you the truth." The room instantly felt sombre. "I know that Jason knows everything and I just found out. I think it's right that you all know everything as well."

Emily told them what Roberta had shared about Scarlett, Neci and the battle.

"You?" Wesley gasped. He looked at Jason as if waiting for him to disagree but Jason nodded. "You have to fight Neci?"

"That's what Roberta saw. Unless she got it wrong."

"You're so brave, Emily," Julian said.

"Brave? I don't want to fight Neci."

"But you have Scarlett's power?" Gabriel asked. "You can do what she can do?"

"I don't even know the extent of what Scarlett was capable of but yeah I have her power and you won't ever have to deal with her again." Emily held on to Gabriel's hand and squeezed it. "She won't be here much longer."

"I almost feel bad for her," Gabriel said softly. "That took some serious guts going up against Neci, knowing what it will cost her."

Emily hadn't even thought about it, but Gabriel was right. What Scarlett was doing was incredibly brave. Another person sacrificing herself for Emily because they believed she could win. They truly thought Emily was the one. In that moment, Emily realised that she had a chance to thank someone for their sacrifice.

"I'll be back, guys," Emily said, handing Gabriel the cards she was holding.

She found Roberta handing a sweet to Antonio before he hurried off. She smiled when she saw Emily, but quickly looked anxious when she saw Emily's serious face.

"What's wrong?" she asked.

"Scarlett. I want to see her before she. . . you know. I didn't get to thank Jessie or Alice for what they've done for me and I want to thank her."

"You always amaze me, you know that? Shall we go now?" Roberta said.

"Where's Sally?"

"She's in there with Thomas. Let me just tell her we're taking a quick trip."

As Roberta hurried off, Emily noticed Lox walking towards

her. If he had been crying, she couldn't tell. They hugged without saying a word. All of the emotions Emily was feeling seemed to spill out, and she buried her face into his chest and screamed so it came out muffled, wanting all the pain to leave her. He hugged her tighter.

"You don't have to do this," he whispered urgently. "Screw what Roberta said. We can find another way."

Emily didn't respond. They both knew there wasn't one, but holding on to the idea that there could be made her feel that little bit lighter.

"Are you ready?" Roberta asked softly and the siblings pulled apart from each other.

"Be safe," Lox said, walking past Roberta without saying a word to her.

Roberta smiled sadly, like she understood. She held out her hand and Emily grabbed it. They teleported to see Scarlett one last time.

Scarlett was sitting on the same chair Emily had seen her in the summer but Emily noticed there was an un-made bed in the corner. From a distance, Scarlett looked tiny. She had lost a lot of weight.

Emily walked closer and could see Scarlett's once luxurious mane of red hair was lank and clumpy. Her skin reminded Emily of how Thomas's had looked—grey and sunken. She smelt of death.

"Hi," Emily said and Scarlett nodded at her weakly. Emily looked at Roberta who nodded at her encouragingly. "I just wanted to say thank you. I know the truth now. Thank you for what you've done for us."

"It's okay," Scarlett said, barely over a whisper. "Do you like the fire?"

"It's going to take some getting used to," Emily said, making Scarlett laugh, triggering a coughing fit.

Emily looked around the room and noticed the mattress in the corner and by its side was half a glass of water. Emily picked it up and handed it to Scarlett, who took it and with her other hand she gripped Emily's wrist tight.

"Hey!" Emily said but Scarlett drank her water, keeping her eyes on Emily.

When she was done, she threw the glass on the floor and the shatter made Emily jump. Roberta took a step forward but Scarlett shot her a look that made Roberta stay back.

"Come closer," Scarlett said.

Emily hesitated for a second but slowly moved forward.

"Janet. . . Moore," Scarlett said. She closed her eyes briefly as if the effort of speaking was too much for her. "Find her."

"I've heard of Janet Moore. That's Neci's aunt."

"Kill. . . Neci," Scarlett said through gritted teeth. "Whatever. . . it. . . takes." Scarlett's hold loosened and Emily quickly moved backwards. "Let me see it. . . one more time."

Emily glanced nervously at Roberta before she held her hands in front of her with her palms facing the ceiling. She closed her eyes and focused on the fire and how powerful it made her feel. Slowly, she felt the heat travel though her body and just like during the Dojo match, she didn't feel any pain. She opened her eyes and her hands were on fire.

"So beautiful," Scarlett whispered. Scarlett looked past Emily and looked at Roberta.

"I have it," Roberta declared, walking towards them.

"Have what?" Emily asked confused, closing her fists making the fire flames disappear.

Roberta opened her hand and in the middle of it was a black round pill. Scarlett took it with trembling hands and popped it into her mouth. She locked eyes with Emily and smiled, reminding Emily of her once beautiful face. Scarlett swallowed the pill and at first nothing happened. Then Scarlett let out a gasp. She gripped the chair before letting out a croak. She closed her eyes and slumped over with her head in her chest. Her red hair hanging over her face.

The sun was shining brightly. The sky was blue and clear and there was no wind. Emily stood in her red Dojo kit in the middle of the stadium beside the rest of her team and their opponents, Mentorawth. The team members were each wearing a black armband. The Ogragons had Jessi Kandaschi written on theirs, whilst Mentorawth had Alice Archinia. Julian Kena was standing close beside Emily.

The stadium was packed with students and teachers. Cecil Archinia was floating by the bottom of the stands looking up at the sky. Thomas Knight was standing beside Mr Davon and Lox. Emily caught his eye and Thomas gave her a thumbs up. This was her idea. She had wanted to do something unique to honour Jessie and Alice before their Dojo match.

Mr Davon had cancelled the Dojo season but the Ogragons

had requested a friendly game to honour Jessie. Then the Mentorawths had asked to be the opponents. Even though Alice never played Dojo, she was a fifth year Mentorawth student.

"On the count of three," Ms Macay announced. She was wearing an armband with both Jessie and Alice's name on it. "One-two-three."

The entire school raised an arm up into the sky and shot a fireball. There was a mixture of red, yellows, blues, pinks, purples that swirled together. The sky wasn't on fire like Jessie had made it, but it was still beautiful, alight and bright. The smiling faces of Jessie and Alice floated high above them (courtesy of Jenkins's illusions) and the stadium erupted into the loudest roar Emily had ever heard. She knew that nobody would ever forget the joyful faces of the two young heroes in the rainbow-coloured sky.

Emily couldn't take her eyes off Jessie and Alice. She would be forever grateful that they had helped to keep her alive. Emily was appreciative of Scarlett for giving up her gifts so that they could stand a fighting chance.

Today was a beautiful day. Her dad was healthy and her friends were ready to fight beside her. She didn't know how much time she had until her battle with Neci but she was going to spend as much of it as she could pushing her powers to their limit. Next time she would make sure Neci was gone for good.

Also by A. Bello

Emily Knight I am. . .

Also by A. Bello

Emily Knight I am. . . Awakened

Classroom questions

I know a lot of teachers and librarians have supported the release of the other books in the Emily Knight series, and with the last book being Carnegie-nominated, I wanted to provide some inspiration for talking points for the classroom, book groups, or just for you, the reader, to consider once you've finished reading Emily Knight I am... Becoming. I would love to hear from you, so if you want to email me with your thoughts on the book, you can reach me at info@a-bello.com

What did you think about the moment Emily was reunited with her father and brother? Did it go as you'd imagined?

What scene/moment in the story stands out for you the most and why?

Classroom questions

Who is your favourite character across the series and what do you like most about them?

What do you think about Wesley's relationship with his mother, Lorraine?

Were you surprised by the ending?

Classroom questions

Imagine the Reviving Water was real and you had some. . .
what would you do before drinking it to test it out?

If you could have one super power what would it be and why?

What would you do with that super power?

Classroom questions

Do you think we need more brave females as the protagonist in books?

With one last book in the series left, who do you think Emily will end up with—Wesley or Julian?

Lox and Thomas Knight have a complicated relationship. Do you think Thomas is trying to mould Emily into Lox?

Classroom questions

If it came to it and Lox had to battle Neci, do you think he could go through with it?

Diversity is a massive issue and there are not enough diverse books aimed at young people. Emily Knight is all about celebrating diversity, why do you think that's important?

About the Author

A. Bello is the award-winning author of the bestselling fantasy series Emily Knight I am. . . and Emily Knight I am. . . Awakened, which was nominated for the CILIP Carnegie Medal 2019, Winner of London's Big Read 2019, finalist for Best Children's book for The People's Book Prize 2019.

A. Bello first began writing the Emily Knight saga at aged 12 with the intention of filling the gaping hole in children's fiction for an inspirational, strong, black female, young protagonist.

A. Bello won the London Book Fair's Trailblazer Award 2018. She is the founder of The Lil' Author School, co-founder of The Author School, Hashtag Press, Hashtag BLAK, The Diverse Book Awards and ink!

Find out more at www.a-bello.com
Follow A. Bello on Twitter: @ABelloWrites
Instagram: @abiolabello @emilyknightiam
Facebook.com/EmilyKnightIAM
Facebook.com/A.BelloAuthor